AFTER HOURS TEMPTATION

KIANNA ALEXANDER

WHEN THE LIGHTS GO OUT...

JULES BENNETT

MILLS & BOON

First Published in Great Britain 2022
by Mills & Boon, an imprint of HarperCollins*Publishers* Ltd
1 London Bridge Street, London, SE1 9GF

www.harpercollins.co.uk

HarperCollins*Publishers*
1st Floor, Watermarque Building,
Ringsend Road, Dublin 4, Ireland

After Hours Temptation © 2022 Eboni Manning
When The Lights Go Out… © 2021 Jules Bennett

ISBN: 978-0-263-30382-7

0622

MIX
Paper from
responsible sources
FSC™ C007454

This book is produced from independently certified FSC™ paper to ensure responsible forest management.

For more information visit: www.harpercollins.co.uk/green

Printed and Bound in Spain using 100% Renewable electricity at CPI Black Print, Barcelona

Like any good Southern belle, **Kianna Alexander** wears many hats: doting mama, advice-dispensing sister, fun aunt and gabbing girlfriend. She's a voracious reader, an amateur seamstress, survival-horror gamer and occasional painter in oils. A native of the Tar Heel state, Kianna still lives there while maintaining her collection of well-loved vintage '80s Barbie dolls. For more about Kianna and her books, visit her website at authorkiannaalexander.com, or sign up for Kianna's mailing list at authorkiannaalexander.com/sign-up. You can also follow Kianna on social media: Facebook.com/kiannawrites, Twitter.com/ kiannawrites, Instagram.com/kiannaalexanderwrites and Pinterest.com/kiannawrites.

USA TODAY bestselling author **Jules Bennett** has published over sixty books and never tires of writing happy endings. Writing strong heroines and alpha heroes is Jules's favourite way to spend her workdays. Jules hosts weekly competitions on her Facebook fan page and loves chatting with readers on Twitter, Facebook and via email through her website. Stay up-to-date by signing up for her newsletter at julesbennett.com

AFTER HOURS
TEMPTATION

KIANNA ALEXANDER

For. The. Culture.

One

Leaning her ergonomic work chair as far back as it would go, Teagan Woodson turned the page in the manual she was reading. The LED lights overhead chased away the darkness in the sound booth, allowing her to read the words with ease despite the late hour. The manual, filled with all the details about the Harcroft Diamond Edition Digital Audio Workstation, wasn't exactly light reading, especially when she was this tired. Still, it had to be done. She was known for her adeptness with the sound equipment and she wasn't about to be caught lacking now.

She'd developed a certain fondness for the machine, and even gave it a nickname: Fancy.

Earlier in the week, a cloud-based update had been automatically installed on the system, adding several new features to the already impressive list of what the machine could do. That update, which was extensive enough to leave the system unavailable for an entire day, was her focus now. When the next artist came in to record, she'd be ready, because she knew this machine inside and out.

That artist would be the Bronx-based rapper Sherman "Lil Swagg" Washburn. Known for his recent hits with both new school artists like Paige the Princess, and legendary pioneers like Rakim, Swagg was making major moves in the hip-hop game. He'd come to 404 Sound seeking a full-service, boutique approach, and as the lead sound engineer, it was her job to provide him with the high-quality experience he expected.

She flipped a page, coming to the section on file backups and security. The manual had originally been a PDF file, loaded on to the system itself, but she'd had it printed and bound at the local office-supplies store. She found it easier to read on paper and figured it would be simpler to reference should the time ever come. She'd rather leaf through this 200-page, comb-bound book than scroll through as many pages on the workstation's screen looking for whatever small detail she needed.

She'd spent the better part of the last few months testing out the new equipment, ever since it had been installed. And while part of her felt nostalgic for Old Reliable, the original soundboard that had been in continuous use since the studio opened its doors in the early nineties, that nostalgia did little to dampen her excitement. Old Reliable was now carefully packaged in the storage room, pending physical refurbishment to her original glory. After that, the old board would be placed on display, as a cherished relic of 404's storied past.

The new workstation was top-of-the-line, and she knew she'd oversee the creation of countless hit songs and albums while operating it. She'd been slowly reading through the manual, trying out each feature as she came to it in the text.

She yawned, the breath escaping before she could free a hand to stifle it. She closed the manual and set it on the counter. Scooting her chair just outside the booth's door to the little side table in the hall, she took a sip of her now watered-down iced coffee before replacing it and scooting back inside again. She remembered her brother Gage calling her "extra" for her rule about not having any food or drinks within five feet of the counter, and chuckled. A red tape outline on the carpeted floor clearly marked out the "consumables exclusion zone," and she explained this policy to every single new person who entered the booth.

It might be extra, but I'm not having some slippery-fingered producer or artist manager spilling anything on my equipment. Because at the end of the day, this was Teagan's sound booth. She might be the baby of the storied Woodson family—and only because her impatient-ass twin brother had beat her into the world by three-and-a-half minutes—but she was still chief tech officer and master of this studio. In here, her word was law, and everyone knew it.

She stood, stretched. The workstation's on-screen clock showed the time: 8:32. Everyone else in the building was long gone by now, except maybe security and janitorial staff. She rubbed her eyes, trying to shake off the bleariness, but to no avail. *I've only got ten pages left in the manual. I'm just gonna push through.* She re-opened the comb-bound book, flipping the pages back to where she'd left off.

A few lines in, she heard the telltale click-clack generated only by a pair of heels on the tile floor in the hallway.

She stopped reading, turning her chair around to see her big sister, Nia, coming into the room, pausing in the door frame. Dressed in her typical attire of black cigarette pants and a matching blazer with a soft pink blouse, she looked professional and stylish.

Teagan swept her eyes over her sister, then glanced down at her own gray tunic, black leggings and ballet flats, once again realizing that the two daughters of the Woodson family resided on opposite ends of the fashion spectrum. Nia was all about polish and panache, while she craved comfort and quirk above all else; Nia stuck to 1-carat studs, while Teagan preferred long, flashy dangling earrings that caught the light just right.

Nia eyed her questioningly as she leaned against the door frame. "What are you doing here so late?"

"I could ask you the same thing," Teagan quipped.

"Touché, I guess." Nia chuckled. "But you know a CEO's work is never finished."

"You're the literal boss, sis. You could go home anytime you want. You're just too much of a control freak to delegate anything."

Nia rolled her eyes. "Whatever. Get your stuff. I'm going home, and you should, too."

She glanced at the manual lying open on her lap. Knowing her sister wouldn't take no for an answer, she closed it and set it on the counter. She took a few moments to shut down the equipment, then gathered her purse and keys. Turning the lights off inside the recording suite, she locked the door behind her as she left.

Moments later, she was following Nia as her fast-walking elder sister strode down the corridor. Nia's giant, long-legged steps had always been a thorn in Teagan's side; even fully grown, she was still two inches shorter than her Amazonian sister. She'd always been like that; Teagan's first memories of her sister were of her striding across the house and the yard, and of her barking orders at all the other siblings. Teagan knew her sister loved them all, but she also knew her sister was way too serious.

"Slow down, Nia. You walking or skating?"

Nia laughed but didn't slow down as she breezed through the studio's front door.

Outside in the parking lot, they stood by Nia's car. "Any plans tonight?"

Teagan chuckled. "You ask that as if I have a social life."

Her lips pursed momentarily before she spoke again. "Look, Teagan. I'm the oldest and the highest- ranking among all the siblings. Every day, I feel the weight of the responsibility for the success of this company bearing down on my shoulders, and that's why I work as hard as I do." She paused. "You, on the other hand, are young and carefree. You should be dating. Or at least attempting to."

She sighed. "You sound just like Mom. Did she put you up to this?"

Nia shook her head. "No, of course not. I haven't even talked to her today."

She didn't know if she believed that. "Interesting, because Mom said basically the same thing to me a couple of weeks ago."

"That's probably because she sees it, too. I know it isn't easy, but try not to shut yourself off from the rest of the world too much."

"Gee, you're laying it on thick, aren't you? You make it seem like what I do isn't important. Without a sound engineer and tech officer, this place wouldn't last a week."

"I know, sis. I'm not trying to discount your importance around here. We definitely need you. Nobody understands the sound equipment as well as you." Nia opened the driver's-side door of her black luxury sedan. "But you can work hard here and still have a personal life."

"And you?" Teagan raised a brow as she waited for her sister's response.

Nia shrugged. "One day. It's not a priority for me right now… Maybe after the anniversary celebration."

"What a cop-out." Teagan shook her head. "I think I'll wait, too, then."

"Look around, sis. Blaine and Gage are already happily married, and nobody saw that coming." She winked as she got into her car and shut the door. She started the engine and called through the open window, "You never know when love will come around."

"Neither do you," Teagan shot back as her sister backed out of her parking space.

Heading down a few spaces, she got into her own

car, a white coupe, and fired up the engine, pulling out onto the road behind her sister. At the next light, they parted ways as Nia took a left, headed for her house in the Westview neighborhood Teagan took a right, toward Shimmering Lakes, the quiet, well-established housing area she lived in.

Driving through the brightly lit streets of Atlanta, she thought about her sister's words. It was so funny that everyone thought she could just…go out. As if exploring the city and the world, beyond the safety of the places and people she knew, came easy to her. She might seem like she could conquer anything, but no one had any idea how much work it took to appear that way.

Shaking her head, she pulled into her driveway, pushing her mother and sister's well-meaning but annoying admonishments out of her mind.

Jogging through the front door of his second-story studio apartment, Maxton McCoy locked it behind him. Hanging the keys on the hook mounted nearby, he swiped his hand over his head, knocking down the hood of his jacket as he ran his hand over his sweat-dampened hair. The endorphin high from his four-mile run around the neighborhood still lingered, making him smile as he shuffled his feet, shifting weight from one foot to the other.

The thumping bass and fast-paced lyrics of legendary Cali rapper E-40 filled his ears as the workout playlist saved to his phone continued to resonate. The Vallejo-born lyricist, known for tongue-twisting rhymes, was often credited with helping solidify the Bay area's importance in hip-hop culture. E-40's unique style, along with his contributions, placed him at the top of Maxton's list of favorite artists.

Walking over to the area just beyond his sofa, he sat down on the throw rug. He could feel the sweat running down his body beneath his clothing and was beyond ready for a shower, but he knew if he didn't do his push-ups and sit-ups now, they wouldn't get done.

He got into position, and with the music still blasting in his ears, did his customary one hundred pushups. That done, he flipped over and lay on his back, beginning his one hundred sit-ups.

Suddenly, E-40's rapping ceased, and the sound of his phone's ringer filled his ears, accompanied by strong vibrations in the hip pocket of his sweatpants. Lying on his back, he tapped the button on the side of his headphones to answer the call. "Hello?"

"Hey, man. What's up?"

He smiled, recognizing his friend's voice right away. "Hey, Sharrod. Nothing going on here but them post-run sit-ups. What's going on with you, my dude?"

Sharrod chuckled. "Still going out for those three-mile runs, even though nobody chasing your ass?"

"Nah, today I ran four miles, smart-ass. That bass is heavier than most people think it is. Gotta keep my upper-body strength intact."

"I guess you don't wanna be caught lacking onstage, huh?"

"Hell, nah, dude." He laughed. "Where are you?"

"I'm still in Atlanta. I'm staying at Aunt Judy's place over in Greenbriar."

"Oh, yeah, yeah. I'm still here, too. I took a three-month lease on a studio over here near Virginia Highlands."

Sharrod paused. "Really? You mean you decided to stick around instead of taking off?" His tone of voice conveyed his surprise.

"Yeah, I stayed." Maxton would be the first to admit that he'd lived a life on the go, constantly in motion, from one city to the next. All that had changed eight months ago, when one astronomical loss had rocked his entire world.

"Didn't see that coming. You usually up and disappear as soon as we finish a tour, either to set up for the next one or to visit some faraway place."

Maxton held back a sigh. "Nah, man. I just…don't feel like chasing anything right now, you know?"

"You getting old on me, man." He paused as if realizing. "Oh, shit. Man, I'm sorry. I shouldn't have…"

"It's okay, dude. No worries." Though he and Sharrod had been friends since their college days, he didn't expect him to be able to read his mind. He kept the pain of that day well hidden, and though Sharrod was aware of it, they rarely spoke of the incident.

Sharrod's nervous chuckle broke the silence. "How did you find a place that'd let you lease for only three months?"

"Paying it all up-front in cash probably worked in my favor," Maxton quipped, sitting up and stretching his arms over his head, relieved by his friend's desire to change the direction of their conversation to a lighter topic. "I figured, since we just finished up with Naiya B's first major tour, that I'd just hang here for a bit and see what gig comes my way."

"Yeah, I was thinking the same thing. Aunt Judy's rarely ever home. Right now she's up in Jersey with her sorority sisters. So I knew she wouldn't mind me crashing here until somebody needs a drummer."

"Plenty of artists down here, so it's bound to be some work for us soon." Maxton climbed to his feet and crossed the apartment to the kitchen area. There, he pulled down his single-serve mixer and the container of protein powder from his upper cabinets, then grabbed the almond milk from his stainless steel refrigerator, setting everything on the black granite countertop.

"I thought you'd have to haul ass back down here, but this is perfect," Sharrod said. "We've already got a potential gig."

Adding the milk and powder to the mixer, Maxton felt his brow scrunch in confusion. "It's Tuesday, bruh, and our last gig just ended Saturday night. What do you mean we already have something lined up?"

"I was on the Gram yesterday, and I saw a post by Lil Swagg."

Maxton put the lid on the mixer and pressed the button, searching his memory bank for that name as the motor whirred quietly. "Is he the kid that did the song with Cambria and Paige the Princess? The one about sex in a limo?"

"'Freeway Threeway.' Yeah, that's him. Anyway, he's holding open auditions for musicians to be on his upcoming album, and he posted a link to a sign-up form."

Turning off the mixer, he disconnected the cup from the base and took a sip. The thick concoction didn't taste nearly as chocolaty as the commercial promised, but protein shakes rarely did. "Let me guess. You signed us both up, right?"

"Yep. And it's a good thing, because the sign-ups were full within ten minutes of him posting the link." Sharrod cleared his throat. "Bet you're glad I'm always lurking on social media right about now, huh?"

He shook his head, thinking back on the times he'd chastised his friend for being too plugged into the news-feeds and timelines of various social sites, obsessively following the lives of the wealthy and well-connected. "I mean, a broken clock is right twice a day, so…"

"Whatever. Stop hating. The auditions are Thursday morning at nine." He paused. "Swagg says he's look-ing for a unique sound that he can only get from a full band. If we want this gig, we gotta bring our A-game."

"Understood." Max took another long sip of the shake, hoping his muscles would appreciate it more than his taste buds did. "So, where are these auditions happening?"

Sharrod sounded as if he were reading when he an-swered, "At 404 Sound Recording Studios. Place up near Collier Heights."

Scratching his chin, Maxton nodded. "Oh, yeah. I've heard great things about that place. I know where it is."

"I've still got my rental car. Do you want me to pick you up?"

"That's fine." Finishing the shake, he set the cup in the sink. "I would just take the MARTA, but if you come get me, I won't have to haul my bass on public transport."

"Cool. I'll be there around eight, then." Sharrod yawned. "Let me let you go. After all, you only got a day to get that bass sounding like something."

"Whatever, Sharrod. Do you even know where your sticks are right now?"

"Dude, you know they always in my hand." He tapped them together to prove his point.

"Well, the shower is calling my name so I'll holla at you later."

After disconnecting the call, Maxton took off his headphones, turned off the wireless link to his phone, and left them on the coffee table.

Walking across the apartment and past the dividing wall that separated his bedroom from the rest of the space, he went to the closet to grab clean clothes and a towel. On the way from the closet to the bathroom, he paused at his nightstand and looked at the framed photo displayed there.

He never bothered with decorating, because his work meant never staying in one place too long. If a lucrative touring gig came up, he needed to be ready to pack up and leave, sometimes with very little advance notice. He'd never even purchased a set of curtains or a house-plant. But this picture made wherever he was, no matter how short the duration of his stay, feel like home.

Inside the polished walnut frame was an old photo of him and his family. It was taken when he was about seventeen. The four of them were dressed in white button-down shirts and blue jeans. His parents, archae-ologist Dr. Stephen McCoy and anthropologist Dr. Wanda McCoy, smiled at him from the photo, as did his younger sister, Whitney. Lingering on her face made the sadness rise in his chest once again.

Right now, his parents were home in Calabasas, hav-ing recently returned from exploring the ruins at Pompeii. In the past, they'd have invited him along on the excursion; but they knew things were different now. Since they'd lost Whitney, the entire family dynamic had changed. His parents continued on with their travels in the name of science, and he threw himself into his work.

There'd been a time when he chased adventures, just like his parents had raised him to do. Now he played it safe, colored inside the lines. One event had changed him, made him flee from the risks he once took so freely.

Two

Teagan walked into the recording suite around eight Thursday morning after depositing her iced coffee from the Bodacious Bean on the table just outside the door. Flipping on the lights, she hung her bag on the little metal hanger affixed to the bottom of the counter and sat down on her chair. She'd dressed up a bit today, donning a flowing beige top, wide-legged jeans and brown leather platform heels. Since her hair rarely cooperated when it mattered, she'd wrestled it into a low bun at her nape and put on a pair of dangly gold earrings with a matching necklace.

In less than an hour, the room would be abuzz with activity. For right now, she just wanted to get set up, get her bearings and prepare for a full day at the soundboard.

She'd finished reading up on Fancy's latest updates and felt confident she could run the system properly. Turning on the workstation, she set it to run a system diagnostic. While she waited for it to display a report, she moved around the suite, making sure everything was in place. The custodial staff's handiwork was evident in the freshly vacuumed throw rug, the fluffed pillows on the sofa and the slight scent of lemon Pine Glo hanging in the air.

The sound of approaching footsteps drew her attention to the door, just in time to see Trevor, 404's sound engineer, entering. "Morning, Teagan."

"Morning, Trevor." She walked his way. "Everything good in Studio Two?"

He nodded, shrugging out of his denim jacket. "Yup. Just came from there, and the systems are up and running just fine. I don't anticipate any problem when Gage comes in later for his monthly check."

"Awesome. You know what a stickler my brother is." She shook her head, thinking how little marriage had mellowed him when it came to organizational stuff. "Anyway, can you head on into the booth and set up for these auditions? I'm expecting Swagg, his manager and the musicians to start showing up pretty soon."

"No problem." After hanging his jacket up on one of the three silver hooks just inside the door, he walked past her and opened the interior door to the sound booth.

Teagan sat down at the workstation, watching through the glass as Trevor checked the connections on the various speakers, amplifiers and microphones inside the booth, then adjusted the position of the electrical cords so they wouldn't be in the middle of the floor. He stopped near the microphone, signaling her with his hand.

She engaged the booth's audio system to talk to him. "Give me a sec. I'm still waiting on diagnostics."

He nodded. "I'm gonna do a soundproofing check real quick." He moved away from the mic, circling around the perimeter of the booth, examining the foam barrier on the walls for any sign of damage.

The diagnostic report finally popped up on the screen, and Teagan made note of the pertinent details. The green icon at the end indicated everything was good with the software, so she closed the report and started up the main program. "Okay, Trevor. Give me a sound check, please."

He moved over to the mic and spoke into it. "Mic check, one, two, three."

She gave him the thumbs-up. "Test my headset for me, please. I'm gonna drop a beat." She waited for him to slip on the headset, then touched the screen to start up the last beat she'd played, a trap tune recently recorded by 2 Chainz and Lil Jon.

He nodded along to the beat and gave a thumbs-up.

"Thanks, Trevor. You can come on out now."

He exited the booth. "Looks like you're all good for recording today. I'll head up to reception and help direct the musicians your way."

"Thanks," she called as he grabbed his jacket and made his way out.

She ducked out long enough to take a long sip of iced coffee, then returned to the booth. As she shut off the music she'd played for the sound check, someone tapped on the door.

She turned and smiled. "Good Morning, Mr. Swagg."

Lil Swagg gave her a sparkling, gold-and-diamond-encrusted smile before replying. "What's up, shawty. Call me Swagg, no mister." A pair of sunglasses with blue lenses rested on top of his close-trimmed hair. He was dressed in an oversize gray T-shirt, designer jeans, a leather jacket and a pair of all-black running shoes. The heavy-looking gold chain around his neck had *Swagg* spelled out in black diamonds.

"Got it." She stood, noting that they were about evenly matched in height as she bumped fists with him. "I'm Teagan, chief tech officer and sound engineer. I'll be running your auditions today."

"Cool, cool." He looked over his shoulder, then looked back. "My manager is with me. He was behind me a minute ago." He ducked his head around the corner, calling down the corridor. "Aye, Rick! Hustle up, man!"

Another man appeared within a few moments. "Sorry 'bout that, Swagg. Had to take a call." He nodded in her direction. "Rick Royce." He was shorter and stockier than his client and dressed in khakis and a long-sleeved green polo with brown loafers.

"Nice to meet you, I'm Teagan. I'll be working with you today. Come on into the recording suite and make yourself comfortable."

As the two men moved past her in a haze of expensive-smelling cologne, Teagan returned to Fancy and opened up a new data set where she'd be saving the audition audio for Swagg and Rick's later review. Checking the time on-screen, she noted that it was about fifteen minutes until the official kickoff time for the auditions.

The echoing sounds in the hallway let her know that the group of musicians was approaching. Peeking out the door, she saw Trevor guiding a group of people into an orderly line in the corridor just beyond the recording suite. There were both men and women hauling various instrument cases and more than a few with drumsticks in hand.

She stood, knowing she'd need to inform the musicians of what to expect. Stopping in the doorway, she got a closer look at the man at the head of the line.

He looked tall, maybe three or four inches taller than she was. He had a medium complexion, and she could just see the ends of his short, curly hair peeking from beneath a black beret. A full beard covered his jawline, surrounding full lips that curved up into a half smile, and dark sunglasses obscured his eyes from view. He wore a red shirt with vertical black stripes beneath a silver-studded leather jacket, and a pair of inky-black jeans with studded, coal-colored combat boots. A large guitar case was slung over his shoulder, the strap cutting diagonally across his chest.

As if noticing her attention, he removed the glasses and tucked them into an inner jacket pocket. His soulful hazel eyes met hers.

Is it my imagination, or is he staring at me, too?

She swallowed, trying to shake off the ribbon of heat that snaked down her spine. "Hi, everyone. We'll be calling you into the recording suite in groups, by instrument. Swagg has asked for you in this order, so please line up this way. Bassists, guitarists, keyboard-ists, drummers."

She waited while the group readjusted themselves; Mr. Dark Glasses held on to his spot in the front. *So he's a bass player.* For some reason, it thrilled her to learn that little tidbit about him.

"I want to make you aware that there is no food, drinks or smoking allowed in the recording suite. I'll also ask that you keep quiet while the sessions are in progress. These rules are in place to protect both the integrity of my equipment and of the creative process." She cleared her throat. "I'll begin calling you in shortly. For now, just hang tight." She turned and retreated back into the recording suite, away from the bassist's arrest-ing gaze.

From his seat on the couch, Swagg announced, "I'm ready for the bass players, shawty."

Teagan nodded. "First bass player in line, come on in."

The man in the beret entered, pausing in the door-way. He was close enough now for her to smell the rich, woodsy scent rolling off of him.

"What's your name?" She looked at the printed list on the counter.

"Maxton McCoy."

She crossed his name off. "Go ahead into the booth and set up your bass."

He nodded to her and did as she asked.

She watched through the glass as he opened his case and plugged it into the amp. Taking a seat on one of the three stools in the booth, he donned the headphones and gave a thumbs-up.

She enabled the recording function, then started the track he was to play along with. While his fingers worked over the strings, she found she couldn't take her eyes off his face. His eyes were closed as if the music had snatched him out of this dimension and into another, where only creative flow existed.

Despite the pleased reactions from Swagg and Rick, and the overall purpose of the moment, one thought overrode all.

Damn, he's fine.

In the cool, dim interior of the booth, Maxton listened to the sound coming over his headphones for a few beats. It was a stripped-down, freestyle performance of one of Swagg's songs, one he hadn't heard and assumed was unreleased. The arrangement included only the rapper's voice and a basic treble melody.

The song itself had a brooding tone, and he knew it would require some minor chords to really bring out its meaning. He wriggled and stretched his fingers but didn't pluck the strings just yet, giving himself a bit more time to fully absorb the vibe.

His ears were analyzing the music, but his eyes were on the sound engineer.

In his ten-plus years of touring and recording, he'd only come across a handful of female engineers, but that wasn't what held his attention about her. She was beautiful in a way that almost hurt his eyes. She didn't seem to be wearing any makeup, and she had clear skin, high cheekbones and sparkling brown eyes. Her curly hair was tucked into a low bun, and based on the level of focus she demonstrated at the controls, he could see why. She seemed like the type to concentrate more on her work than her appearance, not that she needed to make much effort in that department. She was already radiant.

Once he wrestled his focus back and picked up on the tone and cadence of the rap, he started working his fingers over the four strings of Joan, his Fender American Professional II Precision Bass. He'd been playing this particular instrument for the last four years, having upgraded from the previous model. He loved everything about it, from the satiny-smooth feel of the rosewood fingerboard to the vintage-style, steel-and-brass bridge to the subtle, just-right curve of the neck board. Right down to the vibrant, three-color sunburst finish, it·fit his exacting tastes and playing style like no other left-handed bass on the market.

He settled into the rhythm, nodding his head along with Swagg's voice as he kept time. The rap, a serious one about the pain of losing a friend to violence in the streets, hit home for him in a way he hadn't expected. Rather than try to tamp down his rising emotions, though, he let them have their moment, using them to infuse his interpretation with something real, something that transcended sound and became feeling.

He closed his eyes as his fingers flowed over the strings in time with the song, keeping a steady bass line while adding improvisation to moments he felt could use it. The vibration from his bass traveled through his fingertips and his hands, up to his arms and down into his chest, carrying him away to another dimension. He always felt like this when he played, and he'd come to truly enjoy this glorious escape into his art.

Anticipating the approaching end of the track, he finished with a flourish and let his bass drop softly at his side. Opening his eyes, he set his gaze once again on the gorgeous woman working the sound equipment.

She gave him a soft smile and a thumbs-up.

He took off the headphones, hung them back on their hook and packed up his bass. Then he exited the booth and approached Swagg, who was gesturing to him.

"That was amazing. You definitely got talent, homie." Swagg stuck out his hand.

"Thanks." Maxton shook his hand. "I appreciate that."

"What's your background? Like, who've you played for?"

"Mostly R & B and soul artists. Johnny Gill, Jaheim, Usher, Charlie Wilson, Lloyd."

Swagg nodded. "Yeah, I can definitely hear that in the way you play. I like your style." He gave Max a pat on the arm. "We'll be in touch with you, playa."

"Thanks again." Maxton started for the door, stepping aside to let the next bass player in before leaving the recording suite.

In the corridor, he sat down on the floor and propped his bass against the wall. The spot he'd chosen gave him a clear view of the beautiful woman sitting at the board.

Sharrod, still in line, said, "Man, why don't you go sit in the reception area or wait in the car?"

He shook his head. "Nah, man. I think I'm good here." He was content to watch the engineer work until she had a little free time between auditions to talk. She might shoot him down, but before he left the building, he had to at least know her name.

He watched the other bassists, then the guitarists enter in turn, all while wondering what made her tick. How had she gotten interested in sound engineering? How long had she been working for the board? How old was she? Did she have a man?

Those last two weren't really any of his business, and he definitely wouldn't lead with them, but for the moment, his curiosity was getting the better of him.

When Sharrod exited after completing his audition, Maxton was standing. "How'd it go?"

Sharrod shrugged. "Pretty good, from what I can tell. Swagg complemented my stick work, so…"

"He had some compliments for me too, so maybe we'll both get the gig." Maxton slapped his friend on the shoulder. "Go on out to the car. I gotta take care of something real quick."

Sharrod frowned. "What are you doing, dude?"

"Don't worry 'bout it." He passed him his instrument case. "Take this with you, bruh. Just put it in the back seat."

"I'm not your butler, you know," he groused. But he took the case anyway and, with a shake of his head, walked away.

Maxton folded his arms across his chest, leaned against the wall and waited for the recording suite to empty out. Swagg and his manager were the last to leave. Swagg extended his fist as he passed. "Thanks for auditioning, homie."

He bumped fists with the young lyricist. "Thanks for the opportunity." Once they were gone, he returned his attention to the recording suite. The engineer was still seated at the monitor, and he could see her typing and clicking away.

Entering the room slowly, he asked, "Do you have to keep working much longer?"

"Not much longer." She glanced up, then went right back to what she was working on. "Just running a few file backups."

He could hear heavy footsteps approaching but chose to ignore the sound. "So, what's your name?"

She opened her mouth, then closed it. Her gaze shifted as if she were looking behind him.

He turned and saw a man standing about six inches behind him. He was tall, of medium complexion and was dressed in a white button-down and khakis. His arms were folded tightly over his broad chest, and his strangely familiar face was folded into a serious expression.

Not knowing what else to say, Maxton said, "Hi."

The man looked right past him to the sound engineer. "Teagan, is he bothering you?"

She chuckled. "Not really."

"Are you sure? Because my twin sense was tingling, and I picked up the distinct feeling of annoyance." He glared at Max.

"It's fine, Miles, so take a chill pill." She shook her head. "This is Maxton, one of the bassists that Lil Swagg auditioned today."

Miles stuck out his hand. "Hello, Maxton. I apologize for my manners. I'm just protecting my twin sister. I'm sure you understand."

"Of course I do," Max said, shaking hands with him. After all, he'd once been that way with Whitney. Tamping down the sadness that often accompanied thoughts of her, he turned his mind back to the matter at hand. *So they're twins?* "You're identical, right?"

"Yep. Right down to the birthmark." Teagan turned her head slightly to the left, revealing a dark, jagged mark on her throat. Maxton turned to see Miles tug down his collar to reveal the same mark.

"Kinda looks like a lightning bolt." Maxton scratched his chin.

"Yes. And if you harm my sister, I'll bring the thunder." Miles smiled, but it didn't quite reach his eyes.

"Noted." Maxton wasn't sure how he felt about this whole situation, but at least he'd gotten an answer to his question, in a roundabout way.

"So, you're alright?" Miles asked his sister.

"Yes, so go on back to…whatever it is you usually do upstairs." She waved him off with her hand.

He shrugged. "Okay, as long as you're good, I'm good." Miles turned and walked down the corridor toward the elevators.

Once Miles was gone, Teagan said, "Sorry about that. You share a womb with someone, and they get a little overprotective, I guess."

Maxton chuckled. "No big deal. At least now I know your name."

She gave him a crooked half smile. "And why were you so interested in knowing my name, by the way?"

He rubbed his hands together. "I just thought it would be good to establish some rapport with you. Since we're going to be working together soon."

She tilted her head to one side, her brow furrowed.

"Swagg auditioned five bassists today. What makes you so sure you'll be chosen?"

"I just know. It's hard to explain." He tugged his lapels, pulling his jacket closer around his body. "I don't want to hold you up from your work, so I'll see you later, Ms. Teagan."

She rolled her eyes. "No miss, please. Just Teagan."

"See, look at that. We've established a dynamic already." With a wink, he turned and walked away.

Outside, he opened the passenger-side door of Sharrod's rented sedan and climbed inside.

Seated in the driver's seat, Sharrod asked, "Did you take care of whatever you stuck around for?"

He nodded. "Yeah, bro. I think I did."

"You care to elaborate on that?"

"Nah." Maxton turned toward the window and smiled.

Three

Teagan sank into the soft, buttery leather of the pedicure chair and immediately reached for the remote. Turning on the chair's massage function, she adjusted the speed and pattern to her liking, then leaned back to enjoy the sensations.

"Ah, I love these chairs," her sister, Nia, who was laid out in the chair next to her, commented. "That's why I always come here. They have the best pedicure chairs in town."

Teagan nodded her agreement. The interior of Nubian Nails and Spa was relatively quiet for a Friday, and she attributed that to the early afternoon hour. The summer sun played over the metallic flecks in the gold paint covering the walls and bounced off the glass fronting the framed African art prints. "I'm glad your half day lined up with my day off this month. If we had waited to come in after five, it would've been super packed in here."

Nia stifled a yawn. "Ever since Mom implemented these 'self-care half days' for me, I've mostly been rolling alone. I mean, she never asked the rest of you to take regular time off like this."

"We both know Mom didn't ask. She just told you." Teagan shook her head. Their mother Addison's strong yet loving presence meant she rarely had to force an issue with her children. "And she didn't make the rest of us do it because we actually take days off."

"Oh, hush." Nia held up her hands, showing off the French manicure she'd just had done on her natural nails. "I did my nails this time, too, so lay off me. I'm maxing and relaxing, just as Mom demands."

Teagan looked at her own full set of medium-length, almond-shaped gel nails in a pinkish-nude color. "I really like how mine turned out. And I'm glad I took the tech's advice and added a little bling to my ring fingers."

"Nah, you know me. If my nails are too long or have too much embellishment, it just slows me down at work."

Staring at her older sister, Teagan wondered if she ever stopped thinking about work. "Were you just, like, born this serious, or did you acquire it before I was born?"

She shrugged. "Probably the first one. There's five of us. At least one of us has to be practical and responsible."

"Don't worry, I think you and Gage have that covered."

The nail technicians began filling the tubs of the

pedicure chairs with steaming water, essential oils and flower petals. Teagan inhaled deeply as the scents of lavender, citrus and sage floated past her nostrils. At her tech's prompting, she placed her feet in the water and sighed as the heat enveloped them. The combination of the vibration of the chair and the hot water threatened to send her straight to dreamland, but her sister's voice postponed the trip.

"It's been such a crazy week. I've spent these last several days chasing down data for the second quarter reports that are due by next Tuesday."

"I know, Nia. I submitted the data from the technology department already."

"Yeah, you did, and I appreciate you being on time. But not all the departments were so fastidious." She ran a hand over her short-cropped hair. "It was pretty touch-and-go for a moment, but I did get the last departmental report this morning. I think we're in line now to have everything ready for the Q2 meeting on Wednesday." She paused. "How are things going down in Studio One?"

"Nothing's happening right now. Lil Swagg booked the studio until the beginning of August, so on days like this when he's not recording, I don't have any reason to be there." The massage program ended, and she grabbed the remote to restart it. "Swagg decided to wait until Monday to replay the recordings and make a decision on which musicians to use in his backing band."

"Okay. But what's this I hear from Miles about one of the musicians lingering after the auditions were over?"

Teagan rolled her eyes. *Dimed out by my own twin. Ain't that a mess?* "The family grapevine strikes again, I see."

"The blessing and the curse of working in the family business." Nia laughed. "So, tell me about this guy. Miles didn't give me much."

She jerked a bit, trying not to laugh while the nail tech worked a pumice stone over the bottom of her foot. "There's not much to tell. We didn't even speak for five minutes before Miles showed up to bully him."

"Sounds like Miles. He's always been very protective of you." She shifted her position in the chair, leaning closer to her little sister. "What's his name?"

"His name is Maxton McCoy, and he's a bass player. He was the first one to audition in that group, and for some reason, he chose to stick around and talk to me after everyone else left."

Nia plucked her phone from the pocket of her denim shorts and began tapping the screen. "Go on. Tell me what he looks like."

"He's, uh, maybe three or four inches taller than me. Lighter complexion. He has this really great hair texture, this loose curl pattern that just sort of hangs down and frames his face." She paused, thinking back to her first look at him. "He has a great sense of style, kind of edgy. You know, the way Blaine used to dress back in the day before he toned it down. And he has the most gorgeous hazel eyes…" She stopped, realizing how much she'd already gone on about Maxton.

Nia stared. "Okay, sis. Seems like he's got some impressive qualities. How was his musicianship?"

"Really great, actually. It's been a while since I've had a bass player in the studio who was that young who had so much… I don't know…soul." She could still hear his playing in the back of her mind. "He's definitely got the chops."

Holding up her phone, Nia turned the screen to face her. "Is this him?"

Teagan balked when she saw Maxton's social media profile displayed on the screen. "Sheesh. Yes, that's him, ace detective Nia."

She nodded, drawing her phone back toward herself. "He's definitely handsome. I can see why you'd be attracted to him."

"Who said that?"

Nia laughed. "Sis, please. You wouldn't have described him the way you just did if you didn't find him attractive."

She looked away, unable to deny the truth in those words. "Fine. He's attractive, we can agree on that. But it doesn't matter."

"Why not? Who says you and Mr. McCoy can't be a thing?"

She swallowed.

"What color did you want, honey?" the tech asked.

"Um, just match my nails, please." Teagan turned back to her sister. "I say we can't be a 'thing.' You and I have grown up in the music industry. We both know that musicians are flighty and unstable. They just don't know how to chill or settle down."

"Teagan, do you hear yourself? You sound like you've totally drunk the stereotype tea." Nia raised her seat back and eyed her.

"Whatever." She hit a button on the remote, matching her sister's posture.

"I'm not saying you have to marry him or anything.

But why not have a little fun with a good-looking man who's interested in you?"

"Is that what you do, Nia? Have little, insignificant flings with guys?" She leaned forward, her eyebrows raised. "Because I'd love to hear about that."

Nia groaned. "You know I don't do that. I don't have time to date, let alone carry on a fling."

"Neither do I."

"Anyway, don't try to turn the question around on me. We're talking about you and your handsome, edgy bassist." Nia slipped her feet into the disposable sandals offered by her nail tech.

The two of them grabbed their purses and shoes and shuffled their way to the drying station, sitting down again. Teagan shivered a bit at the cool air being blown on her feet by the fans. "I haven't been on a date in ages. The quality of guys in Atlanta can be very variable, and that becomes even truer with just the men that hang around the studio for whatever reason."

"True enough." Nia sighed. "Look at us. Turning into two old spinsters while two of our brothers have already gotten hitched."

"Speak for yourself," Teagan quipped. "I'm still young and fresh. I could get a man if I wanted one. Right now, I just don't want to bother with it."

"Not even for the superhot, supremely talented man with the awesome curl pattern and the light eyes?" Nia winked.

"Least of all for him. I'm not about to risk my feelings on a musician. It's like I said. They just can't settle down, and I'm not about to be left heartbroken when he packs up his bass and hits that dusty trail."

Nia rolled her eyes. "It's a fling we're talking about here, girl. Not a game of *Oregon Trail*."

"Maybe so, but dating is way more dangerous. And I'm not fording that stream anytime soon." Shaking her head, Teagan turned her thoughts back to her still-wet toenails, and how she would spend the rest of her day off.

Because I'm not gonna spend it thinking about Maxton McCoy.

With a bowl of popcorn in hand, Maxton walked to his sofa. After setting the bowl on the table between the two glasses of iced cola there, he flopped down on the soft cushions. "What do you want to watch?"

Sharrod, seated next to him, glanced up from the screen of his phone. "It's Friday night, bro. To be honest, I'd rather hit the clubs and see if we can get into some trouble."

Rolling his eyes, Maxton grabbed the remote. "Fine. I'll choose."

"Why you ain't wanna go out this weekend?"

"We just came off tour, and I'm tired, Sharrod. Plus, since we about to start this new gig working with Lil Swagg, I think we need to tone it down. You know, rest up."

Sharrod scoffed. "We don't have the job yet, Max."

"Whatever, bro. I can play circles around those other bassists. I got this gig on lock, and so do you!" He slapped his friend on the back.

Sharrod shrugged in response. "I don't know, man. I feel like my cadence was off just slightly in that third and fourth bar."

"You're such a perfectionist." Flipping through the channels, he settled on a retro station that was playing reruns of the popular early nineties' competition show *American Gladiators*.

Looking up from his phone to the television screen, then at his friend, Sharrod said, "You're not seriously putting this on, are you?"

"Stop hating. This was my joint when I was little." He grinned as he watched Turbo, his favorite Gladiator, take on Laser in the joust. "Besides, I asked you what you wanted to watch, didn't I?"

"And I told you that I wanted to see some T & A out in those ATL streets." Sharrod clapped his hands together.

"Wow, man. Sometimes the San Bernardino Rico Suave really jumps out of your ass, doesn't it?" Maxton ribbed his old friend with his elbow.

"We can't all be from the hoity-toity hills of Calabasas, now, can we?" Sharrod punched him in the shoulder just as playfully.

Maxton stuck out his tongue. The two of them had been teasing each other like this ever since their days as roommates at University of Southern California's Thornton School of Music. They lived far enough apart that had they not gone to school together, they might never have met. "We may be from two different worlds, but we're both Trojans, bro."

"Fight on, Max."

"Fight on, Sharrod." He gave his friend a double fist bump.

He stared off toward the television but didn't seem to actually be watching the vintage goodness being played out on the screen. "Hey, you remember that night junior year, right after the homecoming game?"

"You mean that year we beat the Bruins by fourteen?"

He nodded. "Yeah, that game. Do you recall what we did after we won?"

Maxton scratched his head, searching through his memory banks. "Oh, yeah! Wasn't that the time we went into the city to drink with some of the guys from the football team?"

"Hell, yeah. And we woke up the next morning, lying in the grass in the quad?"

"Shit, I'd forgotten about that. I don't remember much of the night after the game, but I do remember waking up when that cold water started hitting me. I was shirtless, you were missing your left shoe, and somebody had drawn mustaches on us with permanent markers." Thinking back, he could still feel the insistent chill of the water being thrown at his bare chest by the sprinklers and see the look of annoyance on the face of the groundskeeper as he'd stood over the two of them.

"To this day, I don't know if the sprinklers came on because they were on timer mode or because the landscape guy turned them on to wake us up." Sharrod shook his head with a laugh. "That shit was crazy. We were lucky, though. At least we didn't get tattooed like Ross Hamlin did."

Max burst out laughing. "I'd like to think he's gotten that photorealistic lobster lasered off by now."

"Me too. Who would hire him with that thing tattooed on his neck like that?"

"Crazy times, bro. Crazy, crazy times."

"You were like that all through school, man. Always hatching some scheme or dragging me along on some kind of adventure." Sharrod ran a hand over his close-cropped hair. "Sometimes I wonder how we even graduated."

Maxton shrugged. "That summer before senior year, my parents let me know that if I didn't straighten up and save some of my adventures for after I got my degree, they were going to cut me off. That sobered me right up." He took another swig of soda, thinking how he'd grown up in the years since his rowdy days at college. *Real life has certainly sobered me up, just like Mom and Pop did back in the day.* "I go for the sure thing now. That's why I'm glad you got us this audition with Lil Swagg."

"You really seem sure we got this gig, Max." Sharrod eyed him. "You stayed behind for a while after the auditions were over. Do you know something I don't?"

Maxton reached for his glass of cola and took a long drink.

Sharrod's brows furrowed. "Come on, now. What did you do, bribe somebody?"

"No, man." Maxton chuckled. "I'm telling you. We got the gig. Would you just trust me on this one?"

"If you say so." Sharrod shifted on his seat until he reclined against the sofa's plush backrest. "But that still doesn't tell me why you stayed behind for like twenty minutes after everybody else left."

Maxton scratched his chin, feeling the smile tugging at his lips. "I just had to stick around and talk to that fine-ass engineer."

"See? This is why I can't take your ass nowhere."

Sharrod gave him a sidelong glance. "You really used the audition as a pickup spot? And you had the nerve to give me grief for wanting to go to the club and pick up some honeys the old-fashioned way."

Maxton laughed as he grabbed a handful of popcorn. "Yeah, you say that now, but you saw her. You gotta admit she's fine as hell."

"Yeah, alright. I'll give you that. She's definitely easy on the eyes."

Remembering the brief glimpses he'd gotten of her beautiful face and shapely body, Max said, "I didn't go there with the intention of picking up anybody. We went there for a work opportunity. But once I saw her, man, I just couldn't resist. If nothing else, I had to at least know her name."

"I'm listening."

"I got to talk to her for a few minutes. Her name is unique… I've never heard it before."

"What is it?" Sharrod swiped across his phone's screen.

"Teagan. Anyway, she seems very serious about her work and very focused. She stayed after everybody had left, just to make sure her equipment was properly shut down."

"Mmm-hmm. Her name means 'little poet,' according to the internet."

He thought about the way her eyes sparkled and wondered if she had ever written any poetry. "Cool. Anyway, I know she doesn't play about that soundboard. She wouldn't let anybody else touch it. And aside from that, she's a twin. Her brother appeared just as I was starting to get some information out of her."

Sharrod drew back. "Oh, snap. Work obsessed, and with an evil twin?"

"I wouldn't call homeboy 'evil,' but he was definitely overprotective. I guess he's the older twin." Maxton stretched his arms above his head. "He was very concerned that I might be bothering his sister."

"Sounds like Miss Teagan might just be too much woman for you, bro. Better play it safe before she puts your heart in a headlock."

"You know what, Sharrod? I think I agree with you on this one."

Eyes wide, eyebrows raised, Sharrod said, "Come again?"

He ribbed him again. "Stop acting so surprised, I agree with you on occasion. And when it comes to Teagan, you're probably right. Shawty's thick and fine as hell. But I just can't get caught up in any romantic entanglements right now."

"I know I shouldn't question you agreeing with me, but I just gotta know why." Sharrod leaned forward, resting his chin on his hands.

"It's just that this is Atlanta. The cradle of southern hip-hop and R & B. If there's anywhere we're going to stumble on that next big gig, like an international tour, it's here." He rubbed his chin. "If I let this woman take over my heart and mind, how would I be able to focus on the next move in my career?"

"I see, I see. You actually making sense, bro." He chuckled. "Hard to believe from a dude that once locked himself on the balcony of our dorm room."

"Whatever man. I just gotta stay focused, plain and simple. I can't let an opportunity pass me by, not if I'm gonna save up enough to finally buy a house and put down roots somewhere."

"Do you think you'll go back to LA?"

He shook his head. "Hell, nah. I'm going somewhere where property prices are more advantageous, and they don't have wildfires every freakin' summer. Don't wanna deal with tornadoes, either." He watched absently as the credits rolled on television. "As much as I love playing bass, I don't wanna do it forever. I want a little piece of land and some peace and quiet."

"I hear you." Sharrod reached for the popcorn and scooped up the last handful. "Any more snacks, bro?"

"Yeah. There's some chips in the cabinet above the microwave."

As his friend walked off to refill the bowl, Maxton pushed all thoughts of Teagan and her overprotective brother out of his mind.

Four

Scooting her chair up to the workstation in Studio One, Teagan touched the screen to pull up the sound files from the recent auditions. Lil Swagg and his manager Rick were waiting on the sofa behind her, so she opened the folder as quickly as possible. "Okay, gentlemen. I'm going to play the audition tracks of the top two musicians in each category, as you requested."

"Sounds good," Swagg said, lifting his sunglasses from his eyes and placing them atop his head. "Let's hear it."

"Okay. We'll do bassists first." She started the audio file for bassist Allen Wright.

Swagg and Rick listened in silence, their expressions unreadable.

When the file finished, Swagg said, "You know,

hearing that dude again, I don't really feel the vibe from him. Go ahead and play the other one."

Obliging him, Teagan opened Maxton's McCoy's sound file and pressed play. The room soon filled with the deep reverberations of his masterful playing, and she closed her eyes, remembering the look of bliss on his face as he worked the strings. His fingertips were deft and sure, and when he opened his eyes, his gaze had landed squarely on her face, causing a searing heat to rise from the pit of her stomach to the sides of her face.

The audio ended, and she looked to Swagg and Rick for their reactions.

Swagg's grin was as big as the diamond-studded letter *S* hanging from the gold chain around his neck. "Yeah, man. He's got the juice. That's my bassist."

Teagan nodded. "Noted. I'll let you hear the guitarists' audio next." She started the first file for that category. She continued on that way, opening and playing audio files until all eight had been heard. While Swagg and Rick deliberated, she leaned back in her chair and stared up at the recessed lighting above. What would it be like to come to the studio every day for the next few weeks, and see Maxton McCoy's impossibly handsome face with that devil-may-care smile? She inhaled deeply. If she were to remain the poised, professional ruler of this recording suite, she couldn't let him distract her from her duties.

I'd let Trevor take over, but Studio Two is booked solid until September. He won't have time to handle this suite, too. She sighed. Whenever Swagg and his manager decided to begin working on the album in earnest, there wouldn't be any good way to avoid the sexy bassist and his disarming swagger.

"Alright, Ms. Teagan, we've made our decision." Rick smiled in her direction. "Go ahead and take down these names for the liner notes. Maxton McCoy on bass, Brady Farmer on guitar, Sharrod Burton on drums and Mike Mendez on keyboard."

Teagan typed up the names in a text file. "Got it." Saving the text file in the folder with the audition audio, she asked, "When would you two like to start rehearsals for the album?" Silently, she prayed they'd say next week, to give her a few days to prepare herself for what was coming.

"Tomorrow," Swagg announced, standing from his seat. "I want to get this project done ASAP. Inspiration is flowing, and with a band this good, we should be done in no time. Then I can get back home to the BX."

"Homesick for New York already?" she asked.

"Yeah, I guess you could say that." Swagg grinned. "Nothin' like the Bronx, ya know? It's the cradle of hip-hop. You can draw a straight line from the pioneers like KRS-One and Boogie Down Productions, Melle Mel…"

Teagan nodded, picking up the list. "Afrika Bambaataa, T La Rock, Grandmaster Flash…"

"Hell, yeah! I love it when I meet a real hip-hop head." Swagg clapped his hands together. "Anyway, you can draw a line from those cats to Fat Joe and Terror Squad and Swizz Beatz to me." He closed his hands into fists, pointing both thumbs toward his chest. "The legacy continues, starting tomorrow, right here in this studio."

"See why I rock with this kid?" Rick gave Swagg

a hearty slap on the back. "Let me call these dudes up and let 'em know."

While Rick made the calls, Teagan excused herself. "I'll be right back, gentlemen."

She walked down the corridor, turning off at the elevator bank and heading into the small snack bar just beyond it. There, she got herself a granola bar and a bottle of water from the vending machines to soothe her rumbling stomach. Tearing off the wrapper, she admonished herself. *No more skipping lunch, girl.*

She was standing just outside her recording suite, munching on the bar, when Rick and Swagg exited.

"Thanks for your help today," Swagg said, giving her a mock salute before tugging his shades over his eyes once again. "We'll see you at 10:00 a.m. sharp tomorrow."

Swallowing a mouthful of raisins and oats, she smiled and replied, "Sounds great. You two have a good evening."

"You do the same," Rick called over his shoulder as the two of them departed.

Alone in the hallway, Teagan devoured the rest of the granola bar, then twisted the cap on the water bottle. She'd just tipped it up when she heard someone call her name.

Peering around the corner, she saw her mother, Addison, strolling down the hall toward her. "Child, what are you doing snacking on your feet like that? Did you skip lunch again?"

"Hey, Mom." She gave her a sheepish grin. "I might have skipped it a little."

She pursed her lips. "Girl, either you did or you

didn't, and we both know you did." Addison pinched her youngest child's cheek. "I don't know what I'm gonna do with you."

She held back the urge to roll her eyes, knowing her mother would pluck them right out of her head if she did. "I promise to do better with that. Now, what brings you down to the studio?"

"I came to see you." She eyed her daughter pointedly. "Did you pick out a dress or an outfit for the anniversary gala yet?"

She sighed. Her mother had been consumed with planning the studio's thirty-fifth-anniversary bash for what seemed like an eternity. "Mom, that party is still months away."

"I know. But if you end up getting something custom, like your sister and I did, you'll need that extra time for the designer and the seamstresses to get it done." Addison tucked a fallen curl back into her high bun. "So please, please decide what you're going to wear."

"I will. I promise." She tapped her chin, thinking. "Wait, what was the color scheme again?"

"It's purple and gold, Teagan." Addison's eyes flashed. "I can't believe you forgot that."

"I didn't, Mom. I was just kidding." She actually had forgotten, but this was her story and she was sticking to it.

Addison folded her arms over her chest. "Well, that little joke just earned you a personal escort to the family tailor, missy."

Teagan. "Oh, come on, Mom. You're not really going to…" She stopped, taking in the firm set of her mother's pursed lips. "Let me just run in the suite and get my purse."

"You do that," Addison insisted.

By the time Teagan returned with her purse, her mother's expression had relaxed. "Mom, I'm gonna guess you're not doing this to the boys."

Addison shook her head. "No. It takes no time to have a suit tailored, but making something custom is a whole different matter." She started down the hallway toward reception. "Let's go."

Teagan used her keys to lock up the recording suite, then followed her mother outside. In the parking lot, they climbed into Addison's midsize royal blue SUV.

While they drove, Teagan leaned back against the passenger headrest, watching the familiar scenery whizz by.

"What's the matter, honey? You seem distracted."

"It's nothing, Mom." She blew out a breath. "Lil Swagg has chosen his band, and he wants to start working on his album tomorrow."

"That's good news." Addison flicked the wheel to make a right turn. "He's paid for studio time for the next several weeks, so he may as well use it."

"That's true." She kept her gaze out the window, not wanting to look in her mother's direction. *If she sees my face, it will give me away.* "I guess I'm just…a little nervous. It's an ambitious project, and I want things to turn out just right for Swagg. I don't want anything to interfere with getting him the results he's after."

"That makes sense, but it sounds like you're doubting your ability to deliver on this album." Addison stopped at a red light and turned her way. "Teagan, you have to know by now that there isn't a better sound engineer in town. Whatever an artist throws at you, you can handle it."

"You sound so sure."

"That's because I am." Addison winked, then accelerated as the light changed green. "Don't you spend one more minute thinking about what might go wrong. Everyone in that room tomorrow will be there because they earned their space there through talent, and that includes you."

"Thanks, Mom." She smiled, accepting the wisdom of her mother's words.

Come tomorrow, I'm bringing my A-game.

When Maxton walked into Studio One at nine fifty on Tuesday morning, he resisted the urge to linger near Teagan and crossed the outer suite to the sofa. There, Lil Swagg, dressed in baggy jeans, a green polo and matching baseball cap, and an enormous gold chain featuring a yellow diamond-encrusted dollar sign, sat next to Rick, who was similarly dressed, minus the hardware. "Good morning. Thank you again, guys, for the opportunity."

Swagg grinned from behind his dark sunglasses. "No problem, homie. Just go in there and kill."

"You got it." He shook hands with the two men and returned to the soundboard, where he smiled in Teagan's direction. "Good morning, Teagan." He paused, letting his eyes delight in her appearance. Today, she wore a sleeveless orange silk blouse with a navy pencil skirt. Small polished-gold hoops sparkled in her ears. The outfit, along with the thin gold chains around her neck and wrists, accentuated her toned arms and long, shapely legs. Lowering his voice a bit, he said, "Told you we'd be working together."

"Morning, Maxton. And yes, I think I recall you saying that." She flexed her ankle as she crossed one leg over the other, showcasing her stylish orange-and-gold, color-blocked pumps. Giving him a quick nod, she let her glossy lips form a ghost of a smile.

Sharrod, who was right behind him, chuckled. "Let's keep the line moving, bro. You got three dudes and their equipment behind you."

Maxton rolled his eyes. "Please. You're carrying two wooden sticks."

"Four," Sharrod corrected. "I brought two pairs of sticks, just in case."

"Whatever, man." Reluctantly, he moved past Teagan at the workstation, passing through the open door into the booth.

The booth was set for recording, with two amps on either side of the space. There were two tricked-out drum sets positioned next to each other, one Tama Starclassic Performer acoustic set and one Roland V electronic set, both in rich black with pearl-and-silver detailing. He could easily identify both sets after years of knowing Sharrod. There were also five stools positioned around the space, one of which was stationed near the mic and headphones that Swagg would use to lay down his verses.

Carefully maneuvering his instrument around the various items in the room, he started setting up by removing his bass from the carrying case and connecting the cable to the amp he'd used during his audition, the one to the far left. Then he took a seat on the stool next to it.

Sharrod seated himself on the low stool behind the acoustic drum set while the keyboardist and guitarists made their preparations as well.

Swagg entered the booth then. "Y'all ready to do this?"

Maxton and the other musicians all responded affirmatively.

"Cool. Let's make sure you all know each other's names. You gonna be spending a lot of time together."

As the introductions were made, Maxton learned the names of the keyboardist, Mike, and the guitarist, Brady.

"Alright, now that we got that outta the way, let me run down my goals." Swagg clapped his hands together. "This album is eleven tracks, and I want to have it done in sixty days or less. I know that sounds like a lot. But before I left NYC, I worked with Chanel the Titan to produce eleven stripped-down beats. We'll use those as a basis and flesh them out into full-fledged songs."

Maxton nodded. "I see. We're just bringing the tracks to life, then."

"Right, my dude." Swagg pointed his direction. "The work is already started. Now we're gonna finish it."

Rick entered then, handing them each a slip the size of an index card. "These are the tracks we'll be recording. As we move through them, lean into your artistry. Feel free to improvise and add a little spice wherever you think it's needed. That's why we hired you."

"Now the engineer will talk with y'all for a minute,

then we'll get started," Swagg said as he and Rick left the booth.

Glancing at the card, Maxton eased over to Sharrod. "See the name of the fifth track?"

"Yeah. Very colorful." Sharrod chuckled.

Most of the tracks had ambiguous or even undecided titles. But track five, called "Eff Money J," had a pretty transparent purpose. "Ever worked on a diss record before?"

Sharrod shook his head. "Nah, but first time for everything, I guess."

Teagan entered then, holding a tablet close to her chest, and Maxton couldn't help staring at her legs as she walked.

"Okay, gentlemen. Swagg has generously added a bonus to your payment due to the tight turnaround he's asking for on this album. You should already have received an email from me detailing the terms, the compensation for the sessions tied to this project and the royalties going forward. Are there any questions or concerns about that?"

No one had any, and Maxton surmised that was because they were making about 20 percent over the typical fee for album work plus a pretty fair royalty on the finished project. Even if Swagg worked them for twelve hours a day for the whole month, Maxton knew the compensation would still be fair.

"Great. I'm going to pass my tablet around, and if each of you would sign and date by your names, to indicate that you're good with all the terms, we can go ahead and get started."

They passed around the device and the sleek black stylus, then Maxton handed it back to Teagan.

Their hands momentarily brushed during the exchange, and he felt a twinge go through him. Her skin was so soft and warm against his that his brain short-circuited for a beat.

"Maxton, are you going to let go?"

Realizing he was still gripping the stylus, he released it into her hand. "Sorry about that. Just checked out for a minute."

"Try not to do that while we're recording." Her tone light and teasing, she took the stylus, turned and walked away, returning to her workstation in the outer suite.

He swallowed. When his gaze shifted to Sharrod, he saw his friend sitting behind the drum set, shaking his head. The other two musicians were surreptitiously watching as well, and Mike, the keyboardist, wasn't even doing a good job of hiding it.

Maxton cringed. *Guess I gotta be a little less obvious about my fascination with our illustrious sound engineer.*

The session got underway with Teagan first playing a track, then allowing the musicians to improvise accompanying music. They spent the better part of the day working on the first track, and by noon, Swagg was satisfied enough to lay down his chorus over the music.

They continued working on the song until just after two when Swagg took off the headphones and set them on the hook. Raising his hand above his head, he said, "Alright, y'all. Take a lunch. My stomach 'bout to collapse."

Chuckling, Maxton propped his bass in the stand behind his amp and headed with Sharrod toward the door.

In the hallway, Sharrod asked, "Where do you wanna eat?"

Maxton shrugged. "I could go for a burger and fries, but I'm not picky about where we get it."

Teagan exited the recording suite and walked by them carrying an insulated lunch bag. She nodded to them as she passed and disappeared through the rear door.

Maxton started walking in that direction.

Sharrod said, "You really following shorty?"

"Not really. We parked on the side, so this door's closer, remember?"

Rolling his eyes, Sharrod said, "Whatever. I'll meet you in the car. Don't spend our whole lunch break mackin', either."

"It won't take but a minute."

They exited, and Sharrod went right, toward the parking lot, while Maxton went left, toward the courtyard behind the building. There, Teagan sat on a bench, using a plastic fork to eat from a clear container.

Walking up to her, he said, "Looks good. What is it?"

She held her hand over her mouth as she finished chewing, then swallowed. "Just some leftover chicken alfredo I made last night."

"You always bring lunch?"

She shook her head. "To be honest, I usually skip it. But my Mom ain't having that, so I'm trying to get better about it."

"Your mom. You mean, Addison Woodson, right?"

She nodded. "Yes. 404 Sound is a family-owned

business, has been for over thirty years. All my siblings work upstairs in the c-suites."

"Including your overzealous twin?"

"Yeah. Don't mind Miles. He can't help himself."

"He wants to make sure you're good. I can respect that." An image of his own sister came to mind, but he didn't want to talk about her for fear of dredging up that same old pain that had become his constant companion these last eight months. "Seems like the Woodsons really look out for each other."

"We do." She set down her fork, gesturing toward the parking lot. "Your friend looks a little agitated."

Maxton glanced that way to see Sharrod flagging him down, air-traffic-controller-style, from the far end of the parking lot. Shaking his head, he said, "Yeah, let me go. We do need to eat before we go back in session. See you later."

"Later." She raised her hand, giving him a small wave as he walked away.

Five

"Come on, Teagan. Keep up."

"Sheesh, I'm coming." Teagan picked up her pace to keep up with her twin brother's long strides. "You know, you could also slow down a bit. Not all of us are triathletes."

Miles chuckled. "Sis, I can see why you kept blowing me off, or agreeing and then flaking on me, all these months. You're out of shape."

She stuck out her tongue. "Shut up, Miles, before I bop you."

"You gotta catch up to me first." He laughed and sped up to a jog.

"Ugh." She picked up her pace again, thankful that the path was paved. They were making their way down Proctor Creek Greenway, a two-lane walking trail in the northeastern part of the city. It was closer to work than Piedmont Park, so she'd taken that into consideration when she finally agreed to come with her brother on one of his weekly fitness walks.

As she dashed along on the right side of the broken yellow line separating the lanes, she took in the scenery. The scorching heat of the July day was finally beginning to wane, and the sun was sinking lower on its trip toward the horizon.

The greenway, which had only opened in the last few years, was certainly not the most pristine or scenic of them all. It wasn't anywhere near as manicured as Piedmont Park's trails. That was largely due to its location in an old industrial area of town. The grassy expanse along the path was dotted with the ruins of many aged factories, warehouses and the like. Towering overhead were the silvery-white poles of power lines, which, while providing vital electricity to the city's ever-expanding power grid, did nothing to add to the scenery.

Still, the trail had its own, unique brand of urban beauty. The winding path took them through deep wooded groves where kudzu and English ivy climbed the hilly banks of the creek, rising up to shroud the trunks and branches of the willow trees. The water, somehow both murky and clear at the same time, babbled as it flowed over the rocky creek floor toward the Chattahoochee River.

Finally, mercifully, she came abreast of her brother, and as she'd promised, used her open hand to pop the back of his head.

"Well, look at that. You finally caught up!"

"I can do anything with proper motivation," she

quipped. "And nothing pleases me more than going upside your big head."

He laughed. "Whatever works, I guess." He blew out a breath and slowed his pace a bit. "Alright, we can ease up now. We're already about a mile in."

"Meanwhile, have I mentioned how much you resemble a highlighter today, Miles?"

He glanced down at his electric green T-shirt and running shorts. "No, but I appreciate the feedback." He eyed her. "By the way, you look like a housewife on a run to the warehouse store."

"Whatever." She'd chosen her fuchsia tank and purple cotton shorts for comfort, not fashion. "It's too hot to think too hard about what I'm wearing. I just tossed this into my bag before I left the house this morning so I could come out here with you." She adjusted the hook-and-loop closure at the back of her visor, which kept threatening to undo the low ponytail she'd slapped her hair into. "And now that I have, it's my supreme hope that you will stop inviting me."

"Nah, sis. I need you healthy, just as healthy as me." He reached over and squeezed her cheek. "That way I can pester you well into our nineties."

"Sounds delightful," she said with mock disgust.

A breeze blew through, rustling the leaves of the trees and providing momentary relief from the oppressive humidity. "Don't worry. About this time of year, I take my walks indoors, because it gets too hot to be out here for very long."

"That's a relief." The temperatures had fallen off since noon but were still in the low eighties, even as sunset approached. "Because I'm not doing this again unless it's in an air-conditioned location."

"Gotcha." Miles lifted his baseball cap, using the small towel he'd had slung over his shoulder to mop his brow. "I love coming out into nature. I need this break from the finance department. Do you know that we were the last department to turn in our quarterly reports?"

She shook her head. "Nia mentioned that somebody was late, but she didn't say who."

"Ugh. I was so annoyed. But my best accountant just had a baby, and things have really been backed up since she left on maternity leave." He sighed. "I had to lean on my other three staff accountants to pick up the pace, just for us to still be late. But at least we showed a rise in profits since the first quarter. I think it could have been a bigger gain if we just…"

"Miles, hush. Didn't we just go over all this at that 7:00 a.m. meeting this morning? I don't want to rehash it, even though I wasn't caffeinated enough to process most of it."

"Yeah, you're right. Tell me about what's going on in the studio. How are things going with Swagg's album?" He sounded genuinely interested.

"That's still shop talk, but I'll indulge you. I think things are going well, for the most part."

"What's the hang-up, then?"

"Today, we recorded the second track six times because the bassist couldn't decide on an interpretation to stick to."

"The bassist keeps tempo for everybody else, so I can see how that would be annoying." He scratched his chin. "The bassist, huh? That wouldn't be the guy in the leather jacket that I saw sniffing around you last week, would it?"

She stared. "How do you know that?"

He shrugged. "Word gets around the 404 building pretty fast. His name's Something McCoy, right?"

"Maxton McCoy." She blew out a breath. "And yes, he's the bassist Swagg chose. Anyway, Swagg ended up choosing the second version out of the six we tried, so it seems to me that we went on with the improvisation for far too long."

"Maybe a little."

"I mean, Swagg wants this album done in less than two months, and I don't want to miss the deadline because we're dawdling in the studio, you know?"

"Makes sense to me." Miles stopped as they reached the crosswalk at Johnson Road, turning toward his sister and grasping her shoulders gently. "I'm going to ask you this again. Is he bothering you? Because if he is, I'm happy to make him eat some sheet music or something."

She laughed. "No, he's not bothering me, Miles. This is just par for the course, a part of the creative process. While it's frustrating, it's not a problem." She grabbed his hat brim and tugged it down. "And if you're worried about us getting together, don't be. If he can't even make up his mind well enough to settle on a bassline, he probably isn't the settling-down type."

"I'm glad you can see that."

"Why must you always resort to threats of violence, anyway? You've been that way since we were kids."

He readjusted his hat. "Probably because I'm serious. You're my twin, so if somebody hurts you, they're essentially hurting me, too." He gave her shoulders a squeeze. "Frankly, sis, I'm not having that."

"I appreciate that, chucklehead." She leaned up and gave him a peck on the cheek.

They crossed the two-lane road, continuing down the trail on the other side. "Are we almost at the end?"

He nodded. "Yeah. It's not much farther to Sanford Road, and once we get there, we can take the MARTA back to the building to get our cars."

"Great, because I'm exhausted." She could feel the sweat rolling down her back but decided not to share that little detail with her brother. "I feel like I should get to eat pizza after this. I'm sure I already burned it off."

"Throw some veggies on it and I'll allow it," Miles replied.

"Fair enough."

They finished the rest of the trail in silence, then took the Green Line back to 404 headquarters. As Teagan trudged to her car, sweaty, tired and hungry, she heard her brother call her name. "What, Miles? And make it quick, because I'm starving and you're the only thing standing between me and a hot pizza."

He laughed. "I just wanted to say, thanks for coming on the walk with me, grumpy. I know you hate working out, but walking is a good way to ease into it."

"I suppose. I just hope your indoor trail is much shorter."

"It will be. Hard to cram three miles inside a building." He tapped his chin as if thinking. "Although, if we did enough laps, we could still make three miles…"

She pursed her lips. "Bye, Miles."

"Bye, sis. Love you," he called as he marched off toward his jet-black pickup.

"Love you, too." She opened the driver's-side door of her white coupe and climbed inside. As soon as she started the engine, she cranked the air conditioner as high as it would go. Snatching off her visor, she looked in the rearview and shook her head at the sight of the curls plastered to her sweaty brow. "Dang. I definitely gotta wash my hair." Wash day was an ordeal she was too tired to carry out, so she resolved to do it tonight but sleep in her turban and deal with the detangling in the morning.

After taking a few moments to let her body temperature drop enough for her to focus on the road, she backed out of her parking space and headed for home.

Maxton sat on one of the tall leather stools at the bar inside Rogue Sports Pub, his eyes glued to the television. The anchors on SportsCenter were busy bantering about the latest baseball matchup between Atlanta's hometown team and the team from Miami.

"Yo, Maxton."

He turned to his left, his attention drawn away from the commentary. "What's up, Sharrod?"

"Are we gonna order? Or are you gonna just keep staring at the TV?"

The bartender, Nick, stood nearby, rubbing a drying cloth over the glass in his hand. "You ready to order, playa? You've had my menu for like twenty minutes. Besides, weren't y'all in here last week?" He set the glass down in the rack, then pulled out his pen and pad from his apron pocket.

Maxton chuckled. "Yeah, my bad. Anyway, let me just get the chicken nachos and a glass of Lee's finest."

"And I'll have the same. Just make my nachos with steak, please."

"You got it." Nick took their menus and slipped them into the holder on the far end of the counter. Then he disappeared behind the bar to deliver their order slip to the kitchen.

Maxton let his gaze sweep over the interior as the sports show went to a commercial break. The brick-red walls were covered with pennants, posters, jerseys and other collectible items representing the four main professional teams that called Atlanta home: baseball, football, and men's and women's basketball. Neon signs advertising popular beers and the occasional photograph of some famous athlete who'd stopped in for a bite to eat punctuated the collection of memorabilia.

"You've been unfocused all day today, bro." Sharrod poked him in the shoulder with his index finger. "What's up with you?"

"What makes you say that?"

"Oh, please. Did we not have to slog through six takes of one song, just because you couldn't settle on a bass line?" He stared. "I'm sure I'm not the only one who noticed, my dude."

Maxton sighed. "Fair enough. I was a little distracted today."

"And I bet I know why, since you spent the entire session staring at the sound engineer." He stared, then gave him the slow blink.

"You have to know her name is Teagan by now."

"I know her name. You sure as hell mention it

enough." Rolling his eyes, he drummed his fingertips on the bar.

Maxton tilted his head to one side. "Stop hating. Either way, she can't be blamed for how distracted I was today. Not all of it."

Sharrod scoffed. "She can't be blamed for any of it. How is it her fault you can't stop staring at her like you're the bear and she's the pot of honey?"

Maxton frowned. *Why is Sharrod making such a big deal about this?* "Anyway, that song is really special. Because of the subject matter, it required a lot more thought to determine the best interpretation."

"I guess," Sharrod said with a shrug.

"Come on, man. Have you really listened to the lyrics? That song is all about the pain of losing someone close to you. I don't know what they used for you drummers, but that's the song I was asked to play along with for my audition."

"Nah, today was the first time I heard that track." Sharrod tapped his chin. "But if you heard it before, why didn't you feel confident about how to work with it?"

"It's pretty heavy material, man. I just wanted to do it justice. There's a lot of pain in that song, and I wanted to make sure I conveyed it while still keeping true to the overall tone of the album."

"Here you go, guys." Nick slid them their beers.

"Thanks," Sharrod said as he gripped the handle of his mug. "I can see that. I know it's important to get the vibe right. It's just that you seemed like you were floundering there for a minute. I've never really seen you lose your cool like that."

He ran a hand over his hair. There was a certain cluelessness in his friend's words, a sign that he was still blissfully unaware of the full measure of pain Maxton had suffered when he lost Whitney. And since he'd never let himself fully vent that pain to his closest friend, he supposed he had only himself to blame. "I didn't know it was that bad from the outside. But I'll be on my toes from now on. Promise."

"Good, because we've still got nine more tracks." Sharrod raised his mug.

Maxton grabbed his own and took a long drink. The citrusy flavor of the Rogue's signature IPA invaded his taste buds, carrying with it the hints of vanilla and the spicy cinnamon that gave the beer its bite.

"Listen. Do you remember when we were on tour with BJ the Chicago Kid, and I missed the last show?"

"Yeah, of course I do," Maxton replied. "They had to replace you with a damn drum machine at the last minute."

"I know." Sharrod shook his head. "And I'm ashamed of that, believe me. Did I ever tell you why I didn't show up that night?"

Their nachos arrived, just in time for the story. Maxton reached for a chip laden with grilled chicken, cheese sauce and jalapeños. "No, you didn't. So what happened?"

"I got caught up with one of the groupies. There were these two girls who had been following BJ's tour bus for the last three stops. I'd seen them hanging around the venues, and I just assumed they were BJ stans. But that night when he did his final stop in his home city, I found out that one of them was only interested in 'the hot drummer.'" He made air quotes around the last three words.

"Oh, boy." Maxton shook his head. "Go on."

"Anyway, I was hanging out behind the theater before the show. Me and a couple of the roadies were just chilling, trading war stories. We'd already moved the equipment onstage, so there really wasn't anything left to do, and it was still, like, two hours before showtime. The two girls come twisting across the parking lot. I mean these girls are looking for something, and the shorter one was just bold about it. She walks right up to me and says, real sultry, 'What are you getting into tonight, drummer boy?'"

Maxton crunched on another chip, nodding. Sharrod's stories were always wild, and though he was never sure if they were fully true, that didn't diminish the entertainment factor.

"So now the roadies are laughing and joking while she's introducing herself. Said her name was Candy. But this girl was thick, with this cute little leather dress on. She had the boom and the pow, you know what I mean?"

"Yeah, I get it," Maxton said. "Go on."

"So I was like, 'Hopefully, I'm getting into you.' Well, after I said that, it was on. We left, got a rideshare over to a hotel a few blocks down the street and that girl spent the rest of the night turning me inside out." He rubbed his hands together. "Shorty showed me some new things, that's for damn sure."

Maxton chuckled around a mouthful of food.

"When I woke up the next morning, she was gone. No note, none of that. Looking back, I'm lucky she didn't take my wallet while I was asleep." He shook his head. "I called up BJ's people, and they were understandably pissed. I had to reimburse them what they paid me for the missed show."

"Dude. Why are you telling me this now?"

"Because there's a lesson in there, man. I screwed myself over by letting a pretty girl distract me from work. And if you ever get the call to go back out on tour with BJ, I can't go, because they banned me from touring with him. Permanently."

Maxton winced. "Ouch. I didn't know you got blacklisted."

"Yeah, I did. I missed out on touring with Only the Family and Lil Durk because of it. Apparently, Chicago dudes are comparing notes and whatnot." With a solemn shake of his head, Sharrod dug into his nachos. "Messed up my money for the honey. Bad move."

While he continued eating his own food, Maxton thought about Sharrod's rather crazy story. He was right. He was lucky "Candy" hadn't robbed him blind; that probably wasn't even her real name. Sharrod had taken an extraordinarily dumb risk to get in a girl's panties, and even though he hadn't gotten jacked, he hadn't escaped unscathed, either. "Please tell me you'll never do that shit again. What if she had bad intentions? We could have found your ass dead in a ditch somewhere."

"You don't have to tell me, and no, I won't be doing anything that stupid ever again." He took a drink. "I know it's an extreme example, but you should still take it as a cautionary tale. Don't let a pretty face keep you from meeting your professional goals."

Maxton nodded but didn't respond. Finishing up

the last of his nachos, he pushed the plate away before draining his beer. "Hey, Nick, can I get another?"

While the bartender refilled his mug with the golden brew, he thought about his recent promise to Sharrod. His friend's crazy-bananas story had served as a firm reminder that he should stick to his goals, not to Teagan.

That might be easier said than done, but he had to at least try.

Six

Passing by the reception desk Thursday evening, Teagan could see that Barbara had already gone home for the evening. Glancing at her phone, she checked the time. It was twenty minutes past six, well past business hours. But it had still been a short day in the studio compared to the previous day. The band had invited her out for pizza with them, but she'd stayed behind to get things ready for tomorrow's session.

She swung open the glass-paneled door and stepped outside. The oppressive heat and humidity of the Georgia summer greeted her, and she groaned. Even with the lightweight fabric of the knee-length sage-green sundress she'd worn into work, there was no escape from the oven-like atmosphere. She picked up her pace as she walked to her car, anticipating the glorious relief of air-conditioning waiting inside the cabin.

She sniffed, inhaling the familiar, unwelcome aroma of cigarette smoke, and cringed. Unlocking the driver's-side door of her car, she reached for the handle and stopped short when someone called her name.

Turning toward the sound, she saw her father's personal secretary jogging toward her. She wore her typical work attire of a black button-down shirt and matching slacks with low-heeled pumps. She pinched the filter of a lit cigarette between her fingers. *That explains the smell.*

"Teagan, hold on a minute." Gloria stopped on the sidewalk in front of her.

"Hey, Gloria, haven't seen you in a while." She couldn't help noticing the way the older woman's voice wavered.

"So, how was your day today? Is everything good in the studio?"

"Everything's fine. I think we're making good progress on Lil Swagg's album."

"That's good to hear." Her head bobbed with approval.

She eyed Gloria for a moment, then asked the question lingering on the tip of her tongue. "You're…smoking again?"

Her gaze skittered around, and she let out a humorless chuckle. "Haven't smoked in months. It's my nerves, you know. When they get frayed, I slip up."

Teagan frowned. "Is everything alright? What's going on that's made you pick up smoking again?"

She nibbled her bottom lip before turning away to take another pull. With her back turned, she blew the smoke toward the building before facing her again.

"You're about to find out. It's the whole reason I stopped you." Reaching into the back pocket of her slacks, Gloria handed her a folded, bright white square.

"What's this?" Teagan opened it up and saw that it was an envelope, addressed to her father. There was no return address.

"I...think it's better if you just look at it." Gloria shifted her weight from left to right, then back again. "You know your father asked me to start screening his mail years ago, back when he was still CEO. To cut down on wasted time, I read his mail and only bring him the important stuff. And doing that for him has never been a problem for me." She shook her head solemnly. "Until today."

Teagan shifted her focus from Gloria's drawn face to the unremarkable-looking envelope in her hand. Taking a deep breath, she extracted the folded letter and opened it, reading aloud. "Dear Mr. Woodson..." She stopped speaking the words but kept reading through the first four sentences. Her heart climbed into her throat like a squirrel charging up a tree. "Holy shit."

"Yeah, that's about the same reaction I had when I read it over my lunch break. I've been trying to figure out what to do since then." Gloria tossed the cigarette on the sidewalk and twisted the sole of her shoe over it. "So, I'm gonna go and leave this to you." She turned away.

"Wait a minute." Teagan touched her arm. "Why me? You screen his mail for a reason. Why didn't you give this to him? It obviously falls in the 'important' category."

"I can't, Teagan. I can't take this to him." Gloria's lips

twisted into a sad frown. "I've known him for years. And the best way to soften bad news is to get it from his baby girl." She stepped back. "Please, do this for me, as a favor."

Seeing the discomfort written all over Gloria's expression and her slumped shoulders, Teagan slowly nodded. "Fine. But I think you're putting too much faith in this making the news any easier to take."

"Thank you." She spun and speed-walked to her small sedan. Within the next few minutes, she'd peeled out of the parking lot.

Guess she didn't want to give me a chance to change my mind. With the letter in hand, Teagan locked her car and reentered the building with her key card. Taking the elevator up to the fourth floor, she walked past her unused office. Her parents gave her an office, just like the rest of her siblings, but she preferred to spend all of her time in the studio. She continued down to the end of the corridor and entered her father's office.

Caleb Woodson was seated behind his big oak desk, talking on the phone. Wearing a dove-gray suit with a charcoal-gray shirt and pocket square, he looked every bit the old Southern gentleman she'd always thought he was. His short black curls were gray around the temples, and a full, salt-and-pepper beard surrounded his smiling mouth.

He glanced up when she entered, gesturing her to the chair across from him.

She watched him while he finished his conversation, thinking of the way his deep skin tone had mixed with her mother's fairer one to produce the medium tones that she and all her siblings had. Or so she'd assumed.

The longer she stared at him, the more aware she became of just how awkward things were about to get.

He finally ended the call, replacing the handset in the cradle. "Hey, sweetheart. To what do I owe the pleasure of this visit from my little princess?"

She gave him a half smile. "Come on, Dad. I'm a long way from my castle playhouse at this point."

"Maybe so, but I'll always see you that way." He winked. "So, what do you need?"

"Can I ask you something?"

"Sure, honey." He settled back in his chair, tenting his fingers.

She paused, thinking of how best to phrase her question. "Did you…ever have any other serious relationships? You know, before Mom?"

He shrugged. "Sure, I suppose. I mean, I had a couple of long-term girlfriends, but I've never proposed to anyone else but Addy." He gave her a sidelong glance. "Wait a minute. What brought on this newfound curiosity about my past?"

Looking into her father's eyes, she searched for any inkling that what she'd read in the letter might be true. Could this really be happening? Now that she was past the initial shock, her mind was free to process the further implications of this whole situation. Was it possible that the man she'd loved and looked up to her whole life wasn't the man she thought he was? Knowing she wouldn't find the answer any other way, she resolved to cut to the chase. She drew a deep breath. "Gloria asked me to…well… I have something to give you."

His brows scrunched together. He extended his hand. "Alright."

Handing over the letter, she rested her hands in her lap and waited.

In the silence, she could hear the moment he reached the second sentence. His breath grew louder, more erratic. Watching his face, she saw his nostrils flare and his eyes flash. Moments later, he forcefully pushed back from his desk and jumped to his feet. "What the hell is this?"

She swallowed. "It's a letter. It came for you today, and Gloria wanted me to give it to you…"

He read aloud, "Dear Mr. Woodson, my name is Keegan Woodbine and I have reason to believe you are my biological father." He balled up the paper and tossed it into the wastebasket. "This is absolute bullshit."

"I told Gloria that having me bring this to you wouldn't make it any easier to hear." Teagan ran her hand over her hair. "I'm sorry I upset you, Dad."

He shook his head. "This isn't your fault and I won't have you taking any blame for it. It's not Gloria's fault, either." He touched his fingertips to his temples. "There's no way this is possible. I've loved your mother for most of my life, and I've never got any other woman pregnant." He looked at his daughter, his eyes pleading. "You have to believe me, baby girl. Please say you believe me."

She nodded slowly in response to his earnest declaration. "Yes, Dad. I believe you."

He laid his hand over his chest. "Good. I'm relieved to hear that."

"There's still the matter of this accusation, though. How are you going to handle this? What are you going to tell Mom?"

He gestured to the wastebasket. "You just saw me .

handle it. That letter was nothing but lies, and there's nothing further to do. And I'm certainly not going to needlessly upset your mother by telling her about this."

She balked. "Dad. If this person went to the trouble of sending that letter, do you really think they won't pursue this claim further?"

"It isn't true!" He slapped his hand on his desk.

"Regardless of that, I don't think they're going to just let it go. What happens when they send another letter? Or escalate this thing somehow?"

His shoulders slumped, he turned toward the window behind his desk and opened the blinds. "Teagan, I already told you. It's all lies, and I don't want to hear another word about it." He stuffed his hands into the hip pockets of his slacks.

She'd come face-to-face with her father's famous stubborn streak, but she still tried to make him see reason. "But Dad…"

"Young lady, if you 'but Dad' me one more time, we're going to have a problem." He kept his back turned to her as he spoke. "It's late, Teagan. Go home and get yourself some dinner."

She knew a dismissal when she heard it. Rising from her seat, she stood and walked out of the room.

Maxton slung the strap of his bass's carrying case over his shoulder and followed Sharrod from the court-yard behind 404 to the front parking lot. "You know what? Mike and Brady are actually fun guys. I'm glad we went for a pizza with them after the session."

Sharrod nodded. "Yeah, they seem like good dudes." He scratched his chin as they rounded the corner to the front of the building. "Hey, isn't that Teagan over there?" He pointed.

Maxton's gaze followed the gesture. There she was, sitting in the driver's seat of her little white coupe. "Yeah, man. That's her. What is she doing there alone?"

They walked closer, and the picture of her became clearer. She was reclining there, her thick curls against the headrest, looking straight ahead. As they approached from the passenger side, he could see the tears streaming down her face.

"Oh, snap. She's crying," Sharrod said.

Maxton slid the strap of his bass off his shoulder.

"Let me guess," Sharrod said, tucking his drumsticks into the back pocket of his cargo shorts. "You want me to take this so you can run to her rescue, right?"

Handing over his instrument, he nodded. "Call me crazy, but I can't just leave her here like this, man."

Sharrod took the bass. "I'll leave it in the trunk for tomorrow's session, then. And how are you getting home?"

He shrugged. "I'll take the train if I need to. Just be at my place at the regular time tomorrow to pick me up, and we're good." He kept his eyes on Teagan as he spoke.

"No romantic entanglements, my ass." Sharrod snickered as he walked away toward his rental.

She finally noticed his presence, and her eyes slid shut.

Maxton walked around to the driver's side of the car. He tapped gently on her window with his knuckle.

Her eyes popped open, and she swiped her hand over her face before rolling the window down. "Hey, Maxton, what's up?"

"That's what I came to ask you." He watched her intently. "What's wrong?"

"Nothing." She shook her head, wiping away more tears. "I'm fine."

"You're sitting alone in your car, crying, so we both know that isn't true."

She cringed, and he couldn't tell if the change in her expression was brought on by embarrassment, annoyance or both.

"Listen, I'm not trying to get in your business or anything like that." Maxton crouched so they could be at eye level. "But I am concerned that you seem so upset. Do you maybe wanna talk about it?"

She sniffled. "Do you want to listen?"

He nodded. "I do."

She jerked her head toward the passenger seat. "Get in. Just watch out for my purse."

He did as she asked, carefully avoiding her bag as he joined her in the car. After he buckled up, she pulled out of the lot. Before he had a chance to ask where they were headed, she spoke.

"There's a coffee shop right around the corner. We can go there."

"Sounds good."

As they drove, she took several deep breaths and, from what he could tell, composed herself. The tears were no longer flowing, but the sadness remained in her eyes.

Soon, they pulled into the parking lot of a small, one-story building with a glass door and plenty of windows along the front. He read the sign affixed to the roofline and smiled. "The Bodacious Bean? What a name."

"It's family-owned, and it's been here for decades." She cut the engine and undid her belt. "Best lattes in the city." Grabbing her bucket-style black bag from the floorboard, she opened her door.

"It's been a long day. I could use a little pick-me-up."

He walked behind her and couldn't help observing the sway of her hips in the short green sundress she wore and the way her calves flexed as she walked in her high-heeled sandals. They entered the place to the sound of a tinkling bell. Maxton inhaled, and the rich aroma of the coffee awakened his senses. "Damn. It smells amazing in here."

"They use their own crossbred bean. Can't get this stuff anywhere else." She approached the counter with all the confidence of a regular and greeted the barista. "Hi. Can I please get a medium iced–caramel latte?" She started fishing around in her purse, probably for her wallet.

Maxton sidled up next to her. "I'll have what she's having. And add a couple of croissants, please." He waved his credit card over the contactless processing machine and paid before she could.

"You didn't have to do that." She eyed him as she dropped her wallet back into her bag.

"I know." He shrugged. "But it's not a problem, really."

She observed him for a few silent beats. "Let's get a table."

He followed her to a two-top in the back, positioned beneath the last window along the coffee shop's eastern wall. He pulled out the chair facing the windows, and after she sat down, he took the seat across from her.

They watched each other quietly for a few moments.

"Whenever you're ready to talk," he assured, "I'm ready to listen." The barista called out their order, and he stood. "I'll grab it. One sec." He returned with a small tray holding their order and set it down. "Here you go." He slid one tall glass, a straw and one ceramic plate her way.

"Thanks." She opened the black straw, stuck it in the glass and took a long sip through it. "It's been a hell of a day."

"How so?"

"Everything was pretty normal until I was on my way home. My father's secretary stopped me as I was getting into my car, and from that moment on, my day turned to a pile of crap."

"Yikes." He drank some of his latte and found it to be just as good as she'd promised. The sweetness of the caramel balanced nicely with the rich bite of the coffee. "Go on."

She sucked her bottom lip. "Basically, she asked me to deliver some bad news to my father, something about his past actions that may have come back to bite him in the rear end." She shook her head. "I don't want to say too much about the details."

He held up his hand. "That's fine. Feel free to tell me as much, or as little, as you like."

"Anyway, it was news to me, too. I don't even know if what I was asked to relay to him is true." She took a bite of her croissant and chewed.

"How did he react to this news?" While his curiosity grew by the second, he didn't feel it was his place to press her for more details about this mysterious bad news.

"He was angry, but he insisted it wasn't true." She

sighed. "All I know is, just the knowledge that it's even a thing has changed the way I look at my father."

"Wow. It must be pretty serious."

"It is, and I wish my father could see it that way." She took another sip of coffee. "I tried to tell him that if he doesn't address this thing, true or not, it's not gonna just go away. He dismissed me." Her frustration came through in her tone.

What in the world is the big secret? Is the man sick? Did he commit a crime? There was no telling. So rather than press, he commiserated. "That sucks. Sounds like your dad and mine are cut from the same stubborn cloth."

She gave a little chuckle. "Oh, really?"

"Absolutely. Last year my dad had pneumonia. Two days after he got back on his feet, he went on a dig in the South American rainforest. Just gallivanting around in all that dampness, as if he didn't just get out of the hospital." He shook his head. "Still can't believe my mom let him go."

Her brow inched up. "Dig? What exactly does he do for a living?"

"Oh, my parents—or 'the Doctors McCoy' as they're often called—are super nerdy. My dad, Stephen, is an archaeologist. My mom's name is Wanda, and she's an anthropologist."

Wide-eyed, she said, "Wow. Those sound like some pretty interesting jobs."

He shrugged. "I guess so, I'm just used to it since I grew up around it."

"Any siblings?" She posed the question with genuine interest.

His heart squeezed in his chest. "Um, yeah. I had a younger sister, Whitney. Unfortunately, we lost her in an…accident last year."

The sadness returned to her eyes. "Maxton, I'm so sorry. I hope I didn't upset you by being nosy."

He shook off the pain that coiled around his rib cage, threatening to strangle him like a snake. "Nah, it's cool. There was no way for you to know. It was an innocent question."

"I don't know if it'd help, but you could always borrow one of my siblings." A small grin showed on her face. "Take Miles. Hell, you'd be doing me a favor."

He laughed, amused by her offer. "No thanks. Ya brother a little too extra for me."

"That he is." She giggled.

He sat, watching her, in awe of the way the sound of her laughter warmed the places inside of him that were cold and soothed the ones that hurt.

Their conversation continued on, flowing as naturally as if they were two old friends who'd recently reunited. He didn't realize how long they'd been chatting until a barista alerted them that the coffee shop was closing.

"My bad. I hope I haven't kept you out too late," he said as he rose from his seat.

She shook her head. "I had a good time. I feel better now that I got some stuff off my chest." She paused, looking up at him through a fringe of dark lashes. "Thank you for listening."

"No problem." He tried to ignore the way his pulse quickened at her words. "I'd better go so I won't miss the next train."

"Where do you live?"

"Virginia Highlands," he answered.

She pulled her keys from her purse. "I'm in Druid Hills, so you're on the way. I'll drop you off."

They rode in companionable silence, and when they reached his complex, he started to get out. Pausing, he said, "Teagan, I hope this isn't too forward. But—"

"I'd really like to see you again." She lowered her eyes for a moment before meeting his gaze once more. "Do you want to hang out Saturday?"

Now it was his turn to be taken aback. "Yeah."

"Good." She smiled. "We'll work out the details tomorrow."

They said their good-nights, and with a wink, she drove away.

He stood on the curb for a long time, contemplating Sharrod's chastisement.

Yeah, I remember what I said about no romantic entanglements. But Teagan and I are just having fun, and there's no law against that. We're just hanging out, and that's all it is.

Seven

Saturday morning, Teagan answered the knock on her door with a smile. The smile fell when she was greeted by the retreating back of the delivery guy. Looking down, she saw the box containing the fancy litter and treats she ordered for her cat.

She hauled the heavy box inside, then closed the door with a sigh. Grabbing her keys from the hook on the wall, she used one to cut through the tape. Clicking her tongue, she called, "Here, Luna."

Moments later, her favorite hunk of black fur came hurtling in her direction. The cat tried to perch on top of the box…and promptly fell in with the contents.

Teagan laughed, tearing open the zipper pouch of treats and tossing some in the box with the cat. "Here, girl. Have a snack." Leaving her cat to enjoy the goodies, she turned toward the full-length mirror mounted on her coat-closet door, checking her appearance once more. The blue-floral romper she'd chosen had a muted print and covered everything that needed coverage while still leaving enough skin exposed so she wouldn't spontaneously combust the moment she stepped into the Georgia heat.

Another knock sounded, and she went to answer it. Luna scrambled past her feet, retreating for the safety of the bedroom.

Guess that's why nobody has a "guard cat." When she opened the door this time and saw Maxton standing on her porch, she smiled. "Hey."

"Hey there." He grinned. "Did you remember to wear your bathing suit?"

She eased aside the corner of her romper's sleeve, showing off the black-and-white strap of her suit. "Yep."

He stared at her bared shoulder for a few long seconds, then blinked a few times. "And do you have a bag to bring it home in?"

She held up her duffle bag. "I've got all my essentials right here." She eyed him. "So, do I get to know where we're going now?"

He shook his head with a laugh. "Nope. It's a surprise."

Stepping out of the house, she locked the door and pulled it shut behind her. "Let's hope it's a good one. I can definitely see the appeal of getting in the water, with it being this hot." She wondered which pool or swimming hole he planned to take her to. Atlanta had plenty of them.

"That's the spirit." He held out his arm and escorted her off the porch to the driveway. "Nice house, by the way."

"Thanks. It's just enough space so I don't feel confined." They approached his car and she whistled. "Nice wheels, playboy." She gestured to the sleek black convertible parked behind her coupe. The car's top was let down, revealing the tan leather seats and lacquered wood-grain paneling inside.

He chuckled. "Thanks. I just rented it until the end of the month. I'll decide whether or not to extend my rental based on our progress with Swagg's album." With a flourish, he opened the passenger-side door. "You may enter the chariot, my lady."

Giggling, she let him help her into the buttery-soft seat, buckling herself in. Taking a pair of sunglasses from her purse, she slipped them on and prepared to enjoy the ride. Once he was in the driver's seat, she contented herself with watching the scenery fly by.

They left Druid Hills traveling west through Atkins Park, then going slightly south through Old Fourth Ward. Once they passed Central Park and headed into Sono, she said, "Are we going somewhere in Midtown or downtown?"

He nodded. "Very astute, Teagan."

Without any further clues, she returned to watching the familiar places they passed. As they slowly navigated through traffic on the northwest end of North Avenue, she realized Midtown was out. *Where could he be taking me in the downtown area that I need a bathing suit? It could be anywhere from a poolside bar at one of the fancier hotels to the MLK Natatorium to the facility at Centennial Park.*

Mercifully, her curiosity about their destination was soon alleviated, as he turned off of Luckie Street at the Georgia Aquarium. Still, that left her with a whole other set of questions. "When are you going to tell me what we're doing today?"

"I'm not. I'm just going to show you."

She blew out a breath. "Maxton."

"Just try to be patient. It'll be worth it, I promise." He pulled up to the entry of the parking deck, scanned a prepaid ticket and drove forward when the striped bar lifted to allow him inside.

Once they were parked, they headed inside the main building and she followed him to the second floor, to a reception desk marked Animal Interactions.

The moment she read the sign, something clicked in her brain. "Oh, snap, Maxton."

He glanced over his shoulder at her. "Hmm?"

She poked him in the back with her index finger. "We're going to interact with animals here? That sounds so cool!"

He laughed. "Yeah, when I heard you talking the other night at the coffee shop, I thought this sort of thing might be your jam." He handed his ID over to the woman behind the desk. "She'll need yours, too."

With excitement humming through her like a current, she fished her driver's license out of her back pocket and handed it over. He returned it to her shortly, and the aquarium employee then gestured for them to follow her.

She felt like a kid as she walked with them through the corridors of the aquarium, finally arriving at an area that felt decidedly behind the scenes. Joining a group of four others, she listened as a wet suit-clad aquarium diver briefed them on what they'd be doing.

"Welcome to the Shark and Ray Encounter at the Georgia Aquarium," she began. "Today, you'll get a chance to put on a suit just like the one I'm wearing and interact, up close and personal, with some of our sharks and rays." The woman continued on, talking about how they'd be given all the necessary equipment and allowed to change, but Teagan spent the rest of the speech half-listening, staring at Maxton.

He met her gaze. "You okay over there, shorty?"

"Rays? Really? They're my—"

"Favorite sea creature. I know, I remember you telling me that." He grinned, gave her shoulder a squeeze. "I called to see how many types of rays they have here—eleven, by the way—and the man on the phone said if rays were your thing, he had two spots left for this encounter."

Something inside Teagan bloomed, and at that moment, she could barely compose herself against the swelling excitement. Another feeling rose, too. Gratitude. "Thank you, Maxton. This is the most thoughtful date I've ever been taken on."

He tilted his head to the side. "Fine as you are? Damn shame, but I'm glad I could be the one to do it for you."

For the next two hours, they learned about the various facets of shark and ray biology, their natural habitats and worldwide conservation efforts to keep their numbers up in the wild. During the second half, they changed into the provided wet suits so they could enter each animal's respective habitat in turn. The best part, however, came when Teagan got to stand between Maxton and an aquarium diver in chest-deep water, sprinkling plankton into the water. Two female rays circled around her, gliding through the water while devouring the treats, and as she watched them, she felt herself ascend to the halls of nerd Valhalla.

After the program ended, they returned to the locker rooms to dry off and get back into their street clothes. She got dressed quickly, wanting to warm up from the lingering chill, and waited in the hall for Maxton. Seeing his sneaker lying in the hallway, she went to pick it up. Dang, he must have dropped it.

She looked up to find him approaching her, wearing nothing but a pair of orange swim trunks. Beads of water clung to his muscled upper body and powerful thighs. Her eyes lingered at his waist for a moment, and the closer he got, the more she realized she was wet again, for entirely different reasons.

"Hey, you found my shoe." He reached for it. "I was looking all over for it."

She handed it over.

"Thanks. I'll be out in a sec." He turned and reentered the men's locker room, showing off a back view that was just as delightful as the front.

She flopped down on the single bench in the hall, doing her best to recover before he came back. As it turned out, Maxton had quite a body beneath his stylish wardrobe. And even though she knew it was too soon to be thinking that way, parts of her wanted to see more of…what he had to offer.

He emerged again, fully dressed. "Ready to go?"

She nodded and stood. "This was amazing. Thank you again."

He stuck out his arm. "You're welcome. The date's not over, though. I'm taking you to lunch." As they started to walk down the corridor toward the reception desk where they'd checked in, he said, "You know, you liked this so much, it's gonna be pretty hard to top it on a second date. That is…if you wanna do this again."

She smiled up at him. "Oh, I'm sure you'll come up with something, playboy."

Seated at a secluded table inside Hudson Grille on Marietta, Maxton looked across the table at his companion. Her attention was on the menu lying on the table in front of her; his attention was on her face. She was so beautiful, and the lingering joy in her expression made her even more so.

She looked up as if she felt his gaze on her. "What is it, Maxton?"

He shook his head, focusing on his own menu. "Nothing."

He had a few minutes to study the menu before the waiter returned with their drinks. "Here's your Sweetwater IPA, sir, and your iced tea and water, ma'am." Sitting the glasses down, he pulled out his pen and pad. "You folks ready to order?"

Maxton looked at Teagan.

"Sure. I'll have the jerk-spiced salmon sandwich with the regular fries on the side, please."

The waiter jotted that down. "Good choice. And you, sir?"

"Let me get the Four Horsemen burger with a side of sweet potato fries."

"Gotcha. I'll get that right out to you." Taking their menus, the waiter disappeared.

She leaned forward, resting her forearms on the table. "I had so much fun at the aquarium today. I never even knew I had an interest in sharks, but I learned so many neat little facts about them."

He smiled. "I see you're going to keep talking about this forever, and I love it." She radiated delight, and it warmed his heart to see her so happy, so far removed from the moment he'd approached her car and found her sobbing.

"Probably." She laughed. "I couldn't help noticing how comfortable you seemed in the water. Are you an avid diver or something?"

He shrugged. "I wouldn't classify myself as avid, but I've been on three or four scuba dives since I was about ten. You should really take lessons, considering how much you enjoyed today. I mean, that was just in a tank. Imagine how geeked you'd be in the open ocean."

She tilted her head slightly to the right as if thinking it over. "I'll have to take that into consideration."

"This wasn't my first time swimming with rays. Or sharks, for that matter. This was just the first time I did it in a controlled environment."

She leaned forward, her brown eyes sparkling, "Well, tell me all about your last ray encounter, Jacques Cousteau."

Laughing, he launched into the story. "Word. So this was about three years back. Mom, Dad, Whitney and I were in Jamaica on a family trip. We were snorkeling at this place called Doctor's Cave Beach, right by Montego Bay. We're all swimming in a line, basically, to make sure we stay together. Anyway, we swam through a cave and came out on the other side. There were these two young rays, circling and playing in the water. We kept our distance but followed them for as long as we could. My dad took, like, a million pictures with his underwater camera. Finally, they sped up and zoomed off, leaving us behind." He paused, realizing what this moment represented. "You know, this is the first time I've shared a memory of my sister with someone, without getting upset, in a really long time."

Her expression softened, but her smile remained as she reached across the table and grasped his hand. "I'm honored."

Their food came, and as Maxton sank his teeth into the juicy, flavorful burger, he immediately felt the burn. It was one of the spiciest on the menu, featuring jalapeño, red pepper, habanero and a house-made special sauce called Scorpion Stinger—who knew what kind of spices were in that. Even as a lover of spicy food, he had to admit that this packed the heat. Swallowing, he said, "Yikes. I can see how this burger got its name."

Smiling, Teagan asked, "Too spicy?"

He shook his head, raising the burger for another bite. "Nah. I can hang."

"You sure?" She looked skeptical. "Because you're sweating."

He chewed and swallowed another mouthful of beef, tomato and spiciness. A trickle of sweat slid down his face, and he grabbed a napkin from the pile in the center of the table. Mopping his brow, he grinned. "That's how I like it. Keeps the sinuses clear and the mind sharp."

"If you say so." She folded a crisp fry into her mouth and washed it down with tea.

By the time he finished his food, he'd built quite a pile of napkins to keep the sweat out of his eyes. "Whew. The fries helped, but not as much as I wanted them to." He signaled the waiter for a glass of water and drank it in one long swig.

Pushing aside her own plate, Teagan remarked, "The jerk salmon was really flavorful and delicious. And not too spicy," she added with a wink.

He chuckled. "Whatever. I finished the burger, didn't I?" He knew he'd probably pay the price in heartburn later, but she didn't need to know that.

After he paid the check and left a nice tip for their server, he stood next to the table and extended his arm. "Ready?"

She smiled up at him as she stood and looped her arm through his. "You're such a gentleman."

"Just one of my many sides," he said as they walked out of the restaurant.

He drove her home, pulling into her driveway just after two. There he opened the passenger-side door, helped her to her feet and escorted her onto the porch. The house, a decent-size ranch with charcoal- gray siding, blue shutters and a decorative stone walkway, looked like the perfect little starter home for a small family. "This seems like a big house for one person. Do you have a roommate or something?"

She shook her head as she pulled her keys out of her purse. "Nope, it's just me and Luna, my cat. The house has two bedrooms and two baths, and that's perfect for us."

"Gotcha."

The lock clicked and she pushed the door open. "If you've got time to come in, I'll show you around."

He followed her inside. For the next few minutes, she showed him her home. The interior was much more modern than the exterior, indicating a recent remodel. "The house was built in the eighties. I bought it two years ago. I upgraded the flooring, the cabinets and the countertops myself, with a little help from my dad and my brothers." She gestured around. "I'm really proud of the way it turned out."

"I can see why." The sealed, ash-gray wood flooring complimented the soft yellow paint on the walls. The open layout allowed him to see straight through the family room and dining room into the kitchen, which had soft gray cabinetry, granite countertops and stainless-steel appliances.

She took him through an arched opening on the left side of the dining room, into a hallway, as a black streak raced by their feet. "That would be Luna. She's shy. There's a bathroom here," she gestured to the only open door. "The other one is in the primary suite." Cracking open a door, she let him look inside. "This is my home-office-slash-craft room."

He looked inside, noting the neat, meticulous setup. One side of the room had her narrow, whitewashed desk with her laptop, a printer and chair, and the opposite wall hosted a similar desk, the top of which was covered with various bins and cups holding art supplies. The wall directly across from the door had a picture window with a bench seat in a small niche, the walls of which held mounted shelves holding various books and knickknacks. "Nice."

She took him back to the front door.

He eyed her and asked, "Isn't there something I didn't get to see?"

She smiled. "If you mean my bedroom, you gotta earn it, playboy."

"Sounds like a challenge," he quipped.

She shook her head. "No. More of a requirement."

He laughed, then gently dragged the tip of his index finger along her jawline. "You're going to make me work for this. I just know it."

Her only answer was a sultry smile. "We'll just have to see what happens."

"Truth is, I really don't have the time for a relationship right now."

If she took offense at his statement, she didn't show it. "Neither do I."

"So, what are we doing here?"

She shrugged. "A fling? A dalliance? I don't think it really matters what we call it, so long as we both understand what it is…and what it isn't."

Their gazes met and held, and the sparkle of mischief in her eyes threatened to do him in. "Enlighten me, Teagan. What will we be doing, exactly?"

"We hang out…have a little fun. No strings, no commitments. And above all, we don't let this thing interfere with our work or our lives." She pressed her open palm against his chest. "That is, if you think you can handle it."

"Seems reasonable." *I like this approach. Seems like we're on one accord.*

Her smile deepened. "Tomorrow is my only other free day for a while. Why don't you meet me at the Creamery, right near Piedmont Park? Say, around 7?"

"I'll be there." He wanted to kiss her but couldn't read her thoughts on the matter. So he grazed his fingertip over her soft, glossy lips instead.

"See you then," she whispered.

Satisfied, he opened the front door and stepped out into the afternoon sunshine.

Eight

Teagan stood near the main entrance to Piedmont Park on Sunday evening, placing herself out of the flow of traffic. The day was slightly overcast, mercifully lowering the temperature into the upper seventies. After a day spent in her office/craft room, working on an abstract watercolor she'd been tweaking for a few weeks, it was nice to get some fresh air.

She'd chosen a simple but stylish white maxi dress, printed with black roses. The thin straps left her arms bared, and the bejeweled white sandals on her feet had a thick, contoured sole that made them comfortable for walking.

She let her eyes scan the clusters of people passing through the entrance until, finally, she spotted Maxton across the street. Holding her hand up high, she gestured to him. She watched as he waited at the crossing signal, and when it was safe, he jogged over to her.

"Hey there. Have you been waiting long?"

"No." She shook her head. "I've only been here a few minutes."

"Good. Wouldn't want to keep you waiting."

She let her gaze over him. He wore black twill slacks with a silver chain dangling between two of the loops on his right hip. He'd paired the slacks with dark sneakers and a black T-shirt with an interesting design. "Is that Jimi Hendrix on your shirt?"

"Yeah. If you look closely, you'll see that his portrait is made up of..."

She leaned closer. "The lyrics to the song 'Purple Haze.'"

"Good eye." He winked. "Now, let's get some ice cream, shall we?"

She linked arms with him and they walked the short distance to the Creamery. The brightly painted food truck often set up in the park during the summer months and usually drew quite a crowd with its homemade ice cream. "Oh, good. There's only, like, four people ahead of us."

"They've got a lot of good flavors," Maxton remarked, scanning the menu painted on the side of the truck.

When it was their turn, she stepped up to the window. "A double scoop of fudge ripple on a waffle cone, please."

"I'll take a double scoop of pistachio in a waffle bowl." Maxton pulled out a few bills from his wallet. "We're together."

The worker cashed them out, and they moved to the left window to allow the next person to order while they waited. A few minutes later, a second worker handed them their order with a smile. "Enjoy!"

Taking their treats to a bench parked beneath a shady willow, they sat down. Neither of them spoke as they dug in. The breeze rustled through the tree's branches as she enjoyed the cool, creamy flavors of vanilla and chocolate dancing across her tongue. Before she knew it, she'd devoured the first scoop.

She glanced to her side and saw Maxton staring at her. He was still eating, but his gaze was locked on her face so intently, it was a miracle he could still guide his spoon to his mouth. At that moment, it occurred to her how she must look to him, dragging her tongue over the heap of fudge ripple. She paused. "Sorry. I must look like a moose licking ice off a windowpane."

He chuckled. "That's a very creative metaphor."

"I saw it on a television special about Alaska once, and I've never been able to get that image out of my head."

"I definitely wouldn't make that comparison." He passed his tongue over his lower lip. "I think it's kinda sexy."

She swallowed, not sure how to respond to the tingle of arousal that went down her back.

"So," Maxton said, spooning up some of his ice cream, "tell me about your family."

She drew a deep breath. "Describing my family members can be a little hard, so I'll try to be succinct. There are seven of us. My mom, Addison, is a martial arts and vegan food enthusiast. My dad, Caleb, is an old-fashioned gent who still owns seersucker and occasionally smokes cigars. They founded 404 before any of us were born."

"I see. And your siblings?"

He appeared genuinely interested, so she continued. "There are five of us. The oldest is Nia. She's uptight. Major oldest-sibling syndrome. Next is Blaine. He's the rebel. Then, there's Gage. He's overly serious, although his recent marriage seems to have made him a little less anal. Then, there's Miles and me. He's the older twin because he used my head as a launchpad so he could be born first. He's a fitness buff and something of a player."

Maxton laughed, hard. Setting his ice cream down on his lap, he said, "What?"

"Stop laughing. I'm serious. He just bogarted his way out, it's something he still does to this day." She shook her head. "You met him."

He recovered from his laughing fit, grabbing his waffle bowl again. "That I did, and he does seem like… a handful."

She sighed. "He is. But I still love him. I love my whole family, even though they get on my nerves sometimes."

"You gave me some…rather colorful descriptions there." He snapped off a piece of his bowl. "But now I'm curious to know how you describe yourself."

She sucked on her lower lip. "I don't know. That's kind of a tall order on such short notice. I exist in multitudes, you know."

"I sensed that." He gave another low, rumbling

chuckle. "How about this. Describe yourself with three adjectives."

"Hmm. Let me think about it while I finish this." She ate the remainder of her rapidly melting ice cream, turning slightly away from him. Then she crunched on the top half of the waffle cone. Folding up the rest in a napkin, she tossed it in the metal wastebasket positioned nearby. Tapping her chin, she said, "I'm gonna go with *focused*, *practical* and *intelligent*."

He nodded. "Okay, I see. From what I know of you, I can agree with all of those. But I think you're definitely leaving some things out."

She punched him playfully in the shoulder. "That's your fault. You only gave me three adjectives."

"You're right, you're right. My bad." He rubbed his upper arm. "Ease up on me, slugger. I'm gonna add some descriptors if I may."

"I'll allow it." She noticed a light green streak near the right corner of his mouth. "Hold on." Reaching for a napkin, she swiped the stain away.

He gave her a soft smile, one that made the skin around his eye crinkle. "Thanks. Anyway, I'd say you're beautiful, witty, thoughtful and—" he paused, letting his gaze move slowly over her form "—shapely."

Warmth bloomed in her chest, and she knew it wasn't a result of the Georgia heat but rather the hungry gaze of the handsome man sitting next to her. "You're laying it on thick today, I see."

He shrugged. "Maybe, but I'm honest."

"I suppose. I'm everything you described me to be, and more." She giggled. "Wanna hit the trail before it gets dark? Walk off some of these calories?"

"Sure."

They walked to the trailhead of the shortest trail and entered it. The sun was sinking low on the horizon, though it was mostly shrouded by clouds. She looked up, seeing the oranges and pinks of sunset had begun to paint the sky, visible through the canopy of leaves above.

He reached for her hand and held it within his. "This cool with you?"

She nodded.

"Just checking. I know we're still working out the details of our little liaison." He winked.

She looked his way, taking in his profile, the strong jaw, the thick brows and the full lips. "I like your approach. Since you're a light touch, I might be giving you a little more leeway than you imagined."

He stopped walking, looked at her. "Oh, really."

"Really." She wriggled her hand free from his, then traced her fingertips up both his arms. Hooking her hands behind his neck, she asked, "Can I have three words to describe you now?"

He nodded, never taking his eyes off her.

"I'm gonna say *handsome*, *talented* and *irresistible*."

He opened his mouth to respond, but she covered it with hers before he could. His strong arms wrapped around her waist, pulling her body against his. She relished the feel of his firm, muscled torso pressed against her.

The kiss deepened, and she was so swept up in it that it took her a few beats to notice the first round of drops of water hitting her skin.

She drew back from him, touched his cheek. "I think it's raining."

"It is. We'd better go."

As they dashed back up the trail toward the entrance, the rain grew heavier, fat drops pelting them at every step. Running over the wet grass, they passed a few other folks in the same situation, picking up their pace or ducking beneath trees or other structures to find shelter from the weather.

"Where did you park?" he called to her over the rain.

"In the deck on Monroe!"

By the time he left her at her car, she was soaked to the bone, and shivering. But she knew the sensation rocketing through her body had nothing to do with being cold and everything to do with the irresistible man she'd just dashed through the park with. Something was happening between them…something special.

Monday evening, Maxton shut and locked his front door behind him, sighing into his empty apartment. He leaned his back against the cool metal door for a few moments, trying to gather his rollicking emotions.

He couldn't recall ever experiencing a day that seemed so long. Since the moment he'd dragged himself out of bed this morning, he'd been fighting to stay focused, to remain upbeat. Now, alone in his home, he felt the weight of keeping up the appearance finally lift from his shoulders.

Unfortunately, the sadness remained.

Today, Whitney would have been twenty-seven.

He pushed himself off the door and trudged to the living room, setting his bass on the armchair before taking a seat on the sofa. He pulled off the black sneakers he'd worn into the studio, then buried his sock-clad feet in the thick pile of his throw rug as he slumped against the backrest.

The ball of tears stuck in his throat threatened to rise at any moment, and after keeping them in all day, he was too tired to care anymore. His eyes welled, and he sprawled there, letting the tears slide down. It wasn't like the last time he'd cried, all those weeks ago. He didn't sob, didn't wail. Just silently mourned his little sister, his gaze on the ceiling, his vision swimming.

His phone rang then, the steady vibration against his thigh drawing him back to reality. Brushing away the lingering wetness on his face, he took his phone out of his pocket and answered the incoming video call. "Hey, Ma. How are you?"

Wanda McCoy's face came into view, or at least the lower half of it. "Hey, Maxie. I'm alright, you doing okay?"

"Yeah, Ma." He cringed. "Ma, you're too close to the camera again."

"I can see you. Matter of fact, when's the last time you shaved, boy?"

He shook his head. "I'm growing out my beard. Fix your camera, Ma. All I can see is your mouth."

"Oh, for goodness' sake." The picture on the screen became shaky and shifted around, going from her mouth and chin to the ceiling, to the floral wallpaper in the kitchen before finally settling on her full face and upper torso. She was sitting at the kitchen table, inside their family home in the suburbs of Calabasas. A black-velvet headband held her salt-and-pepper curls back from her aged brown face, and her dark eyes squinted as she looked into the camera. "How's that, son? Can you see me now?"

"Yes, Ma, that's better." He smiled. "Sorry I couldn't make it home, but I'm just getting into the thick of this gig with Lil Swagg."

"Lil who?" Her brows eased together, a show of genuine confusion.

"Lil Swagg, Ma. He's a young rapper out of the Bronx. And even though you're not into that kind of music, at least the kid's got a good ear. Not many artists his age would go to the trouble and expense of recording with a live band over a drum machine and some manufactured beats."

She pursed her lips. "Hmm. That does set him apart from the rest, I suppose." She reached off-screen, then raised a glass of dark-colored liquid to her lips.

"Ma, are you drinking soda pop?"

She frowned. "Oh, hush. It's that sugar-free cola, so don't you fuss."

"Alright, I won't. So, how's Dad?"

"He's still with Dr. Sutton in Sicily. They're working in the Valley of the Temples."

He scratched his chin, thinking back. "Oh, yeah, I remember him talking about that. He's been trying to get in on that action for a while now, hasn't he?"

She nodded. "Yes, child. Talked about it nonstop for weeks. I'm just glad the department chose him to go this time so I can stop hearing about it."

"Ma, you know he'll come home with a million stories and probably a few souvenirs."

"I know. But I enjoy that part." Her lips tilted up into

a small smile. "He always brings me back something I can use, whether it's an artifact or an anecdote."

She quieted, her smile fading.

For a few moments, they simply looked at each other. In the silence, an understanding passed between them, one of shared grief.

Finally, she spoke. "I...went by Whitney's grave this morning."

He nodded. "The headstone in place, right?"

"It's there. I had no idea having a custom one made with her image engraved on it would take so long." She sighed. "Anyway, it's there now, and it looks so nice. I'll text you a picture of it later."

"Okay."

Her eyes grew damp. "I took her some flowers. I had the florist make me up an arrangement of orange mums with a birthday ribbon around the pot."

"Her favorite color. I'm sure she would love it, Ma." He paused. "Thanks...for going over there."

"Of course."

She quieted again, and the corners of her mouth drooped. Her eyes began to dampen, and she sniffled. But she quickly plastered on a smile as she got up, taking the phone with her on a walk through the house.

He watched the screen as she entered his sister's childhood room. The space remained untouched, down to the bed being unmade from the last time she'd slept in it before the accident. "I keep saying I'm going to clean this room out, donate some of her things. Lord knows there are folks out there who could use them."

"There's no rush, Ma." He wanted her to know she didn't have to bear the burden alone, as she was apt to do as the family matriarch. "When I finish this gig, I can come home. You know, help you go through it and make some decisions."

"Closet full of clothes in here," she said, turning the camera toward the open closet door. "Stuff she couldn't wear anymore. Old baby clothes, even."

"Keep the baby clothes, Ma."

"I probably will. Myrtle was saying something about getting them put in a shadowbox or something like that."

He nodded at the mention of her good friend and colleague, Dr. Myrtle Reeves. Myrtle taught in the English department at Cal Lutheran in Woodland Hills, where his mother taught in the global studies department. "Sounds like a good way to preserve them."

The image panned around the room, showing the familiar lavender walls. Taped to them were many of her school awards, her dreamcatcher that she'd made one summer at camp and a good eight or nine posters, all of the same artist. "Wow. I'd almost forgotten how obsessed Whit was with Tupac."

She sighed, still off camera. "Yes, yes. She loved him, even though I thought his lyrics were a little too brash. I never made a fuss because your father and I tried to let you kids enjoy things, let you explore and develop your own personalities."

That was true; he couldn't ever remember his parents forcing them to do anything. They'd discuss; they'd explain; they'd even ask firmly. But they never pushed. And in response, he and his sister had, with few exceptions, remained on the straight and narrow. "You're right, his lyrics could be a little rough at times. But Pac was a wunderkind, a true poet. Did you know there are entire college courses devoted to his lyrics now?"

She turned the camera back to her face, showing her wide eyes. "No, I didn't. Obviously, we don't have those classes at Cal Lutheran."

"Yeah. But they're a thing. I think after he was gone, people started to look back and see his genius." He thought back on the late-night conversations he'd had with his sister about Tupac's songs. "But Whit knew back then. She had good taste."

The tears filled her eyes then, and her breathing grew heavy. "I miss my baby girl, Maxie. I miss her so, so much."

He felt his own eyes watering again. "I know, Ma. I miss her, too."

She sat down on the end of the twin bed and sobbed.

There was nothing he could do, no comfort he could offer. They were both caught in this storm of pain and grief, this dark chasm that he feared had no light at the other end. He wished he could reach through the phone and pull her into his arms. But that was impossible. So instead, he simply let her cry, watching over her as she emptied out some of the hurt. He felt that familiar squeezing in his chest, and he set his phone down and drew several long, deep breaths.

She wiped her face, getting up from the bed. As she left Whitney's room, closing the door behind her, she said, "Sorry about that, son."

"Don't apologize, Ma. Do you remember what Pastor Yates said about grief?"

She nodded. "It's love with nowhere to go."

"Right." He dried his face with the tail of his shirt.

"It's hard now, and it might be hard for a long time. But we're going to get through this."

"I know we will. Sometimes, I just can't see that." She ran her hand over her hair. "Let me go on and get this laundry done. Have you eaten?"

"No, not yet."

"Well, eat something, baby. And try to involve some vegetables."

He chuckled. Same old Ma. "I will, Ma. I love you."

"I love you, too, baby." She offered him a watery smile before disconnecting the call.

Taking a deep breath, he got up from the sofa and went to see what he had in the fridge. Removing a bagged salad from the crisper, he poured some on a plate. Teagan's face popped into his mind.

He recalled their lunch on Saturday and the way he'd just naturally told her a story about his family, about Whitney. She'd listened and, in doing so, had given him a gift: a chance to relive the moment and feel the love he had for his sister, without the pain and guilt of losing her.

As he poured the dressing over the salad, he smiled.

Teagan Woodson was nothing less than incredible, and he knew this would be an unforgettable fling.

Nine

Teagan stood by the sofa inside the outer suite of Studio One, listening as Lil Swagg and Rick compared notes on the project at hand.

"I think we're making good progress," Rick said. "We've got the first two tracks in the bag, and we'll get the third and maybe the fourth done today."

Swagg nodded, his eyes still locked on the screen of his phone. He wore a black tracksuit with purple piping, and the words Bronx Swagg emblazoned across his chest. The words were partially hidden by yet another heavy, jewel-encrusted chain, this one featuring a large pendant in the shape of a microphone. "You right, Rick. We're looking good right now. We just need to keep up that momentum."

Wondering how he could even see the screen through the lenses of his dark sunglasses, Teagan nodded her agreement. "I think we're right where we need to be. I'm cleaning up the files as we go, so the finished song files should be super clean and easy for Chanel to put her finishing touch on."

"I'm sure she'll love that." Swagg glanced up, smiled. "And if that's the case, I can definitely recommend 404 to some of my homies back home that's looking for that upscale recording experience."

Teagan grinned. "Thanks. We'd be honored to get that endorsement."

"No problem, Miss Teagan." He raised his fist and bumped it with hers. "You got real skills at the board, and I respect your professionalism. Real talk."

"I'm happy to help. I'm a total nerd for sound engineering. That's why I work in here instead of in the c-suite upstairs." She felt the bounce in her step as she made her way back to the workstation and sat down. The on-screen clock displayed the time: 9:32. The musicians would be there within the half hour to get the day's session underway. Deciding to use this bit of downtime wisely, she opened the file for track one of Swagg's albums and ran it through the system's automatic optimization program. The program displayed an on-screen graph, showing its progress, and she watched it for a few beats before taking out her phone.

A text message from Miles appeared on the screen.

Hike this week?

Swiping the message away, she shook her head. *I barely made it on the last walk, and now he's asking me to hike with him? Sheesh.*

Rick's voice cut into her thoughts. "We've got a guest coming today, to lay down a verse."

She turned her chair to face him. "Did you talk to the guys at the security desk about that?"

"Yeah, I did."

"As long as Tate and Owen know, we should be good." She turned back toward the workstation, anticipating how crowded it would be with more people in the room. It wasn't ideal, but she tried to respect the wishes of her artists so as not to interfere with the creative process. *That reminds me, it's about time I lobby Nia and my parents about moving to a newer, bigger building so I can have more space in my studio.* Whenever the next true hip-hop supergroup came along, she wanted to be ready. Keeping her eyes on the screen, she kept her ears open.

Swagg said, "Rick, who the hell is coming here today? I didn't request anybody for a guest spot. I thought we were gonna record that stuff later when we got back with Chanel in NYC."

"Don't worry, man. It's all arranged. Trust me, this collab is gon' set the hip-hop world on fire."

"I hope so." Swagg sounded less than convinced. Mike walked in then, carrying his keyboard case. The other three musicians followed behind him in a lopsided line, with Maxton bringing up the rear. Teagan exchanged greetings with each of them as they passed. As usual, Maxton lingered.

Today, he wore a pair of black jeans that sat just at the top of his hips, showing off the gray waistband of a pair of designer boxer briefs. His black tee had a grayscale image of The Notorious B.I.G.'s face on it, along with the quote It's All Good, Baby, Baby. His shiny dark curls were swept to one side, and she could see something silver dangling from his left ear. "Hey, Teagan."

"Hey, yourself." She pointed. "New piercing?"

He grinned. "Yeah, got it last night. It's a letter W."

She nodded, understanding the meaning. "I like it. Looks good."

She heard Swagg whistle, then say, "I see my bass player got the juice with the ladies, too! I see you, homie!"

Maxton laughed. "Let me get my ass in the booth."

She stifled a giggle. "Yeah, you do that."

He went inside and shut the door behind him. She watched through the glass partition as the musicians set up to start the session. When everyone was in place, she engaged the suite's intercom-enabled sound system. "Y'all ready?"

A chorus of affirmative answers came over the speakers.

"Good deal. I'm gonna start playback on track three." She tapped the appropriate icons on the touchscreen of her workstation. The band picked up on it immediately, which didn't really surprise her considering the amount of time they'd spent working on it already. *They probably have the melody memorized by now.*

Swagg got up and stood near the counter, bobbing his head in time with the music. "Man, they're sounding good today. I like this."

"I agree. Maybe they practiced in their spare time," she joked, knowing full well Maxton had spent the better part of his weekend with her. That, however, was privileged information.

It took about ninety minutes before the instrumental track was completed to Swagg's satisfaction. He clapped his hands together. "That's it. That's the one right there."

"Great." Teagan saved the audio file.

Rick appeared beside them. "Right on time, too. Vic Grip and his people should be here any minute."

"Vic Grip? Hell, yeah!" Swagg nodded.

A knock sounded at the door. Rick opened it.

Teagan looked toward the three men who entered, all of them dressed similarly in baggy jeans and over-size tees, heavy chains around their necks. The one in the front declared, "What's up? Vic Grip and Money J are in the building."

Swagg frowned, turning to Rick. "What the fuck, Rick? Money J? I hate that crazy motherfucker."

Rick held up his hands. "I didn't know Money J was coming, I swear. I only invited Vic. He said he'd be bringing a couple folks with him."

Swagg's eyes flashed. "And you didn't ask him for names or nothing?"

"My bad, Swagg. I didn't even know they hang to-gether." Rick's eyes darted back and forth between his artist and his guests.

Rick moved quickly to stand between Swagg and his guests, and the gaggle of bodies effectively blocked Tea-gan from scooting her chair away from the workstation.

Teagan, aware of the rising tension, turned her chair as much as she could. "Gentlemen, do we have a prob-lem here?" She poised her hand over the handset of the desk phone next to her station.

"Nah, shawty," one of the visitors said, stalking closer to Swagg. He was the smaller one of the group but still wide enough to take up space. He wore a backward cap and had two teardrops tattooed beneath his right eye. "Ain't no problem, if Swagg keep my name out his mouth."

·   "It's not my fault your bars are garbage, J." Swagg folded his arms over his chest.

A vein popped in the man's neck. "See, that's that shady shit I'm talking about."

"It ain't shade. I'm just spittin' facts." Swagg's lips curled into a disdainful smile.

Money J pounded his fist into his hand. "Okay. I see I'm gonna have to knock that smirk off your face."

Teagan stood then. "Oh, no. Take that mess outside before you damage my equipment." She pointed at the door, and in doing so, touched one of the men's chest.

He sneered at her. "Don't touch me." He raised his hand.

The door to the booth swung open and Maxton strafed through a narrow gap in the tangle of bodies.

A second later, a flying fist hit Maxton square in his right eye, and he cursed.

All hell broke loose then as the men began swinging their fists and shouting obscenities. Teagan felt the backs of her knees being pushed into her chair as the men rumbled their way past her. Rick backed up toward the sofa only to have Swagg pushed into him. The entire time, Maxton kept his body wrapped around Teagan as the chaos and noise swirled around them.

Mike and Sharrod came from the booth and entered the fray, trying to pull Money J and Vic off Swagg and Rick. Brady hung back, his eyes darting toward the door.

The brute who'd tried to hit her remained there, effectively blocking the way out. He wore a crooked grin on his face, and she could tell he was enjoying the carnage he'd visited upon her domain. *What a grade A, first-class asshole.*

Enough of this. Teagan stretched past Maxton's hold, reached back and grabbed the handset, using the bottom of it to bang the number two key. Holding up the receiver, she shouted, "Security! Studio One!"

Maxton ignored the throbbing in his head, watching through his watery, partially closed eye as two burly, uniformed security officers elbowed their way into the room, with one guard slapping a zip tie around the wrists of the man who'd been trapping them all in the suite. Brady helped the guard drag him away while Sharrod and Mike helped the other guard subdue Vic and Money J.

He could feel the slight tremor in her body as he held her and hear the rapid breaths she took. She was afraid but refused to let it show on her stony face. She was a trooper, and he respected that. But the fact remained that she shouldn't have been subjected to such base behavior, especially not in her place of work.

It was the peak of immaturity. They were grown men, carrying on a pissing contest in the middle of the workday, like a bunch of bored youngsters. *This is precisely why I don't do that macho bravado bullshit. It's all fun and games until somebody gets hurt.* And as irked as he was by the shiner he'd gotten, he knew he'd have been even more pissed if Teagan was the one nursing the bruise.

As the so-called guests were dragged out, cursing, Maxton finally released his hold on Teagan. She flopped onto her chair, dropping her head in her hands.

"What the hell was that?" Maxton couldn't remember the last time he'd been so pissed. "I think you two owe Teagan an apology for this bullshit."

Rick, righting his clothing, shook his head. "Apparently, it was very bad judgment on my part. I apologize, Teagan."

It was quiet for a moment, so Maxton eyed Swagg.

Swagg, wiping a bit of blood from his lower lip, offered a solemn nod. "I'm sorry about this. I'm so freakin' embarrassed."

"Y'all brought way too much excitement into my studio." Her voice was shaky but determined. "See that you don't do it again. And I hope you know whatever damage was done will be billed to you and your artist." Teagan fought hard to keep the anger out of her voice. "I'm going to suspend recording for now, pending a final decision from the CEO."

"Got it," Rick said as he and Swagg departed.

Left alone with Teagan, Maxton let out a pent-up breath. "Are you alright?"

"I'm fine, thanks to you." She stroked her fingertips along his jawline.

Her touch soothed the ache in his head. "I wasn't about to let that jackass hit you."

"Chivalry is alive and well, I see." She gifted him with a soft kiss on the cheek. "I'm more concerned about you. That eye is about four shades of purple." She stood up. "Let me get you some ice, and then I'm taking you to urgent care."

He shook his head. "I don't want you to trouble yourself. Sharrod can take me."

"Did you take a fist to the eye for Sharrod?" She looked at him pointedly.

"No."

"Then, hush, and let me do this for you." She spun and marched out of the room.

After she left, he eased himself onto her seat. *What a day.*

Sharrod entered a moment later. "Damn, Max. You look a hot mess. You alright, bro?"

"Obviously, I got a black eye outta this deal." He resisted the urge to touch his eye. He could feel the tightness in the surrounding skin and had only a sliver of vision left on that side. "You think it's gonna heal well?"

Sharrod grimaced. "I don't know. It's pretty gnarly." He gave him a gentle slap on the shoulder. "Good looking out for Miss Teagan, though. Come on, I'll swing you by the ER."

"She's gonna take me to urgent care."

"You sure? It's no problem." His friend appeared genuinely concerned.

"She insisted. Trust me, you don't want the smoke with her." He chuckled, shaking his head. "This whole mess got her low-key pissed."

Sharrod threw up his hands. "Alright. Well, let me make myself scarce. Call me when you make it home, okay?"

"I will," Maxton promised. After his friend left, he had a few moments alone to process what had happened. He'd been in the center of an actual, real-life rap beef. And as cool as it sometimes seemed on social media, he found the consequences of such an encounter to be far more inconvenient than entertaining.

She reentered the room then with a stack of napkins and a plastic bag filled with crushed ice. She stooped, bringing a napkin to his face, and dabbing gently. "Just cleaning up the blood a little bit."

He nodded, his eyes locked on the swell of her cleavage that was visible above the square neckline of her short-sleeved top. The garment's golden hue accentuated the glow in her skin.

"Here, hold this against your eye." She stood, handing him the baggie of ice.

He dutifully pressed it to his swollen eye, wincing at the blistering cold.

"Okay. I'll grab your bass and walk you to my car."

"Alright," he said, standing. "Are you sure my case will fit in your car?" He tried to imagine how the bulky shell would fit in her little two-door coupe.

"We'll make it work unless want to leave it in the booth." She shrugged. "The doors will be locked."

He shook his head. "Nah. We don't really know when we'll be back in session yet, right?"

"That's true. Wait here. I'll go grab it."

He watched while she entered the booth, slipped the bass into the hard-shell case and snapped it shut. As she maneuvered it around the space, she said, "This isn't even as heavy as I thought it would be." She grabbed her purse from the counter and slung the strap over her shoulder. "Come on, let's go."

He followed her outside, still holding the ice pack to his eye. In the parking lot, he saw the police talking to the security guards while Money J and his crew cooled their heels in the backs of two separate squad cars.

It took some work, but they managed to get his instrument into the back seat. After that, they climbed inside and she drove him away from the studio.

They entered the semi-empty interior of Quick Med Urgent Care and walked over to the check-in desk.

"Can I help you folks—?" The scrubs-clad employee behind the desk stopped midsentence as she looked up from the paperwork in front of her. "Ouch."

Maxton chuckled. "Yeah. It's been a bit of a day."

"How long is the wait for someone to patch him up?" Teagan asked.

The nurse typed into the computer in front of her. "It's not too bad. About twenty or thirty minutes."

"That's fine." Maxton stayed at the desk long enough to fill out the paperwork on the tablet she handed him, then he and Teagan took a seat in the far corner of the waiting room. There were only four other people there: an elderly couple and a woman with a small child on her lap.

"You know, I think you're pretty brave for stepping in the way you did. I respect that."

He shrugged. "As I said, I could tell he was going to swing and I wasn't having it. I was brought up better than that. I'd never raise my hand to a woman."

"Being around my brothers all the time, I think I take for granted that men will do what's right when it comes to how they treat women. Today, I got a pretty unpleasant reminder that's not always the case." She offered a crooked smile. "I appreciate what you did, Maxton."

"Guys are quick to say, 'not all men,' but I believe

in putting my principles in action rather than standing by and watching other men misbehave." He stared at her with the only good eye he had at the moment and felt his heart do a somersault. "Thank you. For bringing me here and for being so kind."

She smiled. "A girl's gotta treat her knight in shining armor special, you know."

"McCoy?" someone called. "Maxton?"

The moment fizzled as he turned toward the sound, raising his hand instinctively. "I'll be back."

"I'll be waiting."

He followed the nurse and, over the next half hour, sat while his eye was cleaned, treated with ointment and patched up. When he emerged, Teagan stood. "Very fashionable," she said, gesturing to the small bandage beside his eye.

"You know it. All the cool kids are wearing these."

"Looks like the swelling has gone down, at least."

He nodded. "It has. I can open my eye halfway now, so that's an improvement." He shook the bottle of pills he had. "They gave a few pills for the pain and swelling. Said the meds might make me a little dizzy."

"No worries. I'll keep you upright." Laughing, she grabbed his hand. "Let's get you home."

She drove him across town to his complex in Virginia Highlands, then helped him up the stairs to his second-floor unit while lugging his bass behind her. Her free hand resting on his back, she applied gentle pressure as they ascended. "Careful, now."

He smiled. "I'm good." He inserted his key in the lock and let the door swing open.

She followed him inside, easing the bass around the door frame. "Where do want this?"

He gestured to the corner of the living room area. "Just set it in that black metal stand."

She passed him and deposited the instrument case in the designated spot. "Do you…think you'll be okay?" She looked at his face, then the front door, then set her gaze on him again.

"Yes." Swollen eye be damned, he wouldn't let this moment pass. "But I'd be better if you stayed."

○

Ten

Teagan felt the smile curl her lips in response to his softly spoken invitation. "You really want me to stay?"

He nodded. "Only if you want to. If you're uncomfortable, just say so and I'll take my bruised eye and go to bed, alone." He grinned.

She laughed. Feeling the boldness rise within, she eased closer to him. "I'd like to stay, Maxton."

He closed the distance between them and pulled her into his arms.

For a moment, they just stood there, holding each other. Teagan felt the warmth of his body against hers, and it felt safe. It felt right.

He stepped away and led her by the hand to the sofa. "Do you…wanna watch TV? Or hear some music?" He sat down and tugged her hand.

Sinking into the soft cushion, she cozied up to his side and kicked off her gold pumps. "Music, please."

He turned on the television and flipped to a satellite music station playing classic soul and R & B. An old Isley Brothers tune filled the room. "How's that?"

"Good." She smiled, resting her head on his shoulder. "Now that we're settled, I wanna hear the story behind that new earring."

"Yesterday was my sister's birthday." He sighed. "After the session, I spent a lot of time sitting here alone, feeling the weight of my sadness. I video chatted with my mom. After a while, I started to get restless, you know. So I decided to go do something in her memory, and I already had a tattoo." He touched the tiny letter, and it dangled. "This was the next thing I could think of."

"I like it. It's not too big, and it fits your style." She paused. "What's your happiest memory with your sister?"

"Odd question, but an easy answer." He let his head drop back against the sofa cushion. "Back when she was a senior in high school, she won homecoming queen. Even though it's tradition for the winner's dad to walk the queen across the field, she asked me to do it. I drove home from USC. She was so beautiful in that gold-sequined dress, and the cheers were so loud from the stands."

She felt the smile tugging at her lips and her heart. "That's so sweet."

"I can still hear them chanting her name. Yeah. I was so proud of her and so honored that she chose me." He gazed straight ahead as if replaying the moments in his mind. "Afterwards, I asked her why she asked me instead of dad. She said 'because you understand me better than anybody and I look up to you.'"

"That's really beautiful."

"You know, she would've turned twenty-seven yesterday." The darkness of his pain threatened to rise again, but he forced it down. "I just wish… I wish things could be different."

She sensed there was something more, something he was holding back, but she didn't want to press him. The last thing she wanted to do was intensify his grief. "You know, my grandmother used to tell me that no one ever really dies as long as they're remembered in love." She touched his face, gliding her palm along his cheek. "Whitney lives, Maxton. Right here." She moved her palm down his upper body until it rested against the center of his chest.

He swallowed, and his eyes glistened.

"I can see now that your music, your beautiful artistry, has been forged in the fire of pain. You're so strong, in ways you don't even realize."

His eyes locked with hers as he raised his hand, cupping her cheek. "That may be true. But I'm not strong enough to fight off what I'm feeling right now."

Her tongue darted out to sweep across her lower lip.

"Will you let me make love to you tonight, Teagan?"

Her pulse quickened; her nipples bloomed. "Yes."

He smiled and tilted her face to his liking before pressing his lips to hers. The moment their mouths connected, she felt the arousal shoot through her body like an electric current. She opened her mouth and his tongue slipped inside to twist against her own. Soon, he drew her into his lap, and she went willingly, giving herself over to him without hesitation.

His hands caressed her fevered skin as he kissed her, moving from her lips to the hollow of her neck, to her collarbone. He placed a sultry lick along the line of her cleavage, and she sighed aloud.

When he pulled back, he tugged the hem of her top and she raised her arms, allowing him to take it off and toss it aside. He kissed along the scalloped edge of her bra while simultaneously reaching behind her to undo the hooks. As her breasts bounced free, he growled before closing his mouth over one aching, hardened nipple.

Her head dropped back, and she moaned as he licked and sucked, enthralled by the searing pleasure of his warm mouth. He switched to the other nipple and gave it the same loving attention, and her back arched in response. "Oh, Maxton."

His face buried between her breasts, he murmured, "You like that?"

"Mmm."

"Then, you'll love what's next." He eased her off his lap, kneeling on the floor in front of her.

She trembled as he slid his large hands over her, gliding from her ankle up to her knee. There, he lingered on the hem of her black A-line skirt. "Open for me, shorty."

She widened her legs, and the trembling increased while he made slow, small circles along her inner thighs. Tugging her panties to the side, he slipped beneath the fabric and she shuddered at the first contact of his fingertips against her womanly heat.

He swirled his fingers around the already tight bud of her clitoris, and she could hear her own rapid breathing. When he dipped one long finger inside, her moans rose, drowning out the music.

"So wet," he mumbled as he tugged at her waistband.

She lifted her hips, allowing him to free her from the panties. Moments later, he draped one of her legs over the arm of the sofa and leaned into her. The moment his hot mouth came into contact with her sex, she cried out.

He swept his tongue through her folds, tasting her, worshipping her, and she could feel the power of ecstasy rising within. She widened her legs, her hands gripping the soft curls at the back of his head, and pulled him in, craving more even as he drove her closer to madness.

He growled into her as he pushed his tongue inside her and she screamed as a warm gush spurted from her. He eased back, licking his lips. "So, you, uh…"

"Yeah," she said breathlessly. "I did."

"I'll take that as a compliment." He grinned broadly.

She stared at the shine still lingering on his lips and felt her pulse pounding all over again. Her body still humming, she was barely aware of him sliding a tray from beneath the sofa, then sliding it back. "What is it?" He asked.

She parted her lips to say two simple words. "Get naked."

He did as she asked, stripping off his black sneakers, tee, jeans and the designer boxers beneath, with his back to her. She heard the crinkle of a foil packet, and he turned around as he finished rolling on the protection. Her eyes widened when she saw his dick, hard and sheathed in black. She wrapped her hands around the thickness for a moment, giving it a gentle squeeze. "Sit down."

Once he was seated, she straddled him and used her hand to guide him inside. They groaned together as he filled her, and her internal walls expanded, then contracted to welcome him. She circled her hips, treating him to a slow ride while his big hands gripped her hips. Her fingertips dug into his strong shoulders, giving her leverage as she continued to grind against him, feeling the growing swell of pleasure. She picked up her pace, leaning forward and moving her hips up and down like a piston, racing toward the orgasm she felt building in her belly.

"Shit!" The bubble burst, and her being shattered into light and brilliance.

"Teagan," he rasped, and his body stiffened beneath her as he found release.

She leaned forward, resting against him and enjoying the feeling of simply being held in his arms. He remained inside her, and just as the post-lovemaking drowsiness began to take hold, she felt him thickening and growing again. "Maxton?"

"Looks like we need to take this party to the bedroom." He gave her ass a firm squeeze before scooting forward and standing. Instinctively, she wrapped her legs around his waist and tightened her grasp on his shoulders. He began walking with her in his arms, but soon her back came to rest against the wall.

"Just one more time," he said throatily as he began to pump, "then I'll take you to bed."

Her eyes rolled back as he stroked the fire inside her once again.

Later, as they lay, spent and sweat-dampened in his

bed, she whispered, "You have even more talents than I thought."

He chuckled in the darkness. "And you still haven't experienced them all."

She took a deep breath, settling into his arms. *Yes, this little arrangement could lead to a lot of fun...if we do everything just right.* To that end, she said, "I'll have to leave pretty early in the morning since I have to go home, get a shower and all that."

"I get it. And I'll wait to hear from you, to see when we'll start recording again." He yawned. "It's all good."

"Thanks." She was glad he seemed to understand the importance of discretion, and that he didn't make a big deal of it.

Yes. This was going to be a lot of fun.

Taking a sip from the cup of chamomile tea in his hand, Maxton looked at the circle of metal folding chairs beyond him in the meeting room of Neal Wellness Center. Once he'd finished the tea, he tossed the foam cup into the trash can, then settled onto the seat of an empty chair. Immediately, the coolness snaked across the back of his thighs, a stark contrast to the mid-July heat outside that had driven him to dress in shorts. Looking around at the small circle of men, he thought back to last week's meeting, which had been his first, and tried to place names with the faces surrounding him.

He could remember two of the other four men present: Bill, who was in his early forties, had a kind face and ice-blue eyes. Kip, the youngest of the group at only nineteen, had brown hair with frosted blond tips and wore a leather jacket and matching pants despite the intense heat of a Georgia summer lurking just beyond the building's doors. *How does he wear that this time of year without passing out?* He wasn't particularly fond of summer, because he felt his style was best expressed in darker clothing that covered more skin. However, there was only so far he would go in the name of fashion. At some point, practicality had to come into play.

The other two men, he remembered their stories rather than their names. One, an older Black man, had lost a mother to a tragic robbery-turned-murder, and the other had spoken about his daughter's unfortunate death after a night of drinking. He assumed everyone present was a patient of his therapist, but he didn't know that for sure and didn't feel it was his place to ask. Besides, how they came to attend the meetings didn't matter. They were all here for the same reasons: to heal, and to grow.

The room's door swung open, and Dr. Alan Tyndall entered, carrying his clipboard case. A Black man in his early sixties, he had a short graying Afro and a mustache. He wore black slacks, a white button-down and a simple red tie. "Good evening, everybody." As the therapist took the last empty seat in the circle, everyone exchanged greetings.

Dr. Tyndall had been Maxton's therapist for the past six months, having worked with him in teletherapy while he was out touring with various musical artists. Now that he was in Atlanta for a time, Dr. Tyndall had suggested Maxton join his small support group, Men Managing Loss.

"So, gentlemen, who would like to be the first to share this week?" Dr. Tyndall let his gaze touch each face in the group and waited for a few moments. When no one volunteered, he pointed to Bill. "Bill, why don't you tell us how your week went?"

Bill drew a deep breath, clasping his hands together. "It's been three years now since I lost Ida in that car accident, so that means I made it to another milestone." He paused. "I also…think I might be ready to try dating again."

The other men offered smiles and words of encouragement; Bill's responding smile was a bit crooked but genuine.

"That's wonderful, Bill. What brought this on?" Dr. Tyndall leaned forward. "Was there any particular thing this week that gave you the final push?"

He nodded. "I was talking to my sister-in-law, and she told me for the umpteenth time that Ida wouldn't want me isolating like this. She'd want me to move on. But I think this time when she said it, I was finally ready to hear her."

"That's a very encouraging sign of growth, Bill. Is there anything else you'd like to share?"

Bill shook his head. "That's all for me."

"Maxton? How about you?" Dr. Tyndall looked his way. "I see your eye has healed up."

Maxton nodded. "Yeah. Well, we're on the eighth song of that album at work. We had to take two days off because of that incident, but I think we're back on track now."

Dr. Tyndall nodded, resting the eraser end of his pencil against his chin. "That's good to hear. But I'm curious to know how you're dealing with the mental and emotional aftermath of that incident."

Maxton swallowed. "I guess I'm doing alright. I mean, it's been hard to focus in the studio at times. We haven't had any more problems. Swagg isn't going to allow any more guests in there during our sessions."

"That's good, but it's less about what's happening in the studio now and more about how you're processing the underlying emotions brought on by what happened."

"It's hard to explain. But I…get angry, almost irrationally so, when I'm by myself." Maxton folded his hands into his lap. "I mean, it just pisses me off. How could a man even think it's okay to just swing on a woman like that? I had to stop him. I had to…" He stopped, midsentence, as realization hit.

"What?" Dr. Tyndall pressed. "What did you have to do, Maxton?"

"I had to protect her."

"Why?" He narrowed his eyes, the way he often did when analyzing what he heard.

The lump formed in his throat, and he felt his shoulders slump. "Because I couldn't protect Whitney. And I just couldn't bear failing again." He folded his arms over his chest, angry that he couldn't stop the tears.

"Whoa. Major breakthrough, my guy." Kip whistled.

"You're safe here, brother," another man added. "I wrestled with that guilt after I lost my little girl to alcohol poisoning. I beat myself up for months, wondering if there was somewhere I went wrong. I worried that I should have made her go to college closer to home or checked up on her more, anything that would have kept her away from that damn fraternity kegger." He shook his head.

"I've journeyed through the valley of guilt myself, Maxton." Dr. Tyndall straightened, tenting his fingers. "I'm a therapist. Mental health and wellness are my life. Yet I lost my own wife to suicide. I should have been better equipped than anyone to help her, to save her. But sometimes, life simply doesn't give us that chance."

Looking around at the faces of these men, of varying ages and from all different backgrounds, Maxton felt seen, heard, understood. Their shared experience of grief and loss, of powerlessness and regret had brought them all to this small room inside a nondescript building in Midtown. And though his journey in the group, and in a way, through his grief, had just begun, he felt grateful for them, nonetheless.

"We've all gone through some form of guilt," Bill stated solemnly. "I gotta tell you, it's a dead-end street. Nothing good can come of it."

Running his hand over his head, Maxton sighed. "When I remember that moment when the zip-line equipment malfunctioned, and I heard her scream… I just can't help wishing I could have stopped it from happening. I would even have taken my sister's place. But since I couldn't do that, I'm just…stuck. Stuck with the guilt, the pain, the sadness that seems like it will eat me alive sometimes."

"Thank you for your honesty, Maxton." Dr. Tyndall crossed his legs. "I think this is a good place to remind ourselves that there are two useless emotions—guilt and shame. These are the feelings that feed off the darkness inside of us, then use those regrets against us, to tell us that we aren't enough. But that's not true. We are enough."

The men around the circle nodded and murmured their agreement.

"And beyond that, we must make friends with time. As it passes, it naturally facilitates our healing. Let go of the worry that you'll forget your loved one. They were much too important for that. The mark they left on your lives is a legacy, something you can share and pass on to others. Tell your children about them. Tell your neighbors and friends about the lives they lived. Do good works in their name. Let the love you have for them stamp out the pain and the guilt, and let the joy of knowing they were a part of your life override all else." Dr. Tyndall let a small smile tug his lips. "My work in my wife's name is here, in this group. Have you ever read the sign above the door of this room?"

Most of them shook their heads.

His smile broadened. "This is the Elise Valmont Tyndall Room for Restoration and Recovery. I funded this space in her honor, to create a safe place for men to heal from loss. And this work, as hard as it is sometimes, fills me up with something I can hardly describe. And it leaves very little room for guilt."

When the meeting ended, Maxton hung back. "Dr. Tyndall, can I ask a quick question?"

"Go ahead." He snapped his clipboard case shut, resting it in the crook of his elbow.

"I'm not sure what my work will be. You know, the thing I do in Whitney's honor."

"You're already in a creative profession," the therapist pointed out. "Why not think of ways you can use your talent to honor her and perhaps help others in her memory?"

He nodded. "I'll think about that. Thanks, Doc."

"No problem." He patted him on the shoulder. "I'm sure you'll come up with something."

Eleven

Thursday afternoon, Teagan was back at the workstation for day sixteen of recording Lil Swagg's album. And based on the expression on the young rapper's face, the workday would soon come to an end.

The musicians were now recording their fifth iteration of the album's eighth track, and she could tell that everyone's patience was thin at this point. Peering through the glass into the booth, she could see the tight expression on Maxton's face. Something was off about his playing, though she couldn't quite name it. Where he usually fingered his instrument deftly and smoothly, today, his movements seemed stiff, almost rote. His improvisations were almost absent, and his cadence was slightly skewed.

She sighed, thinking back on the last two weeks with

him. They'd spent a good amount of time outside the studio together, hitting up the city's restaurants and taking long walks in the park. When they weren't out and about, they'd convened at his place for some smoking-hot sex. They kept their interactions professional at the studio, but when they were alone together, behind closed doors, all pretense was dropped as they gave in to the passion simmering between them.

Swagg rose from his seat on the sofa and came to stand next to her. "What is going on with them today?"

She shrugged. "I don't know. Something is definitely off, though."

"They usually sound so dope, but they don't really seem to be feelin' it today." He raised his index finger above his head, circling it around. "Yo, that's it. Cut the playback."

She tapped her screen, ceasing the stripped-down melody that the band members had been building around.

Swagg gestured to the intercom. "May I?"

"Sure. I'll press the button. You talk." She pressed the green button.

"Listen up, y'all. I don't know what the problem is, but y'all just not hittin' the mark today. So why don't we knock off early, y'all rest up, fill your well and whatnot, and just come back rested and ready to do this shit tomorrow? Everybody good with that?"

All four of them gave the thumbs-up.

"Cool."

Teagan pressed the red button to end his broadcast.

The booth's door opened with the musicians filing out. Maxton was last to leave.

"See you tomorrow," she called to him.

He glanced her way. "Yeah. You too."

She cringed inwardly, noting how his words lacked their usual warmth. *What's going on with him? Did I do or say something wrong?"*

Swagg stopped Maxton on the way out. "You good, homie? Because a track can live and die by the bass line, and you weren't at your best today."

Maxton nodded. "Yeah, I was just a little distracted. Got a lot on my mind." He hoisted his instrument case from one hand to the other. "I'm good, though. Tomorrow, I'll be ready."

Swagg waved. "See you tomorrow."

"See ya." Maxton turned and walked out.

While Swagg and Rick gathered their things, Teagan tried to focus on making sure today's work was properly saved and cataloged, but her mind kept going to Maxton. If he were her man, she'd have every right to follow him and press him for answers about whatever seemed to be bothering him.

But he's not my man. This is a fling. No strings attached, not even if I'm concerned. She simply didn't have a leg to stand on, because keeping things casual had been her idea in the first place. If she started making exceptions to their agreement now, who knew where it would lead. Probably not anywhere she was ready to go. So she pushed the thoughts away.

Left alone in the studio after Swagg and Rick's exit, she ended her session and set the workstation in shutdown mode. While she waited for the on-screen prompts to indicate the process was finished, she heard the echoing sound of someone shouting in the hallway. Considering her encounter with Money J and his thugs a couple of weeks ago, she didn't want to wait and see what the source of the sound was. At least Vic Grip, while misguided in his decision to bring the other men to her studio, had been gentlemanly enough not to participate in their childish brawl.

Rising from her seat, she went to the studio door and peered down the hall.

There was her father, walking in her direction from the elevator bank. He was shouting into his cell phone, and she immediately became curious as to why. It wasn't like her father to do something so unprofessional in a public space, so she assumed it was something pretty serious.

She turned back to see the screen go black on the workstation, then grabbed her purse and keys. Locking the door behind her, she headed toward her father, who'd now stopped in the hallway to carry on his angry phone conversation.

"No! Don't you dare come here. You won't be allowed on the premises!" His face twisted into a scowl; he stabbed the air with his finger. "Now, you listen, and you listen good. I don't know how you got my number, but don't you ever call me again. And don't come anywhere near me or my family, or I will have you arrested!" He took the phone away from his ear and jabbed the screen to end the call.

She looked at her father's untied necktie, sweat-dampened brow and his flashing eyes, wondering what was going on. Soon, though, she remembered. "Was that him, Dad? The man that claims you're his father?"

"Yes, that was that lying miscreant." He stuffed the phone into his pocket and marched past her.

She followed him into the security office directly adjacent to the reception desk. Only one officer was currently on duty, and he looked up from the camera monitors as soon as they entered.

"Mr. Woodson, is there a problem?"

"Owen, I need you to implement a one hundred percent ID check on anyone entering this building. If they're not staff or a member of the Woodson family, check their identification. I don't want anyone with the last name Woodbine on 404 Sound property, for any reason."

"Yes, sir. I'll take care of it right now." Owen spun his chair from the security monitor to the computer and began typing.

Teagan backed out of the way as her father exited the security office, then followed him as he stalked through the main door of the building. "Dad, slow down."

He stopped on the sidewalk and looked at her. "What is it, Teagan? Can't you see I'm in the middle of something?"

"Yes, and it looks like that something is a nervous breakdown." She shook her head. "Dad, you know I love you so, so much. But I tried to tell you that this guy wasn't going to stop."

He grimaced as if hearing her words caused him physical pain. "Please spare me the I-told-you-so, child. My pressure is already up."

She rested her hand on his forearm, giving it a gentle squeeze through the fabric of his light blue button-down. "What did he say to you that got you so upset, Dad?"

"He just restated the same lie that he wrote in that letter. The only difference is, he claims to have proof."

She stilled. "Proof?" That was a pretty bold claim to make, especially since her father was so insistent that there was no veracity to the claim. "That's...troubling."

He huffed. "It's absurd, that's what it is. None of this is true, so the proof he's talking about doesn't even exist or is faked." He shook his head solemnly. "Whoever this young man is, he missed his calling as an actor."

She asked the question that to her seemed the next most logical. "Okay. Now that you see this isn't going away, are you going to talk to Mom about it?"

He sighed. "Why must you keep bringing your mother into this? I've already told you this is all some elaborate lie. Why should I drag her into this, knowing she'd be just as upset as I am? I'd rather spare Addy this nonsense."

Teagan sucked in a breath. "Yes, I'm sure Mom would be upset to learn about this. But can you imagine how absolutely livid she'd be if she heard it from someone other than you?"

He frowned. "How would that happen, Teagan? You, me and Gloria are the only ones who know. My secretary knows better, and so do you." He looked at her pointedly. "Don't interfere with this, Teagan. This is my issue, and I'm going to handle it as I see fit."

She released his arm. "Dad, I'm not going to go behind your back. But I am gonna keep nudging you to tell Mom about this. Please. We don't know what this guy is capable of."

He hesitated, and she saw the contemplation play across his face. "I'll think about it."

"That's all I ask." She pecked him on the cheek. "Love you, Daddy."

"I love you too, baby girl." With a forlorn smile, he turned and walked to his car.

As she got into her own car, Teagan couldn't help thinking of Maxton again. Part of her wanted to call him, wanted to ask what she should do about this whole mess with her father. She didn't like keeping secrets from her mother, but she also didn't want to break her word.

She grabbed her phone out of her purse to call Maxton but stopped short. After the way he'd acted toward her today, she had no reason to believe he'd be interested in hearing about her problems. Besides, that would probably exceed the parameters of their little fling.

She put her phone away and started the engine. As she pulled out of the parking lot, she couldn't help thinking of how this thing seemed determined to outgrow the box they'd tried to put it in.

Sitting on his sofa, Maxton used his small laptop to perform an internet search. Dr. Tyndall's advice had been bouncing around in his head for a couple of days now, and he wanted to go ahead and make some moves toward building something meaningful in Whitney's name.

Ever since the seed had been planted in his mind, he'd been thinking about it. Admittedly, his preoccupation with this new mission had contributed to his less-than-stellar playing in the recording session today. *I don't want that to happen again, so I need to get this together so I can concentrate on my work.*

He wasn't going to rush the process, not with something as precious as his sister's legacy at stake. What he needed was a firm plan, a solid foundation. Once he had that in place, he knew he could go back to putting his heart and soul into his current gig.

He clicked on a link to the home page of a website explaining how to form a nonprofit organization. He leaned back against the cushions, slowly scrolling as he read the information on the screen. *Damn, this is a lot. Better take some notes.* He opened a text file, snapped the two windows next to each other, and typed up a few pertinent items.

The sound of someone knocking at his door drew his attention. Setting the laptop aside, he stood and went to answer it, expecting some salesperson or a local churchgoer passing out tracts.

As he checked the peephole, he got a surprise. Opening the door, he said, "Teagan? What are you doing here?"

Still dressed in the knee-length purple sheath she'd worn at the studio earlier, she offered him a crooked smile. "I was going to call, but... I thought this would be better."

"Um..." he glanced at his computer, then back to her. *She did drive all the way over here... I guess my planning session will have to wait.* He took a big step back. "Come on in."

"Thanks." She entered and closed the door behind her. "I hope I'm not interrupting anything."

He jogged over to the sofa and shut his laptop. "I was just poking around online. So, what brings you here?"

She approached him and dropped her handbag on

the coffee table, her hand coming up to stroke his jaw-line. "I just…really need a distraction right now." She grabbed his hand, moving it to her thigh and curling his fingers around the hem of her dress. "Do you think you can help me out?"

He swallowed, looking down into her sultry eyes. "Yeah."

"Good." She gave him a peck on the cheek, then turned away from him.

He felt his brow furrow, but confusion quickly turned to arousal when he saw what she was doing. She kicked off her sandals, went to the arm of the sofa and bent over it.

Blood surged into his dick at the sight of her up-turned hips. No woman had ever approached him so boldly, and he'd never been this turned on. As he palmed her ass through the thin fabric of her dress, she widened her stance.

"Please, Maxton. I need it," she crooned, her voice low and sultry.

He quickly grabbed a condom from the secret drawer under the sofa, snatched down his shorts and boxers, and sheathed himself. That done, he lifted her dress, bunching the fabric around her waist. Hooking his thumbs under the band of her lacy black bikini under-wear, he dragged them down her legs and watched her step out of them.

He licked his lips, anticipating the feel of her as he rested one hand on the small of her back. Using his other hand, he guided himself inside her tightness.

"Oh, yes," she purred, as he reached the deepest part of her.

He began his work then, at first using a gentle, slow stroke that tested the limits of his self-control. He gripped her waist, drawing her body in closer to his with each thrust. Her soft moans filled his ears, spurring him on.

Soon, keeping his pace slow became impossible, and he sped up to match the desire roaring through his body like wildfire. The pitch of her moans changed, growing higher as he put even more power into the movements of his hips. Her body, so wet and tight, threatened to drain him of every ounce of strength he had, but he didn't care. Nothing mattered but her cries of ecstasy and the release he felt building inside.

She screamed as her body clenched around him. That was enough to push him over the edge, and moments later, he felt his own body pulsing inside her as he came. He eased away from her, disposed of the condom, then returned and slipped back into his boxers.

As she stood, tugging down her dress, she giggled.

He raised a brow. "That's not a critique of my performance, is it?"

"Of course not. You were amazing." She shook her head, still laughing. "I just can't believe I did that. I must really be stressed-out."

He chuckled as he flopped down on the sofa. "I guess so." Patting his lap, he said, "Sit down. Tell me what's on your mind."

She sat on his lap sideways and settled into his embrace with a sigh. "Look, Maxton. I know this thing between us is all about keeping it light, no strings, all of that. But I'm sitting on a huge secret, and I don't really have anyone else I can unburden myself to."

"Nobody?"

She shook her head. "Miles and Nia are family, so they can't know. And unfortunately, I don't really have any close friends, just acquaintances." She inhaled deeply. "A lot of that is my fault. I'm probably the least social of all the Woodson kids."

"Okay." He scratched his chin, wondering what was bothering her so much. "Let me guess. This has something to do with your Dad?"

"Yes. That situation I told you about before. It's back, just like I said it would be."

"Are you going to tell me what this 'situation' is, Teagan?"

She nodded. "I will if you promise me you won't tell anyone else."

"I won't." He held up his hand. "I don't have any reason to go telling your family's business."

"A young man has come forward, claiming that he's my father's illegitimate son."

His eyes grew wide. "Oh, snap."

"Yeah. My father denies the whole thing, even going so far as to say it's impossible that this person is his child. But he won't let up. First, he sent that letter a couple of weeks ago. Then, a few hours ago, he called my dad's cell phone to make the same claim directly to him."

"That seems like more of your dad's problem than yours. So why are you so upset?"

"For starters, the mere existence of this accusation has shaken my view of the man I thought my father was. But the absolute worst part is that my father refuses to tell my mother about it, so she's totally in the dark about this whole mess." She shook her head. "And that puts me in the very awkward position of lying to my mother. It isn't a position I want to be in."

"That's...a lot. I can see why you'd be stressed-out by it." He ran his hand over her hair, playing with the few tendrils that had escaped her low bun. "So, what are you going to do?"

She shrugged. "Nothing, right now. I told Dad I wouldn't say anything to Mom. But I just know this is gonna blow up in his face, and I told him as much."

"Then, there's really not much you can do."

"I guess you're right." She cupped his face in her hands. "Telling you did help, though. So thanks for listening."

"You're welcome." He gave her a soft, gentle kiss on the lips.

Looking at her, so comfortable in his arms, made him think very seriously about their arrangement. The more time he spent with her, the more he felt his heart opening to her. They'd begun with a promise to keep things casual, to keep things fun. Now here he was, re-considering the very foundation of what they'd agreed to.

His feelings for her were growing, and if she could trust him enough to share with him what she just had, he may as well take a chance and trust her with what he felt. There was something between them, something real, something works more than a fling.

"Teagan, I need to tell you something."

"Go ahead. I'm listening."

"I've been thinking we should..." The sound of the

alarm on his phone going off interrupted him, and he cursed, remembering. "Shit."

"What's wrong?"

He shifted, scooting from beneath her. "It's almost six, and I have an appointment."

The corners of her mouth fell, and her shoulders drooped. "Do you have to go?"

He nodded as he stepped into his shorts and dragged them up. "Yeah, I do. It's really important. I'm sorry to rush you off. It's just that when you—" he pointed to the sofa arm "—did that, I totally forgot about it."

"I can see how that could happen." She sighed but got up and slipped back into her panties and shoes. "I'll let you go. See you tomorrow at the studio."

"Yep. See you there." He pulled his shirt over his head and tugged the tail down.

She gave him a quick peck on the cheek, grabbed her purse and left.

A few minutes later, he grabbed his wallet and the keys to his rental and ran out the door.

Twelve

"So, it's true, then. You and the bassist?"

Teagan shook her head in response to her older sister's voice coming over her car's speakers. "I thought we were being discreet, but I guess not."

"Come on, Teagan. 404 is a family-owned business. You know how fast word gets around the building." She chuckled. "I gotta admit I'm surprised. I didn't think you had it in you to have a fling."

"I didn't, either." She thought back to last night, and how quickly passion had turned to awkwardness. "It's funny, though. Just when people start talking about our little arrangement, things get weird between us."

Nia sounded confused. "What do you mean?"

She signed. "I went over there yesterday to…hang out. Anyway, when we were just chilling on the sofa, his phone went off and he jumped up, saying he had an appointment. Then he basically put me out so he could go."

"What's weird about that? Maybe he really had an appointment."

"Maybe, but that's not the issue." She turned right, onto the side street where 404's building was located. "Just before the phone went off, he got this really serious look on his face and started to tell me something. When he jumped up to get ready, he never finished his sentence."

"He didn't call or text you last night to clear things up?"

"Nope. So now I'm just left wondering what he was going to say." She shrugged, pulling into her designated parking space. "I'm gonna see him shortly, so I suppose I can just ask."

"Hmm. You'd better brace for impact."

"Why?" She cut the engine, switching her phone to speaker mode, and reached into the passenger seat for her purse.

"You say he had a serious look on his face. What if he wanted to end things and was trying to let you down gently or something?"

Teagan felt a twinge in her chest at her sister's words. As much as she didn't want to think about it, she'd started to get attached to Maxton in a way she hadn't intended. "Who knows what was on his mind? I just wish he'd said it, so I wouldn't have to be worried about it now." She blew out a breath. "With Swagg's album and everything going on with Dad…" She clapped her hand over her mouth, but it was already too late.

"Yeah, what's up with Dad? He's been a little extra salty lately."

"I, uh, nothing," she stammered. "Listen, I'm here. So I gotta go."

"Teagan, wait—"

She disconnected the call. *Yikes. I can't believe I slipped up like that.* As she reached for the door handle, she glanced in the rearview and saw Maxton's rented convertible pull into the lot. Getting out of the car, she walked down the sidewalk toward the right side of the building where he'd parked.

The air felt hot and sticky, despite the early hour. She'd dressed in lighter colors, donning a yellow pencil skirt with a striped, yellow-and-white button-down blouse and nude pumps, in an attempt to reflect rather than absorb the searing Georgia sunshine. Her heels clicked on the concrete as she moved toward her objective: answers.

Moments later, she met him near the southeast corner of the building.

Dressed in denim shorts that revealed his hard thighs, a black polo and black sneakers, he wore a thick silver chain with a three-dimensional skull pendant dangling from his neck. Dark sunglasses over his eyes, he gripped the handle to his instrument case as he strode toward her. "Good morning."

"Morning." She eyed him. "This is a pretty tame look for you."

He shrugged. "I agree. But it's getting too hot for the kind of stuff I like to wear."

"I see." She paused. "Before we go inside, can I ask you something?"

"Sure. What's up?"

"What were you going to say to me last night? You know, before you had to rush off to that appointment?"

He sucked in his lower lip. "Yeah, again, I'm sorry I had to run out the way I did. You were…very distracting."

She offered him a small smile. "I figure it must have been important. Anyway, it's fine. I just wanted you to finish saying whatever it was you started to say before you left."

He shifted his weight, looked away. "I…don't think this is a good time to talk about that."

Her sister's warning echoed in her ear, and she bristled. "Oh, so it's like that? Are you at least going to tell me where you went in such a hurry last night?"

He titled his head to one side. "Not that I owe you an explanation, but I have a standing Thursday-night therapy session."

She frowned, narrowing her eyes. "I never said you owed me anything, I simply asked a question. I'm just trying to get a little clarity here."

"Clarity on what, exactly?" He rested his free hand on his waist. "Why would you even care where I went?"

Noticing the change in his stance, she said, "Wait a minute, Maxton. I don't like your tone."

"You don't like my tone? Really?" His lips curled into a sarcastic smile. "That's rich, considering your tone right now, not to mention how you just showed up at my apartment yesterday unannounced. Not even a text to let me know you were on your way."

"I asked if I was interrupting, and…"

"No." He cut her off. "I may have been raised in Cali,

but I know it's rude to just dismiss a visitor. So I wasn't going to just dismiss you, the way you dismissed my time and convenience by showing up the way you did."

She stared. "I'm sorry. I didn't realize I'd inconvenienced you. I didn't hear any complaints when you were making love to me." She cringed, realizing she should have left that last part as interior monologue, but she couldn't unsay it now.

His brow creased; his jaw hardened. "You know, you're a real piece of work. You insisted from the beginning that we keep this thing casual…"

Teagan heard the telltale creak of the side door being opened but didn't turn toward the sound.

"Yet you appear at my home, distract me from what I was working on, then proceed to drop this whole mess with your dad's outside child in my lap…"

"What outside kid?"

Teagan's heart dropped so fast, she was sure it bounced off the pavement. Turning toward the door, she saw her mother standing there, a few feet away. She must have just exited the building from the side door.

Addison, dressed in a bright red pantsuit with her hair up in a high chignon, walked a few steps closer to her daughter. "Teagan, what is he talking about? What's going on?"

Glancing back at Maxton, she gritted out, "Thanks a lot."

He rolled his eyes. "Shit! I'm going inside. The session is gonna start soon." He strode past her and went around to the front of the building.

Teagan didn't know if he went that way because he

always entered through the front or because he didn't want to get any closer to them.

Addison grabbed her daughter's hand. "Teagan, can you please tell me what the hell is going on? I clearly heard that young man say something about your father and an outside child!"

Squeezing her mother's hand, she said, "Mom, let's go inside to your office. I'll explain it to you there."

Entering through the side door, she popped her head inside Studio Two. Trevor, sitting at his old faithful soundboard, turned around when she entered. "What's up, boss lady?"

"Can you get the session started in Studio One, please? I need like half an hour."

"I gotcha covered." The longtime employee glanced between their two faces. "Everything alright?"

"That remains to be seen," Addison said.

"Thanks, Trevor. I'll be back ASAP."

She and her mother boarded the elevator, taking it to the fourth floor. There, Addison let Teagan into her office. As Teagan sat down, Addison closed the door behind her.

"Are you going to tell me what's going on now?" Addison sat on the edge of her desk.

She looked up at her mother, towering over her due to her position, and had a flashback to her days as a little kid. Back then, her mother had seemed like a superwoman. But today, with the worry and concern lining her face, Teagan could see that her mother wasn't nearly as impervious to damage as she'd once thought. "I can't, Mom."

Folding her arms over her chest, she asked, "And why not?"

"I gave Dad my word that I wouldn't speak to you about this." She drew a deep breath. "My best advice is to just go talk to him."

Addison sighed. "I just can't believe this is happening. I'm walking out for a coffee run, and I overhear you arguing with…" She paused. "Wait a minute. Why were you two arguing? Isn't he one of the musicians working on that album in your recording suite?"

She nodded. "Yes, he is."

Addison rolled her eyes. "You know what? Never mind. I don't have the mental capacity to handle whatever you've got going on on top of what I just overheard." She stood, pacing the room's hardwood floor, her heels clicking in time. "Did I hear it right? Please tell me I'm mistaken."

"I can't do that, Mom." She rested her cheek in her hand. "Please, just go talk to Dad. I'm already way more involved in this than I ever wanted to be." *If only Gloria had just handed over that letter, maybe I could have avoided getting ensnared in this whole enterprise.*

"Don't you worry. I'm going to Caleb's office right now and getting some answers, straight from the source." Addison opened her office door. "Go on downstairs and handle the session. I'll deal with your father."

Cringing inwardly, Teagan got up and left the room.

Max sat on the low stool in his corner of the booth, his bass across his lap. He'd practically slid into the room not too long ago, not wanting to hold up the recording session. In his haste to remove the instrument from its case, he'd accidentally knocked it out of tune.

He strummed each of the strings in turn, listening to each note as it reverberated through the booth. All four single notes sounded off, though in different ways. He didn't bother with chords right now, knowing they'd sound like a chorus of alley cats. *Better to just tune the thing than subject everybody in the booth to that noise.*

Opening up the smartphone tuning app made by his bass manufacturer, he began the process of getting her back in tune. Left-handed guitarists were a rarity, and every time he took his bass in his hands, he remembered how hard it had been for him to learn to properly tune and play his instrument. With his left hand on the strings and his right hand on the tuners, he played the notes one by one. The E and A notes were sharp, while the D and G were both flat. Following the on-screen prompts, he loosened the first two tuners, then tightened the last two. With that done, he closed the app.

"Hey, Brady," he called.

"Yeah?" The guitarist turned his way.

"Can you give me a little Deep Purple, so I can test my tune?" He readied his fingers.

"No prob. First tune I ever learned how to play." Brady strapped on his guitar, a B.C. Rich Warlock Extreme edition in rich black lacquer, and began to play the famous opening stanza of the British rock band's hit "Smoke on the Water." Maxton picked up the bass line at the appropriate moment, and soon, the entire band was running through the 1972 classic. Mike used his keyboard to simulate the vocals, and the vibe was definitely there. They were all along for the ride, grooving, caught up in the magic of a familiar yet extraordinary piece of music. Four musicians, four instruments, all combining to create one awesome sound.

Swagg switched on the intercom as they wrapped up. "Yo, that was hot. Seems like y'all back in top form."

He hoped the rapper was right because he was determined to make up for the previous day's lack of progress. Swagg had given them an ambitious goal. Maxton wanted them to succeed in meeting it. *Challenge is good for a musician. It keeps you focused, keeps you learning, keeps complacency away.*

He was too young and too early in his career to start resting on his laurels. He wanted to always be learning, always be growing as a bassist. And in order to do that, he had to take the hard gigs, put in the long hours, play the pieces that made him nervous or fell outside his comfort zone.

Trevor, seated behind the workstation, held up his hand. "Let's pick up where you left off and run through track eight." Playback on the melody track started, and Maxton began picking out a bass line.

The rest of the band joined in, and Maxton felt the synergy inside the booth growing. He added a little flair to his line as the track reached its bridge, then eased up for the return to the chorus and the next eight bars. As the song's final eight bars played, he kicked it up another notch. The rest of the band followed his lead. Each musician added their own special touch to the combined sound. The music swelled, and the track ended with a rich, intense finish.

Swagg clapped his hands, nodding his approval as he reengaged the intercom. "Hell, yeah! That's what I'm talking about, y'all." He eased over to Trevor, touching his shoulder. "That's a wrap on that song, homie. I'm ready to get in the booth and lay my verses down."

Trevor nodded, and Swagg stepped into the booth. Maxton and the other musicians sat down on their stools and listened while he rapped his verses over their newly created track. Maxton bobbed his head in time, enjoying the way the music and Swagg's vocals blended together, complementing each other so well, with neither element overpowering the other.

As Swagg went into the song's bridge, the suite door swung open and Teagan walked in.

Maxton felt the smile slip from his face as he took in her gloomy expression. *Boy. I laid a big-ass egg with her today.* She looked stressed-out, and because of his careless blunder earlier, he knew he was to blame for that, at least partly.

Maxton watched Teagan for a few minutes as Swagg finished his vocals, and it soon became obvious that she refused to look in his direction. When they convened work on the album's ninth track, he found it difficult to regain the focus and flow he'd had just a short time earlier. His fingers slipped a few times, screwing up his chords and throwing off the cadence of the rest of the band.

Even as things inside the booth started to go to the left, Teagan's gaze remained locked on her screen. She never looked up, not even a glance.

Swagg held up his hand, extended his index finger and swirled it around his head. Teagan gave him a subtle nod, then restarted playback on track nine's melody.

Once again, Maxton couldn't find his groove. He

looked down at his fingers, minding their progress over the strings. But when he hazarded another glance at Teagan, he found her looking straight ahead through the glass. Her expression was one of utter boredom and disinterest.

Seeing that expression took him back to his days at Mrs. Hardy's Music Academy. He'd studied under her as a young, impressionable bassist, starting his lessons at the tender age of seven. His parents, while both scientists, had encourage his artistic interests and had paid the exorbitant fee allowing him to enter her elite academy. Years of absorbing his father's love of funk music, particularly the animated stylings of the legendary Bootsy Collins, had fueled Maxton's desire to play bass.

He'd taken lessons four days a week for ten years, completing Mrs. Hardy's Young Master's Program a few months before he started his senior year in high school. His parents, as well as his sister, Whitney, had praised his playing at every opportunity. But not Mrs. Hardy. While he was one of her star pupils, she rarely doled out praise. Even when she did, it usually came paired with some criticism or another. For years, he labored at improving his skills, filled with confidence and fear in equal measure.

She'd watch his recitals, stone-faced, as if she had somewhere else to be. And while her strict standards had helped him secure a spot at his dream school, he could still feel the sting of her disapproving stare whenever he made a mistake. This many years and this many miles away from Mrs. Hardy, he knew he shouldn't be feeling this way again.

Faltering beneath the weight of his frustration, he plucked his E string so hard, he snatched it right out of tune again. Even with the sounds of all the other instruments around him, he could hear how flat the note played. He cursed inwardly.

Sharrod dropped one of his drumsticks. As he snatched it up and started playing again, he glared at Maxton. "Get it together, bro!"

He did his best to salvage the piece, but his out-of-tune string made his bass line sound tinny and strange. He tried adjusting the tuning peg on the fly, but it just wasn't working.

Swagg gestured for them to stop, then spoke over the intercom. "You know what? Y'all slipping again. It's cool, though. We got a track done, so I'm good with reconvening Monday." Swagg looked pointedly from Teagan to Maxton. "Use the weekend to deal with whatever tension or hang-ups y'all might have. Because next week, we gon' blast through these last three tracks. Y'all feel me?"

Maxton swallowed. "Yeah." His bandmates offered their affirmatives as well, and he could feel their disapproving stares burning his face.

Teagan offered a tight nod.

"I'm glad we all on the same page. See y'all Monday." With that, Swagg departed.

Feeling chastised and embarrassed, Maxton settled onto the stool again and flipped open his instrument case, setting the bass inside. He snapped it shut and stayed seated as the other musicians packed up.

Sharrod eyed him. "Man, what's going on with you two? I told you this was a bad idea."

"Don't start with me, Sharrod." Taking in the tight set of this friend's face, he added, "I'll handle it. I promise."

"I hope so." Sharrod shoved his sticks into the back pocket of his jeans. "Because whatever you two have going, it's not cool to put the gig at risk for the rest of us." He turned and stalked out.

Alone in the booth, Maxton watched Teagan through the glass partition. She was still busying herself with anything else other than looking in his direction, but by now, he'd grown tired of it.

Getting his case, he left the booth, passed her in the outer suite and sat down on the sofa. "Teagan, can we talk about this?"

She ignored him, continuing to tap the touchscreen at the workstation.

He sighed. "Teagan, I know you can hear me."

Thirteen

Staring at the screen of her workstation, Teagan pretended there was no one else in the room. For a while it was easy, as she ran file cleanup and optimization on the track-eight audio they'd created today. She simply tuned out the insistent voice behind her, choosing instead to focus on the colored patterns flashing across the screen, tracking the process as it happened.

Upstairs, her mother had probably already read her father the riot act, and she was pretty sure that the only reason she hadn't heard it all go down was the soundproofing in the recording suite. Or maybe Mom hadn't talked to Dad at all. Maybe she'd gotten halfway down the hall, decided to it wasn't a good time to discuss it and gone back to her office to simmer quietly, like a pot of Aunt Gracie's Brunswick stew. She glanced up at the ceiling as if she could see through it, wondering what was going on in the executive suites right now. Knowing she'd find out soon enough how it all had gone down, she returned her attention to the screen.

Behind her, Maxton called her name yet again.

She released a long, drawn-out sigh. It was obvious he wasn't going to go away and leave her in peace to figure out what to do next, so she finally turned her chair around and faced him. "What is there to talk about, Maxton?"

"We need to talk about whatever is going on between us." He gestured with his hands to himself, then to her.

"What we have going on isn't the problem." *Is he really going to make it about us?*

"It's creating a tension between us that is now encroaching on our work, our livelihood. That makes it a problem."

She stared at him, noting the hard set of his jaw and the stiff way he sat, perched on the edge of the sofa. "I don't want to talk about this."

"What is it you're avoiding here, Teagan?" He held her gaze. "I'm trying to get some clarity."

"On what?"

"On why you came in here acting the way you did." He rested his elbows on his thighs, tenting his fingers. "You were so obviously ignoring me that even Swagg picked up on it. You heard what he said to us when he told us to wrap up for the day?"

She rolled her eyes. "Of course. How could I not have heard it, when he was hovering over my workstation?"

He tilted his head slightly to the right. "If you say you heard that, then you should understand that it's a problem, and we should be able to act like adults and talk about it."

"That's pretty big talk, considering the fact that your big mouth just caused a whole lot of trouble for my family."

His expression changed, a crooked half smile flexing his lips. "Oh, I'm the big mouth? You came to me and told me your darkest family secret, but I'm the one with the big mouth?"

She cringed, feeling the sting of his words and of her own regret. "I thought I could trust you. Thought I could unburden myself to you. Apparently, I was wrong."

"See? That's just it." He shook his head. "When I came to you, asking your name, it was because I wanted to know you better. I felt there was a connection between us." He paused, his gaze linking with hers. "You were the one who suggested a fling. No strings, no commitments."

"I know what I said, Maxton." A twinge of tension went up her back, coming to rest between her shoulder blades. She shifted in her chair, attempting to alleviate it, but to no avail.

"Do you? Because when you showed up at my place last night, it sure as hell seemed like you'd forgotten."

She closed her eyes. *I really stepped in it, didn't I? I never should have gone over there.*

"You asked me what I was going to say before I left for my appointment, but the truth is, I'm glad I didn't finish. You're not ready for what I was going to say, and that's crystal clear to me now." He stood, wrapping his fingers around the handle of his instrument case. "I can't do this with you, Teagan."

She felt her heart squeeze in her chest, and she didn't like feeling at all. "Can't do what?"

He gestured around with his free hand. "I don't know—whatever it is we've been doing for the past month."

She felt the squeeze again. "You mean, going on dates? Having deep talks? Making love until we're both exhausted?"

"Yes, that. This fling, or sneaky link, that we've been doing." He sighed. "Call it whatever you want. Either way, I'm out."

She stood, effectively blocking his only exit. "Why? Why don't you want to keep seeing me? Is it because of what happened this morning?"

He shook his head. "No, Teagan, it's all of it. I'm sorry for the awkwardness I caused today, but you gotta realize that even that situation began with you."

She frowned, folding her arms over her chest. "That's not fair."

"I think it's very fair. You dumped the drama in my lap. Otherwise, I wouldn't have known about it. I shouldn't have blurted it out the way I did. That's on me." He shook his head. "But it doesn't matter. This just isn't going to work, and we both know it."

She chewed her lower lip. "I don't see why we can't just renegotiate the terms of our arrangement."

"Because I don't want to, Teagan. I've had enough of this." He drummed his fingers on his instrument case. "I made a mistake in agreeing to the first set of terms, and now it has blown up in both of our faces. It's not the worst mistake I ever made, not by a long shot. But I don't want to make it worse by prolonging it."

"Don't I get a say?" She was pouting and she knew it, but she couldn't control it.

"I've already given you plenty of 'say.' You said you don't want strings or attachments. Those were your words. Well, here's a news flash—if there are no strings, then there are no explanations, either." He fixed her with a penetrating stare. "So when I tell you I'm done, that I don't want this anymore, I shouldn't have to face an inquisition. You should just step aside and let me go."

She swallowed, cursing inwardly at the traitorous tears she felt rising in her throat. "But Maxton…"

He held up his hand. "No. I'm out." He broke eye contact with her and looked past her as if she weren't even in the room anymore. "Now, please step aside."

She angrily wiped away the single tear that fell. She wanted to change his mind, but that didn't seem likely. So rather than make a fool of herself, she stiffened her spine and gave him a curt nod. "Fine. If that's what you want, then it's over."

"Good. Thank you."

She took a giant step to her right, coming to a stop as her hip bumped up against the counter supporting the workstation.

With the path cleared, Maxton and his bass disappeared through the recording suite's outer door. After he turned the corner, she walked to the door and peered up the corridor. He probably knew she was watching, but he didn't stop, didn't look back, didn't acknowledge her in any way. She caught a fleeting glimpse of his back as he turned the other corner near reception and left the building.

She flopped back into her chair and let the angry

tears fall. Part of her felt insulted by the dismissive tone he'd used, and yet another part of her was angry with herself. She knew this was a bad idea from the very beginning; it was why she'd never involved herself with any of the people who came to her suite to work. She'd never dated anyone she worked with, not an artist or producer or manager or session musician. Now that she'd broken that streak, the very first one she'd gotten entangled with turned out to be a dud. *The one time I let my attraction to someone overrule my good sense, this happens. Go, figure.*

It had proven to be a painful mistake, one she didn't plan on making ever again.

She thought about the conversations they'd had, the meals they'd shared, the nights she'd spent lying in his arms. She remembered the way his body felt next to hers, the thrill of having him inside. Was this what it meant to have a fling? To lose yourself in something magical, to the point that you forgot it was only meant to be temporary fun?

Was it supposed to turn out like this, or am I just bad at it? It must be the latter because who would sign up for this? Who would willingly subject themselves to the regret and sadness she felt right now?

Saturday night, Maxton sat at the bar at the Rogue, his hand gripping the handle of a frosty, half-filled mug. Turning it up, he downed the rest of the contents and slammed it down on the counter. "Can I get another?" Nick wasn't working today, but the guy behind the counter seemed cool, nonetheless.

"Number three, coming up." The bartender grabbed his mug, filled it at the tap and slid it back his way.

"Thanks." He grabbed the handle, blowing out a breath. Just a few days ago, everything had been great. He'd had a challenging, well-paid gig with a rising star in hip-hop and a sexy liaison with the world's hottest sound engineer. Now he'd lost one of those things, and as it turned out, it wasn't nearly as expendable as he'd first thought.

The weeks he'd spent with Teagan had been some of the best in his life. Since the loss of his sister, he'd closed himself off from the world, developed a tunnel-vision-like approach to his work, and tried to run from his sorrow. Teagan had made him laugh, made him think. Most of all, she'd made him live again by giving him a reason to get out of his apartment and see what life outside had to offer.

He prepared to hoist the golden liquid to his mouth again but was interrupted by the sound of someone calling his name. Turning his head, he saw a confused-looking Sharrod coming his way.

"Maxton, what the hell's going on with you?"

Maxton shrugged. "Just chilling, man."

"The hell you are." He pointed to the mug. "How many of those have you had?"

"This is my third. But trust me, it won't be my last." He raised the mug in mock salute, then took a deep swig. "Ah, refreshment."

Sharrod didn't appear amused. His face twisted into a sort of disapproving grimace. "I've been calling and texting you all day." He sat down on the stool next to him. "I thought it was weird that you didn't respond, so I went by your place. When you weren't there, my next thought was to check here." He shook his head. "What's going on with you?"

"Nothing. Why were you so pressed to reach me, anyway?"

"Brady and Mike invited us out for the night. You know, drink, eat, maybe hit a club or two." He sucked his teeth. "I see you already got the drinking part started."

He laughed with all the bitterness he felt. "Yeah, I suppose. But I don't wanna go to any club. This here is a party for one." He drained the mug again. "Hey, bartender!"

The bartender returned but paused when Sharrod made eye contact and gave him a solemn head shake. "Sorry, compadre. Maybe dry out a little, okay?"

"Whatever," Maxton groused, shoving his empty mug away. "Thanks a lot for spoiling my fun, Dad."

Sharrod frowned, watching him intently. "You weren't having any fun here, and we both know it."

Maxton shifted his gaze away from his friend's penetrating stare, scratched his nose. "Let me get a ginger ale."

"That, I can do." The bartender whisked the old mug away and soon replaced it with a fresh mug full of the subtly tart soft drink.

"You gonna tell me what happened between you and Ms. Teagan?" Sharrod adjusted his position on the seat.

"I thought you were going to hang out with Mike and Brady tonight?"

"I did, too." He folded his arms over the image of

Snoop Dogg on his T-shirt. "But since my homeboy is in trouble, it's been a change of plans. So, speak."

He shook his head, thinking back on their conversation. "I never should have gotten involved with her, man."

"I know that." Sharrod threw up his hands. "I literally told you that from the beginning."

He rolled his eyes. "I bet you're enjoying being right, huh?"

"No, I'm not, for two reasons."

Maxton braced for some smart-ass response, likely accompanied by one of Sharrod's worry anecdotes.

"It's actually kind of weird, being right at this magnitude. Things played out almost exactly as I said they would. That makes it a little too strange to be satisfying."

He drew a deep breath, surprised by the direction this was taking. "What's the other reason?"

Sharrod scratched his chin. "Honestly? It pains me to see you hurting, which you obviously are right now. That takes all the joy out of it. I'm not even gonna say I told you so."

Maxton's brow inched up. "You just did."

"Fair enough, but I won't say it again." Sharrod chuckled. "Anyway, just tell me what happened."

He recounted yesterday's disastrous conversation with Teagan. "Bottom line is, I just can't do this with her. She's asking me for something I just can't give."

"Which is...?" Sharrod eyed him questioningly.

"She wants to keep things casual." He shrugged. "Turns out I can't do that, at least not with her."

Sharrod's brow knit together. "What? Why would you…?" His eyes grew wide. "Bro, you didn't."

In response, Maxton leaned forward, resting his forehead onto the cool marble surface of the bar. "I'm afraid I did."

"Oh, snap." Sharrod's voice was filled with surprise. "I can't believe you fucked around and fell in love."

Maxton felt the groan rising in his throat before it left his mouth. "You and me both. It's the stupidest mess I've ever gotten myself into," he murmured. Before yesterday's ill-fated tête-è-tête, he'd thought the worse part of it was that he'd never gotten to tell Teagan that he loved her. Now he knew better.

Sharrod pursed his lips and blew out a breath. "Damn, that's rough. I do have some good news, though. Maybe it will cheer you up."

"Nothing can cheer me up," Maxton griped, "unless you're willing to let the bartender bring me another beer."

"Come on, Maxton. Hear me out." Sharrod pulled his phone out of his jeans pocket. "When Brady called me, he told me all about it. He's got a connection to a producer out of Houston, through a friend of a friend. Anyway, Brady's producer buddy got him a spot on a nationwide tour. It's an old-school-versus-new-school, festival-type show. This is gonna be epic. I'm talking big names. LL. The Roots crew. That young guy out of Chicago with the blond dreads… Damn, I can't remember his name, but you know who I'm talking about. They even got the Houston hottie herself in the lineup."

Without lifting his head, Maxton sighed. "Sharrod, did you know that when you get excited, you talk fast, and I don't know what the hell you be saying? I got like the first ten words and the rest was gibberish."

Sharrod jabbed him in the shoulder with his finger. "You'd get more of it if you were looking at me while I was talking."

"Sharrod just give me the short version, dude." He dragged himself back up and faced his friend. "You're killing me."

"Short version is this—we have a chance to go on one of the biggest hip-hop tours the country has seen in years. All we gotta do is give our decision by the end of next week so Brady can let the producer know and make the arrangements."

He thought about it. Based on his friend's excitement level and the big names he thought he'd heard him say, it could be a very lucrative gig. "I don't know, man. I'm just not in the right headspace to say yes to this. At least not right now."

Sharrod nodded. "I get it. You gotta work some stuff out." He flagged down the bartender and ordered himself a lemonade. "But I'm definitely gonna take it. I hope you'll be able to come with me."

With a nod, he took a sip from his slightly watered-down soda. Usually, he was quick to say yes to gigs like this. A tour like this was manna from heaven for a working bassist, providing not only income but an opportunity to enjoy some free travel while building relationships that could lead to the next gig.

I just...can't right now. He needed time, time to nurse his bruised heart the same as he'd nursed his black eye, the one he'd gladly taken in Teagan's defense.

"You look a mess, Maxton." Sharrod put his hand

on his shoulder. "Look, I'm willing to sit here with you as long as you want. But honestly, I don't think it's the best way to help your situation right now."

"What would you suggest, Sharrod?"

"Let's just go meet up with Brady and Mike. Brady can give you more info about the tour, you can keep drinking without looking sad and pitiful, and we can have some fun." He held up his hands. "I mean, it ain't gonna mend your heart, but the boys and I can certainly dampen the pain for one night."

Maxton locked his hands around his mug, taking a moment to think about it. Sharrod was right, going out with the guys wasn't going to fix it. But neither was sitting here, running up a tab alone. Draining his ginger ale, he pulled out his wallet and tossed down a couple of folded bills to cover his drinks and a tip. "You know what? You're right. Let's go."

Sharrod stood. "Bet."

Sliding off the stool, Maxton did his best to push all thoughts of Teagan Woodson and her beautiful smile out of his mind as he and Sharrod left.

Fourteen

Teagan awakened while it was still dark Monday morning. Glancing around the room, she cursed silently. Too many nights in a row of sleeping like trash were starting to take effect. So she lay there, staring at the ceiling, counting imaginary bunnies jumping over a fence, hoping she'd fall asleep again. By the two hundredth bunny, it became clear that wasn't going to happen. With a deep sigh, she rolled onto her right side and grabbed her phone from the nightstand to check the time.

Five twenty-eight. Great. She usually got up around seven thirty to get dressed and be at the studio by the time it opened at nine. *Looks like I've got some time to kill.*

Free, uncommitted time was the last thing she wanted right now. Because every moment that she didn't keep busy, her mind filled the space with thoughts of Maxton. She sat up in bed, resting her back against the headboard and yanking the covers up around her neck. Bending her knees, she pulled them close to her body in a sort of upright fetal position. The inky darkness surrounding her felt heavy, oppressive. So she switched on the small lamp on her nightstand and picked up a book she'd been trying to finish.

Her attempt at reading was short-lived, and she soon marked her page and returned the book to its spot on the nightstand. *I doubt Maxton is losing any sleep over me.*

It wasn't a relationship; they weren't soulmates or anything. Or at least, that's what she kept reminding herself every time an image of him popped into her mind. It was just a little harmless fun. But now, as she faced a feeling of loss that she'd never expected, it seemed like much more than that.

It seemed getting tangled up with Maxton had been akin to bringing a kudzu vine into a Georgia forest. It seemed like a swell idea at the time, but the next thing you knew, the vine took over every tree for miles. He was the vine; her heart, the unsuspecting forest.

She finally drifted back to sleep, still sitting up. When she startled awake again, it was almost seven, so she got out of bed and took a hot shower. She was standing in her closet in a bra and panties, rifling through her clothes when she heard her cell phone ringing. Searching through the blankets, she found it on the bed and answered it. "Hello?"

"Teagan." Her mother's voice sounded relieved. "Good, you're up."

"What's up, Mom? Is something wrong?"

"Yes and no. How soon can you get to the building?"

She frowned, confused by her mother's somewhat cryptic words. "Maybe twenty or thirty minutes. Why?"

"Listen carefully. Come to the building as soon as you can. I want you to park, come in through the back door in the courtyard and come directly upstairs to your father's office."

She blinked several times, still processing all of this. "Yes, I can do that. But are you going to tell me what's going on?"

"We'll explain when you get here. Just make sure you do exactly what I say, and don't stop and talk to anyone on the way, okay?"

"I won't. I'll be there as soon as I can."

"Good. Love you."

"Love you, too."

Addison disconnected the call, and Teagan returned to her search for an outfit. Settling on pink blouse and cream-colored slacks made of lightweight material, she got dressed. Stepping into a pair of pink pumps and sliding on a pair of dangly silver earrings fashioned to look like long feathers, she got her purse and keys and left home to drive to the 404 building.

Luckily, the fates granted her a somewhat easy commute through the demolition derby known as Atlanta rush hour traffic, and she made it from her neighborhood in Druid Hills to the building in the northwestern corner of Collier Heights in around twenty-eight minutes.

As she drove down Sound Avenue, the private side street where the company headquarters sat, she saw something odd. Slowing her car near the front of the building, her eyes widened.

What the hell?

There, in the center of the sidewalk, a man reclined in a collapsible camp chair. It was a fancier model of camp chair, with an attached sunshade that enveloped the man's upper body in shadow. He wore dark shorts, a white tee and white sneakers. His face, obscured by a baseball cap and sunglasses, bore a rather silly grin considering the early hour. His legs were extended in front of him, revealing his above-average height, and what looked like a small cooler was set up next to his chair.

Teagan stared as she passed. The man lifted his hand, offering a friendly wave as she drove by.

Shaking her head, she pulled around to the side lot, turned in and parked as close as she could to the courtyard. After locking up the car, she entered the rear door using her keycard, then took the elevator upstairs to the fourth floor.

Entering her father's office, she found her parents inside. Her mother sat on the right side of the room, near the bookcases, while her father stood at the window behind his desk, peering out.

Addison stood when her daughter entered. "Hey, Teagan. Thanks for coming in early."

"You're welcome. Does anybody want to tell me what's going on? Because there's a man on the sidewalk in front, and he looks pretty dang comfortable."

"We know," her father called over his shoulder. "It's him."

"Who?" Teagan looked from her father to her mother

and back again before realization hit her like a wet towel across the backside "Oh, snap. It's—"

"Yes. It's Keegan Woodbine, the crazy person who claims to be my son." Caleb shook his head. "The nerve of him, showing up here at my place of business."

Addison snorted. "It's your fault he's here."

"Addy, I told you already. I don't have any other children. It simply isn't possible."

Addison slapped her hand down on the small table she'd been sitting at. "Then, damn it, Caleb, go tell him that. Go down there and talk to him."

Caleb bristled. "I don't want to talk to him."

"And I don't want to call the police on him, either, because we all know how that could end." Addison sat down in the chair, her shoulders drooping.

"He's smart, I see." Teagan walked closer to her mother. "He set himself up on the sidewalk because it's just beyond our property line."

"Right." Addison shook her head sadly. "Caleb, this is the last time I'm going to say this. Carry your stubborn ass down there and talk to that boy. I'm not gonna have him sitting here when Lil Swagg and his musicians start arriving."

"Addy…"

"If you 'Addy' me one more time…" Her voice was hard, cold. "Get out. Go deal with him, or he'll be the least of your worries."

Caleb sighed. Straightening his sports coat, he left the room.

Teagan grabbed her mother's hand, gave it a squeeze. "Mom, are you okay?"

"No." She ran her free hand over her face. "I waited

to talk to your father about this until we were at home because I didn't want to cause a scene. He spent all weekend telling me it's not true, that it's impossible. We came in early this morning to inventory the storage room, and that boy was already sitting there."

Teagan asked, "Why did you call me?"

"Because you're the only child that knows about this mess so far, and I don't want to pull your sister and brothers into it any sooner than I have to." She blinked rapidly, tears welling in her eyes. "This whole thing is so upsetting."

Teagan bent and hugged her mother tight around her drooping shoulders. "It's going to be okay, Mom. Somehow." Easing away from her mother, she walked to the window. She could see Caleb talking to Keegan, who'd stood and folded his chair. Both men appeared calm, at least from her vantage point, but there was no telling what they were saying to each other.

"What's going on out there?" Addison asked.

"They're talking. Calmly, from the looks of it." They went back and forth for a few minutes, then Caleb watched while Keegan packed up his chair and his cooler and crossed the street. Caleb started back toward the building, and Teagan watched Keegan climb into a Jeep parked at the dry cleaners across the road and drive off.

Caleb returned to the office, swinging the door closed behind him. "There. The problem is solved."

Addison looked at her husband with narrowed eyes. "Just like that, eh. And how do you figure it's solved, Caleb?"

"He showed me a birth certificate with my name on

it as his father." He shrugged. "That's far too easy to fabricate, so I dismissed it."

"And how did he react to that?" Addison pressed.

"He seemed offended, but I certainly didn't care. I demanded a DNA test. I told him that if he could prove he was my son, we'd sit down and talk about his inheritance." He eased over to his desk and seated himself in the big executive chair, looking rather self-satisfied. "That was enough to get him to leave."

Addison rose slowly from her seat. "You told me it's not possible for him to be your son."

"It's not." Caleb picked up a pen from the cup on his desk and tapped it his forehead. "That's why I agreed to do the test. Once we have concrete proof, you'll be reassured that I'm telling the truth, and he won't have a leg to stand on to make any further claims."

Addison stared at her husband but didn't utter a single word.

Teagan swallowed, sensing her mother's rising anger. She sidled closer to her, locking an arm around her waist. "Mom, let's go get a cup of coffee."

"Sure, honey." Her voice dripped with false pleasantry. "But first, let me tell your father something." She took two steps closer to his desk, resting her palms on the other side. "There is no way I can explain to you how hurt and embarrassed I am. You knew, for weeks, about this accusation, and you hid it from me. Now you think everything is fine." Her words dripped with icy intent. "You may think your problem with that boy is over. Your problems with me, however, are just beginning." She stood, turned and sailed out.

Unsure of what else to do, Teagan followed her mother and closed the door behind her.

Keeping his eyes focused on the cars flowing around him, Maxton navigated the gauntlet to reach the designated pickup area of Hartsfield-Jackson Atlanta International Airport on Monday evening. He couldn't think of anyone else he'd go through the trouble for, other than his parents. So when his dad had called, he'd sucked it up and prepared to make the drive.

Scanning the sidewalk in front of the terminal doors, he saw a woman in profile. Her little black dress, bouncy curls and long legs reminded him of Teagan, and he sighed aloud. Working with her today had been difficult, to say the least, but he'd put on his blinders and focused on the work at hand. As a result, track nine of Swagg's album had now been completed, and only two tracks remained before they could officially put this project in the books. Shaking off those thoughts of her smile, and of the tears he'd seen standing in her eyes when he broke things off, he went back to searching for his father.

After a few more laps around the pickup zone, he finally spotted his dad. Dr. Stephen McCoy, clad in his starched khaki shorts and matching short-sleeved shirt, stood out among the more comfortably dressed travelers. Maxton slipped into the nearest empty spot and got out, opening the hatch.

"Hey, Dad," he said, reaching for a hug.

Stephen smiled and embraced his son. "Evening, son. Good to see you."

Maxton took his father's two duffle bags and tucked

them carefully into the back. Closing the hatch, he got into the driver's seat, buckled up and pulled away from the curb.

They drove through the city, headed back toward Maxton's place. "So, how was the flight?"

"Long." Stephen chuckled. "International flights are always like that, though. Luckily, I booked a first-class seat that folds into a bed, so it wasn't too bad."

Maxton nodded. "Any idea what you want to eat?"

"Something other than Italian," he quipped. "I've had my fill of pasta over these last couple of weeks."

"I got you." He chuckled, glad he'd made other arrangements for his father's brief visit.

Later, at his apartment, Maxton whipped up a simple, classic-Southern feast for his father. When he presented him with the plate of fried chicken wings, cinnamon waffles and green beans seasoned with onions, his father whistled. "Wow, son. When did you learn to cook like this?"

He shrugged, sitting next to his father on the sofa, holding his own plate. "Being on the road as much as I am, takeout gets old quick. So I took some time between tours to learn how to cook for myself."

"Wise decision." Stephen munched on a wing, the crisp skin crackling as he chewed.

"I take a few shortcuts here and there. Like using frozen waffles." He winked.

His father laughed. "Hey, I'll allow it."

"So, tell me," Maxton said, sipping from his glass of iced water, "what kinds of cool stuff did you come across on your trip? Mom told me you were itching to get to the Valley of Temples."

"I was, and I've made some very interesting finds over there." Stephen clasped his hands together. "I'm so glad I finally got the chance to go."

Maxton settled back against the cushions. He loved hearing about his parent's travels, and now he could use any distraction he could get from thinking about Teagan. "Alright, let me hear it."

"I spent most of my time on the western end of the valley. There's a garden down there, called the Garden of the Kolymbethra. It's huge—five hectares. That's over ten acres. Anyway, this place is so lush. It has so many varieties of trees—white poplar, willow, myrtle, broom. Then, there's an orchard full of citrus trees. They have almonds and olives and so much good stuff growing there." He smiled. "I just wish your mother could have gone to see it. She'd love it. I'm gonna go back, take her with me, when I get around to it."

"I think that's a great idea. She'd probably love that."

"I also spent a good amount of time exploring the ruins of the Temple of Castor and Pollux. That place is huge. It's a two-mile walk just to cover the span of the inside. I was able to collect a few soil samples as well as some fragments we think might be ancient pottery. We tagged everything, turned it over to the proper authorities for analysis."

"How long will it take to find out what it was?"

He shrugged. "Few weeks to months. I'm a patient man. I can wait." He scraped up the last of his green beans. "Enough of my adventures. What's going on with you? Are you enjoying your time in Atlanta?"

He thought about how he'd answer. "It's been mostly good. I've really been enjoying this gig. Sharrod and I are working with a rapper out of the Bronx who brought in a full band for his next album. It's really been an experience."

Stephen nodded slowly. "Okay. Now, tell me what's not going so well."

"I…got involved in something I shouldn't have."

His gray brow arched. "Is it legal, son?"

"Yeah." He chuckled, in spite of his somewhat somber mood. "I realize now how that must have sounded. What I meant was, I got into a sort of romantic entanglement, and I'd have probably been better off just walking away in the beginning."

"Oh, now I definitely want to hear about this." Stephen shifted in his seat, resting his back against the armrest and faced his son. "Tell me about this woman."

"Her name is Teagan, and she's the head sound engineer at the studio where I've been working."

"Lord have mercy. Not a workplace fling."

Maxton cringed. "I'm afraid so." He recounted the story of his brief affair with Teagan in as much detail as he felt was appropriate to tell his father. Starting with that first day, when he'd asked her his name, he described their time together up until last Friday when he'd broken things off. "I could tell I wanted more than she was willing to give, and I didn't want to stick around and get my heart stepped on."

Stephen scratched his chin. "So what you're saying is you weren't supposed to be together in the first place, but you couldn't resist her. And now, even though you're apart, you realized you love her. Is that right?"

"I never said I loved her, Dad."

"Maxton, you didn't have to. If you didn't love her,

you wouldn't be struggling with the situation the way you are." Stephen shook his head. "Did I ever tell you how your mother and I met?"

"She told me you met at UC Santa Cruz."

"We did." He nodded. "But did she tell you that we started out competing against each other for a single scholarship to the humanities department?" He looked off into the distance. "I first saw her on the quad, the summer before sophomore year. I asked her out and took her on two dates before I found out."

"And how did that go down?"

"We had to give a presentation to the award committee, as a last step in the process of potentially earning the scholarship, which was for upperclassmen in humanities. I'd already given my speech when your mother came running into the auditorium. She was late for the presentation. But she still got up there and nailed it."

Maxton leaned in. "Okay, so did she fuss you out?"

He shook his head. "No. I fussed her out, idiot that I was. Told her I couldn't see her anymore. I blew my presentation and I blamed her for it. She was a 'distraction,' or at least that's what I told myself. I still can't believe I said that to her."

Now the parallel between these stories was becoming much clearer.

"I spent the next three weeks throwing myself into work, miserable. I lost her and I lost the scholarship. But you know what? Your mom won it. Even though she was late, she made a hell of a presentation. Won the committee over just like that." He snapped his fingers. "When I finally got my head out of my behind, I crawled back to her and asked her to be my girlfriend. Lucky for me, and for you, your mother's forgiving spirit overrode her annoyance with me. By the time school started in the fall, we were an item."

Maxton whistled. "I see you two got off to a rocky start."

"We did. But I'm glad I had sense enough to realize how important she was to me before she got away."

He thought about that for a moment, thought about how he would feel if Teagan found someone else. How would he be able to accept that, knowing he hadn't even told her how he felt? "I don't want that. Dad. I don't want Teagan to be the one that got away."

"Then, I think you know what you have to do." He stood, gathering their plates. "Listen, son. I'm not going to tell you what to do. You're a grown man. But I will say this. If you really love her, you'd better tell her that." He stood in the arched doorway leading to the kitchen, his gaze intent. "Sometimes, you have to be willing to go to a woman with your hat in your hand and tell her you were wrong. And there's no shame in it."

As his father washed the dinner dishes, Maxton let his head drop back, his gaze resting on the ceiling. He'd understand if Teagan told him to kick rocks, but he had to at least try. No other woman had ever made him feel the way she did, and he didn't want to walk away, didn't want to wait and see if someone better came along.

He wanted Teagan.

I love her. Now I just have to figure out how to get her back.

Fifteen

Munching on the last bit of a croissant, Teagan stood in the hallway just outside Studio One. It was Tuesday morning, and she'd just arrived to prepare for today's recording session. Only two tracks remained to be finished on Lil Swagg's album, and she hoped they'd finish this week. If they didn't, she'd have to call the next artist who'd booked use of the studio and see if they were willing to move up their slot so Swagg could have more time.

Hopefully, these next few days would be super productive.

Draining the last of the coffee in the paper cup she'd brought from the Bodacious Bean, she tossed the empty cup and the crumpled pastry wrapper into the trash, dusted off her hands and entered the studio.

She was seated at the workstation a few minutes later when Swagg and Rick walked in. She waved to them as they headed for their usual perch on the sofa while continuing to let the workstation run through its daily start-up protocols.

The musicians began trickling in with Mike arriving around nine thirty and Brady around a quarter till. Five minutes before ten, Sharrod entered, drumsticks in hand.

Teagan surreptitiously watched the door without taking her eyes off the screen, knowing Maxton wouldn't be too far behind.

A few long seconds passed.

Finally, she saw someone entering, their face obscured behind a huge bouquet of orchids.

Her heart turned a flip when she saw the vase lower to reveal Maxton's handsome face and the huge grin he wore. "Good morning."

"Morning," she stammered, captivated by the beauty of the blooms. "What's...all this?" She gestured to the flowers.

"That would be thirty Ocean Breeze orchids," he said, handing the clear crystal vase to her. "Your brother was kind enough to tell me orchids are your favorite flower."

She frowned, confused. "Which brother? Gage?"

He shook his head. "No. Miles."

She gasped. "Wow. I've never known my twin to like any guy well enough to help him out with that sort of thing."

Miles peeked his head around the door frame at that precise moment. "You're right. I deeply dislike most men who try to date you." He patted Maxton on the shoulder. "But this guy makes a hell of a case for himself. Give him a chance, sis." With a wink, he strolled off toward the elevators.

Maxton jerked his thumb in the direction Miles had appeared from. "How's that for an endorsement?"

She giggled. "It's pretty damn good." She looked him over, taking in the black jeans, distressed black tee shirt and the black-and-white bandana tied around his forehead, keeping his curls out of his face.

He squatted, hanging on to the armrest of her chair as he came to her eye level. "I wanted to apologize for the way I acted Friday."

She shook her head, feeling the tears form in her eyes. "No, you were right. I contradicted myself and put way too much on you, considering the parameters I set."

He grabbed her hand. "But that's just it. I don't want parameters with you, Teagan. I want it all. All the secrets, all the excitement, even all the sorrow. You're too special for a fling or an affair."

"And what makes you say that?"

"I love you, Teagan." He squeezed her hand inside his own. "I don't even know when it happened. Maybe it was the first time I saw you, working so hard and looking all serious. Or maybe it was the smile on your face when I took you to swim with the rays. Or maybe, it happened that day in Piedmont Park, when we kissed in the rain."

She was full-on crying by now. "Damn it, Maxton. I'm gonna look like a raccoon if you keep this up."

"Sorry 'bout that, baby. Rest in peace to your mascara." He brushed away a few tears from her cheek.

"Anyway, it doesn't matter when or how it happened. All I know is that I love you, and I want a full relationship with you. Give me all the stings, all the commitments. I'm ready."

"You have no idea how relieved I am to hear this," she said, sniffling. "Because I love you, too, Maxton." He drew her into his arms and held her tight while everyone in the studio cheered.

"That's what I'm talking about! Get ya lady, homeboy!" Swagg's exuberant declaration rose above every other sound in the space, and Teagan laughed as she pulled back from the hug.

A smiling Maxton reached into the hip pocket of his jeans and pulled out a small box.

She drew back. "You didn't."

He laughed. "No, I didn't. I'm not about to jump straight to the proposal, I mean, unless…"

She punched him in the shoulder.

"Ouch." He rubbed the shoulder, feigning injury. "It's not a ring. It's this." He opened the small blue box and held it up so she could see the contents.

She sucked in a breath. "Oh, my."

Inside the velvet interior was a beautiful charm bracelet with alternating silver and gold beads. Three charms dangled from it: a sea turtle, a great white shark and a stingray. She lifted it out of the box, admiring its beauty and detail work up close. "This is gorgeous. Thank you so much."

"You're welcome. You do understand that if you put that on, you're officially my girlfriend."

She slipped the bracelet over her hand and onto her

wrist without a moment's hesitation. "Good. Because that's just what I want."

He pulled her close again, but this time, he kissed her on the lips. The hoots and hollers of the men present filled her ears, but she didn't care. She couldn't remember the last time she'd felt so happy, so at peace.

Eventually, they parted, and Maxton grabbed his bass from the hallway and took it into the booth, and she turned her chair back around to face the workstation and clicked on the intercom. "You guys ready to finish this album and make it a hit?"

Swagg was on his feet, and he strolled up to the partition with a broad grin. "Listen. With all these good feelings and good vibes floating around the room right now—" he paused, giving Teagan's shoulder a gentle pat "—I think we should be able to just knock out these last two tracks right now, today. You feel me?"

The band seemed to agree, based on their boisterous reactions.

Laughing, Teagan said, "Okay, boys. Let's get it." Touching her screen, she started playback on track ten's melody file.

Swagg's proclamation turned out to be right, because the day quickly became a real, honest-to-goodness jam session. Bobbing her head along to the music, Teagan could feel the rhythmic energy flowing through the space. It seemed as if the good vibes Swagg had described, vibes she was at least partially responsible for creating, were fueling the musicians to play at the top of their skills. They ran through a few versions of each track and found the sweet spot where Swagg, his manager and the musicians were happy. That done, everyone left the booth and congregated in the outer suite to watch Swagg as he laid down his verses over the album's last two tracks.

"Looks like Swagg is feeling the flow today, too," Rick quipped as his artist effortlessly laid down bar after bar. He did so well, he was able to record his verses on both finished musical tracks in only a single continuous take.

By 4:00 p.m., Teagan had completed the final file cleanup and combined all the finished audio files into a folder. She turned to Swagg. "As soon as you tell me where to send these, you can consider your album finished."

Rick slid her a card. "Send everything to Chanel the Titan, and cc it to Big Apple Records. Here are the website addresses to the encrypted upload portals."

"You got it." Teagan set to work on the uploads. "So, Swagg, does the album have a title yet?"

He shook his head. "Nothing official, but I can feel some ideas forming in my brain. Gotta give them some time to marinate."

"I can't wait to hear what you come up with." She reached out and shook his hand. "Thank you so much for the opportunity to work with you on this project. I'm really proud of how it turned out."

"So am I." Swagg turned to Rick. "Let's go celebrate, man."

Rick clapped his hands together. "I'm definitely down for that." He looked to the band members. "You guys coming?"

Everyone filed out of the room, with Sharrod hanging back to fist-bump Maxton. "Catch up with us later." With a wink, Sharrod disappeared out the door.

Standing in the doorway of the booth, Maxton smiled at Teagan. "What a day, right?"

"Right. It's been a wild ride." She raised her wrist, admiring the way her bracelet caught the light. "Where on earth did you find these sea-life charms?"

"I made it to the jewelry store last night before it closed." He approached her chair. "I couldn't believe they had those charms for my girl."

She could feel the grin spreading across her face. "That's me. I'm your girl."

He gently tugged her out of her chair and into his strong arms. "All mine."

She didn't know what it was about his possessive tone that seemed to touch her like a caress, but as their lips met, she realized she didn't really care.

Ten Weeks Later Houston, TX

Maxton kept his eyes straight ahead, effectively staring at LL Cool J's legendary back as he plucked out the bassline to the rapper's 1995 hit, "Loungin." Because this was the last show on the Hip-Hop Classic vs Current Tour, the members of the nineties girl group Total had joined LL on the stage, to reprise their harmonies on the song's catchy hook.

Sweat ran down his face, a common predicament when he played under stage lights for hours at stretch, but he paid it no mind. This was what he loved most, performing with an artist he respected, in front of a crowd of true fans.

As the tune ended and LL walked offstage to the roars of the crowd, Maxton set his bass down and flexed his fingers.

"Hell of a night," Sharrod shouted from his seat behind the drums set.

"Yeah," Maxton called back, nodding. "That's how you close up a tour."

The stage lights went down as the curtain dropped, and Maxton carefully placed his bass inside the case and snapped it shut. Carrying it with him, he walked off the stage, headed for the greenroom.

Passing some of the artists on his way down the narrow corridor, he waved to them. Finally arriving, he opened the greenroom door.

Teagan sat on the black leather sofa, her open laptop on her thighs. Her hair was up in a messy bun on top of her head, revealing the graceful line of her jawline and neck. Dressed in dark-wash skinny jeans and a sparkly silver tank top with black ballet flats, she looked both stylish and comfortable. "Hey, you."

"Hey, baby." He walked over, propping his bass on a stand in the corner and flopping down on the couch next to her. Giving her a quick kiss, he asked, "What are you up to?"

"Just got off a video chat with Nia. She's ready for me to come home. She says Luna misses me."

"She's guilt-tripping you with your cat? I'm guessing she wants you back at work?"

She laughed. "Yes. Trevor's been running both studios, and apparently, the engineer the temp agency sent over to help him isn't up to par."

"Are you ready to go back?"

She shrugged. "I mean, I miss Luna. And I don't like other sound engineers touching Fancy. She's mine. Plus, I've never taken this much time off work before, so I can understand why they'd be floundering without me."

"I guess they really need you around, huh?" He kissed her again. "I'm still glad you decided to come on the road with me for a few weeks. Having you here has made the last part of the tour even more amazing."

She smiled, and he melted inside. "I'm glad I came, too. I needed a little adventure in my life. Nia was right. I work too hard."

"Well, it's officially the end of the tour, so we can hop an early flight back to Atlanta tomorrow." He stopped, hearing the muffled sound of the crowd as it seemed to rise again. "I guess folks are still out there."

Sharrod walked in, still clutching his sticks. "We're on, bro. Crowd wants an encore."

Maxton stood. "Looks like I'm on again. Why don't you watch from backstage this time?"

"Sure. I'm game." She shut her laptop, tossing it into her large purse. Slinging the purse over her shoulder, she followed them back down the corridor. Taking up a post near the stage crew, she stopped and watched as they returned to their places on stage.

Maxton was seated on his stool, bass in hand, when the curtain rose again. The DJ dropped the intro to LL's classic, "I Need Love," and the man himself returned to the stage to the sounds of loud cheers and thunderous applause.

The DJ spoke into his mic. "Y'all know this jam is about something we all need. Right, Uncle L?" LL raised his mic, nodding his head to the music.

"That's right, so let's give some love to our band to-night. Y'all know me, DJ Bigg Stuff, on the ones and the twos. Let's give it up for my man, Brady, on the guitar."

The crowd cheered as the DJ went on to name each musician individually, then gave them a few seconds to show off before moving on to the next. Maxton watched as Sharrod played his drum solo, and took a deep breath, knowing he was next.

"And last but not least, we got my man Maxton McCoy on the bass. Take it away, Max."

Max stood as the spotlight landed on him, but instead of playing a bass solo, he took the mic Sharrod handed him and spoke into it. "Y'all good out there tonight?" Pausing a moment for the crowd's roar, he raised the mic to his lips again. "Our illustrious DJ is right. We all need love. And when you find it, you better hold on tight." He gestured, and a burly stagehand escorted the bewildered-looking Teagan out on the stage.

Teagan stood in front of him, her eyes the size of a bass drum, and mouthed, "What's going on?"

He took her hand. "Y'all see this fine woman? She got my heart on lockdown. And today, I'm trying to make it all the way official, right here in front of the great city of Houston."

Teagan's hand began to shake inside his. He dropped to one knee, pulling the black box out of his pocket. Popping the lid open, he held up the brilliant cut, tear-drop-shaped two-carat diamond ring for her to see. "Teagan Woodson, will you marry me?"

Her lips trembled, the tears streaming down her cheeks illuminated by the spotlight. Taking the mic, she spoke into it. "Yes, Maxton."

The crowd roared, the band cheered, even LL clapped for them as Maxton slipped the ring on her finger. Once that was done, he stood and drew her into his arms for a kiss. They ran offstage, finding a dark, semi-quiet corner away from the noise and the prying eyes. There, they embraced again, kissing passionately.

She pulled back, looking up into his eyes, with tears sparkling in her own. "I can't believe you did all this."

"Believe it. A woman like you deserves something really special. I just hope I pulled it off well enough."

She gave his waist a squeeze. "Trust me, you did everything just right." She touched his face. "I love you, Maxton McCoy."

"I love you too, baby."

She leaned up to kiss him again, and time seemed to stand still. Being with her felt natural because her love provided the most perfect melody to complement his bassline.

And he couldn't wait to experience the beautiful music they would make together.

* * * * *

WHEN THE LIGHTS
GO OUT…

JULES BENNETT

To my girls.
As you grow into amazing young ladies,
I pray you always take the chance at life and love.
You two are my everything.

One

There could be worse places to visit than an old castle turned into a distillery. The sprawling stone structure nestled among the rolling hills of Benton Springs, Kentucky, and was quite a pleasant surprise. The story behind this structure from centuries ago was rather fascinating…almost as much as the ladies who now owned the place.

Antonio hadn't known what to expect when he'd fired up his private jet and departed Cadaqués, Spain, two days ago, but the beauty of this centuries-old building and lush surroundings reminded him so much of home.

Which was the one place he was trying to break free from. Well, maybe not the picturesque coastal town itself, but the legacy that loomed in front of him. He had no clue how to break the devastating news to his parents that he would not be taking over the family business they'd created...a family business that should have been handed down to his brother, but tragedy had robbed them all of the future they'd envisioned.

"You must be Antonio Rodriguez."

Antonio turned from admiring the scenic view and nearly stumbled as he took in another stunning sight. The redhead with a wide smile striding toward him was the very woman he'd been corresponding with via email for the past couple of months.

"And you would be Elise Hawthorne," he replied.

He'd not only done his homework on this distillery and the variety of spirits they offered, but he'd also checked out the three dynamic women behind the Angel's Share label.

Elise held the prestigious title of CEO and was the direct contact for all VIP accounts. They'd bounced messages back and forth for some time now and she'd been nothing but professional and accommodating.

Still, nothing had prepared him for that instant punch of arousal to the gut. Who knew tortoiseshell glasses could be sexy?

Elise empowered both brains and beauty...two qualities he found absolutely irresistible, and if he didn't keep his focus on work and his own issues, he'd find himself wrapped up in a tangled mess he didn't have time for.

Shame that. He wouldn't mind getting to know Elise Hawthorne outside of working hours.

She closed the distance between them and extended her hand. "It's a pleasure to finally meet you in person, Mr. Rodriguez."

"Antonio," he insisted, offering her a grin, mainly because he wanted to see her smile in return. He wasn't disappointed.

The photo of the sisters on the company website had been difficult to really hone in on the features of each woman. They all stood in front of the castle and the castle had been the focal point of the image.

But Elise had stood out with that vibrant red hair and in person...she was a damn stunner.

Antonio took her hand and immediately admired the soft, yet firm shake. A powerful woman with confidence and a killer smile...maybe this trip of his to America would be even more enjoyable than he first thought. A little flirting wouldn't hurt anybody.

There was still that fine line, though, and he'd vowed to keep this trip strictly business. This was his last deal before pulling out of the family business for good. He owed this trip to his parents, and he owed it to himself, to push aside his personal wants and focus on the pub side of their restaurants and bringing in new labels never before purchased in their area of the world.

And that was the easy part of the trip. Roaming across the States, going from distillery to vineyard, doing sample tastings and getting to meet new people, was everything that gave him life. He just had no clue, once this trip was over, where he'd ultimately end up.

Grief had him all confused lately, doing more out of guilt and obligation than anything else. Taking over the chain of posh restaurants his parents had started decades ago was not his idea of how he wanted to spend his life. He wanted his own goals, his own dreams... he didn't want to fall into the title that was meant to be shared with his late twin brother. For now, though, Antonio was in charge of upgrading the pub side of each of the family's five restaurants.

If only Paolo hadn't died...

Throughout Antonio's entire life, he'd enjoyed the traveling and experiencing different cultures. He'd never wanted to be in one place and spearhead a dynasty meant for someone else. He thought he could do what his parents wanted and be the son they needed.

He always felt he owed it to Paolo to try. Antonio had put all of his own selfish thoughts and wants aside, thinking he would grow into this role they'd created for him, but that hadn't been the case.

And the longer he let these feelings fester, the more he resented everything about this business. He was going to have to do this last trip and finally have a talk with his parents about the realistic vision he had for his future.

Family was absolutely everything, so how did Antonio break his parents' hearts by walking away from this mega dynasty they'd built? They'd trusted so much to him, hoping to retire soon and leave him in possession of their precious legacy. The last thing he wanted was to be married to a woman...or to a business. He enjoyed his freedoms, always had, and once his brother passed, Antonio realized the importance of living each day like it was your last.

Yet, guilt over being the son who survived had him fulfilling his parents' wishes instead of living his own life.

"Angel's Share is nothing like the photos online," he claimed, refocusing his attention on the breathtaking surroundings. "This is really quite extraordinary and must be seen in person to truly appreciate."

Her smile beamed even wider. Her shy beauty couldn't be denied, but there was something about a powerful, dynamic woman he'd never been able to resist.

Too bad he wasn't here for play. Jet-setting playboy was definitely not the next business venture he wanted to get into.

"Thank you," she replied. "The castle dates back to the late 1800s. Obviously, there have been some renovations and changes, but the structure remains original. There have been some additions to the outbuildings around one hundred years ago, but those are holding up well, too. We're quite proud of the operation we have and how everything seemed to fall into place for us."

"As you should be."

Elise gestured toward the stony walkway. "It's such a beautiful day. Would you like to start the tour outside around the grounds?"

"I'm at your disposal." He offered a mock bow. "Show me everything you have."

Elise quirked a perfectly arched brow and he realized his words might have come off as offensive, or could definitely be construed a different way.

Instead of saying a word, she merely nodded. He really needed to keep the mood light since they just met. He might have vowed to himself he wouldn't get involved with a woman on this trip, but he hadn't expected to be face-to-face with such temptation and have such a strong urge right out of the gate.

"It's nice to get out of my office once in a while, so

we'll start right here." She gestured with her hands out and glanced around the sprawling piece of property. "As I said, the castle dates back well over one hundred years. A Scottish family migrated here in 1845 and took a few years to build this replica like what they'd left behind right down to the drawbridge, which is a fun feature we still love."

As Elise spoke, Antonio tried to focus on her words and the background for Angel's Share Distillery. But there was something so soothing and almost...sultry about her lilt. He always found American women fascinating. They were bold, dynamic, and unapologetic for their ways. Antonio had taken more than one lover here in the States as he'd passed through over the years. This trip, however, was meant for business for his family and for him to possibly explore other business opportunities—something he could do completely on his own.

Unfortunately, there would be no flings while here in Benton Springs. But that didn't mean he had to avoid all temptation.

Elise Hawthorne was definitely someone he wouldn't mind getting to know a little more intimately, and she could certainly make his time here more interesting. Flirtatious smiles and fun banter were still his default mode...it wasn't like he could just turn off who he was.

"What started you in the world of distilling?" he asked as he followed her around the side of the castle.

Elise came to a stop on the path, turning to face him fully. "Oh, well, my sisters and I have always loved this abandoned place. In high school we used to hang out here with our friends and sneak drinks on the weekends and party. Several years ago, when it came up for sale, we all knew we wanted to do something remarkable with it. I guess, in a ridiculous way, you could say we came full circle."

Antonio nodded and chuckled. "That, you did."

"Besides, there's no better location than Kentucky to start a distillery and with this unique setting, we're drawing quite the crowds and business." She beamed as she spoke. "This castle was once a distillery, but when Prohibition shut everything down, they never reopened. A private owner lived here until the late '90s. When he died it stayed empty until we bought it. So, when my sisters and I decided to dive into this man's world, we wanted something more romantic and unique. Since this place was still sitting vacant, we knew we had something special."

"This is definitely unique," he agreed.

"We even have interest in weddings, but we haven't opened up our grounds to that type of venue yet. I guess our romantic angle is working."

Antonio studied her once again, realizing there was something different he kept taking away from her looks. She was quite polished, yet casual, and all business. There were layers to this woman and he wondered just how many he could peel back before his time here was up in a few weeks.

"You mentioned your sisters. When I looked Angel's Share up online, I noticed you all are quite different from each other."

Elise's smile widened and she quirked a brow. "We are very different from our looks to our personalities. But we were raised together. Adopted, actually, when we were only infants. We're closer than any blood relation could have ever made us. I'm the oldest, then Delilah, then Sara. They say I mother them, but I guess that just comes with the territory."

The conviction and love in her tone was definitely something he could appreciate and resemble. A pang of jealousy speared through him, though. Having lost his twin at only thirteen years old from meningitis, Antonio didn't have stories of milestones or accomplishments he could share.

Growing up an only child, losing the bond of a twin, had been life altering for Antonio and had shifted the dynamics with his parents, as well. Now he was the only one they had and that heaviness weighed on him, growing more so with each passing year.

His restlessness and need for freedom started after Paolo's death and he didn't need to pay a psychiatrist to inform him the two were related. He'd needed to get out of the house where so much pain and so many memories were stored, but then after he started traveling he realized he could escape the heartache even if for a short time.

Family meant absolutely everything to him, which was why he'd gone so long with keeping this secret from his parents. Running the chain of restaurants was certainly not his desire. But he couldn't disappoint them and he needed a solid plan of action before he could even entertain the idea of leaving the family business. He didn't want them disappointed, but they deserved to pass their legacy on to someone who would feel just as passionately about it as they did.

"You have certainly created quite a stir in the media

and the bourbon circles considering this is typically a male-dominated industry."

Her smile turned to a sneer and he could tell she was fighting back her true thoughts.

"That might be, but we're running circles around them and they can't keep up." She adjusted her glasses and held his gaze. "It's actually been rather enjoyable watching those seasoned veterans try."

Antonio laughed and shook his head. "I meant no disrespect. I'm actually in awe of what you three have done here. Not only have you created the promise of a top-notch bourbon, along with an amazing gin that everyone is talking about, but the world is anxiously awaiting your ten-year bourbon reveal, too."

"Between us, I'm more of a gin girl, so thank you for that." She started walking again down the path, heading toward the back of the castle. "We are really proud of our bourbon and have had tasters from all over the globe come in for samples before we unveil our ten-year. The buzz generated is worthy, I believe. Our products are perfection and I'd put them up against any distillery."

Antonio wished he could have gotten in on that initial elite group, but maybe having this exclusive one-on-one time would prove to be even more beneficial. He wasn't too keen on sharing, especially where intriguing women were concerned.

They reached a back door and Elise typed in a code, then opened and gestured him in. "This may be an old castle, but we have state-of-the-art security. After you."

As soon as he entered, a sense of home overwhelmed him. Antonio couldn't quite put his finger on it, but the old meeting the new really took him back to Cadaqués.

He loved his hometown and the rich history with the rolling hills that eased down onto the coast. The old stone paths that led to quaint businesses and homes. His town was not only rich with history, they were also rich with generational families who continued to grow and prosper. Perhaps that was just another draw for him to come to Angel's Share first on his American tour. He could see himself here, as odd and unexpected as that sounded. Other than having a coastline, the similarities were cozy and made him feel welcome.

"I can see why you all love this castle," he told her as she came to stand beside him. "And why you were eager to purchase and find a use for it."

"Oh, you haven't seen anything yet," she beamed. "I'm saving the best for last."

He shifted his attention from the exposed stones and high beams to Elise, who stared back at him. There it was again. That punch of lust he'd gotten when they'd first met. Thinking of the photo he'd seen on their company website, Elise posed with her sisters. She hadn't stood out to him at the time. But now, in person, she pulled him in, captivating him with some invisible power.

"How many tours do you give here?" he asked.

"Oh, we average about ten per day. We like to keep the groups small and intimate so the customers feel like they are getting a VIP treatment. We might be growing fast, but we still want to maintain that small-town, friendly atmosphere."

"No, I mean you specifically."

She blinked, clearly taken aback by his question. "Oh, well, I never give tours. I mean, when we first opened, my sisters and I took turns when we would have one group a day or something like that. Then we started gaining momentum and ultimately hired some younger college kids to do the public group tours. They have vibrant energy and go through a history and spirits training before they can start."

While Antonio was eager to see the rest of this amazing castle and learn all about Angel's Share, he wanted to know more about Elise Hawthorne and what made up this fascinating woman. If he kept asking questions, maybe he'd chisel away the professional exterior and dig deeper into the woman beneath.

He took a step closer, not even realizing he'd done so, but he wasn't sorry.

"The public is missing out on your personality and beauty," he told her. "You are who they would want to see."

She shrugged as if unsure of what to say. Her red hair slid over her shoulder and he wanted to reach out and touch those silky strands.

Oh, man. He was in trouble and he was only on day one of this tour. How the hell was he going to make it staying in this town for weeks?

At least he was only at Angel's Share for this week before moving on to other distilleries in the area. But he'd be in the same town with this temptation for longer than he was comfortable with.

Elise tipped her chin. "Are you trying to flirt with me?"

Antonio couldn't help but laugh. There was that bold American attitude he found so fascinating. "Trying? If you have to ask, maybe I should do a better job."

She quirked a brow, maybe trying to intimidate him, but he only found the gesture sexy. "Is that why you're here? To flirt?"

"I'm here to find the best brands to take back to Cadaqués. I'm here to work my ass off like I always have, and if I just so happen to encounter a captivating, beautiful woman, you can sure as hell bet I will not turn down the opportunity to flirt."

Elise Hawthorne wasn't quite sure what to think of this unflinching, charming visitor, but there was no way to ignore his toe-curling statement…just like there was no way to ignore how sexy and captivating he was. The dark Mediterranean skin, the thick black hair. And the eyes. There was no way to ignore that deep, piercing stare framed with midnight lashes.

And then there was that accent.

Mercy. From the start she'd been trying to focus on being a professional and showing off the work she and her sisters were so proud of. But the man had a thick Spanish accent that only added to his sex appeal.

Sex appeal? How did those words even enter her mind right now? She was too busy to think of having a social life, let alone a sex life. Elise had rearranged weeks' worth of schedules to make this meeting with Antonio Rodriguez. His parents had been famous actors back in the day, and now they owned a wide chain of restaurants across the coast of Spain in tiny towns that were quickly becoming tourist hot spots. And now they could potentially be Angel's Share's first global account. With the Rodriguez name in their repertoire, that would only help to add more accounts across the globe. She needed to land this deal.

Following the Rodriguez family was easy to do, considering they were in the public eye and all over social media. Ignoring all the press that family received would be virtually impossible. Antonio had not only been deemed the golden child, he'd also been given the titles playboy, jet-setter, and wild child.

All of those descriptions were the exact opposite of her and certainly nothing that would make her want to get involved…though she could easily see why he'd become the fantasy of any woman he came in contact with. But she wasn't looking for a man, especially one with such a naughty reputation.

Get your head back in the game, Elise. No more thinking of his bedroom eyes.

Her sisters would absolutely die laughing if they knew Antonio Rodriguez was flirting with her. Of the three girls, Elise was the calmest, the driest, the one who always put work and responsibility over anything else. Sara often called her *boring*. She wasn't wrong, but *boring* got the job done. Elise preferred a nice, tidy world with structure. She didn't like too much shift, and getting infatuated, or anything else, with Antonio, would definitely be a shift.

"Flirting will not get you a discount on any future orders," she told him with a smile, wondering where her own saucy attitude came from. Maybe this banter was contagious. "So you might want to save that for another company you're visiting."

His mouth quirked as if he fought back a grin, but before he could say anything, Sara came through the back door, her hands full of folders, her purse, a laptop case, and her coffee mug, and she nearly dropped everything when she came to a complete stop upon seeing she wasn't alone.

"Oh, sorry," Sara gasped as she blew her hair from her eyes. "I didn't expect to see anyone in here."

Elise welcomed the interruption. She needed a reset to get her thoughts firmly under control. Clearly staying in her office behind the desk day in and day out had clouded her mind. Perhaps she should start doing more tours and interacting with the customers. Then the sexy sight and charming chatter from one charismatic man wouldn't throw her mind into a tailspin.

"No worries," Elise replied. "Actually, I'd like to introduce you to Antonio Rodriguez. You remember me telling you about his arrival."

Sara's eyes widened as she no doubt found Antonio her type. Sara was the one who fell in love easily, who never turned down the chance to let some man charm her. She was always looking for love, but had yet to find the real deal.

"It's a pleasure to meet you," Sara stated with a grin that only accentuated her dark, wide eyes. "I'm—"

"Don't tell me." Antonio held up his hand. "You're Sara Hawthorne."

Sara attempted to situate everything in her hands and get her chaos back in order.

"Let me help," Antonio offered as he reached out and straightened the pile of folders and adjusted her purse strap on her shoulder. "There."

Sara's red-lipped smile widened as she stared at Antonio from beneath her lashes. "Smart and handy. You are a great man to have around."

Elise had no idea how her very unorganized sister could always look so adorable, sultry, and a hot mess all at the same time, but the woman managed to pull it off.

Elise had seen her sister flirt before, but right now Elise wasn't really finding this cute like usual. Anytime they went out for dinner or just to unwind, Sara was always the one men came to, so it was no surprise that Antonio was returning Sara's very friendly smile.

Sara beamed. "You've done your homework. Have you met Dee yet?"

Antonio's thick, dark brows drew in.

"Our other sister, Delilah," Sara corrected.

"We actually just started our tour," Elise informed her. "I covered a little history of the castle, but we haven't done much else. Antonio only arrived about thirty minutes ago."

"Well, I'm sure you will absolutely love everything about Angel's Share, and Elise is literally the brains behind the operation so you are definitely in good hands."

They all had their special talents and area of skills for the business. Elise was proud of her quirky brain and the random factoids. With an undergraduate degree in History and a master's in Business, she had put her crazy-high IQ to good use and was proud of being known as the "brain" of the group.

She'd never been nearly as stunning as Sara with that flawless skin and glossy dark hair and she certainly couldn't even compare herself to Delilah with her sweet smiles and genuine, natural beauty. Both of her sisters were striking without even trying.

Elise, on the other hand, always tried to find the best pair of glasses to fit her face shape and not make her look like an old lady. She might have a boring lifestyle, but did she have to look the part, as well? Not to mention how she'd just had to make an emergency hair appointment because she'd seen a wiry gray hair this morning and had to pluck the damn thing out with tweezers.

She used to think being so stuck in her ways and not as lively as her sisters was her downfall. But over the years, she'd come to the realization that they were all uniquely different and complemented each other. They each were strong in their own ways and hers just happened to be organization and timeliness.

"I have no doubt I'm in the best hands."

Antonio's comment pulled her back into the moment and she found that midnight gaze locked onto hers. A shiver raced down her spine and she couldn't recall the last time any man elicited such a reaction simply from a stare.

The man was a professional panty-melter and she was too smart to fall into that devious web.

No matter what emotions Antonio pulled from her, Elise knew more than anything else, she wouldn't be bored during this visit.

Elise didn't know if she should be afraid or thrilled.

Two

"And that covers everything we keep open to the public."

Antonio stood at the entrance to the gift shop as customers came and went. He'd seen several groups on tours while he'd walked around the grounds, both inside and out, with Elise. The atmosphere could only be described as electric and the initial tastings had been far beyond his expectations.

"So what questions do you have for me?"

Antonio shifted his attention to her and took a step closer. Her eyes darted to his and he had to give her credit, she kept that professional smile in place. But he'd heard that sweet tone of hers for hours, he'd been enveloped by some fruity perfume, and that striking red hair all pulled back in a low bun only made that sexy, studious side of her even more prevalent. And the way she'd tip her head or adjust her glasses to fully look at him and give her undivided attention had been a hell of a turn-on.

There was something to be said about an intelligent, independent woman who downplayed her beauty or, further still, didn't even recognize the power of it. Antonio wondered if she even realized how stunning she was.

"I only have one question."

She tipped that pointy chin. "And what is that?"

"Join me for dinner this evening."

Her lips pursed as if she was either trying to come up with a reason not to or trying to hide a smile.

"That wasn't a question," she informed him.

"I wasn't giving you an option to say no."

Her eyes widened behind those dark frames. Good. He wanted to keep her on her toes, and a little surprise statement would surely do just that. Although, was she actually surprised that he'd brought up the personal topic? Had he not been forward enough the entire day?

"I don't date," she replied.

And now he was the one who was surprised.

"Ever?"

Elise shrugged a slender shoulder. "I don't give it much thought, actually. I stay pretty busy here."

"Too busy to eat?"

That got a slight snicker from her. "Of course I eat. I have a nice selection of frozen dinners at my house that I can pop in the microwave at any time no matter when I get home. The steak tips with broccoli is calling my name."

"That sounds…well, disgusting and extremely disappointing." No way was he letting that atrocity happen tonight. "Why don't you show me the town and take me to your favorite restaurant, my treat."

Her eyes darted away for a fraction of a second before meeting his once more. "I can't go on a date with you."

But she wanted to…and she was seriously thinking about it, it seemed. Those slight hesitations and the way she looked at him… Yeah, she was giving his invitation some serious consideration.

He didn't know what he was doing or where he thought this would lead, but Elise challenged him with that stoic, guarded demeanor. How could he just ignore that? There was something about her that really made him want to dig deeper, to fully see behind that mask. With the beauty, the intelligence, and the tug of desire, Antonio couldn't just ignore this magnetic pull…even if he'd vowed to behave on this trip.

Oh well. He wouldn't apologize for who he was and there was nothing wrong with being attracted to various women. He'd never made promises he couldn't keep and everyone always knew exactly where he stood. He respected women…he just so happened to enjoy the intimacy, as well.

"Don't call it a date," he told her. "I'm new to Benton Springs and I'd like to see more of the town. You're my tour guide."

She laughed. "For the distillery."

Antonio shrugged and took another step toward her, totally ignoring the people bustling in and out of the gift shop behind him. He only had eyes for one woman right now and he knew he had her just about where he wanted. She was wearing down on her refusal and he had to believe she was just as attracted as he was. Maybe peeling away her layers would be easier than he first thought.

"What's your favorite restaurant?" he asked.

"DiMarco's," she told him without hesitation.

Antonio pulled out his phone, typed in a few things, and had made dinner reservations within minutes.

"All set." He slid the phone back into his pocket. "Dinner is at eight."

Elise blinked as she shook her head. "You just...you got reservations that fast? When I call, I have to wait a week and I graduated with the owner."

"I have a way," he explained with a slight shrug.

"And does that include not taking no for an answer?" she asked, quirking a perfectly arched brow.

"You never came out and said no," he retorted. "Which means you want to, but you're upset that you want to. Am I right?"

Elise narrowed her eyes. "Are you always this difficult?"

"Difficult? You mean persuasive? Yes, I am."

He waited, letting her mull over whatever thoughts were racing around in her mind. He'd never force a woman to do anything, but this woman was on the fence and all he had to do was wait for her to tip over to his side.

Elise blew out a sigh and threw her hands up. "Fine. I'll go, but it's not you. It's only because I haven't had good manicotti in months."

Antonio laughed. "You're busting my ego over pasta and cheese."

Humor danced behind that solid stare and this was the first time he'd seen that slip of her professional guard.

"Your ego needed busting, I'm sure. Pick me up here at seven-thirty. I'll be ready."

Antonio was going to take this win and go with it. "It's a date."

"Not a date. A business meeting."

Antonio leaned in next to her ear and whispered, "I have excellent multitasking skills."

A shiver overcame her, vibrating against him as he had barely brushed against her. He didn't waste any more of her time; he wanted to leave on this note…with her wanting more.

Antonio made his way from the building and headed toward his rental car. Day one of his business tour and he'd already broken his vow. Oh well. If he was going to backslide, Elise Hawthorne was a hell of a sexy mistake to be making.

Elise stared at the reflection in the old floor-length mirror in her office and applied a pale gloss…which was absolutely absurd. She didn't get fancied up for anybody, let alone a potential customer with too much charisma who likely never heard the word *no*.

Yet, she hadn't been able to say no to him, so here she was in her office, attempting to refresh herself for her not-date.

Why had she agreed again? Oh right. Because he'd asked. Mercy sakes, no wonder he had a reputation. The man was impossible to deny.

Frustrated with herself for being an easy target, Elise removed her glasses and pulled her hair from the bun. She shook out her strands, cursing when her hand got caught in a knot.

"I'm not surprised to find you in your office, but I am surprised to find you fixing your hair."

Elise caught Sara's reflection in the mirror. "Yes, well, I feel like I need to do something a little more fun for my dinner with Antonio."

Not that the word *fun* suited her, but she felt different around Antonio, so why couldn't she alter her look a little?

"Is that right?" Her sister moved on into the office with a smile on her face and eyes wide. "That man is delicious, and that accent..."

Leave it to Sara to adequately put the perfect adjective to their newest VIP customer. Maybe Elise should put Sara on this dinner. She was always looking for love and was determined to find it. Not that Antonio gave off any vibe that he was looking for such things. Quite the opposite, actually.

But the instant the thought of Sara and Antonio out to dinner entered Elise's mind, a sliver of jealousy shot through her...which was absolutely absurd. There was no room for such nonsense and that was not how Elise's mind worked. She was logical, career-oriented, and determined to make Angel's Share the absolute best distillery in the country.

"What are you still doing here?" Elise asked her sister.

Sara stepped into the room and shrugged. "I'm hiding and trying to ignore the fact I need to go to Milly's house."

Milly. Just the name of the sweetest lady who ever lived put a vise around Elise's heart. She missed her mother every single moment of every single day. She'd been gone for a month now and the girls couldn't bring themselves to finish cleaning out their childhood home.

But Milly, a single woman with a heart for love and nurturing, had taken in three little girls from the foster care system and raised them as her own. They'd formed a family that no biological connection could rival.

"Why don't you wait and we can all go together?" Elise asked.

Sara came to stand behind her and Elise caught her sister's gaze in the reflection. There was a pain there that only they could understand. The pain that went so deep from loving someone so much. That was the price of love, though…ultimately, there would be the loss.

"I think I need to go alone just for myself," Sara explained. "If that makes sense."

That made perfect sense. Elise had been to the house alone, but she hadn't bothered anything. That was definitely something they all needed to do together.

"Unless you'd like me to take your place." Sara winked. "Going on a date with a sexy guy with a hot accent sounds like a better plan."

"It's not a date."

Sara lifted a few strands of Elise's hair. "You fussing with all of this says otherwise."

Elise turned to face her sister. "Listen, simply because I don't want to show up looking like I just left work doesn't mean I'm excited for a date."

"I thought it wasn't a date?"

Elise groaned and skirted around her sister. "Go away."

Sara's laughter mocked her, but Elise didn't care. They

needed laughter in their lives right now, even at her own expense.

"So tell me the business side of Mr. Rodriguez, because I wasn't around him long enough to get a good vibe other than how hot he was."

Business. Yes. That was what she could focus on, what she had control over. Her emotions...not so much.

"You know Antonio's famous parents."

Sara nodded and Elise went on.

"They are expanding their liquor selection and opening more pub-style restaurants and want to add in some bourbons and gins. We are his first stop and he's checking out a few other distilleries in the area while he's in town. He's also going out west to check out some vineyards. My job is to make the best impression for our distillery because our liquor will speak for itself, and we both know it's the best. We are all in agreement of how important an opening up to the global market will be for us."

"Of course," Sara agreed. "So you did the tour today."

"I did." Elise went to her desk and checked the time on her phone. "We're going to do the secured areas after hours, though. I didn't want to hinder production and I want to be able to devote my attention to his questions or concerns."

"After hours sounds—"

"Professional," Elise stated. "And that's all that's happening. This is no different than any other high-profile customer we cater to and show around from the inside out."

Sara crossed her arms and raised her brows. Elise

didn't like this scrutiny, not from Sara. From Delilah, on the other hand, she expected some pushback.

"Except this client is the most attractive one we've ever had and you typically always just stay behind your desk," Sara countered.

Elise squared her shoulders and pulled in a deep breath. "All the more reason to get out and be hands-on. I need the distraction and I need the change of scenery. Besides, I wanted to do the tour, to get back to where I started here. I needed to do this for my sanity."

Sara's features softened as she took a step forward and reached out her hand. Elise took her sister's hand in hers and squeezed.

"I just worry about you and Dee," Sara defended. "It's worse now with Milly gone."

"I get it. I do. We worry about each other and that's okay, but I promise I'm fine. Antonio isn't here for anything other than business and that's all I'm after, too. Getting in with the Rodriguez family in Spain would be a nice feather in our cap."

"I have no doubt you will secure this deal. Just don't fall for his charms," Sara warned. "The media loves to capture him and his arm candy of the week."

Arm candy? Elise nearly laughed at that term being applied to her. She was in a very committed relationship with her desk and her emails. She wasn't looking to change positions anytime soon.

And she sure as hell wasn't looking for love or a fling or anything else other than a hefty order to be shipped overseas for their first global account.

"Well, I'm not looking to be anyone's candy, on their

arm or otherwise," Elise assured her sister, then released her hand. "But he is going to be here any minute so I need to get going."

Elise grabbed her purse and slid it over her shoulder. She reached for Sara and pulled her in for a tight, quick embrace.

"Good luck at Milly's," she said as she eased back. "Text me if you need anything. Family comes first."

Sara nodded. "Go on. I'll lock up everything and set the alarms after you're gone."

Elise stepped from her office and headed down the stairs toward the main entrance of the distillery. The wood doors provided no light because they'd wanted to keep as true to the castle and time period it had been built as they could, so Elise would have to step outside to see if he had arrived yet.

As soon as she opened the door, she was greeted with the dark clouds of a spring storm rolling in. Elise pulled her jacket a little tighter around her as her hair whipped around her head. She should have kept it up like she always did.

A large black SUV turned the corner on the road and into the parking lot. The vehicle seemed just as menacing and sexy as the man. A burst of arousal curled through her just as thunder rolled through the ominous sky.

She wasn't into premonitions or anything like that, but she couldn't help but wonder what she was getting into and why she hadn't just let Sara or Delilah take over this account from the start.

Oh right. Because Elise was the VIP account go-to, Sara was their marketing and social media guru, and

Delilah was a jack-of-all-trades, filling in where the others couldn't.

Just as the first raindrop hit her face, Elise stepped to the SUV, but Antonio was quick to come around and open her door. He'd changed as well, now wearing dark jeans and a black button-up shirt. Everything about this man intrigued her, fascinated her…and none of that was good. She was in a vulnerable, emotional state. She needed to keep her wits about her tonight.

"You look beautiful," he told her as he assisted her into the vehicle.

Okay. While she didn't want compliments, she was still a woman and she couldn't help those giddy feelings that rushed her. But after a compliment always came that awkward few seconds when she had no clue what to say.

"I like to look my best for manicotti," she joked as she reached for her seat belt.

Just as Antonio opened his mouth, the sky opened up and rain pelted him. He shut the door and raced back around to his side and slid behind the wheel. Once he was in, he turned to face her. Water droplets clung to his dark lashes and Elise hadn't thought it possible for him to get any sexier…she'd been wrong.

"You know how to deflate a man's ego."

He likely meant the statement as a joke, but that husky voice sent a shiver through her. Maybe they should have just stayed at the distillery for their after-hours tour. This dinner, this night, was beginning to feel too much like the date she'd sworn it wasn't.

Three

The storm continued to rage as Antonio drove the windy, two-lane roads back to the distillery. Dinner had been amazing, but the company had been even better. Elise had insisted on paying, which went against everything he'd been taught. But he understood her need for professionalism and control.

Antonio found Elise to be even more fascinating than their initial meeting. She knew her business, that was for damn sure. Clearly, Angel's Share was her passion and her sisters were her life. He could completely understand and appreciate that loyalty to family heritage.

And all eyes were on him, as of late, to carry on his own heritage as the Rodriguez heir.

As he pulled into the parking lot, Antonio pushed aside that crushing guilt that threatened to overcome him. There was nothing he could do about his personal life right this minute, and he wanted to just enjoy the company of a sexy woman who could just be the distraction he needed, but shouldn't have.

"Do you want to be dropped off at the door or at your car?" he asked.

The rain continued to pelt the car and in the distance a flash of lightning lit up the sky. He didn't necessarily want her driving in this storm, but he had no place to tell her what to do and even if he did, she'd likely balk at him for trying to help. Which was just another trait he appreciated with Elise. Some may call it stubborn, but he preferred strong-willed and determined. He lived his life with the exact manner.

Elise glanced out the window, then turned back to face him.

"Are you in a hurry to get anywhere?" she asked.

"Back to the rental house? Not especially. Why?"

She pushed up her glasses and smiled. Damn it, there went that trickle of arousal once again. What was it with this woman? He'd been around and with beautiful women his entire life. Did he only want her because he'd deemed her off-limits? He never did like the word *no*, but this was different. This was his own self-control…which seemed to be dwindling with each passing moment.

"I still owe you an after-hours tour," she told him. "Do you have an early morning tomorrow?"

Even if he did, he wouldn't be turning down her obvious invitation.

"I have the tastings of the exclusive labels you scheduled for one o'clock tomorrow," he informed her. "Then my next tour is in three days, just a couple towns over."

Elise waved her hand. "Well, go ahead and cancel that. No need to waste your time when you've clearly had the best."

He couldn't help where his mind went—to an instant image of Elise completely bare for him, wearing those glasses and nothing else. That long, silky red hair all around her shoulders as she stared up at him and he claimed her as his own.

"I can't resist the best."

Her smile froze as her eyes darted to his lips for a fraction of a second, but that was long enough for him to know this attraction wasn't just one-sided. Oh, she was likely fighting an internal battle just like he was. Good to know because he wasn't sure how long he could hold out on reaching for her. What would one kiss hurt? They were adults and clearly, there was already some instant pull they both felt.

"Are you ready to run for it?" she asked with a wide smile on her face.

Antonio nodded with a naughty, crooked grin. "You seem excited."

She shrugged a slender shoulder. "I love a good thunderstorm and I love showing off what we've done here. Of course I'm excited."

Her enthusiasm was contagious. Not that he was a fan of storms, but he was a fan of Elise's. Somehow in this first day of being in her presence, he'd nearly put aside the anxiety he had, thinking about his parents and his next step once he returned home. How Elise managed to hold his attention so completely was a mystery to him, but one he intended to solve.

"I'll follow you," he told her as he shut off the vehicle. "On three. You ready?"

She nodded and reached for her door handle.

"One, two—"

"Three!" she yelled as she jumped from the car.

Antonio raced after her. The cool rain pelted his back as he hunkered against the harsh winds. In an expert move, Elise had the front door unlocked and open just as he got there. They both stepped inside, instantly away from the harsh elements.

Antonio wiped his feet on the large rug with the Angel's Share emblem embossed on it as Elise punched in a series of buttons on one alarm, and then moved to the second panel and did the same. The doors clicked back to locked and lights flickered on.

"This place can be a bit creepy at night when I'm here alone, especially during a storm." She swiped the droplets from her face, removed her glasses, and pulled her hair over one shoulder. "But I can't think of a better time to show you around. I love the history here."

"I admit the castle drew me in immediately when I saw it online," he told her. "But when I pulled in this morning, I felt like I was home."

She cocked her head aside and reached for the hem of her shirt to clean off her lenses. "How so?"

Antonio pulled a handkerchief from his pocket and offered it instead. Her hand brushed his and he wasn't surprised by another shock of arousal, but he was surprised that something so simple could have him so worked up.

This entire day had been nothing but verbal and emotional foreplay.

"My small town is rich with history," he explained, focusing back on her question. "The castle there dates back a little earlier than this one, and we have some amazing architecture as well in our downtown buildings."

She stood there staring, not taking the cloth he'd offered.

"What?" he asked.

"I'm fascinated about your hometown, but are you going to pretend like it's normal for a man to still carry a handkerchief around?"

Antonio took her glasses and cleaned them for her. "It is normal, at least to me. My parents instilled manners and my father always carries one, so I guess it was just passed down. Silly things, really, but I never thought about it."

"They must be proud of you."

Of course they were, they fully expected him to take over their dynasty. As the only child now, they had silently placed a heavy load on his shoulders that he wished like hell he could off-load on someone else. But he couldn't do that to the people who loved him most.

Antonio didn't reply. He stepped forward, closing the gap between them as he eased her glasses back into place. Her eyes met his, locking him in as he was unable to move, unable to breathe.

Thunder rolled outside the castle walls and part of him wanted to ignore everything but the sexual attraction pushing them together. But this was crazy. He'd only met her this morning and he was only here as a family representative, nothing more.

But there was more. So much more than what he'd initially planned or counted on. He wanted to erase that sliver of space between them and cover her mouth with his. The need consumed him. The need to taste her, to taste the rain on her lips and explore her on a whole new level.

Aside from the fact he had a craving for her like no other, he also desperately needed this distraction. There was no better way to forget his troubles than with the affection and companionship of an intriguing woman.

Elise blinked and cleared her throat as she took a step back, breaking the spellbinding moment. Antonio missed his chance and wished like hell he would've just gone in for it. What would she have done? There wasn't a doubt in his mind she would have reciprocated the kiss, and he had every intention of finding out…soon.

Each time he started to get a little closer, that mask went back in place. One of these times he was going to rip it off and see the true Elise. Damn it, that silent challenge she threw down was likely lost on her, but not him. He welcomed the defiance.

"Are you ready to get started?" she asked, adjusting her glasses back into place.

"I'm at your mercy."

Her lids lowered slightly and the pulse at the base of her neck beat fast. Oh yeah. She wanted that kiss just as much as he did. Between the storm outside and the fact they were alone in an old castle, they had the perfect combination for sexual tension.

His body stirred, his desire soared. And he'd done

all of this to himself. Had he not asked her to dinner, had he not followed her inside moments ago, he could have gone back to his rental where he was sure to keep his hands to himself.

But his needs weren't the only issue. No, the issue was seeing that matching passion in Elise's eyes. The pull was too fast, too strong. He couldn't just ignore how she looked at him…and how she seemed to be struggling just as much as he was.

"Let's start at the beginning," she told him. "We'll go to the mash area, which is that amazing scent you get as soon as you step inside the building. We actually have a candle in our gift shop that mimics the aroma."

When she turned away, Antonio followed those swaying hips. He believed that, for the woman who was all business, there had to be some serious pent-up desire inside there. He wanted to be the one to pull that out. No, he *needed* to be the one.

He couldn't describe the all-consuming yearning to have her, to claim her.

Elise led him up the metal stairs toward the scents of yeast and mash. Even this didn't take away from all of his erotic thoughts and images of Elise. While she was trying to maintain a professional exterior, he knew what was boiling deep inside. Maybe they just met, but he knew women, and he recognized that indescribable need.

All he could think of was that they were alone, with a storm raging outside just as it raged inside. The only thing to stop them from crossing that line from professional to personal was themselves…and he was ready to ignore all the reasons why they shouldn't.

"So Angel's Share is a little different in the way we begin our mash process and that is actually kept a secret even from our exclusive clients."

She flashed him a smile he could only describe as proud.

"Even our most important VIP customers aren't in on that," she went on. "But once you visit other distilleries, you'll notice this aroma is fresh. That's the only way I can describe it. There's a subtle sweet undertone, but nothing that will take away from the rich bourbon flavor."

He listened as she pointed toward pieces of equipment, how she discussed their startup and their struggles. How they borrowed so much and called in every favor to get this place up and running. Which was quite an undertaking since bourbon has to age for years before it's ready for public consumption. They'd been smart in also offering gin to get their name out there until their first bourbons were ready, so by the time their ten-year bottle rolled around, Angel's Share would already be well-known.

Brains and beauty. There was no way this operation would fail.

"We have excellent bourbon and gin right now and as you know, we're unveiling our first ten-year at our anniversary gala." She turned to face him fully and kept that megawatt smile in place as she pushed up her glasses. "If you're still in the area, you are welcome to come."

He'd make sure he was in town, no matter what schedule he had to rearrange to be here.

"So where else are you traveling?" she asked. "I need to know who my competitors are."

"Right now I'm not interested in anyone else. You're top of my priorities."

Elise motioned for him to follow. "In that case, let's keep this tour going so I can secure you're mine."

Oh hell. There wasn't much *securing* that needed to be done. As far as he was concerned, Angel's Share would be going into his family's businesses.

Besides the fact Elise had him under her spell, he had loved the tastings he'd done earlier during the main tour. The richness, the subtle char from the barrels and the hints of nuttiness were perfect and exactly what he was looking for in bourbons. He hadn't come here looking for the gin, but since he'd be doing business anyway, the smart decision would be to incorporate all of Angel's Share's products.

Elise led him back downstairs and down a long, narrow hallway lined with old stone. The thunder continued to rumble outside as he followed Elise down another set of steps. They headed toward a basement he hadn't even known existed. When they came to a steel door, she punched in a code. A series of beeps echoed in the hallway before the latch on the door clicked. Elise pushed through the opening and the creaking noise had Antonio chuckling.

"I feel like this is how a missing person's case would start," he joked. "An old castle, a storm, the dungeon..."

Elise snickered as she gestured for him to enter ahead of her. "I assure you, I'm not kidnapping you. This is the room that is my absolute favorite and we don't let anyone down here. Actually, very few employees even know its existence and the ones who do aren't given the passcodes."

Yet, she'd brought him here. That spoke volumes for how well their connection was already. Elise was the perfect distraction. He'd known coming to the States would help keep him busy and keep his mind off a conversation he wasn't ready to have with his parents. Something was missing in his life and he had no idea what the hell could fill that void.

But diversions by way of intelligent women were most welcome until he could figure out his life.

"So what is this special area?" he asked.

Elise led him down another hallway and to another door. With her hand on the knob, she looked back over her shoulder. "This is where all the history is located."

He followed her inside a room with stone walls. An old desk sat in the corner, a floor-to-ceiling shelf nestled in another corner. There was at least a light overhead, but not much else.

"Are you sure you're not about to lock me in here?" he joked.

Elise went to the shelf and pulled out a book before meeting his gaze.

"Do you want to get locked in here?" she retorted.

"Are you flirting with me?"

Elise pursed her pale pink lips. "No flirting. We're here for work, right?"

He was having a difficult time remembering that, and all of her smiles, her wide eyes behind those glasses, and whatever this magnetic pull was, Antonio knew he couldn't stay alone with her much longer.

She sat the book on the desk and carefully eased the cover open. Closer inspection showed the book was definitely old. The yellowed pages with frayed edges had a cursive writing that was both elegant and scratchy. History had always fascinated him and seeing the delight on Elise's face told him this was just one area they had in common.

Not that he was looking for anyone to bond with on a deeper level. He wasn't so sure long-term commitments were for him. Oh, the whole love and marriage thing worked great for his parents. There was no denying how much they adored each other since the moment they'd met while filming a movie decades ago. And it wasn't that he didn't believe in love. Antonio just didn't think he could commit to one person for the rest of his life. All of that sounded so…permanent.

Exposing his heart to someone with the hopes of forever would only lead to pain and loss. He couldn't take the risk of being that destroyed ever again.

Besides, he enjoyed taking off on a whim and traveling and doing his own thing on his own time. Taking over in a position meant for someone else wasn't fair to him or his parents. Surely, they wanted someone who actually had a passion for the business like they did… and that wasn't him.

Maybe all of those thoughts made him a selfish person, but at least he was honest. And any woman he was with knew exactly where he stood. He might not be looking for commitment, but he did respect women and would never lie about something so serious.

"So what are we diving into?" he asked, standing next to her at the desk.

"This is one of the diaries from the original architect of the castle. We found these when we were restoring this place and we keep them locked away."

"Are you serious? That's amazing."

Antonio glanced at the dates just as the lights flickered for a brief moment and came back.

"We should head back upstairs," Elise told him. "You don't want to be down here if the electricity goes."

She'd barely gotten her sentence out before the lights flickered once more and ultimately gave up, plunging them into darkness.

Antonio waited a beat, hoping the power would return, but no luck.

Elise cursed beneath her breath, turned on her cell flashlight, and left the room. The very unladylike groan from the hallway told him this was not a good predicament they were in if she was this frustrated.

Of course not. So…

"Are we trapped?" he asked.

"For now. You're not claustrophobic, are you?"

Antonio shook his head and then realized she probably couldn't see him.

"I'm not," he told her. "Do you have cell service here?"

She turned her phone over and then held it up, walking all around the room. Antonio pulled his out and did the same…all for naught. They were underground and surrounded by old stone.

"Well, the good news is there is a bathroom down here," she told him with a half-nervous chuckle. "The bad news is nobody will be here until morning."

"That doesn't sound like bad news at all," he retorted. "Sounds like you and I are going to get to know each other even more."

Four

Why did that sound like the most delicious threat ever?

Elise certainly hadn't lured him down here for any shenanigans, but now they were stuck in an old dungeon with very little furniture, no lights, and a hell of a lot of sexual tension.

Of all the sisters, Elise was the least likely to find herself in this position. Delilah was always the mischievous one growing up and Sara would welcome the chance to get stuck during a storm with a sexy man. Nothing about this scenario was like Elise.

Growing up, she had been the studious one, the by-the-book one. She'd been the one to make her sisters stay the course and see their dreams come to fruition even when things seemed impossible.

And perhaps that was why she was so damn enthralled and almost excited that she was locked in a castle basement with a sexy Spaniard. Things like this never, ever happened to her.

"I have to apologize." Talk about unprofessional and embarrassing. "When I wanted to give you a tour, this wasn't exactly how I expected things to go."

"Things happen. Even you can't control Mother Nature."

His low voice with a thick accent washed over her in the darkness—the man might as well have reached out and touched her.

"We have power outages with storms, but they usually don't last long. Maybe we'll be saved before morning."

"Oh, I can think of worse situations. This is just an unexpected moment. Life is full of them."

Elise tapped her phone for some light as she crossed the tiny room and took a seat against the wall.

"Are you always this optimistic?" she asked.

"Not always."

He came and took a seat next to her, his thigh brushing against hers. She'd thought coming over here would make him stay over there. How could she keep resisting?

No, the question should be *why* she thought she had any right to have to resist. This was a business arrangement. Elise wasn't looking to complicate things or do anything with Antonio other than land this important account.

"My parents are all business, all the time." Antonio's statement cut through the darkness. "I couldn't be more opposite and sometimes I wonder if I even belong to them. I mean, if I didn't look exactly like my father, I'd question."

"Delilah, Sara, and I were all adopted by our mom, Milly." Elise found herself remembering all the amazing moments from childhood. "Milly was a saint for taking on three kids all under the age of four and sticking by us no matter our crazy ideas."

"Is she part of the distillery?"

Elise swallowed the lump of grief. Time healed all wounds...or some such saying, but Elise's ache continued to grow with each passing day.

"She actually passed about a month ago," Elise informed him. "But she was a huge part in our success and will always be here in spirit. We definitely wouldn't have gotten anywhere without her."

Antonio's strong hand settled on her thigh, sending way too many emotions shooting through her. He was offering comfort and she was having the total opposite reaction.

"Sorry to hear that. Grief can make you really appreciate family and how much they enrich your life."

The conviction in his tone seemed to just tug her even more toward wanting to know more.

"Sounds like you speak from experience," she commented.

"I have my own loss I deal with, but we don't need to get into that. We're talking about you. I'm sure Milly was proud of you and your sisters."

Elise let the conversation circle back to her. She didn't want to push when he obviously didn't want to talk about his own pain.

"Oh, she was. When we first had the idea of the distillery, she told everyone who would listen. Then, once we bought the building, she brought all the members from her yoga classes to tour the place."

Antonio's rich laughter lay like a warm blanket over her. Elise closed her eyes and rested her head back against the cold wall. She supposed if she ever had to get locked down in a century-old dungeon, being trapped with Antonio was the best way to go. At least she wasn't completely alone because being alone right now with idle time only made her think, and thinking led to grieving and she didn't want to go down that path. Even though weeks had passed, if she started giving in to her thoughts, then she'd have to admit the truth and come to terms with what everyone called "her new normal."

"And did the yoga class end up back here for tastings once you opened?" he asked.

"Of course. Not only that, they had a special yoga class on the rooftop at sunset once a week that entire first summer." The moment in time rolled through her mind like an old movie. "I like to think our marketing skills really boosted our business, but looking back, it could have been all the grandmotherly types in spandex and posting on social media that amped up the attention."

He chuckled again. "I'm sure that didn't hurt, but you and your sisters have something uniquely special here."

"We're women, I know. We hear that all the time from shocked potential clients who think we're just a front and there's actually no man behind the operation."

"Believe me, I'm well aware there are three brilliant

women running Angel's Share," he replied. "All of you being beautiful is just an added bonus."

Antonio's hand remained on her thigh and she wondered if he even realized it. She sure as hell did. The warmth, the strength, emanating from him was not helping her ever-growing desire. Because being stranded here for the time being was oh so helpful.

"Working in an industry typically run by men, there have been some struggles and barriers we didn't expect," she admitted. "But I assure you that if you work with us, you won't find an easier company to partner with and you'll have happy customers back home once you introduce Angel's Share."

He gave her thigh a gentle squeeze...apparently, he knew all along that hand was still there. She imagined someone as powerful and regimented as Antonio wouldn't miss any detail—especially when it came to women.

"I have no doubt we will work well together or I wouldn't have made the trip halfway across the world to be here."

Now he did slide his hand away, but his body still aligned with hers. Their arms, their hips, their legs. Elise wanted to shift slightly, not that she wanted to get away from him, but the longer she kept feeling his touch, the more she wanted...well, more. No matter how innocent this all seemed to be, there was no way she could deny the undercurrent and she wondered if they were going to get out of here before anything rose to the surface.

"We're not talking work while stuck here," he told her.

"We're not?"

"I want to know more about you as a person, not as a distiller."

Elise blinked against the darkness, wishing she could see his face, to read his expressions and what she saw staring back at her. But if they were going to have such personal conversations, perhaps darkness was her best ally here.

Elise had always kept her emotions close to her heart. She'd always had her inner circle of those whom she trusted and let in. Her sisters had cared for her like no one else.

Except Milly. Milly had cared.

"I'm a pretty boring person. If you want excitement, that's Delilah or Sara. Dee is in the process of a divorce, though, so I'm not sure how much fun she'd be. I think the divorce is a mistake, but she didn't ask my opinion, so…"

Silence filled the room, far longer than Elise was comfortable with.

"Her husband is a divorce attorney, so there's some irony there," Elise added, wondering what else she could share that kept them off the topic of the fact they were alone or that there was this crackling tension all around them.

Elise sighed and stretched her legs out before her, crossing her ankles as she continued. "Sara, on the other hand, believes love is going to sweep into her life and whisk her away to some royal fairy tale. We've tried to explain to her that she already owns a castle, it just didn't come with Prince Charming. She seriously dates all the wrong men, but she's not about to give up."

"And what about you?"

"What about me?" she asked, her heart beating faster because now he wanted to zero in.

Antonio shifted, his arm brushed hers a few times and she realized he was rolling up his cuffs on his dress shirt. Mercy sakes, the forearms were coming out. She fell into that category of forearm-loving women—she couldn't help herself. There was something so sexy about those strong muscles that were usually under-rated.

"Are you married or divorced?"

"Is that your subtle way of asking if I'm single?"

"I'm not being subtle. I don't play games."

Apparently not, which was just one more layer of appeal she didn't need to notice or find more enchanting.

"I'm single. Never been married, unless you count my office. I'm in a serious relationship with my new cushy leather swivel chair."

Antonio let out a deep sigh as he shifted, his legs rustling against hers. Elise tried to have no reaction whatsoever, but she couldn't help those tingles and happy dances going on inside her. If there had been any question before, there were none now. Antonio Rodriguez was flirting with her and she was absolutely loving it.

"My parents work too hard," he replied. "They say that's so they can leave a legacy to me when they retire. There's so much more to life than working and we've learned that life is definitely too short. Why shouldn't people have fun while working?"

So he'd learned life was too short and he was grieving. He'd definitely lost someone close...but who? If he wanted to reveal or open up, he would, so Elise kept the conversation going and let him have the lead.

"That's a good question," she agreed. "I guess you just have to find what you love in life and then your career doesn't seem like a job. I mean, I definitely put this place and my sisters' needs above my own, but I love what I do and I love seeing everyone around me happy."

"Even at the expense of your own personal life?" he questioned.

Elise shrugged, not thinking he couldn't see her, but he could feel. She grew twitchier sitting here, so she came to her feet and removed her jacket. She didn't know if it was the sexy man or the enclosed room making her hot all of a sudden.

"I'm not sacrificing anything," she defended. "I don't have anything going on in my personal life so there's no reason I can't put everything else first. Maybe once I get all of this on a solid foundation, then I can start assessing my time away from here."

She thought he would stand now that she had, but there was no movement from Antonio. Elise reached her hands out slowly, feeling for the edge of the desk she knew was close by. Once her fingertips hit the curved edge, she turned and eased one hip and then the other up.

There. If she stayed up here, then she wouldn't have to be too close and she wouldn't have to have those "innocent" touches and brushes. Not that she didn't enjoy them…that was the problem. She enjoyed Antonio a little too much and this was only day one of his visit.

She had to start pulling back before she got lost in those thoughts in her head and ended up acting on her sudden desires.

"You're high-strung."

Elise stilled as his accusation wrapped around her. "Excuse me?"

"You're having a difficult time sitting still, you put your sisters and work ahead of everything, and you don't even like to talk about yourself." Now she heard him shifting and knew he'd come to stand. "What do you do for fun?"

"Fun?"

Once again, Antonio's low, rich chuckle penetrated her. It was a laugh, for pity's sake...a laugh at her expense, by the way, and she still found him utterly sexy and irresistible.

"So even the word is a foreign concept," he confirmed. "When you leave work, what's the first thing you do?"

"Take my bra off."

Damn it. That was not what she wanted to come out of her mouth and that sure as hell wasn't what he was asking.

"Fascinating image," he murmured, his feet shuffling across the old stone floor as he came toward her. "And then what?"

Had his voice just taken on a sultry tone? If the power wasn't restored soon, Elise knew she was not going to be able to resist him much longer. How had all of this spiraled so far away from professional and a working relationship to ending up locked in together with an insurmountable attraction?

He was a client, one very prestigious client from another country. This account could open major doors for them and all she could think about was ripping off his clothes and seeing just how sturdy they used to build these old desks.

She circled back to answer his question instead.

"Sometimes I watch historical documentaries or take a bubble bath if it's been a long day."

"Is that right?"

Oh yeah. Definitely more sultry now and he stood much closer. So close, in fact, she could feel his breath on her cheek. Elise closed her eyes as her entire body responded with a flare of arousal she hadn't felt in such a long time.

"I'd say with as hard as you work, you deserve some pampering. Do you ever get a massage?"

"Um…no. I…" *Can't think.* "No massages. I never make time for appointments like that."

His hand smoothed her hair from her shoulder, cupping it just so, then he started kneading. She tipped her head, gladly giving him better access. She should put a stop to all of this, but…why? They were both adults—clearly, he wouldn't be touching her if he didn't want to and she sure as hell wanted him to continue. There was nobody to tell them this was wrong.

So why was she letting those negative thoughts creep in? Just because he was a potential client, one had nothing to do with the other.

Her mind was all over the place, bouncing back and forth on whether she should do what she wanted or stay the course of her usual by-the-book approach. She'd never had to fight against herself before and right now the internal struggle was extremely real.

Then again, she likely couldn't concentrate on any

coherent thought when those magical hands were working her over.

"Maybe you're in the wrong industry," she moaned as he went to the other shoulder. "Have you thought about being a masseur?"

"Making a woman feel good would be an excellent way to make money." His warm breath tickled the bare skin along her neck. "I wouldn't be opposed to a career change."

Elise sighed, or maybe she moaned again. Either way, she wasn't ready to call this quits just yet. As long as he was willing to work out her tension, she was going to let him.

"Turn around so I can do this properly."

She stood and turned her back to him. Then he stepped in closer behind her, so close his long, lean torso brushed against her back and she stilled, her breath caught in her throat.

"I can't take much more if you keep moaning like that," he whispered in her ear.

The heavy silence of the room made that seductive whisper seem like a boom. As with everything else she'd learned from Antonio so far, there was a commanding presence that couldn't be ignored or denied.

Elise pulled in a deep breath and slowly turned to face him. Even though it was dark, maybe because it was dark, she wasn't hiding what she wanted any longer. And she wanted to forget that she was the responsible one, the by-the-book one.

She hesitated for a second before she decided to stop overthinking everything in her life. Now was her time, her night, to live in the moment.

"Then do something about it."

She threw down that proverbial gauntlet and waited. She wanted to forget everything outside this room and let Antonio Rodriguez show her exactly what she'd been missing out on.

Five

Antonio cursed himself, wondering if he'd come on too strong or made Elise too uncomfortable by his blatant words and advances. Those were the last things he wanted. He just couldn't seem to get a grasp on his own control, not when the ache and desire were far too strong.

The second she turned, he waited for her to tell him this was a professional relationship only and that all hands and sexual comments should be kept to himself. But it was dark, too dark, and he could only feel her… which was precisely how he got into this predicament to begin with.

Elise's hands fumbled around over his chest, then flattened as she moved them up and over his shoulders. As much as Antonio demanded control in all situations, this one was quite different and totally new territory. He wanted Elise, there was no denying that truth, but he also wanted her to be comfortable and he didn't want to come across as domineering.

Then her body brushed his from chest to hip as she aligned their bodies, and Antonio came to the realization that relinquishing control could be a very, very good thing.

Her lips brushed along his jaw, then his chin, as she slowly made her way to his mouth.

"We're on the same page, right?" she murmured against his lips.

Oh hell, yes.

Antonio gripped her waist and pressed her even farther into him as he covered her mouth with his. That question was all the green light he needed to act on this attraction. The moment the tip of his tongue touched hers she came alive in his arms. Clearly, her own pent-up desires had been just as fierce and strong as his own.

Her fingertips dug into his shoulders as she opened for him, letting out one of those little moans that had already driven him beyond his breaking point. How could a woman with this much passion hold it all back? She deserved an outlet and Antonio wanted nothing more than for her to use him.

With careful, strategic motions, Antonio turned them around. He kept one hand on the small of her back, while he felt behind her for the desk. Finally, the edge of the desk grazed his fingertips and he took another step until Elise was against the top. He lifted her, setting her on the solid surface, all while keeping his mouth on hers. He couldn't get enough and he'd just gotten started.

The question was, how far did she want to take this? She'd given no indication he should stop or that she was hesitant, but he also didn't want to assume she was ready for everything he wanted to give her.

Elise spread her legs apart, allowing Antonio to step in farther.

But then she eased away from the kiss just enough for him to still feel that warm breath tickle his face.

"What are we doing?" she panted. "I mean, I know what we're doing, but is this smart?"

Smart? Probably not. But what did common sense have to do with any of this? Sure, he'd told himself he would focus on business and trying to figure out what his own next steps should be to break away from the family legacy. But that was before he'd met Elise, and he couldn't think of a better distraction than this fiery vixen.

Who could blame him? There wasn't a man alive that would turn her away. She was the perfect package, especially because she wasn't looking for more than this, either. Her dedication to her work and family made any type of relationship nonexistent...just how he liked things.

"We can stop now if that's what you want," he told her.

Antonio rested his hands on either side of her hips, but didn't pull back. If he couldn't see her, he at least wanted to be near. He wanted to feel her, to smell her. All of his senses were heightened now that one had been removed. But what he wouldn't give to see this body of hers. She'd been driving him crazy all day with those curvy hips and dip in her waist. While he couldn't wait to get his hands on her bare skin, he did wish he could take her in completely.

"What I want is to be responsible and professional, but apparently, I already crossed that line when I climbed up your body a moment ago."

Antonio couldn't help but admire her honesty. It was that transparency of hers that he found so refreshing and perfect. Too many people who surrounded him were either trying to impress him or they wanted something from him. From everything he could tell, Elise was a genuine person with no ulterior motives other than she wanted him as much as he wanted her. And since they were both adults with the same need, there was no reason for them to ignore this connection.

"I imagine you are always professional and responsible," he countered. "Take what you want, *amante*."

"What does that mean?" she asked.

He leaned forward and whispered against her ear. "Lover."

Her body trembled against his and there was something almost on a whole other level that made this moment even sexier, naughtier, than if they'd been in the light.

"You can be whatever you want here," he assured her. "Anything that happens here, stays between us and has nothing to do with the outside world. Not work or family. Just us."

Elise let out a soft sigh and his body immediately responded. He wanted her, but he had to wait to see where her head was at. No way did he want to coerce her into something she wasn't ready for.

"Just this once, right?" she asked. "And nobody has to know."

"Nobody."

"And this won't get in the way of work?"

He had her. They both knew it...and he hadn't even bothered replying to her *just once* question. Maybe once wouldn't be enough, maybe it would, but he was smart enough not to lock himself into anything—especially where a beautiful woman was concerned.

"This won't get in the way of anything we have going on with our business arrangement," he assured her. He'd honed the skill of separating business and personal long ago. "Don't deny what you want when there's nobody here but us."

She shifted against him and then there were two soft thuds to the stone floor. Her shoes were off...now for the rest of her clothes. Antonio waited a beat to see what she'd do next and he didn't have to wait long. She wrapped her legs around his waist and scooted farther to the edge of the desk, securing him perfectly between her thighs.

"I'm not going to deny either one of us." Her hands slid over his forearms and up over his chest, finally landing on the buttons of his shirt. "But since we're leaving all of the outside world out of this room, I'm done talking."

"Sí, señorita." Who knew beneath this professional, conservative persona a sexy vixen was hidden? Aside from her actions, her demands were just as telling as to exactly what she wanted. Why was everything about

Elise so attractive and magnetic? He couldn't figure out how she could pull him in from so many angles, from her brilliant mind to her body to her work ethic and family loyalty. He shouldn't let these overwhelming urges overtake his common sense, but there was no going back now. He was too far in and he couldn't just ignore a woman in need...right?

As Elise toyed with the buttons on his shirt, Antonio eased his hands to her waist and slid up beneath the hem of her top. The instant he came in contact with that soft, velvety skin, Antonio knew this woman was going to be his undoing. He'd been in town less than three days and already had broken the promise to himself, and even though she had said this would only be a one-time thing, he wasn't about to lie to either of them and pretend that was an accurate statement.

He wanted her now and he knew he'd want her again. Turning off this need simply wasn't an option, nor did he want it to be.

Her hands frantically moved to rid him of his clothes and what started as sultry and passionate had quickly turned frantic and desperate...or perhaps the desperation was on his part because he was just as eager to get all of these barriers out of their way.

Antonio worked at the button and zipper of her pants and helped as she shifted side to side to ease the garments down below her hips. His shirt fell to the floor, he yanked her pants off and gave them a toss, and they both went to work on his jeans, but not before he reached into his wallet and pulled out protection.

In a matter of moments they were bare, and he was sheathed and ready, but he'd never cursed darkness more. What had been sexy and mysterious just moments ago, now only left him feeling robbed of the full Elise Hawthorne experience.

Oh, he might not be looking for more than a physical distraction, but that didn't mean he wanted to lose out on seeing this fascinating woman up close and completely bare.

Elise's hands flattened on his chest as her calves slid over his hips and she used the heels of her feet to dig into the backs of his thighs. Her silent demand was sexier than anything she'd said so far and Antonio wasted no time stepping into her.

Her hands traveled down his torso, then back up and over his shoulders, moving around to the back of his neck. She threaded her fingers through his hair and pulled him even closer.

He'd dated women all over the world, he'd bedded quite a few of them as well, but he'd never been with a woman who could pull off being subtle and dominating all wrapped into one alluring package.

And Antonio couldn't get enough of her.

As he eased in closer, he gripped her hips to make sure their bodies were lined up perfectly. She grazed her lips over his, almost as if trying to find her own way and how exactly she wanted to go into this. Maybe there was a slight hesitation because she was getting back into her mind, he didn't know. All he knew was that he wasn't going to let any outside forces into this room or into this moment.

Antonio opened his lips over hers, just as he joined their bodies. And then he stilled. He shouldn't have that immediate sensation of everything being so...perfect.

Yet, there it was and now he had to get out of his own head space and into the moment because emotions or feelings or anything else were totally unwelcome.

All he wanted was to feel and let go, and let Elise do whatever she wanted.

Elise had just started having a panic of wondering if this was the biggest mistake she was getting ready to make, but then Antonio took over and she didn't give a damn if this moment, this night, was a mistake or not. He felt too good, *this* felt too good. She never did anything just because she wanted to. Her whole life had been giving to everyone else, taking care of others, and putting her own social life on the back burner.

For tonight, she was taking and not caring about consequences.

Having Antonio join their bodies so perfectly, and then remain completely and utterly still, was driving her out of her mind. Elise jerked her hips against his and arched against his bare body. What she wouldn't give to see those hard muscles in the light, but she'd have to just use her imagination because feeling them would have to be enough.

After tonight there would be nothing else between them other than setting up a nice VIP account and growing both of their businesses.

That sounded so cold, but there was nothing chilly about what was happening here and she wasn't going to be sorry or have regrets. This moment, this man, was exactly what she needed to get her mind off her grievances and stress.

As Antonio pumped faster, his hands came between

them to cup her breasts. Elise tore her mouth from his, crying out as she dropped her head back and let every euphoric sensation wash over her.

Yes, this was exactly what she'd been missing in her life.

Antonio whispered something in Spanish and she wished like hell she'd paid more attention in school, but most likely her junior year Spanish class didn't go over whatever Antonio was sharing here.

He could be talking about a grocery list for all she knew, but it took this intimacy to a whole new level. Any man she dated from now on had to know another language and whisper something during intimacy. She never knew how much of a turn-on this would be.

His entire body worked against hers, his hands seemed to be everywhere at once, and that talented mouth roamed along her jawline, down the column of her throat, and to the swell of her breasts.

The immense onslaught of sensations hit her all at once from so many directions. She couldn't hold back, couldn't deny the euphoric combustion as she let go and let her body soar.

Elise cried out, reaching to clutch on to Antonio's shoulders for support. He continued to murmur something she couldn't quite understand and she couldn't focus on anything while her body continued to tremble.

Just as her waves started to cease, Antonio jerked harder, faster, then stilled as he rested his head just against the side of her neck. His quick, warm pants covered her heated skin as he struggled to catch his breath during his own release.

Elise wrapped her arms around him, closed her eyes,

and continued to relish in this moment, to try somehow to lock it all in and freeze this portion of time. As ridiculous as it sounded, she wasn't ready to see their intimacy come to an end. She'd needed this distraction from her own grief, from her set ways. She hadn't realized how breaking the rules could be fun, exhilarating even.

And even though they were trapped, Elise wouldn't change a thing. She knew they'd get out come morning at the latest, so she was going to embrace their time together because once they left this room, every other interaction they had would be strictly professional. She'd go back to exactly the way she was before, but with a little secret she would keep locked away.

Silence enveloped them once again and Antonio shifted back, breaking that warm bond they'd created and shared. Now it was over, and she already regretted telling him this night was a one-time-only thing.

Six

His back had certainly had better nights of sleep. Antonio wasn't in his twenties anymore and he was about to say goodbye to his thirties as well, which apparently meant more aches and pains than he was normally used to.

But resting while sitting up against a stone wall with a sexy woman lying on his lap had been about the only option in this small space. Besides, it wasn't like he would have gotten much sleep anyway. His mind was too worked up, spinning in all directions about the quick events that had led them up to this point.

Antonio had certainly taken lovers and one-night stands before, but last night had been new for him. He never slept with someone he was in direct contact with regarding his family's business, and he never slept with someone when he'd been vulnerable, but he'd been getting that same vibe from Elise. She was in a grieving period, so maybe they just needed each other.

It was all of these questions and unknowns that didn't sit well with him. He didn't like these unwanted emotions that had kept him awake and staring into the darkness. What happened to the times when he could just have sex and move on? It was like fate was mocking him by leaving him trapped in this room. Any other time he would have been itching to get out, to put the one-night stand behind him. And for reasons he couldn't begin to comprehend, he had no idea why he was so content still being here with no idea of when he would get out.

In all the hours he'd had to contemplate what he and Elise shared or what he ultimately wanted to do about his family business, he'd come up with absolutely nothing. He had no answers and the last thing he needed was more complications in his life.

Ironically, he'd just voluntarily added one and she currently had her face buried in his lap, letting off tiny snores that shouldn't be adorable, but they were. She'd probably be mortified if he told her she snored, so like a gentleman, he would keep that nugget of information to himself.

The lights flickered once, then went back off, then flickered again, staying on this time.

And the evidence of their passionate night couldn't be more obvious. Their clothes were strewn about all over the tiny space as they lay entangled and still completely bare.

Elise pushed off his lap, sat up, and clearly didn't want to look at him or say anything. She shoved her hair from her face and came to her feet, glancing around, deciphering her items from his. She scrambled to gather her clothes, keeping her back to him the entire time. No words, no smile, absolutely no emotion from the woman who had just bared everything to him.

Okay, then. Apparently, she was sticking to that whole one-night thing and they were not even going to discuss it. He hadn't taken Elise as someone who would turn away from conflict or an uncomfortable situation, but at the same time she was also regimented and a rule follower. She clearly meant what she said.

Antonio pulled his own clothes on, wanting to say something, but not really knowing what because he didn't want to make her uncomfortable.

Shouldn't something be said, though? They couldn't just pretend nothing happened...could they?

Maybe she could, but he couldn't. Something had happened and he wanted it to happen again, but if he couldn't even get her to speak, he'd likely never get her right back where he wanted.

Why couldn't they have both? While he was in town they could have a nice fling, since they both enjoyed themselves, yet still maintain that working relationship and partnership. The idea was perfect, but he had a feeling she didn't want his opinion right now.

Damn it. He'd never been like this before. He never actually cared about post-coital feelings or wanting to have a chat. What the hell had happened last night? When had he transitioned from fast, frantic sex to wanting to discuss it? He almost didn't recognize himself.

Elise smoothed her hair over her shoulder and turned to face him. "The electricity must have been restored."

"Then let's go before we get trapped again," he joked, though he wouldn't mind another night with her. Maybe this time in a more comfortable area with the moonlight on her skin so he could explore every inch and treat her the way a woman should be treated in bed.

Elise smiled, but her eyes darted away and he wondered if perhaps his joke came out completely wrong, like maybe she regretted what they'd shared. He had zero regrets. If he had to get trapped with anyone doing anything, this was the way to go about it.

After getting out into the hallway and then punching the code at the keypad at the end, Elise gestured for him to exit ahead of her. He started to pass by, but then turned to face her.

"I wouldn't change last night for anything."

Her eyes darted up to his, wide and full of shock.

"I didn't want you to leave this place with any negative thoughts or worries," he added.

Then, because he couldn't help himself and she'd still not said a word, he slid his lips over hers. They'd agreed that anything that happened down here stayed here, right? Well, they hadn't gone back upstairs yet and he wanted one last taste.

He swallowed her gasp, took a step into her, and backed her gently against the doorway. He pressed his hands on either side of her head, not the slightest bit ready to end this moment. There was something addicting about her and he had no clue what it was that kept pulling him in. Shouldn't their night together have already gotten her out of his system?

Unfortunately, the memorable experience did quite

the opposite. He wanted more, so much more than those few hours had offered.

"Oh my word!"

Antonio pulled his lips from Elise at the shrill exclamation. He glanced over his shoulder to see Delilah, who looked both shocked and pissed.

Mierda.

Apparently, what happened wouldn't just be staying between Elise and him now.

"What the hell is going on?" Delilah demanded.

Elise pushed against Antonio's chest and took a step away from him and toward her sister. "Just a kiss."

Just a kiss? What?

Antonio nearly laughed, but he didn't say a word. However she wanted to handle this with her family was none of his concern. He had his own family issues to sort out and sex couldn't complicate his future. Hell, this had just been one night, he had no commitments or ties to her...other than that invisible pull he still couldn't quite figure out.

"A kiss?" Delilah huffed. "Is that why your shirt is on inside out?"

Elise gasped and glanced down, but Delilah let out a very unladylike growl.

"It's not inside out, but that reaction tells me more went on down here." Her eyes darted to Antonio, then back to Elise. "I don't even know what to say, but I'll be up getting things ready because Katie called in sick and someone has to head up the first tour of the morning. Maybe you should do the walk of shame back to your office and clean up."

Antonio inwardly cringed at the harsh tone as Delilah turned and left them alone. He glanced to Elise, but couldn't read her emotions. Gone was the passionate woman from the night before. Now she stood with her chin tipped in defiance, her arms crossed, and her shoulders back. A niggle of guilt curled through him, knowing he was the one to drive this uncomfortable wedge between the sisters, and no doubt Delilah would tell Sara, as well.

Family meant everything to him and he knew enough about Elise to know she felt the same. In many ways they were cut from the same cloth, but there was nothing he could do to change what had happened.

"I take full responsibility for all of this," he told Elise. "I can talk to her if that would make things better."

Elise turned to face him and shook her head. "No. We both are to blame and I need to take care of this. As far as work…"

She sighed and shoved her hair away from her face, then readjusted her glasses. The frustration permeated from her and Antonio wanted to take her into his arms to console her. Which would not be smart and he was a fool for even having those thoughts. He needed to push aside their night just as she was doing and focus on everything else going on in his life.

"I'll head out," he told her. "Why don't I come by tomorrow and we'll do the tasting for the exclusive bottles. I know we were down for today, but if that won't mess up your schedule, I'd say your sisters would like to talk to you."

Elise nodded, but didn't offer anything else so Antonio took that as his cue to leave. He should be elated about this easy way of escape, but he couldn't shake that gnawing feeling that he'd damaged something within Elise. But she didn't need or want him to interfere with her family dynamics or try to soothe the hurt feelings. She had to do that on her own and he had to delete last night from his memory.

Unfortunately, that was all he could think about and he knew without a shadow of a doubt that as long as he remained in Benton Springs, he would continually want Elise and that one time had certainly not been enough.

Considering they had a full day of tours and were down one employee, that left Elise stewing in her office until Delilah could come talk to her. Hopefully, by the time that happened, her sister would have cooled off a little.

After a change of clothes and a retouch of makeup and hair in her office bathroom, Elise felt a little more like she was ready to tackle any argument. But she couldn't stop thinking about last night. There was no way to just flip that switch and pretend it never happened. Oh, she'd put on what she hoped was a convincing front for Antonio earlier. She'd told him one night and that was what she had to hold to so she'd put that wall between them.

From here on out, they had to be professionals...no matter how her body still hummed and craved his touch. She'd just been without intimacy for so long, now her emotions had opened back up and she thought she had to have more. There was no way round two was even possible.

How had she gotten into this predicament? Could

she be more cliché? A stormy night, a power outage, a sexy stranger. She'd allowed herself to be caught in that web of desire. Perhaps that was because she'd put herself directly in the path of seduction.

In the back of her mind, she knew what she'd been doing when she invited Antonio back into the distillery after hours. Granted, she couldn't have predicted the power outage, but she'd wanted to be alone with him; she'd wanted to continue feeling that sexual tension that she hadn't experienced in so long.

Elise pulled up her emails, determined to regain focus and get to work like she was supposed to do. They had a gala coming up, they had customers flying in from all over the country and potential customers from around the globe. This monumental night had zero room for error and all eyes would be on the three women who were going up against corporations and a male-dominated world.

Before she could open her first message, her office door slammed shut.

"Tell me this isn't true."

Elise glanced up to see Sara striding across the room, her long bangs flying around her face, as she held her cell up with her text screen open. Elise didn't have to read what the text was or who it was from to know what had happened.

"The kiss?" Elise asked. "It's true."

"Kiss?" Sara laughed. "This is me you're talking to. I'm not stupid and I've seen Antonio for myself. Nobody could blame you for what went on in that cellar. I want details, by the way. But I promised Delilah I would do damage control."

"There's no damage to control," Elise assured her. "Delilah came in at the wrong time and is blowing all of this up into nothing. Antonio and I are both professionals."

"Who just so happened to spend a dark night together in the basement of a castle. It's so romantic and I'm jealous."

Elise rolled her eyes and leaned back in her chair. "Not everything is a romance novel."

Sara gasped. "Why shouldn't it be? This is the greatest thing that's ever happened to you."

Elise couldn't really disagree with that, considering she hadn't been on an actual date in over a year and hadn't had sex in longer than that. Of all the sisters to have a heated one-night stand, Elise would be the last one for that position. But she wasn't sorry it happened. She was, however, sorry she got caught.

"Are you sure this won't mess up our working relationship with the Rodriguez family?" Sara asked, suddenly shifting back to work mode.

"I'm confident we will secure this account. In fact, Antonio is coming tomorrow for the tasting of the exclusive bottles we will make for them. So we need to get those sample batches ready and set up by one."

"Consider it done," Sara replied with a firm nod. Then she tipped her head and scrunched her nose. "Do you want to talk about last night?"

Elise pulled in a shaky breath. "Not really."

Sara offered a soft smile. "Well, my imagination is pretty good and I only have one thing to say. Good for you."

Elise couldn't help but laugh. "I don't imagine this is what Dee had in mind when she sent you to see me."

"Probably not, but she knows me so surely she's aware that I handle things much differently than her. And Camden just had those divorce papers delivered, so the timing couldn't have been worse."

Elise pulled in a shaky breath and closed her eyes. No wonder Delilah had been so harsh earlier. Elise couldn't imagine the pain Dee and Camden were going through. They were two imperfect people who were absolutely perfect together. But they were human and had flaws. Apparently, they couldn't work them out and Elise absolutely hated that for them.

"I had no idea," Elise said, refocusing on Sara. "I'm sure she'll come talk to me once this morning rush is over. What else do you have going on today?"

"I'm actually meeting someone at Milly's place around noon because I finally ordered a dumpster."

Elise didn't say anything; she didn't know what to say. Going through their childhood home and trying to decide what was precious enough to keep or what could be deemed as trash was like continually reliving the fact Milly was gone.

How could someone's entire life just be placed into a container and thrown out? How could years and memories be simplified down to so little and the rest of the world just move on?

"We have to do this," Sara added in that soft, comforting tone of hers. "Putting everything off won't change the fact and she would want us to move on."

"Moving on seems like we're leaving her behind."

"She's always with us," Sara reminded her. "Someone as bold and vibrant as Milly would never be left behind."

"Do you want me to come with you?" Elise asked.

"No. I'm just going to make sure it's dropped off around back and then I'll come back here. I don't plan on going through anything today. Maybe we can all go in this weekend and spend a few hours."

"Doing this together might make things a little easier," Elise agreed. "I'll bring the gin."

Sara laughed. "I'll get the tonic and lime."

"If Dee is speaking to me then, I'll have her bring some snacks."

Sara waved her hand. "You know how she is and she'll need you, especially today. Let her cool off. She'll come around."

Most likely, but Elise had never been one to put herself in drama or conflict. She absolutely hated confrontation, so this waiting game and the unknown of how Delilah would be was weighing heavy on Elise's mind.

"I need to get some work done before I head out," Sara stated. "If you ever want to talk about last night, let me know. And I don't just mean details. This is so out of character for you. If you just need someone to listen, I'm here."

Elise smiled and nodded before turning back to her computer. She wasn't sure she'd ever want to talk about that night with anybody. Discussing the events would only make her relive them over and over.

Then again, she'd be doing that anyway. There was no way she could go on with her life like she hadn't had the most intense sexual night ever. She almost felt like she needed to categorize everything that happened before Antonio and after Antonio. The man was that potent that she couldn't just pretend her life hadn't been altered forever.

And she still had to face him for work…like she hadn't spent a wild night with him and then woken up completely naked in his lap.

Seven

"What are your thoughts on Angel's Share?"

Antonio set his phone on speaker and placed it on the side table next to his Adirondack chair on the deck. He'd wanted to call and check in with his parents and, in true Carlos Rodriguez fashion, his father got right down to business.

But what Antonio thought of Angel's Share today was a bit different than what he'd thought yesterday. Now all Antonio could think of was Elise and all of that pent-up passion she'd unleashed on him. How intense she'd been, even though she tried so hard to shield her emotions…he'd felt them. When she'd initiated that first kiss, Antonio knew that had to have taken all of her courage to just go for what she wanted.

Which meant she'd truly desired him more than he'd first thought.

That in and of itself was one of the sexiest things about her. Aside from the fact she was brilliant and a master distiller, the woman knew what she wanted and went after it…in her personal and professional life.

"It's an impressive distillery," Antonio replied as he looked out over the rolling hills of Kentucky. "The samples I tried were great and just what I think we need to add to our restaurants. I'll be doing the exclusive tastings and will choose the best combination for us."

Most distillers would create a special batch for VIP clients or restaurateurs. Angel's Share was no different. To have an exclusive bourbon for Rodriguez establishments would be a win-win for both parties. Elise would get her label abroad and he would have something no one in Spain had gotten their hands on.

"And how is everything else going? I only traveled to Kentucky once many years ago. Beautiful part of the world."

"It is," Antonio agreed, not really in the mood for small talk with his father. "When I return home next month, I do have a few things I'd like to run by you."

There. He'd planted the seed for a talk. Although Antonio still had no clue what that talk would entail exactly, he was hoping for some eye-opening experience while he was in the States. He was a damn good businessman, he just didn't know where he wanted to invest his time or his money quite yet.

"Sounds serious. Is everything okay?"

"Everything is fine," he assured his father. "Just looking ahead to the future."

"Well, that sounds promising. Your mother and I

can't wait to turn over Rodriguez to the new generation. We're proud of you, *hijo*."

Damn it. He didn't want to feel guilty about pursuing his own plans, but he did. His parents had done absolutely everything for him and he was going to crush their dreams.

His father went on to tell him about some of the things that had happened since he left and how his mother was already booking trips to travel around the globe as soon as they handed over the reins. Antonio simply listened, because there wasn't much he could say and he couldn't get too excited about this transition because if he didn't have a solid plan, something tangible to cling to for his future, he would be stuck in a world he didn't love and didn't want.

He had too many passions, that was the problem. He loved to travel; he loved to meet new people and socialize, and he'd always been comfortable inserting himself into any situation. So staying locked down to one area, one business with many chains, seemed like a prison.

While he was damn proud of all his parents had accomplished, that wasn't his ultimate goal in life. For the past several years he'd done everything just as his parents wished. He didn't know another way without hurting them. Even though Paolo passed years ago, that was something none of them had recovered from. There was no recovery, there was only living a completely new chapter in life.

Grief had always been the driving force behind Antonio's actions. He was the only child left to make sure his parents had the happiness they deserved.

"Make sure to let me know how the exclusive tasting goes and what you decide on," his father said. "We trust your judgment."

"I'll call as soon as I've sealed a deal," he assured his father. "Talk to you then."

Antonio tapped the screen to hang up and stretched his legs out, crossing his ankles. He really had no plans today, though he should come up with something. Staying at his rental with just his thoughts regarding his home life and last night would only drive him mad.

Granted, last night hadn't been planned and today should have been his private tasting. But other events had unfolded and left him and Elise in a compromising position...literally.

He couldn't help but wonder how her day was going and if there was too much of a rift between the sisters. Delilah seemed pretty upset and angry with Elise.

Antonio didn't know how his next visit would go, but perhaps taking a drive to see the picturesque area he'd never been before would clear his mind. Maybe he'd even find another restaurant that intrigued him. As someone who grew up in that business, he was always looking for new foods or atmosphere or anything that kept customers coming back. He might not want to do that line of work for life, but he still admired what his parents had established.

Was that to be his destiny? Should he just take over the life his parents wanted him to, especially now that they were opening pubs as their last big venture before they retired?

Antonio had always prided himself on being in control and making his own way in life. Even though he worked for his parents, he'd never been given a handout. His parents had always instilled a work ethic in him and he'd started at the bottom within the company. They'd wanted him to learn every position so he could fully understand staffing and be more relatable when he took over.

Antonio came to his feet and grabbed his cell from the accent table. He definitely needed to get out, get some fresh air and go for a drive. Maybe then he would have a clearer understanding and could regain focus of the reason he came to the US to begin with. His night with Elise was clouding his mind. When he should be planning his future, all he could think about was the sexy vixen who had seduced him in a mostly innocent, yet demanding way. Then again, how could he not be stuck replaying their night over and over?

"I never said Antonio and I did anything."

Delilah rolled her eyes and snorted. "You can't lie to me, Elise. I know what I saw and that was definitely a morning-after kiss."

Elise resisted the urge to pace her office, though there was plenty of room and she desperately needed to get some energy out of her system. She'd known Delilah would come and talk to her once she got a free minute, but there was nothing Elise could say at this point that would make her sister any less angry.

They all knew there was a different set of rules to live by, considering they were living in this man's world. They had to be careful of every action that could impact this business they'd taken years to build.

Though Elise knew the anger was well placed, all of Delilah's emotions likely stemmed from hurt. Delilah didn't want that divorce, but she was too damn stubborn to say otherwise.

"What were you thinking?" Delilah demanded, then held her hand out. "No, don't answer that. I've seen him, so I know exactly what you were thinking. But this isn't like you. This is something Sara would do."

Elise threw her arms out and sighed. "Fine. I'm human. Happy now?"

Delilah's pale pink lips pursed as her eyes narrowed. "Well, at least you're not lying to me anymore. But seriously. How is this going to affect our working relationship with that family?"

Elise crossed the room to stand in front of her sister, then calmly reached for her hands.

"There's nothing to worry about," Elise assured her. "Antonio and I are adults. We already said anything that happened last night was to stay a secret and had nothing to do with our partnership."

Delilah's worry lines between her brows only deepened. "Partnership aside, what on earth? I mean, seriously. You just met the man and the emails before he arrived do not count. Emotionally, this has to be eating at you."

Not in the way Delilah might think. The only thing that bothered Elise was how much she still desired Antonio. Having him once, okay, she couldn't really be to blame for her actions at her moment of weakness. But still having that need? Those unfamiliar emotions were certainly new for her.

All she could blame this on was the lack of social life and she was still in the grieving process since losing Milly. Vulnerable emotions had to be the reason for acting so out of character.

Fine. Those were all solid excuses, but she was a grown-ass woman who could make her own decisions and shouldn't have to justify or apologize.

"I'd rather just move on and put this behind all of us." Elise released her sister's hands and took a step back. "We have the VIP tasting scheduled for tomorrow. Antonio enjoyed all of the samples he tried yesterday. I really think he's going to have a difficult time narrowing down his decisions with our exclusive bottles. Now, do you want to discuss the papers you were delivered?"

Delilah held Elise's stare and ultimately shook her head. "Not particularly."

"Fine." Elise knew her sister would talk when she was good and ready. "Back to the tastings. Everything will be set up by noon. Antonio is coming at one and with the amount of new pubs his family is opening, I can't imagine he will leave without an astronomical partnership."

"Perhaps you can convince him to sign up for more than one batch," Delilah suggested. "Apparently—"

"You guys."

Elise and Delilah both jerked their attention toward the doorway where Sara stood, her face pale and eyes wide. She had a folder in her hand and she not only shut the door behind her, she also flicked the lock into place.

"What is it?" Elise demanded, crossing to Sara. "You're trembling."

Without a word, Sara thrust the folder against Elise's chest. "I don't know what to believe anymore. I just... I can't... Why all the secrets?"

"Okay, whatever it is, we will get through this." Delilah put her arm around Sara's shoulder. "Come have a seat and tell us what happened."

Elise shot a glance to Delilah, who shrugged, clearly just as confused and concerned. Sara usually wasn't dramatic, so whatever contents she'd uncovered in that folder had to be something rather serious.

"I found that in Milly's basement." Sara took a seat and placed her hands on her lap. "The guy for the dumpster was running late, so I just went downstairs to start sorting and looking. You know that old safe she always told us was empty? Well, I went to move it and heard something inside. It took me forever, and ultimately a hammer, but I got it open and that was in there."

Elise rested a hip against her desk while Delilah took a seat in the chair next to Sara. All eyes locked on the closed mystery folder.

"What is this that you keep referring to?"

Sara pulled in a shaky breath. "Our adoption papers, birth certificates, and look at that photograph of us as babies with a woman who looks like Milly, but that's not her."

Delilah and Elise studied all of the contents, but focused on the yellow-edged photo. Who was the mystery woman?

"Look at all the countless messages and receipts from a private investigator all trying to locate us," Sara added.

"An investigator?" Dee asked. "Why did Milly have an investigator? And what do you mean by *us*?"

"Because she was looking for you guys and me,"

Sara explained. "Before she ever adopted us, she was looking specifically for three girls."

Elise shook her head, having no idea what her sister was talking about. "How is that possible? She didn't even know who we were until she adopted us."

With a quick flip of the folder that she took back from Elise, Sara started sorting through the stack of papers. "That's what she wanted everyone to think. But from all of the papers and documents in here, Milly Hawthorne is our biological aunt."

"What?" Delilah gasped. "That's not possible."

Elise stared at the papers, as if she could see everything all at once and figure out what Sara was trying to say.

"Our birth mother was Milly's sister." Sara pulled out several papers and held them up. "We all have different fathers, but we share the same mother...and I believe that's the woman in the photograph with us."

Elise really wished she'd taken an actual seat before that bomb was dropped into her life. Real sisters? How was that even possible when they were all so different physically? There had to be some mistake, but whatever Sara had read, she firmly believed it to be the truth.

Her focus darted back to the picture as she studied the woman she'd never known. Could this be her mother? Milly's sister? There was so much to process here.

"Let me see," Delilah demanded as she took the papers. "None of this makes sense. If we have the same birth mother, where is she and why did Milly have to come looking for us?"

Sara closed her eyes and sighed before she refocused

on the contents of the folder. She shuffled through once more and pulled up another paper.

"This is our biological mother's death certificate."

Death? They'd just supposedly found out who their birth mother was, one Elise still couldn't believe they shared, and now they discover she's no longer living? Were their lives condensed to this one folder? How could the history and all the answers they wanted be compiled into just these papers?

Elise's mind was spinning in way too many directions for her to keep up with. She wanted answers, but she really didn't know all the questions she wanted to ask.

"Her name was Carla Akers," Delilah stated as she stared at the paper. "We have an actual name to put to the woman we don't even remember."

"She died in prison," Sara murmured. "When she went to prison, that's when Milly started looking for us. We were in different foster homes because of the overload of caregivers. It's all in there. Everything."

Elise rounded her desk and wheeled her chair back to the other side to take a seat next to Sara. Papers, documents, photographs, and photocopies were passed around the trio. Shock settled in quickly, and Elise was only left with more questions than she had answers for.

And there was no one left to ask.

"Am I reading this right?" Elise asked as she glanced to her sisters. "Our mom and Milly were estranged sisters. That's why she hired the investigator to find us after Mom ended up going away."

What kind of life had she led that ultimately took her down a path of destruction? How could she and Milly have been so different? Moreover, how could their birth mother be so totally opposite from each of her girls?

None of them had ever dabbled in drugs, they'd never been arrested. The closest run-in any of them had with the law was when Delilah got a speeding ticket after she'd left her purse at a restaurant and was hauling ass back to get it.

But now, reading all of these damning truths they couldn't deny, it just seemed like too much. There were too many raw emotions, especially coming on the coattails of Milly's death. She wouldn't have all of these papers if this wasn't true. But why hadn't she told them any of this?

"I just don't understand all the whys," Sara whispered, tears clearly clogging her throat. "Why had she never told us we were actually related? I mean, maybe she was protecting us from our mother's harsh life, but to know we are actually sisters…"

Elise thought back to all the years they'd spent with Milly and how she had truly loved and cared for them as her own. How she'd raised them as true sisters and they'd really never known any different since they'd come to live with her when they'd been so little. Of course they didn't remember being anywhere else but Milly's house.

"I agree," Elise stated. "In her own way, she probably wanted to protect us from the truth about our birth mom. Do I wish she would have told us the truth? Yes. But at the same time, she had a sister who was an addict, according to the paperwork here and her prison record. Milly was doing the best she could with three kids. Milly didn't have to come looking for us and I think that shows the love from the start that she had."

There wasn't a doubt in Elise's mind that Milly had moved heaven and earth to find them. The woman had worked as a schoolteacher her entire life and then a yoga instructor for fun on the side. No doubt hiring an investigator took up most if not all of her savings.

Another burst of hurt struck Elise right in the chest. She missed that woman more than she ever thought possible to miss anyone. Would that gnawing ache and black hole ever be filled again?

"So what do we do now?" Delilah asked, her eyes brimming with unshed tears. "Do we pretend like we never saw this or do we try to get more answers?"

"Like what?" Sara asked.

Delilah sank back into her chair and glanced to both sisters before replying, "Find our biological fathers."

Eight

Antonio took a seat at the raw-edge table in the VIP tasting room. There were five tumblers before him, all with the Angel's Share logo etched into the thick glass. When he'd arrived earlier, he was greeted by an employee he hadn't met yet and was escorted into this room. He assumed Elise would be the one joining him, but after the other night, perhaps another sister would be taking her place.

Regardless, he was only here for a job so it didn't matter who showed up.

Which was partially a lie he kept repeating to himself. He wanted to see Elise again. He wanted to know if that sexual pull was still there or if she'd gotten out of his system. The only way to get that answer would be to see her face-to-face.

An entire day had passed without hearing from her or seeing her, so feelings and emotions weren't near as strong as they'd been when he'd left that cellar yesterday morning. The problem? All he'd thought about was what had transpired in the dark behind closed doors. Any other time he'd be thrilled to have one night, no strings, no regrets. But this night had been different in every way imaginable.

He should be amped up to find the perfect batch of exclusive bourbon for his family's restaurants…but he couldn't deny the fact he was much more on edge to see Elise. Ever since they walked out of the cellar, he'd continually replayed their night. As much as he had enjoyed the allure and seductive tone of being in the dark with such a dynamic woman, he'd felt robbed that he hadn't been able to fully see her. When the lights had finally flickered on, she'd been in such a hurry to dress, he hadn't been able to take in much…but it had been enough of a glimpse to make him crave more.

Well, damn. That answered his question. He still wanted her and he hadn't even seen her yet today.

Now, what was he supposed to do? She'd stressed their night was only a one-time thing, but how could she just flick off her emotions like that? She'd turned to fire in his arms and there was no way in hell she could just be done. He refused to believe someone as bold as Elise could just ignore this chemistry.

The door behind him opened and closed and he knew without turning around that Elise was going to be the one joining him today. Her soft sigh and floral perfume suddenly surrounded him. And he wished like hell she wasn't in the forefront of his mind, but she'd been there for two days now.

He was in some serious trouble with this one.

"Sorry I'm a few minutes late," she told him as she breezed by. "We had a slight staffing problem, but that's nothing you want or need to hear about."

As she came to stand on the other side of the table, Antonio noticed two things right off the bat about her. One, she was obviously frazzled and upset, which he highly doubted had anything to do with employees. And two, she was just as stunning and sexy as he remembered. Maybe more so, now that he'd had her.

Was it those glasses she pushed up on her nose? Or perhaps it was the way she'd pulled her vibrant red hair over one shoulder and let the waves fall down. He had no idea what this magnetic pull was or how the force continued to happen, but he did know he was having a hell of a time fighting it.

"I'm actually a pretty good listener," he told her, offering a smile.

She reached into the glass cabinet behind her and started pulling out five different bottles, all with different colored labels with a variety of names and numbers on them. At any other time he'd be thrilled to have this opportunity, but his hormones and this woman were trumping common sense and business right now.

"Yes, well, you're not here to play my shrink or sounding board," she retorted as she carefully sat one bottle by each glass. "You're here to choose the perfect bourbon to be sold exclusively for Rodriguez restaurants."

"I can do both."

He reached forward and took her hand before he could

stop himself. Her eyes darted to his in an instant…and there it was. That fire he'd wondered if she'd been able to extinguish obviously still burned below the surface. No doubt she was trying to compartmentalize everything, but in a short time he already could read her body language.

The flare of her lids, the swift intake of breath, that quick yet subtle way she pursed her lips. The woman had become much too easy for him to read in too short a time.

"We need to focus," she murmured, staring back at him.

"I'm focused." He slid his thumb back and forth over the pulse on her wrist, a pulse that had kicked up. "Don't act like you're not thinking about it."

"Thinking about it and acting on it are two totally different things." Her eyes darted down to where his dark hand circled her wrist. "We can't do anything but put that night behind us."

He released her, only because he didn't want to come across as a complete jerk, but she wasn't unaffected. She wanted more with just the same amount of ache and need that he had.

"And how do you do that, exactly?" he asked. "Turn off desires so easily?"

She eased her hand away and shifted her gaze back to his. "Nothing about me is turned off when it comes to you," she corrected. "But I have a job to do and so do you. So that's what we should be doing."

Elise picked up the first bottle and started explaining what went into this particular batch and how this would be different from the others. As she poured, he didn't miss the way her hand shook slightly. Maybe others wouldn't notice that, but he'd fine-tuned her actions and this was completely out of the ordinary.

Once she sat the bottle down, Antonio eased his chair back, came to his feet, and circled the table. Elise jerked back and turned to face him.

"What are you doing?" she asked, her eyes wide as she took a step back.

"We aren't going any further until you tell me what has you so upset."

She stared at him another moment, then blinked and tried to look away. "I don't know what you mean."

Unable to help himself, he reached up and framed her face. He wanted to see those eyes, he wanted to see her, and he wanted her to see him. Damn it. What was he doing? He should be taking drinks and making notes, then placing a hell of an order.

But he'd be a complete ass if he ignored the fact Elise was hurting. Something had jarred her and he didn't think it had anything to do with him. Sure, their night had been amazing, but she wasn't this rattled when he'd left.

"And you think because we shared a night that you can read me so well?" she asked. "We agreed that was it, remember?"

Antonio slid his thumb over her bottom lip. "I never agreed to any such thing, but that's a discussion for later. You're upset."

There went those pursed lips again, but only for a second. She closed her eyes and blew out a breath before looking back up at him.

"There's some family stuff I'm dealing with that is private," she admitted. "I'm a little off today, but that won't hinder our time. I'm sorry you even noticed and pulled you away from what you came here to do."

"Will you stop?" he demanded. "You don't have to be Miss Professional right now. I know you're human, too. I also know you better than your other customers, if I'm assuming correctly. I can listen if you need to talk or we can reschedule. I don't want to cause more stress."

She opened her mouth, closed it, then shook her head. Antonio dropped his hands, but didn't step back. There was no way any business or work should take priority over what was happening to her internally.

"This is what I need to be doing and this is where I'm in control." She offered him a small smile. "I'm sure someone like you can understand control."

As much as he wanted to press, he had no right to, and if she wanted to dive into business, then that was what they'd do. He'd address their personal time later…because he was definitely not done with that conversation.

Elise waited as Antonio surveyed all the samples he'd had. He made notes on the paper provided by her team so the customers could rate the spirits in various categories and get the best bottle for their needs.

But her mind was on that damn folder in her office. There was so much to do with the gala coming up, their regular accounts and new ones coming in, on top of the public visiting each day, plus cleaning up at Milly's house…now her sisters were contemplating tracking down their biological fathers.

All of this chaos made that one-night stand look like a vacation. She wouldn't mind another vacation to take her mind off all this, but she had too much going on to get sidetracked now.

Although if she was guessing correctly, she'd say Antonio was more than ready for another go-round. How the hell was she supposed to avoid temptation a second time?

"Well, what are you thinking?" she asked, mainly because the silence only made her start living in her own thoughts. "You seemed to really enjoy the gold and blue labels."

He nodded. "I really enjoyed all of them, but I want to narrow this down."

Elise crossed her arms and smiled. "You're used to just taking anything you want, I know. Must be tough to have to give something up."

His eyes met hers and that dark stare seemed even more arousing than before.

"I wouldn't know," he replied. "I've never given up anything that I've wanted."

One shiver after another raced through her. Of course he hadn't. She should have known that and she also should have known that anything she said could be construed as sexual. The awareness was too high and she knew this was not a level playing field. She didn't have experience like this with all the banter and the one-night stand. Someone like Antonio had skills she couldn't even imagine.

And she was falling way too easily into his web. The problem? She didn't necessarily want him to untangle her. Part of her enjoyed this thrilling stranger giving her memories to last a lifetime.

"Focus on the batches," she told him. No matter how much she would love to enter into a hot, temporary fling, she was still a professional in a man's world and she had to live by different standards. She didn't make the damn rules, but for now she had to live by them.

Angel's Share's reputation was everything to her and her sisters. This was all they had and she would not screw it up by letting a sexy Spaniard passing through get into her mind and jumble her priorities.

"Fine." He came to his feet and nodded. "We'll carry all of them and I'll make sure different batches are only available at various locations. Problem solved and everyone is happy."

Elise wanted to squeal with delight. They'd officially landed their first global account and not just a small one, either. She couldn't wait to tell Delilah and Sara. They all needed something good to focus on, especially now.

"All right, let's discuss us."

Antonio's bold statement pulled her attention back to the man who now leaned across the table, holding her steady with that dark, piercing gaze.

This is where things could get even trickier than they had been. The fine line she had to walk now would have to be done slowly or she'd fall off, and no matter which side she landed on, she'd get hurt.

"There is no us," she told him. "There was a night of intimacy when we were both vulnerable and now there is a working relationship. Thank you, by the way. Your contract will be drawn up by the end of the day and ready to sign and then you can travel across the country all you want, but know you got the best liquor right here in Benton Springs."

The muscle in his jaw clenched, his nostrils flared and she couldn't tell if he was aroused, frustrated, angry, or all of the above. Well, join the club because she was on her own emotional roller coaster.

"Tell me you haven't thought of that night every minute since we walked out," he countered. "Tell me you can just ignore the fact you still want me. Go ahead and try to lie to me, but you can't lie to yourself. I see it in your eyes, Elise. You're a passionate woman and you need an outlet."

Elise took in every word, and damn him for being so dead on with his assessment. How could he already know her so well? The fact that he could read her in such a short time should be a glaring red flag as to how many women he'd seduced and given this same speech to.

"Are you offering yourself up as my outlet?" she retorted.

Antonio shrugged. "If you want to use me, then so be it."

"How noble and self-sacrificing of you." Elise tucked her hair behind her ears and adjusted her glasses. She'd been wearing her hair down more since Antonio came into her life. "I'll worry about my passions and wants. I'm setting you free."

That wicked grin she'd seen before spread across his face, and a slow curl of arousal spiraled through her.

"Is that right?" Antonio eased back and stood straight up. "Your loss."

Yes, she was very well aware of that, but that was the choice she'd have to live with and she fully believed she was making the right one. She had to go with common sense over any wants or temporary needs.

"We can send the contract to you or you are welcome

to wait around to sign," she told him, focusing solely on business now.

Something came over his face and that chiseled jawline seemed even more pronounced, his shoulders even more broad and squared, his defiant chin tipped as he stared back at her.

"Send it over," he told her. "I have some work I can be doing from home for the next few days."

"Consider it done," she assured him as she clasped her hands in front of her. Perhaps she did that for fear of reaching out to what she'd just shoved away.

Damn it. Why did she have to be a confused woman? Why did she have to put her career and family over her own selfish needs? Why couldn't she have it all? Who wrote these damn rules?

"This will be a very prosperous venture for the both of us," he told her.

Before she could comment or even think of what to say, Antonio offered her a nod and excused himself from the VIP tasting room. His long stride ate up the distance to the door and then he was gone, closing the door behind him. Elise stared at the closed door, knowing she'd made the best decision. If they'd met under different circumstances, maybe she could explore more.

But Antonio wasn't a *more* type of man. He was nothing but a fleeting distraction and she'd had her fun. Now she had to work and focus on this mess that had just blown up in her personal life…and forget that night with the Spaniard.

Nine

"Are you girls ready?" Delilah asked, shielding her face from the sun.

Elise stared up at the two-story old farmhouse in the middle of the Hawthorne property. She'd grown up here, she didn't remember any other home or anyone else who had ever cared for or loved her. But being back here with her sisters, knowing Milly wasn't on the other side of those doors, now more than ever Elise wanted her inside so she could ask all the questions this folder had produced.

All Elise could hope for was that they could find what they were looking for and then they'd have to deal with whatever truth they were left with.

"We won't find what we need out here." Sara sighed. "Let's head in and see what we can do."

Elise swallowed the lump in her throat as they headed toward the front door. Milly would have already put out her seasonal wreath and decorated her porch. There would be a plate of freshly baked cookies in the kitchen and each girl would be welcomed with a tight hug that would make them feel like they were home.

Death might have robbed them of the woman, but it couldn't rob them of the lifetime of memories they'd created together.

"Should we divide and conquer?" Elise asked.

Delilah turned her key into the lock and eased the door open. "That might be best. I'm afraid if we all stay in the same room, the only thing we'd get done is crying and reminiscing."

Sara laughed. "I'll cry anyway. But I really hope we can find some answers in here."

"I hope so, but if they weren't in that safe or that folder, I don't know where else they could be," Elise added. "This is all still so…overwhelming."

Elise followed her sisters inside and couldn't help but smile. The place still smelled like flowers. Milly always had fresh flowers from her gardens in various rooms. The grand staircase in the foyer led up to the bedrooms, so Elise started toward the steps.

"I'll go up," she offered. "Someone can take the basement and someone can take this floor. I'll be in Milly's room. I know we need to clean out the whole house, but we're in agreement that we're looking for answers first, right?"

Both Delilah and Sara nodded.

"I'm in no hurry to sell this place," Sara stated.

"I'm not, either," Delilah agreed.

Elise bit the inside of her lip as emotions already threatened to overwhelm her. She had to power through. Mourning was a natural process, but there was so much to be done between going through and deciding what to keep or toss, and digging for more of the truth from their pasts.

"Then why are we selling?" Elise asked. "Nobody said we had to."

"Well, we all have our own places now," Delilah stated. "I mean, I guess I could stop renting that house and move back in here. I wasn't sure where to go once my divorce goes through."

Elise hoped the divorce didn't go through, but that was definitely a conversation for another time. There was too much other baggage to unpack today.

"Let's not make any major decisions just yet," Elise suggested. "We don't need the money from the sale, and one of us might just need this place. Let's hold on to it and just focus on finding out about our fathers."

"Is that what you want?" Delilah asked. "To find out who your father was?"

Elise had gone back and forth, wanting to know, but also perfectly content with having Milly as everything she'd ever needed. But did her birth father even know her biological mother had been pregnant? Maybe he didn't know he had a child out in the world, and what if he'd been looking for her?

Or what if he hadn't cared? What if he was just as bad off as her mother, or had his own family by now and was settled in his ways? She wouldn't want to disrupt that.

"I honestly don't know what I want," Elise replied. "I'm just so confused lately."

"Are we talking the fact Milly was our aunt or the fact you're still hung up on Antonio?"

Elise jerked and blinked at her sister's accusation. Pulling in a deep breath, Elise gripped the banister on the staircase and eased down onto a step.

"All of it," she admitted.

"Oh no." Delilah leaned against the doorway that led into the living room and crossed her arms over her chest. "You cannot get attached to a one-night stand. I married mine and look how that has turned out."

"You and Camden are perfect together," Sara chimed in. "But we don't have time to argue about that right now."

Delilah opened her mouth, no doubt to argue, but Elise slid her own troubles in.

"I'm not used to flings, okay? And he seemed caring, like he really worried how I was doing and the impact that night had on you guys with me."

"Men are simple creatures," Delilah told her. "They get what they want and then they move on. Don't read any more into it than that."

Sara rolled her eyes and came to sit beside Elise. "Don't listen to her. She's jaded. If you want to explore something with Antonio, go ahead. No one is stopping you. Do we think it's smart for the business? Probably not, but just think how romantic this could be."

Elise had no clue how her two sisters could be so polar opposite in their take on relationships. In all reality, she could see both of their points of view, which was why she was having such a difficult time figuring out where her head should be.

There was no good answer to be had right now and they each had other things they needed to be doing.

She came to her feet and turned to head upstairs. "I'll be in Milly's room. Let me know if you guys find anything."

The last thing she wanted was to get into a bickering feud regarding Delilah's upcoming divorce or to rehash her night with Antonio. She'd pushed him away from her personal life and neatly compartmentalized him in the professional pocket right where he should be...and where he would stay.

That didn't mean she couldn't keep reminiscing, though. She had all of those memories to last her a lifetime and one day she might actually find someone who loves her and wants to settle down...but would he make her feel so passionate? Would he make her feel so reckless and out of control she didn't care to vulnerably expose herself?

Honestly, she was so married to her career and that distillery, she couldn't imagine a man putting up with being second in her life. So Antonio was pushed aside just like she thought he should be.

Unfortunately, she still wanted him. He'd been right when he said he couldn't just turn off those emotions. She couldn't, either. But apparently, she was a damn good liar.

She didn't much worry for him, though. Antonio would move on to another town, another woman. That was his nature and he likely would forget her as soon as he found his next conquest.

Elise should be thankful her one-night stand was with someone not from around here. Once Antonio was gone for good, the temptation would remove itself and she wouldn't have such a hard time.

She sank down on the edge of Milly's bed and stared around the room. Milly was from the generation who saved everything, so each room would take so much time. Which was fine. At least Elise had something to do with her evenings instead of wonder what Antonio was doing…or whom he was doing it with.

Elise could only do so much and she had to focus on the house and finding answers. At least she could control that, somewhat. Keeping her mind on her sisters and their even deeper bond now was what Elise needed to focus on.

She started working with the narrow closet and the clothes. Each piece held a special memory, not to mention Milly's signature floral perfume. The boxes on the top shelf held old photographs, and before long Elise found herself sitting in the middle of the floor surrounded by pictures of birthdays and Christmases past. As she held a photo in one hand and one of Milly's favorite shirts in the other, Elise let out all of her emotions she'd been bottling up. The loss was too much for her to carry any longer, so she left everything right here where she sat. All of her anger, her emptiness, her sadness, her pain…all of it came out.

Finally.

Now, if she could only rid herself of those emotions for Antonio Rodriguez.

"You look as spent as I feel."

Elise looked up from her pile of photographs. Delilah stood in the doorway, her arms crossed, her eyes red-rimmed.

"This is much more difficult than I thought it would be," Elise admitted. "I'm not sure how far I got. Maybe this first day was just meant for an emotional cleanse."

"If that's the case, I'm pretty cleansed," her sister stated, stepping into the room.

Delilah carefully tiptoed around the memorabilia spread all over the rug and eased down to sit on her knees. Sara popped into the doorway right then as well and had a tissue up to her nose.

"Is this the pity party?" she asked. "Room for one more?"

"Come on in," Elise welcomed. "Move things out of the way for a seat if you'd like. I pretty much made a mess in here as I took a long, painful stroll down memory lane."

Sara circled the bed and ended up climbing on top of it just behind where Elise rested her back.

"This is like when we'd all pile in here when it would storm," Delilah laughed. "Milly always said she needed a bigger bed if we kept growing, but then we grew out of being scared."

"You know she loved every time we came in here." Sara wiped her eyes with a tissue. "She just didn't want to admit it because she was teaching us independence."

"There was nobody like her." Elise shifted her legs and scooped up a stack of photos. "There's so much love in all of these. It makes me think we should just leave things be and not go searching. We had a great life and I just... I don't know."

Sara started toying with Elise's hair. "I totally get it.

I wondered the same thing. If Milly wanted us to know, then she would have told us. But she kept this truth from us for a reason and perhaps she was protecting us."

Delilah shook her head. "I want to know. I need to know. With all the upheaval in my life right now, I want some control and searching for my biological father is the only thing I can think of outside of work."

Elise glanced around to the mess she'd made and still had no clear picture of what she wanted to do. Each sister had to make her own choice as to what was right for her and they all likely wouldn't agree, but Elise knew one thing…they would all support each other no matter what.

"Are we done for the night?" she asked. "I'm exhausted and I'm not sure I can do this anymore today."

"Let's head out." Delilah came to her feet and reached her hand down to Elise. "If you all want to come back tomorrow, let me know. I'm fine taking a break, but I'm also fine doing this again."

Once on her feet, Elise shrugged. "I'll feel better once I get some rest. I will be here tomorrow for a few hours at least. Maybe if we do a little each day, we can find some answers or at least feel some sense of closure. Do either of you care if I take a few of these photos home?"

"Go for it," Delilah said. "I'm sure we'll all be taking some."

Once they all agreed to come back tomorrow afternoon, Elise took the precious photos and went to her car. The sun had long since set and she knew it was late. As tired as she was, she also knew that once she went home, she would be too wound up to sleep. There was simply too much rolling through her head. There were too many memories that had assaulted her over these past few hours. Her emotions were raw, like she'd just opened up her heart to all of the pain surrounding the loss.

From the overhead light in her car, Elise stared down at one of the photographs. This one was Milly with three little girls piled on her lap. Their smiles were all so wide, so happy. Elise didn't remember this day, but she'd seen this picture before. Milly had said this was the day the adoption had been finalized when the girls were toddlers. The day they truly became a family.

But they were already blood related well before then.

Elise sat the stack of images on the passenger seat and started up her car. She wasn't ready to go home and sit in the quiet with her thoughts and her worries. She needed something, needed someone.

So she pulled out of the drive and headed in the opposite direction of her house.

Ten

The soft knock at the front door had Antonio glancing up from his laptop. Who was stopping by so late? He only knew a few people and certainly hadn't told anyone where he was staying while in town.

He ignored it, thinking maybe just kids were playing pranks.

As he shifted his attention back to the spreadsheet he'd been drafting, the knock came again, a little louder this time.

Antonio pushed off the bar stool and moved around the kitchen island where he'd set up a makeshift office. He padded barefoot down the long hallway toward the front of the house and realized he only had on a pair of shorts and nothing else.

But the moment he glanced through the peephole,

he realized he didn't need to be wearing anything more. The woman on the other side had already been all over him.

With a quick flick of the dead bolt, Antonio opened the door. He was about to blurt out some witty comment or something sexual to get their banter started, but he took one look at her and realized this wasn't the time.

Her eyes traveled over his body, then up to meet his gaze and that was when her eyes welled up with tears and she thrust herself into his arms. Antonio widened his stance to catch her as his arms came around her waist.

He had no clue what made her come here or what happened, but she had vulnerability written all over her. This was a bad, bad combo and he'd have to really pull up his willpower to resist her.

Still holding on tight, Antonio walked backward just enough to close the door. He reached behind her and slid the lock back into place. Elise buried her face in his neck and trembled against him. Whatever she'd gone through tonight had her seriously rattled.

"Are you hurt?" he asked.

"Just my heart," she whispered back.

Then she eased back and framed his face with her hands. She stared at him with unshed tears in her eyes and Antonio really wanted to harden himself against this woman. She'd made it clear their night was over and there would be no more. He didn't want to give in to her obvious, yet silent, request. He didn't want to be someone's regret in the morning.

"This is a bad idea," he told her. "Why don't you let me take you home?"

"If I wanted to go home, I'd be there," she murmured, her eyes dipping to his mouth. "But I need you. I need to forget reality for a little while. I'm not asking for anything else."

His body stirred to life and Antonio was trying to remember why this was a bad idea. She clearly knew what she was here for, she knew there was nothing else between them.

But she was vulnerable. Maybe too vulnerable to be making a rational decision.

"I know what I'm doing," she stated, as if she could read his thoughts. "Are you going to help me forget or not?"

Oh hell. He was fighting a losing battle. He knew it the moment he'd seen her standing on the other side of his door. She felt too damn good in his arms and she was on the verge of begging. Who was he to deny a distressed damsel?

Antonio lifted her into his arms. He had never been one for theatrics or romance, but he didn't even think about what he was doing. With one hand behind her back and the other behind her knees, he carried her to the bedroom.

This was nothing more than him helping her…at least that was what he told himself. In all honesty, he was a selfish man who wanted everything she was offering. But she was hurting, that much was apparent. So he had to be attentive and nurturing. He had to let her take total control here.

Elise's fingers threaded through his hair and slid along his neck. Having her here was a total surprise, but he wasn't in the mood to ask questions. She'd come here for only one thing and he was more than ready to let her use his body.

As soon as he stepped into the room, he sat her on her feet at the foot of the bed. The light from the hallway flooded in and the full moon provided a soft glow through the double doors leading to the patio.

Antonio slid his fingertip beneath her chin and tipped her head up to look into her eyes. "You're sure?"

Elise flattened her hands on his chest and eased him back. Holding his gaze, she reached for the hem of her shirt and pulled it up and over her head. She tossed it aside without breaking her stare and then reached for the button on her jeans.

Antonio continued to watch as she rid herself of each and every article of clothing, and then stood before him completely bare. The light from the hall and the patio slashed across her body in various hues…he'd never seen a more stunning sight.

He'd known from feeling every inch of that skin just how gorgeous and curvy she was. But seeing her brought both of them to a whole new playing field. This wasn't like the other night. Oh, they might both be saying this was temporary, and it was, but the night they spent in the castle was spontaneous. Tonight…well, Elise had planned to come here with one goal in mind.

Still keeping her wide eyes locked on to his, she sank onto the bed and scooted until she was in the middle. She leaned back on her elbows and lifted her knees, silently inviting him to join her.

Damn it. Any other woman he would've been undressed and ready to go. But this woman… He wanted to see her, all of her. He wanted to take in each dip and curve.

"How long are you going to make me wait?" she asked.

Antonio remembered he'd vowed to give her the control and she clearly was more than ready for him. He quickly shed his shorts, went into the adjoining bath for protection, and came back in to stand beside the bed.

He looked down at her one last time before placing one knee on the comforter and crawling over her body to straddle her. With a knee on either side of her hips, Antonio placed one hand beside her head and used the fingertips of the other to trail down that smooth, creamy skin between her breasts.

"I can't stop looking at you," he admitted.

A slow smile spread across her face and he'd so much rather that and the passion in her eyes than the vulnerable, hopeless feeling she'd appeared with when he'd first opened his door.

"I was robbed of the chance the other night and only had my imagination to go on since then."

Her brows quirked. "Been thinking about that, have you?"

He realized his mistake in admitting she'd been on his mind. How could he keep their fling isolated to one night, and now two, when she took up way too much real estate in his mind?

"Maybe I have," he whispered, his hand traveling down to her inner thigh. "I'd bet when you're in bed at night, you've been thinking, too."

He slid his fingertip just over her core and she arched her back, letting out a low moan. That was it. That was what he wanted from her. He wanted to make her forget whatever demon chased her here. He wanted her to only have him, have this, on her mind for the rest of the night.

Antonio was having a difficult time taking this slow, but she changed everything when she reached up, wrapped her arms around his neck and pulled his mouth to hers. She opened for him, grazing her tongue against his as she shifted beneath him. Before he knew it, he'd settled perfectly between her spread thighs and she'd locked her ankles behind his back.

"I need you," she panted against his lips. "Now."

He'd never found dominating women sexy before, but Elise had a way that made him want to give up everything and just let her go. She had total control here and that was the biggest turn-on.

Antonio pushed into her, which elicited another cry from her as she reached up and gripped his shoulders. She tipped her hips and started working her sweet body against his. He kept the majority of his weight off her, using his hand to stay propped up. But he shifted and gripped the back of her thigh with his free hand, needing to be even closer, even deeper.

Elise's short nails bit into his skin, her head thrashed from side to side. He could watch her all night, but he wouldn't last...neither would she. Right now this was all about forgetting. Maybe in the morning they could explore even more.

Because she wasn't going anywhere tonight.

When she worked her hips even faster, Antonio eased down and kissed just below her ear, then along her jawline, and finally landed on her lips. She moaned into his mouth and Antonio wasn't sure how much longer he could hold back. When she panted like that, clutched onto him, jerked against him…she utterly consumed him and he still couldn't get enough.

Finally, her body stilled and she arched back even farther, breaking the kiss. Antonio couldn't tear his eyes away from the passionate woman beneath him. She'd shown up here needing him, but maybe it was he who needed her.

When she looked up at him with those expressive eyes and smiled, something flipped in his chest…which was ridiculous. That was just desire and want. Nothing more.

He jerked his hips as she whispered, urging him on. She pumped even harder against him until he completely shattered and let the climax consume him. He leaned down and rested his forehead against hers, trying to catch his breath, trying to figure out how to keep her here because he still wasn't done.

One time hadn't been enough. Two times hadn't been enough. At what point would he be willing and ready to let her go?

Elise lay in the crook of Antonio's arm, wondering how long she could stay wrapped in his embrace and in his bed. She'd come here looking for an escape, and she'd certainly found just that, but he'd been even more. There had been a gentleness to him that she hadn't expected. She'd assumed he'd open the door and she'd proposition him and they'd have frantic sex right in his entryway.

But no. He'd carried her to his bedroom like she was a prize he'd been waiting on.

She shouldn't let herself get giddy or read any more into this than what it was. All they had between them was just sex...and a working relationship. He wasn't going to fall madly in love with her and be by her side during all the difficult times. He didn't even live in this country, for pity's sake. So any form of emotional attachment was only asking for heartache.

As much as she wanted to remain right here, Elise couldn't let herself take more from Antonio. She'd gotten what she needed, a break from reality. She'd been so depleted after leaving Milly's she just had to have some sort of distraction and outlet. There was nothing more for her here.

Elise sat up and swung her legs over the side of the bed.

"Where are you going?"

Glancing over her shoulder, her heart flipped at the sight of Antonio. All of that dark skin glowing in the moonlight, his hair all messed from her fingers, and those heavy lids half shielding dark eyes as they stared up at her.

"Home."

Before she could come to her feet, his arm snaked around her waist and eased her back.

"Stay."

His lips grazed the small of her back, sending a shiver throughout her body. She closed her eyes, trying to hold on to the moment because all of this was fleeting and she had to lock in this intimate memory.

Oh, how she wanted to stay. But making that bold decision wasn't smart. If she stayed, they would be taking this from just physical to something more...at least she would. She made attachments, she'd never been one to have flings and she had a sinking feeling she was already getting too involved with this man.

"I should go," she countered.

Another kiss on her back, this one higher. Then another, and another. Finally, he reached her neck. Easing her hair aside and flipping it over one shoulder, he feathered his lips along that exposed skin.

"You should stay."

His hands came around from behind and captured her breasts. Elise dropped her head back against his shoulder and knew she was fighting a losing battle.

"I'm not done with you," he growled against her ear. "And we both know you don't want to go anywhere."

No, she didn't. And she wasn't.

Antonio slid one hand down her torso toward her core and Elise instinctively spread her thighs. The moment he touched her, she couldn't stop the cry of passion. He already knew her body so well and had spoiled her for anyone else.

"That's it," he murmured as he worked his hands all over her body. "Don't hold back."

As if she could. She had no clue how he managed to turn her on so fast and had her so achy in a matter of seconds. She started to think she was fighting a losing battle, but quickly realized she wasn't losing anything.

Elise let the euphoria take over, she let Antonio have his way as he selflessly pleasured her. And when her body peaked, he murmured something in Spanish in her ear. She had no clue what he was saying, but that accent, that husky voice, was sexy as hell.

The moment she stopped trembling, Antonio shifted

behind her and turned her in his arms. Elise came up to her knees, straddling his lap. She hovered over him and looped her arms around his neck.

"I guess I'll stay."

She smiled and eased her body down to join them. Antonio gripped her backside and worked his hands in a magnificent way that had her body already humming once again. His mouth found one nipple and Elise had to hold tight to his broad shoulders to remain in place. He totally consumed her and she wouldn't have it any other way.

She moved fast, harder, needing another release, and just as her body started climbing once again, Antonio released her breast and captured her mouth. His body tightened beneath hers as she let herself go. Strong hands covered her back, holding her even closer to that strong, hard chest.

The crest seemed to last longer this time, much more intense than ever before.

And when they both came down, Antonio cradled her in his arms, covered her with his blankets, and kissed her forehead before dozing off.

Elise lay there in the glow of the moonlight, wondering how she was ever supposed to let this man walk out of her life and go back to just a working relationship.

Eleven

The robust aroma of coffee pulled Antonio from his sleep. He blinked against the sunshine streaming in through the patio doors. He would have thought he dreamed of having Elise multiple times in this bed if not for his sore body and the rumpled sheets beside him.

She'd stayed. He didn't know why that had been so important to him, but he heard her bustling around in the kitchen and cursing beneath her breath. She shouldn't be so adorable, but he couldn't help but smile.

His mother would love her.

Antonio stilled. Where the hell had that thought come from? He'd only met Elise in person days ago and was already thinking about his mother and her meeting? That was a big *hell no*. There was nothing more here than a fling and two people who needed to distance themselves from reality. That was all this ever could be.

Before he could get out of bed, Elise came back in holding two mugs of coffee.

"I assume you like it black?" she asked, then stopped in her tracks. "Or maybe not at all. I have no idea."

Ah, now a little bit of insecurity crept up. She wasn't acting so insecure last night when she showed up at his door. That was the bold, take-charge Elise. The woman who stood before him was having doubts and that was the last thing he wanted.

"Black is perfect," he told her, reaching for the mug.

She handed it over and he used his free hand to curl around her hip. She'd put on her T-shirt and underwear, but he could tell she hadn't bothered with a bra. Maybe she wasn't as conflicted as he'd thought.

"I'm surprised you didn't run when you woke up."

She offered a soft smile and shrugged. "I thought about it. I've never spent the night with a man I wasn't in a relationship with, so I wasn't sure what the protocol was. Especially considering our unique situation."

He sat his mug on the nightstand, took hers from her and did the same, before urging her down to sit on the edge of the bed.

"There are no rules here, Elise. We both obviously have turmoil in our personal lives. There's nothing wrong with finding an outlet for escape."

Her green eyes seemed even more vibrant this morning than he'd seen before. Though they were still a little puffy from whatever had upset her before she arrived.

Do not get involved. Do. Not. Do. It.

"Want to tell me what had you showing up at my door so late?"

He couldn't help himself. He wanted to know what

had happened to make her do a complete one-eighty from the last time he'd spoken with her. She'd been adamant they keep this relationship completely business. She wasn't even entertaining flirting...yet she'd spent the night in his bed.

Elise's eyes darted away and she pulled in a shaky breath. Antonio rested his hand on her bare thigh. Having this conversation while he was completely naked and she wasn't far from it was teetering extremely close to relationship status and deeper than he wanted to go.

Damn it, though. There was something about seeing her hurting that didn't sit well with him. He wanted to see the passionate, smiling woman who had all the confidence in the world...and she was still in there. He just had to pull that side back out.

"My sisters and I were at Milly's house yesterday," she finally stated, turning her attention back to him. "There's just so many memories left in that house."

"That has to be tough."

He couldn't imagine losing the foundation of his life. His parents had done everything to provide for him, they had made him the successful, determined man he was today. Which is why the guilt was so all-consuming and damn near crippling. He had to be honest, though. If nothing else, his parents had always demanded respect and honesty so there was no dodging this conversation.

Elise reached for her mug and took a sip of coffee before setting it back on the nightstand. He had no idea what to make of the fact she chose to turn to him when she was so upset. There had to be more than sex for her. She'd stated more than once that she didn't do flings, but they were sure as hell excelling at just that.

"How did Milly pass?" he asked.

"She had a stroke in her sleep." Elise slid her finger over his hand on her thigh and started drawing a pattern. "I should be glad she didn't know it was coming or wasn't in pain. But I'm selfish and I want her here. I have so many questions for her and after what we discovered..."

Antonio waited, but she stopped. He gave her thigh a gentle squeeze. "What did you find out?"

She pursed her lips and shook her head. "We decided not to tell anyone, but it's something that's changed all of us forever."

Disappointment hit him harder than it should have. There was no reason for him to care about her personal life. There was nothing he could do to help and he wasn't staying in town long enough to get involved.

Yet, he was a little upset she felt she couldn't confide in him. Who did she have besides her sisters? Who would she have turned to last night had he not been here? The idea of Elise turning to another man did not sit well with him. He didn't know why, there was no logical explanation, but he couldn't help how he felt.

Likely he was just too damn confused between his own life, which was up in the air, and the unexpected spin his world took when he met Elise. He'd told himself not to enter into any flings while here on work, but that was well before he'd been locked in a castle cellar with a vixen.

"My parents are expecting me to take over their family business in the next couple years."

He found himself opening up and he certainly hadn't

planned to. But Elise was too easy to talk to and he wanted her to feel comfortable with him.

"That's actually the last thing I want," he admitted. "I love them, I love the empire they've built, but it's not the life I want to live."

Elise's eyes widened. "Oh wow. What do they say about that?"

Antonio shook his head and sighed. "Haven't told them yet. I was hoping to use this trip and some distance to figure out what I want to say and really where I want to go. I just know being married to a business and having to nurture it until I retire sounds like a bore."

She let out a soft sigh. "That's why I love being in business. I need a commitment and since I don't have any relationships, Angel's Share is all I have."

And that was just one way he'd found their differences. He didn't know why he was so restless, nothing in his past created that line of thinking. Quite the opposite, in fact. Family dynamics and solidarity had been ingrained into him since birth, even more so since the loss of his brother. But this was just not a legacy he wanted to carry on himself.

"When are you going to talk to your parents?" she asked.

"When I talked to my *padre* the other day, I mentioned enough to let him know we needed to talk about the future and the takeover. I don't want to blindside them."

Elise turned his hand over and laced their fingers together as she offered him the sweetest smile. And there went that flip in his chest again. He refused to believe his heart was getting involved. He'd never let that happen in his life, let alone with a woman he'd only known a few days.

"You don't want to disappoint them," she countered.

Antonio swallowed. "That, too."

"I can't imagine they'd be upset with whatever you decide. They love you and while I don't know them, I bet they want to see you happy."

He couldn't help but smile. "I don't doubt that's all they want, but if I don't take over, then who will? I'm all they have now since Paolo is gone."

"How did he die?" Her hand tightened slightly as she shifted a little closer to him.

"Paolo was four minutes older than me," he heard himself saying. "He was the best oldest brother, and I always reminded him he was older. We had the best childhood and did everything together, but he passed when we were thirteen from meningitis. Knowing my parents are looking to me as the next generation of all they've accomplished...it's overwhelming at times."

Damn it. He hated that he sounded like a jerk.

"I don't mean to be ungrateful," he went on. "There's nothing I wouldn't do for my mom and dad, but this wouldn't be fair to any of us if they handed the businesses over to someone who didn't want to be in that position. I keep hoping for a happy medium...which is why our inevitable conversation has to happen sooner rather than later."

"I think if you are completely honest with them, the three of you can find a solution," she offered. "Did you ever think they just assume they are doing you a favor? Maybe they think this is something you've been wanting. If you don't tell them your real feelings, they can't help you."

Antonio slid his other hand over their joined hands. "You're pretty damn smart. Have you ever thought of being a parent? Or do you even want a family?"

Well, hell. Why did he ask that? With every personal question, he dug himself deeper and deeper into her life. Pretty soon, he wasn't going to be able to see the top of this hole he'd dug for himself and there would be no way out.

The odd thing? He wasn't panicking about this. Not yet anyway. He enjoyed his time with Elise. There was something calming about her, something that seemed to temporarily fill a void he hadn't known he'd had.

Being here was good for him. When he left, he'd have all of these memories of their time together and he knew he'd met her, in this manner, for a good reason.

"I'd like a family someday," she told him with a shrug. "But I'm in no hurry. I'm terrified, actually. All I know is what I learned from Milly and now all of that turned out to be a lie."

What the hell had happened to her yesterday? Whatever she'd uncovered was life changing and he wanted to know. He wanted to help her just like she'd helped him. Words from a virtual stranger seemed to go a long way in balming the wound.

"I'm a good listener," he offered. "I have nobody to tell your secrets to and sometimes an outsider's opinion goes a long way."

Elise pursed her lips and he could practically see that internal battle she waged with herself. She wanted to talk, to get this problem off her chest and seek some sort of relief, but he also knew enough about her to know she put her family above all else.

Just another way they were so much alike.

"Something like this could harm our business," she murmured. "I mean, maybe not, but other than promising my sisters, I also have to look out for Angel's Share."

Family and business. Of course. He couldn't be upset with that and he had to respect her decision. That didn't mean he liked it, though.

"First of all, I'd never turn any information on you or your business," he told her. "I respect your decision to keep this private, but you need to know that."

She nodded and removed her hand from his as she came to her feet. Before she could reach for her coffee mug, Antonio slid his hand up the hem of her shirt, instantly finding that curve of her backside. His body stirred to life and with no sheet or blanket to cover him, there was no hiding the effect she had on him.

"Where are you going?"

Her eyes traveled over his bare body, which sure as hell didn't help to curtail his desire.

"I'm supposed to meet my sisters this afternoon back at our old house," she told him.

He glanced at the clock on the nightstand and back to her. "Looks like you have plenty of time left."

He didn't want her to walk out of here, not yet. He needed more and had no idea when that ache of wanting *more* would cease. Regardless, he had a timeline here and there were other places in the States he was set to explore before heading back to Spain.

"Is it a good idea if I stay?" she asked.

Oh, he had her. He curled his other hand around her

opposite hip and turned her body to face him. Staring up at her, he lifted that tee until it was around her neck, then she finished removing it, and flung the garment across the room. Antonio hooked his thumbs into her silky white panties and jerked them down. Elise scissored her legs to let them drop before she kicked them aside.

She climbed onto the bed and covered him completely.

"We didn't use protection the last time," he murmured against her ear.

"I'm on birth control and clean, but I guess it's too late for that conversation." She lifted her eyes to his. "Do we need something?"

"I've never gone without," he told her honestly. "I'm clean."

And there was that wide, sexy smile he'd come to…

No. He hadn't come to love it. He didn't *love*.

But he did want to see more of that happiness from her. He wanted to see all of her passion, all of her desire. And he wanted to be the one who gave her all of that.

As she joined their bodies and stared down at him with her heart in her eyes, Antonio knew he was in trouble…and he had no clue how the hell to make sure nobody got hurt when he left.

Twelve

"You have to wear blue," Sara told Delilah. "That's so your color."

Delilah stood in front of the floor-length mirror at the boutique dress shop and stared at her reflection. Then suddenly burst into tears.

Sara and Elise shot each other a quick glance before going to their sister.

"Don't wear blue," Sara corrected. "It's horrid. We'll find you something in black."

Delilah covered her face and sniffed. The sales associate came around the corner, but Elise smiled and waved her on.

"We're fine," she told her. "Maybe a glass of champagne?"

"Of course." The associate nodded and scurried away.

Surely this wasn't the first breakdown they'd had in the dressing area. They did cater to high-society women, after all. Queen was the store everyone went to when they wanted something different, something one-of-a-kind, and where they could be pampered while shopping.

With the posh pale pink velvet sofas, the crystal chandeliers, and mirrors all around, it was impossible not to fall in love with this place. Just the atmosphere made you feel beautiful and they wanted their customers so happy, that if they didn't have a dress you loved, they'd call in their custom seamstress to make the perfect dress happen for the client.

Elise had never gone that far. Anytime she'd come in, she fell in love with too many things and couldn't narrow her choices down. Although she'd never cried over anything, so something more than dress shopping was going on with her sister.

"I love the dress," Delilah stated with a sniff.

Elise patted her sister's back and honestly had no idea what had set her off right now. Maybe because of all of this going on with Milly, perhaps the divorce papers she'd been handed, or the fact they were each trying to find that perfect dress for their gala. This was about the only day they could carve out of their schedules to shop together. A sister's opinion was worth more than anything.

But right now Elise wasn't so concerned with finding the perfect piece for their bourbon reveal. All she cared about was the welfare of her two best friends because that was all she had left in this world.

"Blue is Camden's favorite color," Delilah admitted. "It was just instinct to grab this and try it on."

Sara glanced to Elise behind Dee's back. Elise just

wanted to fix this for Dee and Camden, but there was nothing she could do.

"Then you should wear it," Elise offered. "You look gorgeous, for one thing. And for another, Camden will be at the gala. I mean, I'm not a marriage counselor, but maybe something as simple as a blue dress could get the two of you talking or reconnecting."

Delilah stared at her sisters in the mirror and patted her damp cheeks. "It's going to take more than a dress to repair this marriage and since he already sent me divorce papers I'm not even sure he wants to. We just have totally different ideas of marriage at this point."

She pulled in a deep breath and smoothed her hands down the front of the low-cut, floor-length dress. She turned from side to side on the large, round pedestal, and Elise and Sara took a step down to give her room.

"Honestly, it's really stunning on you," Sara stated. "You look hot."

Delilah laughed and turned to face them. "I actually do like this one. But maybe I should try more just to be sure. This was only my first one of the day."

She slipped into her dressing room just as a tray of champagne with cheese and crackers was delivered by the associate. Perfect timing. Champagne would surely help Dee not only get into the mood of trying on dresses, but it might also lift her spirits and help her forget just for a bit. That was what Elise wanted for this day. They'd all been bogged down with so much that they needed this relaxing, fun girl day away from work and life.

"What else can I get you ladies?" the associate asked.

Elise leaned in to whisper, "If you could spend more of your time on Delilah, that would be great. Sara and I can help each other. We just want Dee to feel extra special today."

The young, adorable associate nodded. "I can certainly do that. Just let me know if there's anything else I can get either of you, as well. I'm scheduled to cater to the three of you for as long as you need. You are my main customers today. I'll just go grab some of our accessories and shoes for your sister."

There were definitely perks to being a local celebrity. Or that was what the media had dubbed the sisters when they'd first opened. Anytime they went shopping or even out to dinner together, they were given the best treatment. Elise wasn't about to balk at all the people who were eager to help them. Queen did have appointments for their shopping experiences because they wanted each shopper to feel special and like they were looking through their own closet and not have to worry about bumping elbows with other women or vying for the same dress.

Once the associate had left the area, Elise turned to Sara and smiled. "So, which one are you trying on first?"

"That two-piece hot pink number is calling my name," she beamed. "It's sexy and romantic. It was made for me if I can get my top half shoved in there."

"Not all of us were blessed with such things," Delilah called from her dressing room.

Sara laughed. "They can be a blessing or a curse. I'll let you know which as soon as I try on the pink number."

Elise grabbed a glass of champagne and went into her own dressing room. As she stood there looking at the variety of dresses, she couldn't help but wonder what Antonio's favorite color was. That wasn't something they'd actually talked about. They seemed to have glossed over basics and gone straight to sex and heavier topics.

When she'd left his place two days ago, she'd so wanted to tell him her secrets. She wanted another opinion or just a listening ear. But she had to put her family, her business, first. Antonio wasn't staying, he wasn't a permanent part of her life so she'd had to take a mental step back.

He'd texted her yesterday, saying he was touring a vineyard about thirty miles away and then he'd sent a goofy selfie. She hadn't quite seen that playful side, but damn if she didn't immediately make that his contact profile picture.

Before she could think of it, she shot off a text.

Favorite color?

By the time she'd undressed, he'd sent his reply.

Your bare skin

Damn. He was good at this. But she could play this game. Something about Antonio made her bold, brazen, and a little more daring than she'd ever been before.

As luck would have it, she had a nude dress in here with a gold shimmer overlay. The deep V in the front dropped well below her breasts, and material would hug her every curve. Elise quickly threw the dress on and turned toward the mirror.

Wow. Even she had to admit she looked killer in this. But probably not the best dress for a professional gala for her distillery. Absolutely perfect for a selfie, though.

She cocked a hip, tilted her head so her red waves fell over her shoulder, and put on her best heavy-lidded bedroom look. She snapped the pic and sent it before she could talk herself out of it.

Just trying on dresses for the gala. Thoughts?

Elise did a quick glance at the back of the dress, which was just as revealing as the front. She had no idea what she'd ever do with this one, but she'd never felt sexier.

She slipped out of it and put it back on the hanger just as her phone vibrated on the small table in the dressing area. She picked up her champagne and nearly choked on her drink when she read his message.

Buy it and I'll show you my thoughts

How could she turn down an invite like that?

"Oh my word," Sara squealed from the other side of the door. "The pink has won the battle, ladies."

Elise reached for the green off-the-shoulder dress with low, scooped back and fitted bodice. The satiny fabric looked like emeralds and she figured it would show off her eyes and hair.

"I'll be out in a second," Elise called. "Don't move."

She hung the nude-and-gold dress off to the side. She'd somehow have to sneak buying two dresses and not give her sisters any clue why she needed the other. That might be the most expensive piece of bedroom attire she'd ever invested in, but the fact that he wanted to see her again had her more than ready to splurge.

She quickly put on the green gown and stepped out

of her room. Her eyes instantly took in Sara in the pink and Delilah, who now wore a short white cocktail dress with one full sleeve.

"Well, damn." Sara laughed. "We look amazing."

Elise went toward one of the free mirrors and stepped up onto the pedestal. She turned from side to side and really liked the feel of the gown; she also couldn't deny that green was definitely her color.

But it wasn't the nude and gold. Pretty much nothing would compare to that one because she was sure nothing else would elicit the same reaction from Antonio.

"I think the pink is it for me." Sara spun around and posed for her sisters to see. "Elise, you have to get that green. Tell me you love it."

"I definitely want this one for the gala."

"Delilah?" Sara asked, turning her attention from Elise.

Dee stared at herself in the mirror and wrinkled her nose. "I don't know. I like this, but I felt beautiful in the blue."

Elise rolled her eyes. "You're stunning in everything."

"Says the woman who is drop-dead gorgeous in that emerald green dress," Dee replied. "I guess I can't blame Antonio for seducing you. You are pretty gorgeous."

Elise chewed the inside of her cheek to keep from giving any indication that something was still going on with her one-night stand. She never hid things from her sisters, but she truly didn't think they'd like her and Antonio still carrying on the fling.

"Her face is red," Sara murmured a second before she clasped her hands together. "Something is going on. I knew it! Give us all the details."

Delilah jerked around. "Elise, are you serious?"

Elise darted her gaze between her sisters and there was no need in lying. They knew her better than anyone else and she had nothing to be sorry for. She was living her life, taking what she wanted that had nothing to do with family or work. This selfish decision was all about her personal life—one she'd put on hold for far too long.

"We have a mutual understanding," Elise explained.

"How is that going to work with the distillery partnership?" Dee asked, clearly skeptical.

"We have two separate relationships."

Sara stepped off her platform, still wearing that wide, giddy grin. "So you're admitting there's a personal relationship?"

"Having sex doesn't make two people in a relationship," Delilah retorted.

"Um…should I come back?"

Elise turned to see the associate with a soft grin and clearly wondering if she should come on in or turn and run.

"Oh, just girl talk," Sara replied. "But I will definitely take this dress if you'd like to help me with some shoes, size seven, and jewelry."

The associate nodded. "I know what would go perfectly with that. Give me just a minute."

Once they were alone again, Elise turned back to her sisters and shrugged.

"There's no relationship," she assured them. "We're just…enjoying each other."

"But you like him more than just physically." Sara tipped her head and narrowed her eyes. "I can see it written all over your face, so don't deny it."

"Please tell me you're not getting attached," Delilah pleaded. "Getting attached only leads to heartbreak and broken dreams. Trust me when I say all of this. The ending is always tragic."

Yet again, her sisters had totally different outlooks when it came to love.

Elise gasped. Love? Where the hell did that thought come from?

"What is it?" Sara asked. "What happened?"

"I've seen that look," Dee groaned. "Don't even say it. Don't think it, either."

Elise closed her eyes, as if she could reverse that thought. Clearly, she wasn't able to keep her facial expressions a secret, and if Antonio could read her like she thought he could, there was no way he could ever see that. The last thing she needed was for him to think she'd fallen for him.

And how was that even possible? After months of emailing, a few days of face-to-face, and some intense sex...that all couldn't lead to love. There was simply no way.

Yet, she felt something so deeply, something she'd never experienced with another man, and she had no clue what label to put on it—other than love.

"You cannot be in love with a man you barely know," Delilah stated.

"You think I don't know that?" Elise cried. "I mean, realistically, that doesn't make sense. But there's something so much more than the distillery and sex between us. I can't explain it."

Sara moved across the spacious dressing room area to the table with the champagne. She grabbed a flute and took a sip, her eyes holding on to Elise in the reflection of the mirror.

"That means it's real," Sara finally told them. "If you have all of those emotions and you can't describe it, then you're definitely in a relationship, Elise."

She thought back to their intimate conversation the other morning. He'd been so open with his past and his emotions. She hadn't expected that from him and she hadn't given anything in return. She'd so wanted to tell him what was going on with her family and she trusted him to keep her secret. Antonio knew the value of family and business, and she didn't think she was being naïve here.

"I don't know what to call it," Elise admitted.

"Trouble," Delilah answered.

Yeah. No doubt this could end up being trouble. What could come from a man who lived thousands of miles away and had commitments where he lived? Neither of them would up and move across the globe.

All of this was madness. Completely absurd. She should just tell him there would only be professional business from now on.

Her mind instantly went to that dress, that text, and she knew she wasn't done with Antonio Rodriguez.

As she met her sisters' worried stares, Elise realized Delilah was dead on. This was all trouble.

Thirteen

"So what are we doing about seeking out our fathers?" Sara asked.

Elise had barely gotten her cushioned chair scooted in at their favorite lunch hangout. Trinity had been open for only a few years, but already this upscale restaurant was thriving. They were another of Angel's Share's clients so the girls always tried to support them when possible.

Not to mention the atmosphere was absolutely adorable. Everything was set up in threes. The seating, the table groupings, the flowers on the tables, even the appetizers came out in threes.

"Right now I'm not ready to look." Elise reached for her menu, though she always ordered the same thing. "Maybe in the future, but the more I think about it, the more I feel that Milly had a reason for keeping this from us and with her death still so recent, I'm just not ready to open that box."

"I agree with you," Delilah admitted. "But the selfish part of me wants to know."

"I'll support anything you guys decide to do," Elise added. "I just wanted you all to know where I stood here."

Sara tapped her fingers on her menu and sighed. "I can't help myself. I've given this a great deal of thought and I want to know. I understand what you're saying, Elise, but I just have to find out for my own peace of mind."

Elise reached for her sister's hand and smiled. "Then I will help you with whatever you need."

"Terrible timing," Dee added. "I've just got so much going on right now to even think of digging into my past. I can't get a grasp on my present and future."

"Have you talked to Camden since the papers were delivered?" Sara asked.

The waitress came just at that moment to take their orders and once they were alone again, Delilah shifted in her seat and rested her elbows up on the table.

"No," she answered. "I don't know what to say and I guess part of me was hoping he'd reach out, but I guess sending the papers was his only form of communication."

Elise hated hearing that; she truly hoped some miracle happened and Cam and Delilah could make up and get back to where they used to be. Delilah obviously hadn't signed the papers yet, so there was still hope.

"Let's not talk about that," Dee stated as she straightened up and shifted her attention to Elise. "I want to hear about what is and isn't going on with Antonio."

Great. That wasn't something she wanted to dive into

and she'd thought they'd laid that topic to rest back at the dress shop. There was sex and a couple of conversations, then there was the business side. There really wasn't much else to tell...or at least nothing she wanted to share.

"You already know everything."

Sara cocked her head. "I doubt that."

"Well, everything you need to know," Elise amended.

"I'm worried about you," Delilah told her. "The last thing any of us needs is more hurt in our lives."

"I don't plan on getting hurt." Though she really wasn't quite certain that was in her control. "Just let me have a little fun."

"I think that's what we're most worried about," Sara added. "This is so unlike you that we're just afraid when Antonio leaves, you'll be crushed. You've fallen for him."

Maybe she had. So what? She was also a very logical person and she knew how all of this would play out. He would leave, she would stay, and they'd communicate via emails for business purposes only.

"No matter what my feelings are for him, I can handle it," she assured them. "Listen, we have something, I won't deny that. The physical is just one part of it. We've also had some pretty in-depth conversations and I just feel like he understands me."

"Did you tell him about what we found at Milly's?" Sara asked.

Elise shook her head. "I just told him we were dealing with some things that changed our lives and everything we thought to be the truth. But I didn't want to share too much since we agreed not to say anything for now."

"I wouldn't care if you told him." Sara reached for the

pitcher of water on the table and poured three glasses. "I actually put out some feelers for an investigator. I hope that's okay."

"You want to find your biological father and that's the first step," Delilah told her. "And as far as Antonio, you do what you feel is right. I just don't want our business affected."

Elise would trust Antonio with anything and part of her did want his opinion, or maybe she just wanted an outside shoulder to lean on. Or maybe part of her just wanted that bond of theirs to go even deeper. She didn't know the exact answer, but she did know she couldn't wait to see him again.

"There's that look on her face again," Sara whispered.

Delilah nodded. "I see it."

"Oh stop." Elise rolled her eyes and reached for her water. "We're all trying to get through this crazy time together. Just let me have my fun."

Sara winked. "Oh, I'd say you're already having it. But I'm glad. I'm still holding out hope that this will be some dramatically happy ending and the two of you will fall in love."

Delilah opened her mouth, but Sara held up her hand. "No, don't say it. Just let me have my moment and let Elise enjoy this."

"While it lasts," Dee muttered under her breath.

Yeah, while it lasted. The clock was ticking and much too quickly, in her opinion. She wanted more time with Antonio, she wanted to get to know even more about his life and his family. She wanted him to not live so far away because there was no way a long-distance relationship would work with an ocean between them.

The man hadn't even mentioned anything about any type of relationship, so the fact that she was even thinking in that manner should be a glaring red flag that she was going to get hurt. But Elise took a chapter from Sara's romance book and chose to live in the moment and soak up all the happiness this time had to offer.

Antonio had left Twisted Vine Vineyard and returned to his rental, but he didn't like the emptiness or the silence that greeted him. Even though this was only his temporary home, having Elise here for a time had changed the dynamics of his entire stay.

What the hell would he do when it was time to move on from Benton Springs? He was due in Tennessee in just a couple of days, but he had promised he'd return for the Angel's Share ten-year bourbon reveal gala. His pilot was well compensated, so going back and forth would be no trouble. But at some point he would be leaving here for a final time and that idea didn't sit well with him. There was a knot of anxiety and confusion where Elise was concerned.

One thing was certain, though. He wanted to see her. He wanted more of her for as long as he was here and for as long as she'd allow.

Antonio unbuttoned the cuffs of his sleeves and rolled them up as he headed toward the bedroom. His eyes instantly landed on that bed, and an image of the two of them and all they'd shared instantly filled his mind. The time he'd spent with her in the cellar and here in this room had been the most memorable, erotic moments of his life. He couldn't ignore this ache of desire, not to mention whatever hell else was happening between them.

Antonio waited for about a half second before he pulled out his cell and texted her.

I need to see you. Are you coming here or should I come to you?

He sat his phone on the dresser and stripped from his dress shirt and pants as he headed toward the shower. This had been a long day and he just wanted to decompress and change his clothes. Then he'd be ready for Elise. He'd thought of her all damn day.

No, that wasn't true. He'd thought of her since the moment she left the other morning. Their conversation replayed over and over in his head. But even more than all their time conversing, he'd told her things he'd never told anyone. She'd truly listened to him, she'd offered advice, she'd even comforted him. None of that had to do with sex or their business arrangement. Elise was truly a phenomenal woman.

He wasn't looking for this…whatever *this* was. When he'd come to the States he'd been dead set on figuring out his own life, working on the pub side of his family's business, and keeping the entire trip professional.

Then Elise landed in his lap—quite literally—and he hadn't been able to concentrate on much else. Even during his touring and tastings earlier today at the vineyard, his mind had been elsewhere and that was the first time in his life he'd ever let a woman cloud his professional mind.

Part of him wondered how this happened in such a short time, but the other part of him knew there was something special about Elise and she just had that impact that was impossible to ignore.

After his shower, Antonio checked his cell and there was nothing. A surge of disappointment hit him. But he had no actual ties to her. They hadn't made any commitments to each other or even discussed meeting up again. He'd just assumed they would carry on this intimate relationship for as long as he was in town.

Maybe he should have specified exactly what he wanted from her. He'd thought from her sexy text earlier that they were on the same page. He'd been in the middle of his tastings when he'd checked his cell and nearly choked on his Cabernet. That damn dress made her body look like she'd just stepped from every fantasy he'd ever had. Antonio hadn't even thought it possible she could look even sexier than he'd seen her, but she sure as hell managed just that.

Right as he turned to his closet to get dressed, his cell rang. Gripping the towel around his hips with one hand, he picked up the cell, only to see his mother's name popping up.

He shouldn't be disappointed, but he'd thought for a second the caller was Elise. Then a sliver of worry hit him as he answered.

"It's late there. Is everything okay?"

"Of course. I just couldn't sleep and wanted to talk to you."

"Of course." Antonio sank on the edge of his bed, still holding on to his towel. "What's on your mind?"

"That's what I wanted to ask you," she retorted. "Your father mentioned you wanted to talk to us when you returned home about the business. I've been thinking about that since he told me. I want to know what you're thinking because I have anxiety and can't wait for you to return."

He knew his mother was a worrier, what mother wasn't? But he didn't want to get into this on the phone and when it was nearing midnight back home.

"There's nothing to worry about," he assured her. "Just some life choices I've been thinking on and would like to run by you guys."

"I see," she murmured. "Are you having second thoughts about taking over or do you have bigger plans for what we already have?"

Antonio glanced up to the ceiling and pulled in a breath, trying to weigh his options and choose his words wisely.

"There's just a good bit to discuss in person," he replied. "I've had some eye-opening experiences here that have me thinking and my mind is in all different directions."

"What's her name?"

Antonio stilled. "Excuse me?"

"The woman you met," his mom replied. "What's her name?"

"How do you know there's a woman?"

His mother's soft laughter came through the line and he knew there was no lying here and no trying to talk his way around the answer.

"*Carino*, you're talking to me, so you might as well just say it. You have a different tone in your voice and something has changed about you."

She could tell that just by the five minutes they'd been

chatting? What did that mean? What did she hear that could possibly make her think he'd changed so much?

Before he could answer, his doorbell rang. His stomach clenched because he knew exactly who would be on the other side. She was the only person who knew where he was and he hadn't exactly sought out other friendships.

Antonio gripped his towel and padded barefoot toward the front door. After a quick peek through the peephole, he nearly dropped his cell and the towel.

"*Hijo*, are you still there?"

He flicked the lock and opened the door to Elise...who stood before him wearing that damn dress that looked like she wore nothing but glitter.

"I'm here," he replied, his eyes locking on to Elise's.

She held her arms out wide and did a very slow spin right there on his front porch before turning back to face him and sauntering right on in like she owned the place.

"Mom, I'll call you tomorrow," he finally replied.

"With more details about this woman, I hope."

He couldn't tear his gaze or his attention away from those swaying hips as she made her way toward his bedroom.

"Yes, of course."

He hung up, not really comprehending what he'd just agreed to, but he didn't care. This woman was going to be the death of him, but he wouldn't want to go any other way.

Fourteen

Elise didn't know what had come over her, but there was some serious power in this dress. The way Antonio had answered the door, phone to his ear and gripping that minuscule towel that barely covered him, it had been all she could do to just walk in and not jerk that white terrycloth out of the way.

But she'd refrained. She wanted him to want her. She wanted him just as needy as she was. And from his text earlier, she had to assume he was exactly that. The moment she'd read his message, she'd thrown on the dress, brushed out her hair, and headed on over. She didn't want to think about it and she didn't want to give herself time to back out. If she'd put too much thought into this, she'd start feeling silly. Never once did she dress up for a man before. Lingerie wasn't practical and she had nobody to wear it for.

Antonio had loved this dress, so here she was, more than ready for him to peel her out of it and show her exactly how much he'd missed her touch.

She never would have had the confidence to do this with another man. How had he pulled her so far out of her comfort zone without her noticing?

"I'm glad that wasn't a video call with my mother."

Elise turned to see Antonio in the doorway of his bedroom, still clutching that towel in one hand and his cell in the other.

"That would have been an awkward moment," Elise agreed, propping her hands on the dip in her waist and cocking her hip. "Do you often answer the door wearing just a towel?"

In an instant, the towel fell to the floor. Antonio took a step into the room, put his phone on the dresser, and took another step toward her. Those dark eyes never wavered.

As her stomach quivered with anticipation and her heartbeat kicked up, Elise was so glad she'd opted to just go on gut instinct and show up here without replying to his message. This might be temporary, but she wanted to hold on to each moment she could. And maybe Sara was right, what if something came from this?

Elise didn't want to get her hopes up too high, but there was that flutter of excitement she couldn't help but cling to. She'd never had so many emotions, such a high, from one man before now, so ignoring any of this would only cheat herself out of something amazing.

"Do you often show up at a man's house wearing a dress that was made for sex?"

Elise shivered, but still managed what she hoped was a saucy smile. "You're my first."

He reached out, curling his fingers around her hips and hauling her against him. His mouth hovered just over hers.

"Right answer," he murmured against her lips.

His hands roamed up over her waist, to the curve of her breasts, and back down.

"How the hell do I get you out of this?" he asked.

Elise flattened her palms against his chest. "And here I thought you loved this dress?"

Antonio grazed his lips across her jawline and up toward her ear. "Oh, I love it. I've thought of little else since that picture, *pequena marta*."

Another shiver raced through her. "What does that mean?"

His eyes came back to hers as he framed her face between his strong hands. "Little minx."

And then his mouth covered hers completely, demanding her to open for him, demanding she make good on that unspoken promise that had gone right along with her sending that photo from the dressing room.

Elise gripped his bare shoulders, relishing in the fact that he had answered the door knowing she'd be there. They'd already fallen into sync with each other, especially where intimacy was concerned. But other things just didn't need to be said or discussed.

Antonio broke away from the kiss and spun her around. His hands were all over her back, her sides, then he cursed beneath his breath.

"Where's the damn zipper?" he growled.

Elise loved that she was the one who brought out that

reckless side of him. Who knew she'd possessed such power or that she'd love being so spontaneous?

"There's no zipper." She flashed him a grin over her shoulder and smoothed her hair out of the way. "It pulls on and off."

"Misericordia."

She couldn't help but laugh at his whisper. "You speak more Spanish when you're turned on."

"Then it's amazing I have any English left in me right now," he countered.

Before she could reply, Antonio dropped to his knees and eased his hands beneath the hem of the dress. She'd thrown on a pair of heels only because the dress was so long and she hadn't wanted to trip...that wouldn't have made the impression she was going for.

With his eyes locked on hers, he slid one shoe off, then the other. His hands slowly slid up her calves, then just behind her knees, to her thighs, and then he stopped. Elise nearly moaned, but she managed just barely to hold it back.

The dress bunched at her thighs as his fingers dug into her skin. She stared down at him, and those dark eyes held her completely captivated. She smoothed a hand over his jaw, then raked her thumb across his lower lip. His tongue darted out and dampened her skin.

"Spread your legs," he murmured.

Elise complied and he moved farther up with the material until it was bunched around her waist. Then he eased forward until his face was exactly where she ached the most. His warm breath fell upon her bare, heated skin and she was about one second away from begging.

When his mouth touched her, Elise had to grip his shoulders to remain upright. Too many sensations hit her all at once. The way he held her in place with that firm grip and his lips had Elise unable to control her emotions. Her body climbed so fast, so intensely, she cried out and it took everything in her not to fall over. Antonio made love to her with his mouth and she'd never in her life had this type of experience. Nothing prepared her for this man and the way she'd connected on so many levels with him.

Elise's body went weak and Antonio came to his feet, still holding on to her. He lifted her in his arms and turned, carrying her over to the bed. He sat her on the edge and finished peeling off her dress. He laid the dress over a chair in the corner of the room before coming back to her and staring down.

"You're quite exquisite when you come undone." He stroked her jawline and feathered down her neck, to the valley between her breasts. "But I'm not done with you."

A shiver raced through her entire body. She couldn't imagine feeling more than she did right now. How could he pull out so many different emotions and thrills?

"You already wore me out." She fell back onto the bed. "I'm not sure I'm ready for more."

Antonio placed his hands on the insides of her knees and eased them apart, then came to stand between. He continued to stare down at her with that dark gaze. Despite being depleted, her body still managed to start humming once again. All it took was a stare, a simple touch, and the man had her turning into a puddle.

"How about you just lie back and relax and I'll do the rest?" he suggested.

Elise smiled up at him. "You've done so much already."

"Good thing I have more to give."

He pulled her toward where he was standing at the edge of the bed. Still holding firmly onto the backs of her legs, he joined their bodies and never wavered that heavy-lidded stare. He moved against her, slowly, passionately. Elise wanted to close her eyes and savor the moment, but she couldn't. Breaking that silent bond would be doing both of them a disservice. There was something so much more going on here, but also something he likely wasn't ready to discuss.

Elise wasn't about to ruin the moment with words that stemmed from her euphoric state. At this point all she needed to do was enjoy the man, the moment, the night. That dress was the best splurge she'd ever made and she'd never look at it the same again.

When Antonio's hand slid between their bodies and touched her at exactly the right spot, Elise could no longer hold herself back. She lifted up to her elbows, now focusing on how beautifully their bodies moved together. With his dark skin in contrast with her creamy skin, they were different, yet so very much the same.

Elise let go of every thought and allowed her body to be all consumed with everything Antonio offered her. He was such a selfless lover and she couldn't imagine ever being with another man after this.

As she cried out her release, Antonio said something again in Spanish just as he held tight to her hips and let himself follow her over the edge. Elise slid her knees up his sides and propped her heels on the edge of the bed for just a bit more leverage…she couldn't get close enough.

Just as her body stopped trembling, Antonio eased down to lie on her. With their bodies still joined, Elise wrapped her arms and legs around him, wanting to keep him right here with her. She'd never wanted time to stand still more than right this minute.

What would happen when he ultimately left? This affair did have an expiration date and it was looming over their heads. Elise didn't want to think about that, she didn't want any negative thoughts to break into this perfect bubble they'd created.

With the way this whole thing started when they'd gotten stranded in the cellar, and then the chemistry… everything just seemed to explode so fast. Slowing down hadn't even been an option. Elise had hung on for the ride and enjoyed that thrilling exhilaration she experienced each time she was near Antonio. She'd never met anyone like him and she doubted she ever would again.

"I can hear your mind working," he murmured into her ear. "I must not have been thorough enough."

Elise laughed as she trailed her fingertips up and down his back. "You were thorough. My mind is always working."

Antonio pressed his hands on the bed on either side of her head and pushed up slightly. With his hair all mussed, those dark eyes framed by inky lashes, and a slight sheen of sweat, she'd honestly never seen a sexier, more breathtaking sight.

"Do those thoughts include you staying here for the night?" he asked.

Every day, every moment, she seemed to get deeper and deeper, but she just couldn't say no to him. Well, she could, but why? She wanted this, she wanted him, even if all of this beautiful mess was temporary. They each had hectic lives, both personal and professional, but everything they'd created together was something only for them. Nobody could take this away and she fully intended to lock these memories in forever.

So of course she'd be staying the night. She still had more memories to make.

Fifteen

"Did you talk to your mother about what you want when you get home?"

Elise extended her feet in front of her on the chaise. It was well after midnight, but neither she nor Antonio were tired. She'd thrown on one of his white T-shirts and he'd pulled on a pair of gym shorts and they had moved out to the balcony off his bedroom. He relaxed in the chaise next to her and their glasses of wine sat on the table in between.

There was something even more intimate about this moment than all the sexual encounters they'd shared. Talking and diving deeper into each other's lives only pulled them further over the relationship line, though she wasn't about to bring up that uncomfortable topic.

"I didn't get a chance." He shot her a smirk and a wink. "Someone showed up at my door and distracted me."

"Oops." Elise lifted her hands in a mock shrug. "Bad timing on my part."

"Perfect timing," he countered. "It was late over there and that was not a conversation I want to have over the phone anyway. I'm grateful for everything they've done and instilled in me, but I have to live my life and not theirs. It's not fair to any of us."

"I don't know your parents, but I would think they'd be proud of you for wanting to live your own life."

Antonio turned back to look up at the starry sky. "I never thought of it that way, but maybe you're right."

Silence settled between them, but there was no discomfort. There was something so easy about talking with him and being with him that put her mind and her heart at ease. She found herself wanting to share more of herself, wanting him to understand her even more.

"We discovered that Milly wasn't just our adoptive mother," she heard herself saying before she could think twice. "She was our biological aunt. My birth mom's sister."

Antonio shifted in his seat and from the corner of her eye, she noticed he'd sat straight up and turned to face her. Elise kept her gaze to the sky as she spoke, trying not to break down because this was the first time she'd said all of this out loud away from her sisters.

"Delilah and Sara are actually my half sisters," she went on. "We share the same mother, but for obvious reasons, we know we had different fathers."

Now he moved and came to sit on the edge of her chaise. His bare hand rested on her thigh and she shifted her focus to him. Those dark brows drew in and the concern on his face was obvious.

And that was why she'd fallen so fast, so hard, for

him. There was more here than sex and she wondered if he could feel that same connection. Surely, he did or he wouldn't have opened up so easily to her.

"So what are you guys going to do with that information?" he asked.

"I'm not doing anything," she told him. "I've had a great life, I love Milly, and I figure if she kept all of this from us, there's a good reason. Delilah is torn, but Sara has already contacted an investigator to find her father."

"And what about your birth mother?"

Elise pulled in a breath and sighed. "She actually passed away in prison. She had a drug problem. That's why we got taken away when we were so young and then Milly had to hire someone to track us down so she could take us in."

Antonio reached for her hand and laced their fingers together, giving her a gentle squeeze for support. "So that's what had you so rattled the other day?"

She nodded and scooted over a bit to give him more room. "I just didn't know what to think or how to react. I wanted to escape and forget."

He leaned in, placing a soft kiss on her lips before easing back. Elise wanted him to say something, but she didn't know what. She also needed to know where they stood. As much as she wanted to pretend this was her life, she also had to be realistic.

"What are we doing here?" she asked before she could talk herself out of it.

The question hovered between them and Elise knew she'd just opened her heart wide, allowing something wonderful to enter or the pain to settle in. His response would only determine which one.

"We're enjoying a drink and the night."

Elise tipped her head and simply stared at him. He knew what she was referring to and she wasn't letting him get off that easy. She wasn't a clingy woman and she didn't need a man in her life to make her complete. She'd gotten along just fine this far with dating casually and staying married to her work. But Antonio was different.

Perhaps part of her felt so comfortable because he wasn't local and she'd always known in the back of her mind this would ultimately come to an end. But she really didn't believe that. Everything inside her just had that hopeful feeling that they had met for a reason, that they had been thrown together for something bigger than just a working relationship.

Good grief. She was starting to sound like Sara.

"What do you want to be going on here?" he finally asked.

Well, damn. She hadn't expected him to turn the question back on to her. She prided herself on being honest, so now that she'd broached the topic, she had to push on through.

"In a perfect world, you wouldn't live an ocean away," she started. "We could see where this goes and we wouldn't have to worry about all the outside problems we have because we could tackle them together."

Antonio stilled and she could have sworn he was even holding his breath. Maybe they weren't on the same page or having similar thoughts. No matter if they were or weren't, she needed to know. They couldn't just ignore the fact that he would be leaving at some point.

"I do live an ocean away," he agreed. He released her hand and just laid his on top now. "I didn't come here looking for anything other than business. I didn't expect to meet someone like you, but at this point in my life, I can't focus on anything else other than my family and everything going on there."

Even though she'd assumed he'd say something like that, the pain of the words still hit her harder than she expected. How could they have so much in such a short time and then let it all go like nothing had ever happened? She didn't work that way. Her heart wasn't wired to love and just let go.

"I wasn't looking, either," she replied. "But even you have to admit this is more than sex."

Antonio nodded. "It is, but this isn't the right time."

"Would there ever be?" she couldn't help but ask.

Antonio reached for her and palmed her cheek, his thumb slid back and forth over her skin. "I love traveling. I love meeting new people and seeing new places. That's why I'm going to step away from the restaurants. There's more for me than staying in one place, and with them wanting my role to change, to be more of a permanent fixture… I just can't be that person."

Maybe he was telling her the truth, but all she heard was that he loved his jet-setting, playboy lifestyle. The hurt that curled all around her heart was of her own doing. She'd let this go on too long, she'd opened herself up when she knew the end result.

But there had been that sliver of hope.

"You're right," she replied. "I deserve more and should be put first in any relationship."

The muscles in his jaw clenched, but he nodded. "You shouldn't settle for anything less."

Elise reached up, covering his hand with hers. "So what now?"

"I'm leaving for Tennessee the day after tomorrow. If you still want me at the gala, I did plan to be there."

The personal side of her wanted to just cut ties because prolonging this heartache would only hurt more in the long run. But the business side of her, the one that always prevailed, knew that having him at the gala would be invaluable. To have potential clients see that Angel's Share was ready to go global would only pull in more business and garner more attention.

"Of course I want you there," she told him with a smile. "I bought my dress earlier today and I'm saving a dance for you."

Antonio glanced over his shoulder to the discarded dress on the bedroom chair. "I hope not that dress."

She reached out and curled her fingers around his neck. "That dress was only for you."

Just because they were calling things off, didn't mean she couldn't enjoy the time she had left with him.

As she pulled him closer, his dark gaze dropped to her lips.

"One last time?" he asked.

She swallowed her emotions and urged him to lie on top of her as she shifted her legs for him to settle between. "One last time," she agreed.

Antonio feathered his lips over hers and Elise savored the moment, knowing this would be their final time together. She had to lock in all of these memories to last her lifetime because there would never be anyone else like Antonio Rodriguez.

* * *

Antonio walked through the vineyard and adjusted his sunglasses.

Just that simple gesture had him thinking of all the times he'd seen Elise adjust her glasses and how damn sexy she'd looked in them.

"We also make an excellent grape juice and bottle it just for kids and that has been a top seller for us for the past ten years."

Antonio listened to the owner of Berry Farm Vineyard and was actually interested in everything the elderly man said. The history of the farm, the way they work and process, to the way they package and distribute. This was a family-run business and something he could appreciate.

But his mind was back in Kentucky, back with Elise. He'd left Benton Springs last night and had hardly slept in his hotel room. He wanted to reach out to her, to text or call or something, but he'd made it clear he wasn't in a place to move beyond physical, and staying personally connected would only confuse her and hurt her more.

And that was the part that really got him. He'd seen that hurt in her eyes when they'd been on his balcony. He knew his words had affected her, but he hadn't wanted to lie and he knew she deserved better than what he was ready to offer.

The thought of her with another man, though, that sure as hell didn't sit well with him. He already hated the faceless guy who would no doubt enter her life and make her smile, pull out that passion, have her dress in killer dresses just to take them back off.

"So what do you think?"

Antonio had to push aside his jealousy and rage and focus his attention back on the reason he was here. He smiled against the sun and slid his hands into his pockets.

"This is quite an impressive establishment," Antonio replied. "One that I think would tie nicely with the way we run our own businesses back home. I'm anxious to get to the tastings to see what we could pair with the various menu items we'll be adding."

The man smiled, causing wrinkles around his eyes to deepen. "I think we can make that happen. Right this way."

Antonio followed behind and slid his cell from his pocket. He tapped the screen, cursing beneath his breath when disappointment hit him hard. There were no messages from Elise. What had he expected? He'd called things off, though he did promise her one dance at the gala.

He was already counting down the days to get her back into his arms again. Though that was utterly foolish, he still couldn't stop himself. He also couldn't help but wonder if he'd made a mistake in ending their personal relationship. Part of him wanted to see where things went, but the other part was much more realistic. Where could they go from here? They lived on two different continents with two different lives. They both had family that depended on them.

As Antonio walked into the tasting room, he attempted to push aside his thoughts of Elise. The problem was, he didn't think he'd ever be able to get her out of his mind.

Sixteen

"This is it, ladies."

Elise glanced around the open two-story portion of the distillery. In mere moments the place would be packed... she hoped.

"I'm more nervous now than I was on our opening day," Delilah admitted.

"I was definitely more nervous then," Sara added as she smoothed her dark hair over one shoulder. "Let's do this, girls. We are about to bust onto this male-dominated scene in a bigger way than ever before."

"That's the plan," Elise said with a laugh. "Go ahead and let them in."

Delilah headed toward the double mahogany doors and cracked them open. She spoke to the employees they had on the outside to monitor the guests and make sure only those who RSVP'd were allowed in. They had security all lined up, the valet drivers, the caterers, the DJ—they were counting on this to be a huge success.

While nerves might be swirling through Elise, she also had confidence that they would no doubt make this next ten years even more impactful than the past ten years. Because this next chapter in their distillery all started with the ten-year bourbon, then the fifteen, the twenty, and they would have a continual momentum that would only propel them to greatness.

She should be thrilled that their monumental night had finally come. They'd worked toward this for so long and sacrificed so much. Hell, Delilah's marriage had fallen apart because of their dedication. Or that was what Elise assumed. Delilah never went into details.

But Elise had her own issues and her own heartache right now. As much as she loved her dress, her hair, she felt gorgeous and was ready for an epic night, she also wondered if Antonio would actually show. She hadn't spoken to him in days, not since she left his house after their last passionate night. That had been the most difficult moment, just walking away like he hadn't changed her entire world. Like he hadn't left an imprint on her heart that no one could ever fill or even come close to touching.

"Might want to smile," Sara murmured. "People are starting to come in."

Elise blinked and pulled herself back to the moment. She couldn't let anything, not even heartache, get in the way of this important night. Her sisters were counting on her.

Once the double doors were propped open, Elise recognized many people, but there were some she didn't know. She crossed the open space to start greeting her guests and thankfully, her sisters were part of this, too. There was no way she could get to everyone. They certainly had to divide and conquer.

As she shook hands and accepted congratulations from her guests, her eyes scanned the room, but she still didn't see Antonio. Maybe he'd changed his mind or maybe he'd gotten busy. If he didn't show, she had to admit that she would be even more devastated, but she had no hold over him and no control. They had a fling, or likely that was how he saw it. Whatever they had, it was over, so dwelling on what might have been or what she was missing would get her nowhere.

All she had to do was go right back to the determined, professional woman she'd been before she met Antonio. Unfortunately, she wasn't the same woman and she never would be. He'd changed her forever and quite possibly ruined her for any other man.

Elise showed guests toward the tasting area on the back wall where staff was lined up to accommodate everyone. There was also an area where they could receive information on partnering and becoming a VIP client. The key for tonight was to get everyone to fall in love with Angel's Share and if they weren't already on their customer list, to get them there.

"There's a couple looking for you."

Elise turned from the tasting area when Sara whispered in her ear.

"A couple?" Elise asked.

Sara nodded. "They're over by the waterfall."

Elise glanced toward the feature wall they'd had put

in when they'd opened. They had the Angel's Share emblem etched into limestone and displayed as a thin sheet of water slid over it and into a rock base. They'd spent a good amount on this feature, but it was still one of Elise's favorites.

As she maneuvered within the crowd, she noticed a tall man with black hair and a crisp black suit, and a very petite woman with long, silky black hair. The lady had on a conservative floor-length red gown with sleeves and Elise wondered why they specifically asked to see her.

"I'm Elise," she announced as she came to stand behind them. "How can I help you?"

The couple turned from admiring the wall, and the woman had a soft smile, while the man was the one who spoke.

But he didn't have to say a word. Elise knew exactly who they were because she could see Antonio in both of them.

"It's a pleasure to meet you." Mr. Rodriguez extended his hand. "I am Carlos Rodriguez and this is my wife, Ana. You know our son, I do believe."

Elise smiled, but the nerves in her gut swirled more than any other time in her life. She shook their hands and tried to remember they were her new customers...not the parents of the man she'd fallen so hard for.

"I had no idea you were coming," she told them. "I would have made special arrangements for you, but I'm so thrilled you're here."

"Oh, nothing special needs to be done for us." His mother waved her hand in dismissal. "We're actually here to see you."

"Me?" Now her nerves seriously kicked in to high gear. "What can I help you with?"

"It seems you've captured my son's attention," Carlos told her. "We've never known another woman to have him so…"

"Flustered," Ana finished. "I believe that's the word you're looking for."

Confused, Elise glanced around to the people milling about. Everyone seemed preoccupied with their own conversations and nobody was paying any attention to hers. Her quick scan also confirmed that Antonio still hadn't arrived.

"We mean that in a good way," Ana quickly added.

Something about her seemed so warm and welcoming. That must be where Antonio got his softer side. But when Elise looked at Carlos, she could easily see how Antonio would look in thirty years. Still handsome with that darker, mysterious air about him.

"I don't guess I know what you mean."

Elise thought she knew, but she certainly wasn't jumping to any conclusions and she was even more confused now. What had Antonio told his parents? He'd ended their personal relationship, so the fact that they had flown all this way surely meant something, but Elise had no clue what.

"Since coming here, Antonio has had a different tone in his voice when we talk on the phone. Lighter. Joyful. Our son has had a difficult time since his brother's death," Carlos offered.

"They were twins. Two peas in a pod. That's why he travels so much," Ana added. "He can still be social, still stay connected with people, but not make any lasting relationships. It's all done in the name of work. We thought when he met the right woman, he'd settle down and commit. But he pushes everything and everyone away."

Everything started to make more sense now. At least, she thought it did. Had he pushed her away because he was afraid? Granted, their time together had been so fast, so intense, she'd been terrified of her own feelings…especially since she'd still been in the grieving process. Elise had wondered if she could trust her feelings, but there wasn't a doubt in her mind that everything she'd experienced with Antonio had been authentic and real.

"But when he talks about you, he's different. We came to find out why."

Shocked, Elise fumbled for how to respond. "He told me about Paolo," Elise finally stated. "I can't imagine the loss you all experienced. He told me you had planned for Paolo to take over the restaurants."

Carlos's dark brows shot up. "He discussed all of that with you?"

Elise nodded. "I hope that doesn't bother you. I've not told a soul and he knows he can trust me."

Carlos and Ana shot each other a look, then smiled. Clearly, they had that special bond where they could communicate without using words. Elise didn't realize she envied something so trivial until just now. She wanted that, and she knew she could have something so special and meaningful with Antonio.

"Mom. Dad. What are you doing here?"

Elise turned, her heart in her throat at the sight of Antonio behind her. His eyes went from his parents to her, then he raked that dark gaze down her dress and back up.

"I still like the other one," he told her, before stepping toward his mom and dad.

Even in the midst of his shock and surprise, Antonio still managed to slip in just enough to have her memories flooding back and remind her just how good they were together. The man was so potent and much too powerful for her to mentally ward off. She had to just stop trying because they were meant to be together. If he was afraid, then she'd help him overcome the fear.

As far as the rest of their issues, well, they'd work on that later. What was important, what she was holding on to, was the fact that his parents obviously knew something substantial for them to show up here on such an important night.

"I'll let you three talk," Elise offered.

"Stay," Antonio demanded.

Elise remained still, but she knew she shouldn't be in the middle of a family conversation, especially when she'd just met Carlos and Ana.

"Why don't I show you all to my office where you can chat in private?" Elise suggested. "And when you're done, come back and find me?"

"That would be perfect," Ana stated with a smile.

Elise motioned for them to follow her as she maneuvered through the crowd. Both Delilah and Sara caught her eye as she exited the main area and went into the hallway, which led to a back staircase to the second floor.

They reached her office and Elise punched in a code, then opened the door wide so they could go in.

"The door will lock itself when you leave," she told them. "Can you find your way back okay?"

Carlos and Ana entered, but Antonio stopped right in front of her. "I know my way."

He looked so achingly sexy in that all-black suit. She hadn't expected him to look at her the way he was now, like he was torn between what he wanted and his duty. She hadn't mentally prepared herself to see him after they broke things off, either.

But all of that would have to wait because clearly there were some family dealings to tie up and once he was free of that and her night came to an end, she had some questions herself.

Namely what he'd told his parents about her and why they were so insistent that he'd fallen for her.

Antonio reached for her hand before she could move away and leaned in to her ear. *"Asombrosa."*

She wanted to ask him what that meant, but he'd already moved away and into the room with his parents. Elise pulled the door and headed back to the gala. She had many guests to see and no doubt questions from her sisters. She'd known going in this would be a memorable night, but she hadn't realized just how much so. Now that she had a little leverage on Antonio, she wasn't going to just let this relationship go so easily.

Both her professional and personal lives were about to change forever.

Antonio slid his hands into his pockets and stared across the room. His heart beat faster than usual and there was a bundle of nerves from so many different angles. He'd start with his parents and then go see Elise and figure out what the hell was going on.

But first, he wanted to know what his parents had said to Elise before he'd arrived.

"Why didn't you tell me you guys were coming to the States?"

"We wanted to surprise you," his father told him. "And we wanted to meet Elise."

"How did you even know her name?"

His mother laughed. "There's not much we don't know about our son, but we figured the woman you'd been talking with regarding the new account was likely the same one who had you preoccupied here."

He'd never said he was preoccupied and he'd sure as hell never even acted like he was seeing anyone.

"What's this really about?" he demanded. "You don't fly this far for a surprise to talk to a woman I'm doing business with."

"But there's more than business, isn't there?" his mother asked.

Antonio crossed his arms over his chest and glanced between his mom and dad. "That's the reason you're here?"

His father took a step toward one of the leather club chairs in the seating area of the office. There were two chairs and a sofa and Carlos gestured.

"Let's have a seat and talk."

Antonio wasn't in the mood for a chat or to be checked up on, if that was what they wanted. He had a gala to get to, a sexy woman to dance with, and a final goodbye to have.

He'd made up his mind that once he left here tonight, he would be moving on to his next destination and wouldn't see Elise again. He'd gone over in his mind if he should stay the night, but they'd already agreed the other night was their last.

He just hadn't had enough of her yet...and while he'd been in Tennessee, he'd not been able to do much other than think of how Elise had flawlessly slid into his world. How, even going through her own loss and sadness, she'd talked him through his own issues.

Something had shifted inside him, something that he could only attribute to having Elise in his life. His future seemed clearer now. Everything about her seemed to fit perfectly...but nothing was perfect. Everything always came to an end...but maybe it didn't have to this time.

"We've been talking about our retirement," his father started after they were all seated. "We know taking over our lifestyle isn't what you had in mind."

Antonio eased forward on the sofa and rested his elbows on his knees. His father sat in the chair to his right and his mother in the chair to his left. He didn't want to hurt either one of them, so he waited until they said more so he could get a good feel for exactly what they were trying to say or what their thoughts were.

"We want you to live your life," his mother told him. "When we started our first restaurant, we wanted to have something to give you and your brother. Then when he passed, you seemed to shut down. Over the years we just knew this life wasn't for you."

Antonio couldn't believe what he was hearing. Never once had they given a clue that they understood he didn't want to take over.

"We tried to push you," his mom went on. "We wanted you to love this life and we wanted to leave you a legacy. We know how much you love traveling and there's nothing wrong with that. Staying in Spain might not be for you, son."

Antonio pulled in a deep breath and tried to process what she was saying. But he knew they still wanted to keep their restaurants open and the pubs they were working toward opening.

"So what will happen with everything you have now?" he asked. "This is still your baby. Your entire lives have been wrapped up in Rodriguez's."

His mother shot his father a glance and Antonio shifted to focus on his dad.

"We've been discussing that," his father started. "We were hoping to come to a solid compromise."

Antonio eased back on the sofa and crossed his ankle over his knee. As much as he wanted to get back downstairs, he also needed to devote his attention to this moment. He loved his parents, would do anything for them, so the fact that they could see his uncertainty without him saying a word really hit him hard. They were just as devoted to his happiness as he was to theirs.

"We'd like to still turn everything over to you." His dad held a hand up before Antonio could reply. "But as you know, we have some of the best managers and they would keep things running when you aren't around. If you want to pop in every month, every other month, whatever. You can easily keep up other ways and make sure the businesses are running smoothly and likely handle any matter from wherever you are in the world."

The suggestion seemed so easy, so perfect for their situation. Could the solution be so clear? Would everyone be happy with this and could they all actually pull it off?

"I don't want to let either of you down," he told them

after a moment. "I wanted to find a way to tell you, but at the same time, part of me wondered if I should just take over and let you all go live your lives. You've worked so hard for years."

"And so have you," his mom countered, reaching to place her hand on his knee. "Without you, one of us would have had to have traveled all over and taken care of getting new and unique things for our restaurants. Without you, we wouldn't be nearly as successful as we are today. So you are certainly no disappointment."

Hearing her say that instantly pulled a weight from his shoulders.

"You flew all the way here to tell me this?" he laughed. "A phone call would have worked just fine."

His mom patted his leg. "Yes, well, I tried calling the other night, remember? When you didn't return my call, I thought I'd try reaching out again."

Oh yeah. He remembered. That night was seared into his mind forever.

"I have to assume you've been a little sidetracked by a beautiful distiller," his mother went on.

Antonio didn't deny the claim, there was no reason to. "She's special."

"I'm thrilled to hear that." His mother beamed. "Perhaps she will be good for you in more than just business."

Oh, she would be, but he wanted to talk to Elise about everything before he fully opened up to his parents. Suddenly, the pieces of his chaotic life seemed to be falling exactly where they belonged.

Seventeen

"What is going on?" Sara whispered as soon as there was a slight lull in the crowd.

Elise waved to a familiar client who had just entered the room. "Antonio's parents surprised him."

"Don't you mean surprised *you*?" Sara asked.

Elise nodded. "That, too."

"What did they want?"

"They're either checking me out or discussing Antonio's role in the family business," Elise stated under her breath. "Probably both, but we'll have to talk later. I'll fill you and Dee in once we close out the night."

Elise followed Sara through the crowd, barely even hearing the music that played at the other end of the room. People were taking advantage of the dance floor and enjoying the classics that Delilah had requested.

And speaking of Delilah, Elise hadn't seen her sister since she'd come back from upstairs. Maybe she was with a VIP client or perhaps she was assisting a staff member.

Several members of the Angel's Share family all worked the crowd, passing out tiny tumblers with sample pours of their first ten-year bourbon. For those non-bourbon lovers, there was also gin. Anything to get new clients or show their current clientele just how epic Angel's Share spirits were. They were unlike any other, especially in this bourbon country territory.

Elise spotted Camden out of the corner of her eye. He came from one of the back rooms that were only for employees.

Camden's eyes locked on to Elise and she smiled and offered a wave. No matter what was going on between him and her sister, Elise did think of him as a brother.

"Well, all of the Hawthorne ladies look absolutely stunning tonight." Camden leaned in and kissed Elise on the cheek before turning and doing the same to Sara. "This looks like a successful night. Your hard work and dedication really shows and this turnout is great. Milly would be proud."

There came that burn in the back of Elise's throat that she didn't want to happen while surrounded by shrouds of people, especially on what should be one of the happiest days of her life.

"Don't get us crying," Sara scolded. "We all had our makeup professionally done and we look damn good."

Camden laughed and nodded. "That you do," he agreed. "I won't stay long and I know things are strained, but that doesn't mean I didn't want to show my support."

Elise spotted Delilah off in the distance, talking to

some guests. Dee's eyes kept darting in their direction and Elise knew having Camden here was difficult.

"You talked to Delilah?" Elise asked, already knowing the answer.

Camden's smile faltered. "We talked, yes."

"Is that all?" Sara asked, which earned an elbow from Elise.

Camden shook his head as he blew out a sigh. "Chemistry doesn't change anything, though. Chemistry was never our problem."

Elise couldn't help but think of her relationship with Antonio. Their chemistry definitely wasn't an issue. The completely different lives, homes, and baggage they each had was.

Still, she couldn't ignore all that worked for them, and all that they'd already shared in such a short time. With such a tight bond between them, Elise couldn't even imagine how amazing a future would be. But she had to talk to him, she had to see where his head space was because she didn't believe for a minute that he truly wanted to push her away. Going back to life before Antonio didn't even seem possible.

"I won't pry," Elise told her still-brother-in-law. "But I'm rooting for the two of you."

A sadness overcame his eyes and he leaned in to give her a hug, then did the same to Sara. "I'm going to head out. Congratulations again."

As he walked away, Sara moved in closer to Elise's side and sighed.

"He's hurting as much as Delilah is."

"And they're both stubborn or something is seriously wrong that she won't talk about," Elise murmured. "But we can't fix anything right now and we still have a couple hours left, so let's focus on this."

Because this moment was all she could concentrate on. They'd worked too damn hard to let anything else interfere with this night. And once this was over, she had to shift to her personal life and make the biggest decision she'd ever made with her heart.

The time had come to lay it all on the line.

Antonio waited until the gala was over. He waited even longer until he knew Elise would be home. He hadn't had to do much digging to find her address and he had to admit, the grounds were amazing. She lived up on a hill and her home was nestled back against the woods. A large pond sat off to the left of her two-story brick house. There was a large side porch that faced the pond and an instant image of the two of them enjoying morning coffee hit him hard.

Even though it was late, her porch lights illuminated the side of the house, the front of the house, and there were lights on inside. She was home and all he had to do was get out and knock on her door. All he had to do to change their lives was tell her everything he'd been mulling over since speaking with his parents.

But would Elise be up for what he had to say? Would she even want to hear his ideas? He'd broken things off and then he'd vanished from her gala. He hadn't seen her since she showed him into her office. He'd had good reasons, but would she understand?

Antonio had never allowed fear or uncertainty to hold him back from anything in his life, but right now he wasn't so sure he could step from his car and walk those few feet to her porch.

Just as he shut off his engine, Elise's front door swung open and she appeared. She still had on the silky green gown, the one that reminded him of satin sheets and how perfect she would be to unwrap. His eyes met hers through the windshield and she remained framed in the doorway with the lights from inside illuminating her. She just stood there, waiting on him, and he knew this was his chance. All he had to do was take it.

He opened his car door and stepped out, then rounded the hood and met her gaze once again.

"My driveway alarm went off ten minutes ago," she told him, still in the doorway. "Were you thinking of leaving?"

"More like thinking of what the hell I was doing."

She crossed her arms and tipped her head with that smile of hers that never failed to punch him right in the gut. She had a power over him, a power no one had ever had before. He never thought he'd like giving up control of any aspect of his life, but he'd quickly discovered there were worse things...like being without the one person who filled a void.

"And did you come to a conclusion?" she asked.

"I did."

He started toward the base of the porch, then stopped. With his hand resting on the railing, he propped his foot on the bottom step. He'd rehearsed his speech in his head on the drive over here, but now that he was in the moment, all of those perfectly placed words failed him and he had nothing. All he could think was how stunning she was, how she'd slid right into his life when he'd needed her most, and where the hell they'd go from here.

"Before you say a word, I want to say something." Elise took a step to the edge of the porch and looked down at him. "I'm not sure why you didn't come back to the gala. I assume you were with your parents and I completely get that. They are lovely people, by the way."

He couldn't help but smile, and he would have told her exactly what they thought of her, but she plowed right on through.

"I know we have totally different lives," she went on. "I mean, we don't even live on the same continent, but I'm overlooking that for now."

She gathered the side of her dress in her hands and came down one step, then stopped.

"I mean, how can we just ignore all of this attraction and chemistry?" she added. "And I'm well aware that relationships aren't based solely on those things, but it's a hell of a start and we pretty much excel at chemistry."

Down another step.

"And I know you wanted to end things and I almost let you—"

He laughed, unable to help himself. "Let me?"

"I figured you knew what you were talking about and that you didn't feel the same way I did. But your parents changed everything."

Down another step. They were only two away now. Still too damn far.

"They said you push every type of commitment away since your brother died. I never thought of that, but it makes sense. With you not wanting to take over their chain, all the traveling you do to keep busy and moving, and then us."

Down one more. She dropped the material of her dress and looked into his eyes.

"There is an us," she insisted. "You might not want to look at our situation that way. You might believe this is all still a fling or I'm just someone you passed the time with, but—"

Antonio framed her face and covered her mouth with his. He couldn't stand not touching her another second and he never, ever wanted her to believe that she was just a fling. That couldn't be further from the truth.

Elise grabbed hold of his shoulders, her fingertips curling in as she held on. There was something so damn soothing about being with her. He still couldn't put his finger on it or even try to label it, but…

Wait. Yes. He could label this.

Antonio eased back, still holding on to her face. "You weren't someone I was just passing the time with. And if you're done talking, I have a few things to say myself," he demanded.

"Am I going to like this?" she asked.

"Depends on how you feel about splitting your time between here and Spain."

Her eyes widened, her mouth dropped to a perfect O and he wanted nothing more than to kiss her again, but he had to keep going.

"I have a solution for us."

"Us?" she whispered, her face still full of shock.

He tucked her hair behind her ears and trailed his fingertips down her jawline. "Us, just like you said, remember?"

"I didn't think you thought we could be one unit," she admitted.

"I didn't," he confessed. "I had no clue how I could have you, have a life that still made my parents proud, and try to figure out what to do with their businesses. Because at the end of all of this, I guess I want my twin to be proud of me, too. Paolo is still such a huge part of my life."

"And are you clear now of what you want?" she asked.

Antonio settled his hands on her hips and placed a kiss on her forehead before focusing back on his speech and her expressive eyes.

"I know that I want to take a leap and commit my heart to someone." He leaned in closer, close enough to feel her warm breath falling on his lips. "And I want to take that leap with you."

"Wait...what?"

"You heard me. I want to take the leap with you," he repeated. "My parents' restaurants and new pubs will all be in my name. I will need to go every now and then to check in, but I can also run things from anywhere in the world since we have trustworthy managers on-site."

Elise blinked. "Wait."

"You said that already."

She closed her eyes, shook her head, then looked back to him. "You mean you want to make this work between us? I had all of my bullet points rehearsed and I was ready to tick off each box to you to prove why we should make this work. The only thing I didn't know how to solve was your parents' business."

His heart opened and he realized that this wasn't painful or scary at all. The only emotions he felt were elation and love.

"Te amo."

A wide smile spread across her face. "I'm going to need to learn Spanish."

"I love you," he repeated in English.

Her eyes filled with tears. "Are you serious?"

"I've never been more serious."

A tear slipped out and trailed down her creamy skin.

"Te amo," she told him.

Antonio bent down and lifted her into his arms. Elise looped her arms around his neck and rested her head against his shoulder as he headed toward the still-open front door.

"You're learning already," he told her. "And by the way, my parents want us to come to breakfast so they can welcome you into the family."

"Breakfast? I'd love to."

With the heel of his foot, he closed the door and glanced around the foyer. "Now, lead me to your bedroom because I have plans for you until we have to meet up with them."

Elise's lips pressed against the side of his neck. "Up the stairs. Last door on the left. And you still owe me that promised dance."

He carried her up the steps and to her room, what would be their room, because he wasn't going anywhere for a while. He would do whatever it took to keep them together because nobody had ever captured his heart, his whole life, the way this woman had. He would give up anything for her, but thankfully, he wouldn't have to. He could still carry the legacy of his family and finally work on settling down with the perfect woman.

"Tell me you love me again," she murmured as he stepped into her bedroom.

"*Te amo.* Always."

* * * * *

COMING SOON!

We really hope you enjoyed reading this book.
If you're looking for more romance, be sure to
head to the shops when new books are
available on

Thursday 7th
July

To see which titles are coming soon, please visit

millsandboon.co.uk/nextmonth

MILLS & BOON

THE HEART OF ROMANCE

A ROMANCE FOR EVERY READER

MODERN

Prepare to be swept off your feet by sophisticated, sexy and seductive heroes, in some of the world's most glamourous and romantic locations, where power and passion collide.

HISTORICAL

Escape with historical heroes from time gone by. Whether your passion is for wicked Regency Rakes, muscled Vikings or rugged Highlanders, awaken the romance of the past.

MEDICAL

Set your pulse racing with dedicated, delectable doctors in the high-pressure world of medicine, where emotions run high and passion, comfort and love are the best medicine.

True Love

Celebrate true love with tender stories of heartfelt romance, from the rush of falling in love to the joy a new baby can bring, and a focus on the emotional heart of a relationship.

Desire

Indulge in secrets and scandal, intense drama and plenty of sizzling hot action with powerful and passionate heroes who have it all: wealth, status, good looks…everything but the right woman.

HEROES

Experience all the excitement of a gripping thriller, with an intense romance at its heart. Resourceful, true-to-life women and strong, fearless men face danger and desire - a killer combination!

To see which titles are coming soon, please visit

millsandboon.co.uk/nextmonth

LET'S TALK
Romance

For exclusive extracts, competitions
and special offers, find us online:

- facebook.com/millsandboon
- @MillsandBoon
- @MillsandBoonUK

Get in touch on 01413 063232

For all the latest titles coming soon, visit
millsandboon.co.uk/nextmonth